Stray

Touchstone:
Part One

November to March

by Andrea K Höst

Stray
© 2011 Andrea K Höst. All rights reserved.
ISBN: 978-0-9808789-9-8
E-Book ISBN: 978-0-9870564-0-5
www.andreakhost.com
Cover Art: Simon Dominic

Author's Note

Touchstone is a diary in three parts, commencing in *Stray*, continued in *Lab Rat One*, and concluded in *Caszandra*.

A glossary of terms and phrases, and a character list, have been included at the end of each volume.

NOVEMBER

Friday, November 16

WTF?

Where the FUCK am I????

Writing that down won't give me an answer, but at least there'll be a record of what happened. Not that I know what happened. I only know what happened to me – and, yeah, I'm not making much sense.

My name is Cassandra Eloise Devlin. Cass for short. Never Cassie.

I was walking home from school. I turned a corner, and I was here. No flashing lights, no warning, no zoomy wormhole: nothing but me one minute in Sydney and the next here.

Here is...*here* is the problem. It's definitely not Sydney. I don't think it's Australia, either, unless it's Tasmania. But I'm sure they'd have gum trees in Tasmania, and that's the thing. The trees are all wrong. Hills covered in trees, too many to describe but none of them remotely like Eucalypt. The birds sound wrong too.

No signal on my mobile. I can't spot any buildings or power lines. No planes have flown over. I haven't been able to see anything at any distance, so I'm trying to get out of these trees, or at least to a lookout. I've been walking for maybe half an hour. My watch says it's 3.30 but the sky thinks it's later. I've found a thread of a track and I'm going to follow it.

I need new feet

Trees, trees, and, oh look, more trees. Green hills in every direction, severely lacking in distinctive landmarks.

All those stories where people navigate by the sun don't take into account crazy, crisscrossing animal tracks being the easiest way to get through all the trees and bushes. I wandered around until I found an overhang of rock, and decided to collapse for the night.

Still no signal on my mobile.

My watch says 6pm. It should be full light, but the sun's fading fast, so I'm not even in the same time zone. An hour or two ahead would put me where? New Zealand? How far ahead is New Zealand?

Of course, having been raised on a diet of *Doctor Who*, *Buffy* and *Stargate*, I've no need to stop at New Zealand. I could be in an alternate Australia, any part of the planet at any time, or a different world entirely. Another planet. Or in a mental asylum, strapped in a straight jacket, giggling.

Since I really don't like that last option, I'm concentrating on gathering details. I was hoping to try and spot the Southern Cross when the sun went down, but it's cloudy. And cool: colder than it should be for nearly Summer. So I'm in a different time zone, in a different climate or possibly at a different time of year.

Today was the last day of exams. History. We were going to go out to dinner to celebrate. Mum will be so worried. Will she have called the police? What will I say, if I get back? No-one will believe I just walked to another...somewhere.

There was a stream a while back, so I'm not dying of thirst, and I filled up the Fanta bottle left over from lunch. The water was probably full of bugs and I'll end up sick, but I was so thirsty and it's not like I'm a smoker conveniently carrying a cigarette lighter so I could make a fire and boil drinking water.

A fire would be damn nice.

A quick catalogue of my wilderness survival gear:

- School uniform: blouse, skirt, blazer, stupidtie, socks, shoes, underpants, bra.
- Ponytail band and butterfly hair clip.
- Backpack.
- Pencil Case of Doom, chock-full of writey stuff.
- 30cm ruler

- Modern history notes – useless (or toilet paper).
- Jenna's birthday present, a blank-paged book with a blue and green patterned cover, which I'm writing in. I was going to give it to her this morning, but she was sick again and didn't come to the exam.
- Little packet of tissues (definitely toilet paper).
- Mobile – close to useless, especially once the battery runs out.
- Wallet – about $20, mostly in coins, and other bits of paper and plastic.
- 600 ml Fanta bottle, full of suspect water.
- Half a forgotten muesli bar, going musty in the bottom of my bag! Yay! (Gone now.)

No knives, no matches, no blanket. No shoes good for walking for miles. This isn't fun. It isn't exciting. I walked into adventure and adventure has given me blisters. I have to try and go to sleep sitting in the dirt in a forest full of things making noises, and I don't know where I am, I don't know why I'm here, and...I don't want to think about it.

Saturday, November 17

SO hungry

How do you tell what's poisonous? Now that would have been a useful thing to learn at school. I've found a couple of trees covered in fruit which look like red pears, and I don't know if eating them will make me drop dead.

The birds seem to like them, anyway. It was hard to find any that hadn't been pecked to death. So here goes...

Floury, but it's been a few minutes and I don't feel any odder than I was before. I've only eaten one, and I'm going to wait a while before eating any more in case there's a delayed effect. I'll take the least pecked with me, since they might be the only thing I can find that's edible.

Last night was a black eternity. I don't feel like I really slept, just dozed, constantly starting awake. I'm heading in the direction the sun rose because it looks flatter that way. No mobile signal. No buildings, powerlines, planes, etc, etc.

I've never walked so much in my life.

Camp

It's an hour or two before sunset, but I've reached a clearing with a stream and stopped to sit with my feet in the water.

It looks like there might have been a fire here a few years ago: the entire slope of this hill is covered in grass and burnt-out trees. The clearing's given me my best view yet of Planet Endless Green Carpet. It's all so empty and untouched. I'm still not 100% certain whether this is or isn't Earth. I've scared off a few animals walking along, but the only one I caught a good look at was a deer, which doesn't exactly narrow things down continent-wise, and I guess there could be deer on other planets.

There's a curving glint of water down below which I'm hoping is a river. I mightn't be able to see any fields or signs of settlement nearby, but I figure if I follow a river I'll find a lake or the ocean and then – I don't know.

My school uniform is nothing but sweat and itches, so if ever a rescue plane wanted to fly over, I'm about to wash everything while the sun's still strong. Never thought to pack a spare pair of undies when getting ready for the exam. There's no cloud today, so at least I can hope to try some star-spotting tonight. Astronomy's not my thing, but the Southern Cross is the easiest constellation in the world – or off it! Too much cloud last night to even see if there's a moon.

Knowing whether this is Earth is really important. If it's Earth, then I might be able to recognise edible fruits and vegetables. And it might be MY Earth. Not another time, or an alternate or whatever. I could just be in somewhere really unpopulated and foresty, and that would mean home is still there waiting for me.

There are no really obvious clues so far. Gravity seems the same, the sun looks the same, the sky is blue, the leaves are green. If I see something which looks totally not from my Earth, I'll have to face not being able to walk back home. Even without being sure, once I follow that river I'm going to have to think about something other than going forward. But until then, just to keep it all in steps that don't overwhelm me, the plan is to get to the river, to follow the river.

Sunday, November 18

Riverward

I'm no good at estimating how far I can walk in a day. I might get to the river today. I'm going very slow because of my feet, plus overall not feeling well. The nights aren't impossibly cold, and I made a nest in the grass which was more or less comfortable, but I woke up covered in dew, and my throat's sore. I'm out of tissues for toilet paper, too. History notes just aren't...up to scratch.

I cut my tie into two pieces and have padded my shoes as best I can. Awkward bandages. Paper scissors don't cut cloth well, but I had to wonder what I would have done if they hadn't been in my pencil case. The things I have with me are irreplaceable.

Better living through bare feet

So here's the plan. Barefoot unless the ground is really rough, and only then the torture devices. My feet are quickly collecting bruises, but I just couldn't go on in my black leather school shoes. My heels are a raw, bleeding mess.

I spotted a tree critter just now, and I'm waiting for it to come out again while wondering if I'm capable of killing animals for food. Food is my biggest issue, since I've finished the last of the red pears. They're not the only fruit I've found – there's lots of green berries, for instance, but they're so sour I think they're not ripe. I picked a bunch of tiny, thumb-sized apples, but they made my mouth go numb.

- Red Pears – good.
- Thumb Apples – bad.
- Green Tearberries – sour/not ripe.

I've been puzzling over catching fish, trying to remember ways that don't involve nets or fishing line. Pears won't last forever. If I'm heading for Winter I'm in such deep shit.

Progress-wise, I'm nearer the river, but have lost sight of it because I'm not up top of a good slope. I'm just aiming in the general direction, which is a lot easier in the afternoon when the sun drops and the shadows point the way. I'm not near anything resembling a good camp – just sitting down for a while – and I need to find water as well. One Fanta bottle doesn't carry nearly enough.

Back in the World

So tonight's the night of the Schoolies' Cruise, and I'm supposed to be celebrating the end of high school. We didn't want to fight the hordes at the beaches, let alone go up to the Gold Coast to be chased by Toolies, so about a hundred of us from Agowla and the Boy's Tech were going on the Harbour. Her Mightiness (Helen Middledell, unofficial Queen of Agowla High School) was the cruise driving force and had all the say on the guest list, but since HM started her thing with Todd Hunter she's been almost human, and didn't try to keep everything to some sort of In crowd.

I was really looking forward to the cruise. I had a great dress, blue and silver and not frilly or little girl. Alyssa's dad was going to drive us in, so we wouldn't have to ride the train, and we had taxi fare home. There was going to be a band, and the way HM was acting, it wasn't going to be Awful Cover Band #36.

Schoolies is a big thing. Not everyone's planning on uni. Not everyone will get in, and not everyone will go to the same uni even if they do. The cruise was going to be the last time most of us would see each other. Nick was going to be there. I hate that I'm missing it. I hate that my unexcellent adventure is probably spoiling it for Alyssa and Nick as well.

I might never see them again. I don't just mean Alyssa or Nick. Or Mum. I mean anyone. Anyone. Ever.

Monday, November 19

Nice place for a holiday

If there was a hotel and people and a way to get back home, I'd probably like it here. It's the sort of place which would be wall-to-wall tourists if it was Earth.

The animal I saw today definitely pushes me toward the not-Earth conclusion. It was pale gold, darkening to reddish along its back and tail and the top of its head. And bouncy. Not like a kangaroo, but like a jumpy lamb or a startled cat. It came down out of its tree and chased insects through the leaves. It has longish legs which look like they should be awkward, but aren't. I'm calling it a tree fox, and even if it hadn't been impossibly cute I don't think I could have brought myself to try and kill it.

Walking for forever

Three days. Three and a bit days. I'm surprised I haven't fallen apart by now. And I've had it easy, really. If I'd found myself in a desert I'd be dead. Even the bush just west of Sydney would be rough in comparison. But here there's lots of water, and the days aren't nearly as hot as Australia in November, though still enough to give me sunburn. I'm trying to make myself a hat.

I found another red pear tree, but most of the fruit had been eaten, or was full of worms. Eating nothing but pears for three days running is NOT good for digestion, plus my throat has stayed scratchy. My horrible blisters are drying out, but it's hard to keep them from becoming dirty, and they're already infected. My feet are holding up otherwise. Sore and bruised, but nothing like so painful as it was wearing my shoes. A bunch of insect bites, too, but nothing fatal, obviously.

I think I'm getting near the river. I'm a lot lower than I was, and the trees are spread out more. Most are a rough black bark, with branches which start spreading out low to the ground. I could probably climb halfway up one easy enough, but the high parts are thin and twiggy, making them not useful lookout points. If I see a wolf I'll climb one. And probably find that it's a tree wolf.

If there were no predators on this world, the deer and tree foxes wouldn't run away from me. That makes sense, doesn't it? I've got to start thinking about trying to make a fire, or a weapon. How to do that with the contents of my pencil case, and a world of rocks and twigs is the problem. I'd make a terrible cavewoman.

Tuesday, November 20

Definitely not Earth

Guess how I know this isn't Earth? Not animals I can't quite identify. Not the stars, which, while Southern Cross-less haven't exactly stood up and looked wrong. Not freaky alien civilisations. No, my watch told me. Each day the sun's set a quarter hour or so later. So this is a world which is really like Earth, but not it at all. Not even an alternate Earth, unless it's one which has a slightly longer day for some odd reason.

I'll have to think up a name.

A whole new world. Other planets, habitable planets, actually exist. There could be anything, anything at all out there. I'm trying to be excited about it, to appreciate what an amazing experience this is. But my feet hurt, and I'm hungry.

As well as discovering a planet, this has been a big day for Survivor Cass. I reached the river at last, at about mid-morning. Since my water bottle was empty, it was great to get to it, and I jumped straight in before the idea of piranhas occurred to me. I seriously needed the bath, though. The river bottom is all small rocks and grit, and the water's very clear at the shallow parts. It's wide, but I've already found a spot where I could wade across. The water is very sweet, no hint of salt, and so long as I follow the river I won't have any more thirsty days (or get so manky!).

I finished my hat while I was drying off. A frame of twigs woven together with grass, and not exactly comfortable, but it does shade my face. Every so often I pull some more long grass to weave into it, and tighten everything up. I've been plaiting skinny grass stalks together to get something resembling twine, and then I'll reinforce it all again. My hat might look like the makings of a campfire, but it's the first thing I've made since woodwork in grade eight, and better than nothing.

During the day I've kept my eye out for:

- Anything edible.
- Rocks that look like flint. Not that I know what flint looks like. Most of the rock here is grey, with some yellow. No really red earth like you'd get in Aus.
- Clay. This involves squeezing any mud I find. Extremely silly.
- Friendly alien civilisations. I could really do with one of these.

It's also been a big day for animals. Plenty of deer, and what I think was an elk, but very big. And grey terrier-sized dogs that run around in groups of three or four. They followed me for a while, and I was a bit worried, but not really because I could send one flying with a good kick, or climb a tree if they came after me. Mid-afternoon I saw paw prints of something larger and spent ages looking for a good place to spend the night. There just doesn't seem to be anywhere safe. Maybe I can weave a hammock? The best I can do is not sleep anywhere close to the river. If all the animals go down there to drink, I don't want to be the after-drink snack.

So new animals today:

- Mondo Elk.

- Grey Terriers.

- Mr Paws.

I'm not even going to start listing the birds, because there's so many. It was a great day for fruit, too. Red pears, berries everywhere, and what I hope are edible nuts. I haven't eaten anything but the pears yet because I'm going to have to be systematic about experimental eating so I know exactly what fatally poisons me. Throat still sore, but my nose isn't blocked. It's sleeping out in the dew which is doing it.

Wednesday, November 21

Handicrafts and cats

Walking along the river is easier than the hills. There's still plenty of ups and downs and rough patches, since someone forgot to install a boardwalk, but overall not too bad.

The big event of the day was the cat. Mr Paws indeed. It was on the other side of the river, which might be the only reason I get to sit around writing this. It wasn't as big as a lion, was more like a leopard, except not spotty. With a golden body and darker brown ears, face and legs, it reminded me of a miscoloured Siamese cat. It watched me across the river, then *flowed* up the nearest tree and was gone – probably to look for a bridge. I dubbed it Ming Cat and I'm going to have nightmares about it tonight. On a less I'm-going-to-die front, there were also otters in the river. Or something like otters. I haven't seen them clearly enough to know whether they're different enough from otters to need their own name.

All the berries I've found continue to be sour, but the nuts were great. Fiddly to get out of their shells, which are like a harder walnut. They taste more like cashews, and would be perfect if I could figure out how to roast and salt them. I'm calling them washews. I wish I'd brought more with me, and if I spot another tree I'm going to harvest as many as possible, since they're light and they'll keep.

Today's home economics project was to grab long stalks of grass and long flat leaves to twist into cords, or to try and weave with. Just sampling which plants work best and don't hurt my hands.

After the Ming Cat, I gave up on weaving for a while and found myself a Big Stick. Then I swapped it for a long, straight(ish) stick. When I'm resting, I rub one end on the nearest rock, trying to make a point. I'm not really pretending to myself that I'd be able to fight Mr Paws off, but I can at least wave it about and look fierce.

Navel Gazing

I've never been the type to keep a diary, so this pile of words is strange to look back over. The first thing which leaps out is how calm I sound. That's a big bluff. I just haven't written down all the shouting and crying I've done. I don't want to write pages about how it feels to wake in the middle of the night, stiff and cold in my grassy nest, to listen to SOMETHING moving around in the dark and hope that if it bites I die quick. Every day, this could be the last thing I write, and no-one would know.

So I don't write too much about the crying and maybe dying. I think about it enough, listening in the dark. During the day, Survivor Cass keeps busy with practicalities because I hate the idea that the whole of my future might be a diary which one day stops.

Thursday, November 22

Life without entertainment

I've been camping a bunch of times with my family, and once on a school camp which of course was wall to wall activities. Even then I brought along half a shelf of books to get me by. Borrowed Mum's iPod. Recorded all the TV shows I was missing, and straight on the comp as soon as we were back to catch up on message boards and all my web comics. I'm the kind of person who watches TV while checking FaceBook, and reads whether I'm having breakfast, or on the bus, or in the loo.

I don't get to find out how anything ends. I don't get to see the next episode, read the next volume, or pick through the latest pile of books Mum brings home to find something new to love. I keep thinking about the book I left sitting face-down on my bed. I'd just reached a scene where the characters were being attacked by these big fleshy bugs which lay eggs in people to make more bugs, but then Mum yelled that I had get in the car RIGHT NOW if I wanted a lift, and now that book is stuck in my head with these bugs chasing people in the rain, and no way to know who gets stung.

Exams are practically the only time I don't bring a novel to school. Theoretically only taking my notes means I'll read them while I'm waiting outside the exam room. Any other day and I would have at least had one book to read and re-read.

So, here I am, Survivor Cass, boldly exploring an alien world. And in between crying, whining and trembling, I'm BORED OUT OF MY MIND.

No remarkable developments today. I've been working on trying to weave bamboo-ish leaves into a mat/blanket/Superman cape. I'm not too bad with the basic structure, but still don't have the slightest idea how to do the edges. I've no needles and no thread. I'm thinking of spending tomorrow not walking, to devote some daylight time to dive-bombing fish and trying to light a fire – something I haven't even tried because reality TV shows have taught me that it's super-hard.

If I catch a fish (my crooked-ass spear has been decidedly ineffective) then maybe I can make the bones into needles. Thread will be hardest – really bad twine I can do, but I don't see how to make thread. I need a horse willing to let me cut off its tail. There's all sorts of things I'm scheming about making, but the bamboo leaf mats are priority number one. Big, light mats I can roll up and take with me, which I can sit and sleep on. One I can use to keep the dew off me, and shut away the night.

Friday, November 23

Treed

The Grey Terriers turned up in numbers. Before today I've only seen them in groups of three or four, but about twenty started following me this morning. I climbed a tree. I'm not sure if they're at all likely to attack me – it's not like they're all gathered around the base of the tree jumping up at me. But every so often they drift back past the tree, and there always seems to be one hanging about watching.

Don't know how long I'll be stuck up here, but I do have food and water – and a sore ass from sitting on this rough bark!

One week

It's been a lifetime. The past couple of days I've been feeling so...annoyed. I mean, if I was going to be whisked off to spend the rest of my life stumbling around the wilderness, couldn't it have happened BEFORE the exams? Or at least after the Schoolies cruise? I don't even get to find out how I did. The whole HSC thing seems pretty minor now. I was going to do an Arts degree while making up my mind where to end up, since there's nothing out there that sounds like an interesting way to earn a living. That I can do, anyway.

The Grey Terriers went away eventually. I waited a long time, not sure it was safe, and saw a new animal as my reward. It must have been hidden in a burrow. It was only the size of a kitten – for all I know it was just a baby, though I didn't see any adults – and was like the tree fox, except smaller with shorter legs and more a creamy manila folder colour with black markings. It was so cute. It leaped about, exploring under the leaves and darting and rushing and then freezing and listening hard and then scurrying back under the tree roots where it lives.

I'm calling it a pippin, and it cheered me up for a while.

The rest of the day was more walking, and finding a rash all over my legs and on my arms. Just pinpoints, but not comfortable. And now I'm sitting here on a hill well away from the river, watching the moon rise. It's the first time it's come up, and if it had bothered to show itself before I would have known straight away that this isn't Earth. It's big, and blueish, and there's a huge scar almost like a bullet hole, or an odd meteor crater, with lines radiating out from it. It's about two-thirds full, and it looks like it'll make the night a bright one. Weird, beautiful. Mum would love it.

Saturday, November 24

I am not my Mother

But sometimes I wish I was.

There was a patch where I hated Mum. My first year of high school, I went to St Mary's. Great school, I really liked it, and April Stevenson was in my class. She was just...there's a certain sort of person who is like a little walking sun. No party feels like it starts until they get there, because they're just so alive. April was full of great stories and ideas and could do anything she set out to. Everyone gravitated to her, like they do with HM at my current school, but April was straightforward nice as well, and a reader, so we were always chatting in the library.

April thought science fiction and fantasy was kid's stuff. She wasn't nasty about it, but she couldn't understand why anyone over ten would read it. So I peeled the fairy stickers off my folders and read other books. She invited me over to her house a few times, and everything was so sophisticated and Mrs Stevenson was like someone off TV. Then we had a parents' day at school and Mum shows up in one of her Celtic dragon t-shirts. She didn't say anything rude, and chatted away with other parents, but I hated her for that shirt.

I said a few things to Mum that year that I can never take back. About how embarrassed she made me. How I was surprised Dad had stuck around as long as he did. Mum doesn't like arguments. She just took me out of St Mary's at the end of the term, and pretty much ignored everything I said for about six months.

Before that I used to think she was the best Mum in the world. When she's not reading she makes jewellery, and eerie but cool little dolls, and sells them online. She plays computer games. She's really bad at racing games, but she'll even play them when Jules bugs her enough. She tries to explain when she wants us to do stuff, and she cares more about what's right than what's in. It's only over the last couple of years that I realised that she wasn't that embarrassing really. And I never got around to telling her that.

I can't imagine what she's doing now. I wish there was some way to at least let her know I'm alive. That no nasty old man grabbed me and did things to me. The worst part about all this is that every day I'm complaining about being Survivor Cass is a day she doesn't, can't, will never know.

Sunday, November 25

One long river

I've been following the river in a loop around the base of a big hill, which is easier than trying a straight line over the top since I get lost so easily once I'm under cover of the trees. The river is narrower and faster than I've seen previously – I'd only swim across it at this point if I absolutely had to – but it's still clear without any hint of salt or tides to suggest that I'm nearing the ocean.

The soles of my feet are black, even after I wash them, and have collected plenty of bruises and tiny cuts, but there's no way I'm putting my shoes on until the sores made by my blisters are better. The rash on my arms and legs went away quickly though. I think it was the tree which caused it. I've lost weight: my skirt keeps slipping down on my hips. I've never been the thinnest girl, though not really fat either, and I wouldn't mind a mirror to see what I look like. Not that I'd pass up a milkshake.

Foliage overload

Another reason I'm glad to stick to the river is it offers a break from the trees. The undergrowth isn't too bad here, but between the trees and bushes it still feels very closed in. Even when I'm up on a hill, I rarely see any distance at all, and big clearings only happen once in a while. When the river's running straight I at least get a reasonable glimpse of what's ahead, but I want a better idea of where I am and whether there's anything out there I should head for.

Which comes down to climbing trees. The problem is, if I fall, if I break a leg or an arm, I'm going to have to fix it. Any accident, no matter how minor, could be fatal. Even the little scratches could get infected, and I don't have the least idea how to make antiseptic, any more than I can figure out where soap comes from.

Anyway, I've found a good tree. It's a kind of pine, I guess. One of the really straight ones anyway, basically a pole with lots of branches sticking out, and if I can use the nearest rock to haul myself to the lowest branch, I should be able to climb up far further than I can on the trees which have lots of low, dividing branches. Time to give it a shot.

View

Okay, just a few scrapes and itches for that effort. And nothing much else. I could see a fair way, but it was all what I already knew – I'm in a lot of low hills covered by trees, and a river is winding through it. Still no sign of farmland or buildings, let alone power lines. I think maybe there's an edge of water ahead. It could just be the river widening again and turning back, but it looked flatter in that direction.

Monday, November 26

Bleaurgh

Very sick. I tried a new fruit, a kind of orange grape (granges). Only ate one, and have been sicking up all afternoon, with the added joy of the runs. I think I'll be okay, but life without toilet paper truly sucks.

Tuesday, November 27

Bad Night

I've made two really large (and very fraying) mats of 'bamboo' leaves now. They're not too hard to carry, rolled up and tied to the back of my backpack. At night I lie on one and completely under the other. It keeps a lot of the dew off, and might even help if it rained: it hasn't rained at all yet, though it's overcast a lot. Even though the mat's paper-thin, it makes me feel safer to be under something.

Last night something walked right up to me, crunching a corner of my mat. I was feeling so awful anyway, and inside I just shrivelled, all while I held my breath and tried to be anything but a big Cass sandwich. For all I know it was a cow, more interested in my mats than me. It was big, heavy. I could hear it breathing, and the tiny sounds it made as it turned its head, right over mine.

And then it left.

I've spent most of today on a rock in the middle of the river, making myself feel warm and safe, and drinking gallons of water. I needed the recovery time from yesterday's food experiment, but it's not bad fruit that makes me stand hunched, cringing from something I didn't even see.

I'll sleep here tonight. I need to. But I know there's no choice but to go on.

Mats

I've been fiddling with my mats, tightening them up again, and wondering how I could make a needle and thread to sew edges. I'd realised I could bend the ends back and thread them through the checkerboard of weave, which keeps them firmer, but mat maintenance is a big part of my day.

My scissors are already showing signs of wear. The kind of paper scissors which fit into pencil cases, even the Pencil Case of Doom, aren't large or strong enough to pretend to be a knife or half the things I've been trying to use them for. The pencil sharpener also has a tiny blade in it, but I'm leaving that alone for the moment, and trying to reserve my scissors for things I can't figure out any other way to cut. Perhaps I'll make another attempt at whacking a stone knife out of the rocks.

Wednesday, November 28

Big Wet

There definitely is an ocean or a lake ahead. I keep seeing the light reflecting from the water, though it's still too far ahead for more. Going to push hard this afternoon, to see how far I can get.

Nature abhors a square

At least, I can't think of any naturally forming squares, except for the occasional odd-shaped rock.

There's a big patch of water ahead. Ocean or a lake, not sure yet. The river's still fresh, without any hint of salt. And to the right, far along the shore, are white, square things. Buildings.

No sign of smoke or power lines or roads or anything but a few whitish squares among the greenery. But this changes so much. Someone made those squares, and although they could be hostile or gecko-men or whatever, it means I'm not the only intelligent person on the planet.

I can barely sit here writing this. I want to run all the way there, I want to scream for help, I want to see a plane fly over, I want it all at once.

I think I MIGHT get there by tomorrow afternoon. I'm definitely going to push as hard as I can, the rest of today and tomorrow.

Thursday, November 29

Water Walk

I'm nearly at the buildings, and should reach them in plenty of time before sunset, though I've yet to decide whether that's a good idea or not.

The lake is enormous. I seem to be walking along an outflung arm of it, and can see a huge expanse beyond the hills directly across from me, so large that I can't see the far shore. It's very cool and still, clear like green tea, and the banks all pebbly. There's these birds which keep flying low across the water in pairs, making the most amazing noises, drawn-out wails. I'm glad I didn't hear that for the first time in the middle of the night.

There are dozens of buildings. And they're old. And obviously empty, with plants growing in all the wrong places. I'm following the shoreline along a road made of white stones which have been set neatly in the ground. It's broken apart in places, where tree roots have lifted the stones, but otherwise it's survived well. There's even what I think must be mile-posts every so often, though whatever is chipped into them is so old and worn I can't tell if it's any kind of script I would recognise.

The buildings are white and blocky, with arched doorways. Most are only one or two stories, with flat roofs, and make me think of Greece, of those pictures of seaside towns. They stretch over the hill, and I think they must continue along the 'main' shore of the lake.

My feet aren't happy with me for walking so hard all day, but I'm going to press on while it's still light. Just to check what's in the buildings, and to see if there's more over the hill. There might be some with people in them. There might be another, occupied settlement.

Dire lack of friendly aliens

No-one's been here for a long time. There's plenty of animal life, though. Ten thousand birds, all singing in the evening. Little pigs which shoot out of the bushes and go racing off, shrieking as if I'd hit them. Chittering squirrelly types jumping from wall to wall. I even saw a cat, a slinky grey one, no different from home. All these different animals, seething through a town overgrown and deserted and empty.

It wasn't a modern town, back when people lived in it. There's no remains of cars or powerlines or anything like that. But it's not caveman primitive either. I can't figure out how the buildings were made, since the walls and roofs all seem to be one single piece of white stone. Like someone took a big block of plaster of Paris and carved out the parts they didn't need to make rooms and doors and windows, and then added pretty decorations around the edges. It's held up really well: worn but solid.

Of the doors and shutters and furniture, most has left barely a trace, making it clear the people have been gone more than a few years. There's little remaining in the couple of houses I've dared to look into, though there's plenty of guck and muck. No visible bones of people, fortunately – this doesn't seem to be like Pompeii.

It's getting dark around 9.30pm (Sydney daylight savings time) and it's too gloomy right now to explore more. I'm going to sleep on the roof of the house nearest the edge, then take a proper look tomorrow. Over the next couple of days I'll hunt for useful stuff and decide whether or not to stay. The fact that this one town is empty doesn't mean anything. Look at Macchu Piccu – it being deserted didn't mean the rest of the world was. And this means there were people here once.

Friday, November 30

Town ramble

The buildings are all made of this white stone, and have pointed arches for doors and windows. Every one where I've bothered to climb up to look has a raised circle pattern in the middle of the roof which I think might represent some kind of flower: each has a central dot and then petals or beams or something radiating out from it to a thick rim. The roofs themselves are slightly indented, and there's drainage holes at each corner, though no downpipes.

The most common type of building is two levels at the front, and one at the back, with a fenced-off bit of garden. They look like terrace houses, but not pressed up against each other. The upstairs windows are pointed arches as well, but much flatter, like someone sat on them. Then there's the buildings which are L-shaped downstairs, with no levels on top, and a wall rounding off a square for their garden. There are other configurations, but almost everything is square. Even the two or three towers are just a stack of slightly smaller squares on top of each other.

That makes it sounds really bare and ugly, but it's not. Partly because there's so many plants growing over everything, but mainly because everything's decorated. Around the bottom of every building, and around each window and door is a border. Geometric shapes, or occasionally little stylised animals. All faded yellow and blue and green, with red-earth tones showing up every so often.

I've been walking around the town for the entire day. The roads make it fairly easy going, but I put my shoes back on because there's occasional sharp rubble. Shattered pottery. After I'd made it over the hill I could see both that the lake is huge, and that the town stretches well along the right side of it. I headed toward what looked to be the town centre, where there were some larger clear paved areas, and two of the four-storey towers.

The tower on the 'north' edge of town is closest to the lake, so I picked it for my basecamp. Fort Cass. I'm sleeping on the roof tonight, since the sky is clear and there's less dirt up here.

I haven't found any bodies, or not obvious ones, though the chance of unearthing some bones is one of the reasons I'm not that keen on kicking through the grot. Did the people choose to leave, and abandon this place? Was it a plague? A war?

DECEMBER

Saturday, December 1

Housekeeping

All this morning I've focused on Fort Cass. First I searched it properly, and took anything that looked useful up to the roof. The bottom of every room is thick with muck, dust and the remains of ancient bug-nests. I'm being extra careful in case of spiders. Or, y'know, mind-controlling tentacle monsters.

Metal objects come in two types: the things that fall into flaky red crumble when I pick them up, and the things which are green-black but whole. Most of the green-black things seem to be decorative, unfortunately. A pretty statue of a pippin, which I've adopted for company. What might be a belt buckle. Some cups. No knives so far, let alone needles. I don't think the tower was a place people lived, but perhaps a place they worked, or a look-out.

After my search I kicked all the big rubble out of the top level and swept it out using the most bodged-up attempt at a broom ever. The handle fell straight off a jug I found, but it would hold water so I sloshed and swept and scraped the floor, and knocked down all the cobwebs. Not too bad.

Next on the agenda are hairy sheep. I spotted them on one of my trips to the lake: a little flock had come down to the bank to drink. They were north, out beyond the buildings, and wandered off when I went near them. I'm pretty sure they *are* sheep, since they looked woolly, but they had horns, and long hair growing in the wool. The horns make me a bit nervous, but I'm hoping I can go and cut some wool off them. Unless they have pointy teeth, in which case I'll pass.

Sheepses

The hairy sheep are guarded by great big hairy rams. All of them except the little ones have horns, but the rams have big twirling ones, and scarred foreheads from bashing up against each other or anything silly enough to come near their ewes. I bet the ewes would give me a good knock too, and in the end I decided not to risk any of them. They might have been domesticated once, but they're not keen on people now.

I still came back with a haul of wool, though. The sheep live on the hills north of town, the biggest unforested patch of ground I've seen so far. Other than a few trees, the grass is broken up by rocks and berry bushes. These are a different sort to the tearberries, also green but going on pink. More sour than cranberries, so I'm guessing they're not ripe yet either. Anyway, the important thing about them is they're thorny, and snag anything which comes near them.

For the price of a few scratches I filled my backpack with tufts of wool, crammed in hard, and there's plenty more back there. The wool is yellow and grotty, but a huge step up from string made out of grass stalks. I have a thousand plans for it, but first on the list is cleaning it. Which means tomorrow I'm going to have to bite the bullet and try to make fire.

If I can manage fire, I should get lanolin as well as clean wool. I don't exactly know what I'll do with the lanolin – keep my skin nice? – but it can't hurt to have it.

Sunday, December 2

Moonfall

Last night was only the second time I've seen the moon. This time it was full.

I was still sitting on the roof of Fort Cass when it rose. All the buildings were slowly picked out in blueish white and it was like looking down at a ghost of a town, everything a shimmering mirage, not real at all. The circles in the centre of each roof became the brightest part of each building, until it looked like the light was *flowing* out from them. And it was. I was sitting right next to one, and didn't know whether to stay or run when a thick mist began to creep out from the centre circle. But who could not find out what it was like to touch?

About a year ago I was friends with Perry Ryan. Her parents were hardly ever home, and she liked to drink and smoke. The smoking I wasn't so keen on, but I thought the drinking was great. It made me feel like I had a personality. I really loved it until Alyssa dragged me out of a party at Perry's house and woke me up enough to tell me I'd been snogging Matt Wilson. The kind of jerk who takes photos. Alyssa went all Mum on me thanks to that, and no more Perry parties.

So the way that cold blue light made me feel warm and happy wasn't exactly new, and I curled around the circle like it was a hot water bottle and let myself enjoy it. After that, I was quickly into the everything's a blur stage. I don't know what made me go looking for more. But I went downstairs (barefoot!) and then to a place I'd only glanced at before, an amphitheatre of step-like whitestone seats in the middle of town. When I'd looked at it during the day, the place had been infested with cats, but that night there was just the light. Gallons of it, drifting off all the buildings and washing into the amphitheatre where a huge version of the circles was glowing so strong the light rose in a column. I went and stood in it, of course, and tried to drink the air, which was more like a heavy fog than a liquid. I've never felt better or happier or more alive than last night, standing there with my arms outstretched and my mouth open, inhaling and swallowing light.

So. I woke up, still feeling really damn good, curled in the centre of the amphitheatre. No hangover. It was mid-morning, sunny. My mouth was dry and the arm I was lying on had pins and needles, but otherwise just Cass, feeling amazed at what had happened.

The amphitheatre is cat central. Their home base, just as the tower's mine. There's dozens of them, all slinky, big-eared, mostly grey tabby but a sprinkle of other colours. No fluffy Persian types here. Some really cute kittens, but the whole lot so feral and wild I wouldn't dare try and pick one up. I got myself out of their territory as quickly as I could, and then because I was feeling energetic I walked back along the lake to a stream I'd passed, and watched otters. It's hard to focus on practical plans when you've spent the night drinking the moon.

Nothing about the moon

Before my attempt at fire, I collected another pack of wool and hunted around for something big and metal which didn't look like it would instantly fall to pieces. I ended up with this flat blue and green bowl which was hell to move since I could only just lift it, and had to put it down every ten steps. I didn't want to risk breaking it by trying to roll it and don't know how it will hold up to having a fire built around it. I'm setting the fire up down on the lake's edge, for ease of access to water.

I wish I knew how to make soap, so I could clean up properly. Even though I wash every day, there's a layer of greasy grime all over me, and the less said about my hair the better. If I can get the fire started, I'll at least have hot water to wash in, before I add the wool. The IF is the big problem here. I tried magnifying sunlight with bits of glass, but either the glass isn't clear enough or the sunlight's not strong enough. I'm having a rest right now after taking up the stick rubbing challenge. I can make the sticks heat up, but all I end up with is hot sticks and very tired arms. I shredded a page of history notes before I started, but I'm going to tear it all up smaller and try again.

Department of Acquisitions

So I have a fire. I'm not altogether sure what to do to stop it from going out overnight, or if it rains. It made me realise that these houses don't have chimneys or fireplaces. My wool-boiling went along merrily, and I now have a lot of very wet wool, and a little scummy yellow stuff I ladled off the top. I've spread the wool out to dry.

While it was cooking I made a start on more mats. I want to cover both the floor and the windows. I'm not sure what to do with the top of the stair to the roof. There would have been something which sealed it nicely before, but I don't think I can make a waterproof mat.

I've never been particularly great at arts and crafts. Not useless, but I'm nothing close to as good as Mum. I'm too impatient. I start out with neatish little stitches, then they get bigger and untidier. But I'm going to make myself a clean wool nest and a blanket and I don't care if it's the ugliest thing around. And I'll fix up my room, and explore this town and get everything useful I can find.

And then–?

My long term options really suck the life out of any feel-good attempt.

Monday, December 3

The Sad Ignorance of Modern Youth

I've seen people shear sheep on TV. And I've seen a picture of a spinning wheel. I know a spindle must be pointy because princesses can prick their fingers on them. The mechanics of how wool goes from fleece to thread, though, is something else. And what is carding? When does it happen?

Anyway, turning all the wool into thread and then trying to weave with it is just beyond me. It would take a century even if I knew what to do. Making a big pile of clean wool so I have something soft to sleep on is part of the plan, but I'm also going to have a shot at making a felt blanket. Of course, felt-making was another thing no-one bothered to teach me, but my best guess is that it might work like making paper, and that at least I've seen someone do.

I thought about it this morning, while collecting more wool and chasing sheep. The sheep, the ewes at least, aren't as aggressive as I thought, though they're skittish as anything. I targeted the middle-sized ones, that don't seem quite fully grown, but aren't being babysat by their mums (and don't have much horn!). My paper scissors aren't nearly as effective as shears, but I can get nice big hunks by sitting on the sheep's back and chopping away. All morning collecting wool, and now I have a massive pile of the stuff and am working my way through boiling it while trying to make a mould for the felt.

I'm using the road for the base, a section of large squares where none of the stones have been displaced. Smaller stones and a log gave me an outline of a big rectangle, and I'll lay out a nice even layer of wet wool and then squish and mush it as flat as I can and let it dry.

I don't know if they use any glues when making felt. Probably, knowing my luck. Just pressing the wool together won't be enough – I need to make it stick together. I may have to do a whole bunch of different attempts, adding different things to the mix, but the first time around I'm going to try without additives. Just lots of water, and heat. I figure boiling all the clean wool again, for a really long time, and stirring it up, might make it break down and go gluey and more like paper pulp. Or not. I'm just guessing, but I have plenty of wool to experiment with, and am going to go find some more big bowls to boil it in. My own lakeshore factory.

I'm so looking forward to sleeping on soft wool tonight.

Tuesday, December 4

The Pre-Industrial Mountain

Today I made another, better broom to sweep out the rest of Fort Cass. It's so stupidly hard to make tools without other tools. Try putting together a broom without large amounts of industrial glue, a nicely finished handle, the straw or whatever it is that they make bristles out of, a drill, a saw, nails, a hammer. Everything I do involves a monumental pile of preliminary tasks, and the simplest thing takes so much time.

The scale of it all got a little much for me this morning, mostly because one of the bowls I was using decided life was too hard and fell to pieces, nearly putting out all the fires and sending me ducking away before I was scalded beyond recognition. I about died of fright, then had an epic tanty and stomped off.

Till now I'd steered clear of doing more than hauling water out of the lake and washing at the edge. This place could be this planet's equivalent of Loch Ness, after all, and I'm not keen on monsters. Even in Australia, it's best not to jump into water unless a local has told you whether there's crocs or stingers or sharks. Since I don't have any locals, I've been watching the wildlife, waiting for a fin to surface or a massive toothy maw to snatch up animals which stray too close. So far I've seen lots of waterbirds bobbing about happily enough, and occasionally fish flipping in the air.

So I went swimming. The water's cold, but since the day was hot and I've been hunched over pots of boiling water, this was a good thing. In a proper story, when the heroine goes swimming naked the very handsome prince turns up to try not to watch. Complete failure on the handsome prince part, but lying back in the water staring at a sunny blue sky, I could pretend I was anywhere. Just Cass, on an extended lakeside holiday.

My school uniform has seen better days. Grubby, worn, with little holes burned in the skirt from all my fire experiments. The jacket's a bit better, since I only wear that at night. Probably I should make more of it just nightwear.

Nutbars

This diary is my volleyball. I didn't get shipwrecked, and I don't have a face painted on it, but it's what I talk to. Did Tom Hanks talk to the volleyball because he'd gone mad, or to stop himself going mad?

Reading back, I see I haven't really talked about myself very much. Me before here. I'm seventeen. Eighteen in February. I have hazel eyes and light brown hair with just a bit of a wave. It goes blondish if I stay out in the sun a lot – I guess it's probably blondish now. Using a lake as a mirror isn't very accurate. I'm 172cm tall, and usually feel a complete hulk around other girls. Mum says I have good skin, but my acne keeps making her a liar. I'm okay-looking; not model material but I clean up all right.

I like The Killers, Gwen Stefani and Little Birdy. Escher prints. Orlando Bloom. Surfing (badly!). But mostly reading. Sf&f, but almost anything really. I was going to study English, history and archaeology at university, and hopefully figure out some way to turn an Arts degree into a job. I'm an above average student, but I'm not brilliant at anything. Partly because I'd rather read than study.

My best friend is Alyssa Caldwell. I like Nick Dale, except when I don't like him. I have one brother, Julian. My Dad left when I was ten, but we see him most months. The thing I wanted most was to be witty and confident instead of just hanging about the edges whenever I'm with a bunch of people, thinking up brilliant things I could say if the right opportunity arose. Guess I don't have to worry about that any more.

Being here is amazing. I'm on a whole new world, and the moonlight is wine. Today it was rough, but I'm coping really well, honestly.

And my period's starting and I hate this. Hate it.

Wednesday, December 5

Felt

I'm now officially sick to death of wool. But I have a blanket, maybe. I'm letting it dry, hoping that it doesn't just fall to pieces when I try and pick it up.

Thursday, December 6

Tissue

Mum talks occasionally about the myth of the paperless society. She means people printing things in offices, but I'm being hit hard by a lack of paper products at the moment. With a choice of washing my butt in the lake or using leaves when I go to the toilet (not even mentioning that the toilet is a hole I scraped in the ground), I miss paper every day. My history notes didn't last long and I don't want to use this diary. Add today's blocked and dripping nose and the failure of my history classes to tell me what pre-industrial women used for their periods, and I really really miss the papered society.

So anyway, since I wasn't feeling well, I spent the morning wandering aimlessly about, scaring the pigsies and annoying the cats. There's a tunnel leading below the amphitheatre, deep enough that it's too dark for me to be keen on more than standing at the entrance peering in. The cats, at least, behave just like stray cats – they watch you, and leave if you get near. Even though there's a lot of them, they don't seem at all interested in hurling themselves at my throat or doing other uncatty things. I wouldn't dare try and pick one up though.

Festering Bag of Snot

The day's gone very black and hot. I rescued my craft project, which fortunately was nearly dry and didn't immediately fall to pieces when I picked it up. It doesn't much look like felt – more like a bunch of wool pressed flat and only just clinging together – but it's still much better than a badly woven mat of leaves. A soft, clean (faintly greenish) piece of luxury.

My blocked nose has turned into a chesty cough. By the time the storm started rolling in I felt absolutely rotten, but made myself go hunting in the nearest gardens, bringing up as much 'trusted' food as possible. I won't have to worry about water, since I still haven't managed to block the stair to the roof. I've set some bowls on the stair to catch water, and positioned my bed against the wall without a window. It hasn't quite started raining yet, but it looks like it will be bad. Like my cold.

Friday, December 7

Rain and Phlegm

All day. So hard to breathe.

Monday, December 10

Not Drowning

When I was in Year 10 I sat next to a guy named David in Science. We weren't friends, didn't socialise outside that class, but we got on well. He was funny and nice, acted the clown to hide he was shy. He moved schools the next year, and early this year I heard that he had died. He'd always had a weak heart, was occasionally sick because of it. I didn't know what to say, what to feel.

Mum says there's three bad things about dying: pain and other unpleasantries, the way your friends and relatives feel after, and the fact that you don't get to find out what happens next. Mum's an atheist – she says she's never met a religion that didn't sound made up. I'm agnostic, because I like the idea of there being something more, but the possibility of it working like Mum thinks it does – that you just stop – doesn't particularly bother me.

I don't remember very much about the past couple of days, but through it all was threaded this horror that no-one would know. That Mum would never know. And, yeah, that I wouldn't find out any of the explanations behind all this.

My family's a healthy one. Colds occasionally, minor temperatures, chicken pox. I've never been to hospital. I needed one yesterday. I don't know the name for what I had. I thought you caught colds or flu from other people, not just abruptly developed them. Whatever it was, I couldn't breathe, could barely move. I don't know what my temperature was, since I felt hot and cold at random, but I'm pretty sure I spent half my time hallucinating (unless there really were dragons and sea monsters spiralling across the ceiling).

Last night was another moonfall. The inside of the building glowed, and I could see the light misting past the windows. I couldn't tell if it was exactly the same, since I couldn't get up to go on the roof. I didn't feel drunk either – I was so out of it I'm hardly sure it happened – but I remember feeling warm and relaxed and not having to fight so much to breathe.

Today I'm not exactly better, but most of the gunk clogging my lungs is gone, and the fever, and I've managed to get upstairs to the roof, and sit here and write this, even if it's taken me half the day. Abandoned as it is, I'm so glad to have found this town. I feel vulnerable enough here. I wouldn't have survived the last few days without solid shelter. I'm feeling very small at the moment, but so glad to be breathing.

All the effort making my felt blanket, and now it really really needs a wash.

Tuesday, December 11

Not entertaining

It doesn't get light till past 10am on my watch now. And dark around midnight. Now that I'm breathing better, it seems to take forever for the night to end. All I've done so far today is lie on the roof watching the birds on the lake. I'm worried that I've hurt my eyes somehow, since random parts of the world are blurry and not quite focused.

I'm going to go down for a forage soon. If I feel stronger later, I might even try to clean my wool collection. Survivor Cass needs some time-consuming projects to keep her sane.

Not that the prospect of trying to relight my fire is anything to look forward to. That's going to have to wait more than a few days – it just takes too much concerted energy to do, and I can't even climb a flight of stairs without having to sit down.

Wednesday, December 12

It's not paranoia if they really are watching you

I'm stronger today – woke up incredibly hungry, which made me realise how little I ate while I was ill. I've been getting a lot done this morning, just by stopping and resting every few minutes.

The idea of lighting the fire is still in the way-too-much category, but I've managed to clean out my room again, and washed my wool mound and blanket. The blanket didn't like that, and has developed splits. Once it's dry I'm going to have to be careful taking it back up to my room, or I'll have felt strips instead.

While it dries I'm searching the nearest buildings. I'm increasing my collection of metal and pottery objects, though, and even have a few knives. They're not very sharp, and the handles have all fallen to pieces, but I have a few ideas on how to fix that. In a few days I'll have a go at making covers for the windows. I also want to make another blanket: if it wasn't such a lot of work I'd make a mound of them. Though I suppose I'll have plenty of time to try.

My eyes are still strained. Not everything is blurry, and not all the time, but I'm starting to wonder if I'll end up needing glasses. That's annoying, but I'm more bothered by a sense of being watched all the time. I'm forever feeling there's someone standing just behind me, or trying to catch movement out of the corner of my eye.

It's not the cats, or not so far as I can tell. There's a few about, but they've never been very interested in me so long as I stay away from their amphitheatre. I've been taking a lot of interest in the birds, hoping they have some nests in convenient spots. After weeks living mainly on red pears and washews I'm really interested in the thought of eggs. I'm also going to experiment more with some of the other possible foods I've found – I've been a bit too scared after the vomiting day, but now I'm starting to wonder if missing out on some of the food groups was the reason I was so sick.

Today's mantra

There are no black things
Creeping
In the corner of my eye
And
There are no claws
Glinting
In the shadow of that door
But
There's nothing wrong with
Me
I'm just fine, I'm
Sane
Normal
Not seeing things.

Friday, December 14

Laying their plans

Mum has a CD of this old musical version of *War of the Worlds*. On that, the Martians make this incredible noise, this 'uullllaaaaa' howl which is so totally unnatural, not a noise anything on Earth would make.

I'm looking for tripods on the horizon.

The noise isn't the one from the CD, of course, but it is super weird. A mournful wail so deep I feel it more in my bones than my ears. I'm sitting on the roof of my tower, listening, watching, but I can't see where it's coming from. It sounds like the hills are moaning.

Whatever it is, it's big. Could even dinosaurs make a noise like this? After spending the last couple of days convinced that something's been watching me, I was creeped out enough already. I wish tonight was a moonfall, or that I'd at least figured out a way to make a light for overnight. I'm not up for fire-lighting. I'm lying here with my pippin statue, pretending it's company.

At this point, I can't decide whether it would be better to be going nuts, or to really have things lurking around every corner, stalking me.

Mouse-like

Is there any difference between being eaten by a bear or a big cat and being eaten by a huge and spooky monster? The monster might even be quicker. You could say that the bear would be more 'natural' I suppose – but that's just familiarity. Bears and cats are the predators which are real to my world, but does it make a difference if the teeth belong to a dragon?

There might be monsters that kill you slowly, though. Or, if there is any kind of soul or afterlife, things which kill you 'wrong' so that your soul is damaged as well.

So can you tell I spent the night obsessing over what was going to come galumphing up to kill me? For all that, it was a good night. The noise stopped when the sun went down, and everything felt lighter somehow. The feeling of being watched had gone, and then the animals came back. I hadn't realised, but the more I felt I was being watched, the fewer animals I saw. Like they were all hiding, while I wandered stupidly around.

The town's main population is all on the smaller side. Sometimes the grey terriers show up and chase things, or the deer or mondo elk wander through, but I don't think they like staying here. It's very open compared to the forest. Birds dive-bomb the little animals and it's easy to see anything approaching if you're high up. What bushes and trees there are aren't so big and thick that anything large could go any distance without being spotted. If the Ming Cats hunt here, they do it at night.

Today's project was to block the windows on the ground floor. Fort Cass is still far from impregnable, but every bit helps. I wish my eyes would stop blurring.

Saturday, December 15

Buttered scones would hit the spot

After winding wool into a rough handle for the longest of my salvaged knives, and 'sharpening' it by scraping it against rocks, I walked back along the lake to chop long poles of bamboo from a stand I'd passed. It was surprisingly easy, but I'm so tired now and it's barely lunchtime. I'm the kind of lumberjack who needs nanna naps.

Sunday, December 16

OMGWTF!

There were two people in my room when I woke up.

They were standing at the top of the stair, talking to each other. Opening my eyes in the grey of just-dawn and seeing these hazy black figures, my heart gave such a thump. And I squeaked and scurried backward and then felt like a complete dick as they just looked down at me and turned out not to be monsters after all.

A guy and a girl, dressed in tight-fitting black stuff, some kind of uniform. They looked to be Asian (black hair and eyes and a creamy-gold skin, though the girl's eyes didn't have that fold). I couldn't understand what they said to me, didn't even recognise the sound of the language, but the tone wasn't threatening. Annoyed or irritated, perhaps, but I didn't get 'prepare to die' vibes off them.

They were surveying my room but not touching anything, and didn't seem too keen on getting close to me, either. I was foolishly glad I'd only just cleaned up, and all my food was neatly separated in bowls with no rubbish lying about. That I was wearing my underpants. One, the girl, started talking to me, asking questions, and I tried talking back, and was trying not to cry because they were people and even though they understood me as little as I understood them, THEY WERE PEOPLE!! It was all I could do not to scream and throw myself at them.

They had a little talk, then the guy went up to the roof and the girl gestured at me to follow her. I put on my shoes first, and packed my backpack since she didn't seem to mind waiting around, though she kept her distance from me and kept scanning the room as if she suspected I had someone hidden behind a jar. I immediately started thinking about plagues, and wondered if that was why the town was abandoned.

She led me down to the lakeshore and stopped at a rock and pointed to me and then to the rock, and when I sat down she walked off. But that was okay because I was busy looking at the ship on the lake.

Not a boat. A narrow metal arrowhead shaped thing, creamy-grey with dark blue side sections. It's big enough to be carrying dozens of people, and is definitely not primitive. Whoever these people are, they're more advanced than Earth.

The two in black weren't overwhelmingly surprised to see me here, or very interested. They acted as if they hadn't expected to see me, and put me aside while they went on with whatever it is they're really here for.

I saw another pair of them, also black-clad, standing up at the central bluff, but then something came out of the ship. A flat platform which floated above the water, and stopped right next to the bank where I was sitting, delivering two women, older than the pair from Fort Cass, and wearing a mix of dark green and darker green, not quite so tight-fitting as the black outfit. Again they were all business, pointing at me and then one particular corner of their platform and very stern about it.

It's not like I was going to say 'no', hopping on very meek, and standing exactly where I was put. The platform began moving straight away, though I couldn't for the life of me figure out what they were doing to control it. Maybe someone back at the ship was steering.

They talked to each other as they went back, and watched me as if they thought I was going to take a knife to them. I saw no more than a corridor of the ship before they ushered into this little box of a room, and shut the door on me. So small it's practically a cupboard, but every few minutes it grows warmer or colder or hums. Maybe they're irradiating me for bugs.

I've been here over half an hour. I wish I'd had a chance to pee before being rescued.

Monday, December 17

The excitement of butterfly grapes

It seems an age since I could write in this book, though my watch says it's only been a day or so. Where to start?

On the ship I was finally let out of my cupboard by a woman in yet another uniform – grey and darker grey with a long pale grey shirt over the top. Just like a doctor's coat, so no surprise that she was some kind of doctor and gave me a medical exam and a bunch of injections. Most of the injections didn't involve needles, but something like a compressed air cylinder. The worst was directly to my left temple, which ached, and then ached worse, and now is a dull persistent pain.

She talked a lot while she peered and prodded, and we did a little pantomime of her pointing to herself and saying "Ista Tremmar" and me going "Cassandra". Then the best part of the day beyond being rescued: a shower and a toilet (hilarious pantomime explanations). The toilet was weird – it was a form-fitted bench with a hole, which doesn't flush or have any water in it – you close the lid after you use it and if you open it again it doesn't smell like it's been used. I couldn't properly see the bottom, but it looked like an empty box. The toilet paper is thickish, pre-moistened squares like baby wipes. And the shower – warm water and soap!

I wanted to stay in there forever, but after Ista had gone through this pantomime of pointing to it and making totally incomprehensible gestures, I'd decided I was supposed to be quick. No towel: the ceiling blew a gale of hot air at me when I turned the water off.

There was a white shift to wear, and I had to put all my clothes in a plastic bag. I couldn't find a comb or toothbrush, so finger-combed my hair into some sort of order before Ista led me off to a room full of chairs. In the medical room, everything was designed to be tucked away neatly and take up no more space than it had to, so I was almost expecting some kind of cattle class cramped airplane seating, but instead there were these long, padded and reclined chairs, like a cross between a dentist's chair and a bed. There were three rows of four, each set up on its own platform. When I lay down the cushions squished themselves in around me like they were trying to hold on – the weirdest sensation ever – but it was absolutely comfortable.

Once I was settled in, Ista gave me another injection, a sedative this time. I was awake long enough to see a plastic/glass bubble thing come up around my seat, and then I was out until waking up where I am now, not on the ship, but on a bed-shelf made of whitestone with a mattress on top, in a small but not cramped room. There's a window, plastic, unopenable and very thick, which looks out over the roof of what seems to be one huge mound of connected building: blockish and white and eerily reminiscent of the town I was in but all joined together and with only occasional windows and doors. The only other thing to be seen is clouds and a black and choppy ocean.

The door is locked, but I found a cupboard which had clean clothes in it (underpants, grey tights/pants and a loose white smock). Other than that, there was only a whitestone shelf before the window and a chair before it which makes me think it's meant to be a narrow table. I tried knocking on the door, but not in a frantic I'm-panicky-and-bothersome way, and searched about, but there was nothing to do except stare out the window. At least my eyes have decided to stop being blurry.

No greenery visible. I can't guess why these people all live mounded up here when there's acre upon acre of lake and forest left to some cats. I keep trying to spot anything which will show me that it's definitely the same planet. But there's nothing but whitestone buildings and water, and it's too cloudy to see sun or moon. Quite a lot of futuristic air traffic. I bounced up and down for a while, thinking that maybe the gravity was a fraction less, but if there's a difference it's subtle enough to be dismissed as imagination.

None of my belongings were with me, not even my watch, so I don't know how long I sat around, but finally a man showed up with a tray of food. He was wearing the same sort of uniform as the rest, but in shades of purple and violet, and was the first person who acted like I was interesting rather than a little problem which had to be tidied away. He gawked at me, in other words, and asked a bunch of questions I had no way of understanding or answering, all in the time it took him to cross and put the tray on the table. One of the greensuits was waiting outside, or I expect he would have stayed and gawked some more. I felt like I was one of those kids found raised by wolves or something.

I dove on the food as soon as the door closed. There were two slices of warm yellow cakey stuff. Not sweet. Some kind of heavy bread? Fruit in jelly where all of the fruit pieces were like butterfly-shaped grapes. A stack of vegetables in sticks – green and white and yellow sticks, all apparently growing naturally to the thickness and length of my little finger. The yellow ones tasted like carrot trying to be celery, the white was zingy and the green very salty. I spent ages on the last of the grapes, trying to work out if grapes would really naturally grow to look so much like butterflies. They tasted like vanilla apples with grape texture.

The way I shovelled all this down my throat, you'd never guess I once wouldn't eat anything other than chips and gravy for dinner. I didn't grow out of that till I was in high school and still occasionally annoy Mum with things I'd refuse to even try. But when you've spent a good half hour pondering whether to eat the wormy bits of your red pears for the protein – and even tried a bite – then no-one gets to call you fussy any more.

After an age the pinksuited person came back and took the tray, and the greensuit gave me my backpack, so now I have this diary again and my watch and everything. Even my clothes, clean but very battered. And next?

Unobservant

After hours stuck in this room I finally realised that the cupboard wasn't the only internal door. I probably wouldn't have even worked out the cupboard if it hadn't been left slightly open. When it's shut, there's just a bit of a dint and if you push the dint the door moves in then slides into the wall. So eventually I spotted another dint, over near the more obvious door to the hall. And it was a door and I have my own bathroom.

Then, after the world's longest shower, I was sorting through my things and I found they'd somehow recharged my mobile. Even though I'd kept it off almost all the time, the battery had run down after a couple of weeks. I immediately played all my song ring tones, over and over. Five whole songs, and a few partial songs. That made me cry.

And now I have games! No mobile signal whatsoever, which isn't a surprise, but trivial entertainment for the win!

You too can have an exciting career in medicine! Join our Test Subject Program today.

Two greensuits came and escorted me to two greysuits: the same woman and a younger man. I think I'm in some sort of security wing of a military hospital. Everyone's in uniform.

The headache from that injection is worse, and wasn't helped by more poking and prodding and taking blood samples and putting me in odd machines. It was very tedious, interesting only because I couldn't see any way they were controlling all but a few obvious devices.

I tried pantomiming that my head hurt and that I would like some Aspro thank you very much, but though they seemed to understand, they just looked sorry and shook their heads. I'm guessing shaking your head means no here. It's hard to describe how my head feels – like a blocked sinus, but above my left eye. It's started to make my sight go all grey with wormy wiggles. I may be having a bad reaction to whatever they were immunising me against, but they didn't seem at all surprised or worried during my exam.

I'm going to have to lie down.

Tuesday, December 18

Skullburster?

I spent the day curled in the bed, being a complete sook about this headache, and not at all friendly when the greysuits came to check on me. I totally feel like a lab rat. I'm sure they've got cameras in here. I can't even turn out the lights. No switches.

It feels like the front-left of my head is pushing out from the inside. Having showers helps a little, or maybe I'm just feeling the need to make up for lost time. The soap is liquid and very spicy-scented. When I'm not showering I'm peering in the mirror in the bathroom. My left eye looks really bloodshot, but not swollen. And I look horrible. I always thought it would be nice to be really thin, but I'm haggard. I had no idea I looked this bad. It's only been a month.

Outside is all storms, the lightning strange and unreal because the thunder is blocked out. The water looks very black and mountainous and I'm glad I'm not in it, but I'm starting to wish I wasn't here. I just can't figure these people out. They weren't at all surprised to find me in that town, though it's obvious none of them recognised my English. One of the shots they gave me seems to have helped bunches in clearing the last of that super-cold away, and they've fed and clothed me and put me in a room. And injected me with something which I can't believe was just an immunisation. Do they find so many random people from other planets that it's normal to use them as test subjects? They're not even trying to figure out a way to communicate with me.

If my head hurt less I'd have the energy to be scared.

Wednesday, December 19

A Vision of Walls

My eyes are going strange again. Not blurriness on random objects this time, but lines. Symbols. It's like I'm seeing an outline of this room overlaid over the room itself, with squiggles in odd spots. I don't know whether to be worried about seeing things, or if there might be some kind of hologram being projected into the room.

My head no longer feels like it's going to explode, though it still aches a fair bit.

Dotty

My headache is more or less gone, but now I have a dot. A green dot.

As hallucinations go, this is an unwavering one. It looks like a piece from a game of checkers, floating at eye height. I can't touch it, and it doesn't seem to cast a shadow. It's been there at least ten minutes.

I've heard of people who see sounds as colours. And of brain tumours pressing in places they shouldn't be and causing problems. The question of what that injection did to me has gone beyond scary now.

The other thing I've noticed is that it's still night-time. It was day before the storm, but I haven't seen the sun since. Possibly I'm on a different world again, maybe. Is the gravity less, or do I just feel more energetic than before? Has it been night for a day straight, or did I just sleep when it was light?

Thursday, December 20

A shot of words

Escorted again to the greysuits, and OW! They had me lie down on another dentist-style chair, this one with its own little helmet. I can't say I was keen, but the greensuits were waiting just outside. Is it better to be a dignified test subject, or a defiant but battered one?

I was just noticing that there was a green dot in the centre of that room too when they turned their evil torture machine on and all these words began to squiggle across the back of my eyes. If I'd thought my head was going to explode before, that was nothing to having a dictionary injected into my skull.

Someone really has to explain the concept of painkillers to these people.

I think I had convulsions. It was a bit hard to tell, but I remember them holding my arms. There was some blacking out going on as well, and a long hazy time after where they were talking about my heart rate and stuff. After a while I must have passed out properly, and now I'm back in my box.

There's a thousand thousand words sitting in my skull. They murmur at me whenever I look at anything. As I'm writing this there's an awkward echo giving me a different set of sounds, and an image of strange squiggles which I presume mean what I'm writing. I don't think I 'know' this language, but sounds are suggesting themselves to me in response to things I look at and even things I think. So I could on one level understand what the greysuits were saying, in the way you half understand those garbled train announcements, where you get the gist and guess the rest. It's not like having an English-Alien dictionary.

I can even read the squiggles I'm hallucinating around the room, in that I'm sure they read 'No Access' when I glance at them, but if I look at them closely they're not letters I recognise, let alone words. Trippy. Still, having a language poured into my skull will save a lot of time, and I'd be 11/10 pleased if my head didn't hurt so much.

Infodump

I was given a few hours to recover from dictionary-injection, and another meal, which helped a lot. Then off to a meeting-type room to talk – actually talk! – to the first greysuit and a new one. Since my internal translation service doesn't automatically make me able to pronounce their words or understand their grammar, I mainly listened and tried to understand what the hell they were going on about. Non-literal phrases especially throw me, just as anything like 'jump the shark' would surely confuse them. They spoke very slowly, and had a plastic sheet on the table which acted like a computer screen and handily showed pictures to help me along. First screen I've seen – all the rooms I've been in are incredibly bare.

The echo in my head had already let me know that the 'Ista' part of 'Ista Tremmar' is a title, a bit like 'Doctor'. The other greysuit was 'Sa Lents', and I think 'Sa' is a general honorific. He's going to be my sponsor.

Centuries ago people called the 'Lantar' lived on the planet I was on. It's called Muina. These people were very learned and in touch with the 'Ena' (which, confusingly, seems to mean 'spaces'). These Lantar triggered a disaster which 'shattered the spaces' and caused thousands of mutant monsters called 'Ionoth' to show up and eat people. So all the Lantar ran away and went to a bunch of different planets. This one is called Tare. They didn't find it a very easy planet to live on, and sometimes the Ionoth things would show up here.

Recently the Tare people started to move between planets again to try and find a solution to the Ionoth problem. They found other worlds where people from Muina survived, but they consider Muina still too dangerous to live on. All the people in uniform I've met are part of Tare's research and defence against the Ionoth organisation (called KOTIS, which must be some kind of acronym, or just doesn't translate).

Remember I said no-one was really surprised to find me at that town? Well, they weren't. They estimate that at least twenty people each year get accidentally whisked off to somewhere else through something which sounds like wormholes: either to Muina or to one of the known worlds or just totally somewhere else. They find about half of them, some alive, some dead, and if they're from one of the known worlds they send them back.

Earth – you probably figured – isn't one of the known worlds. They asked me a bunch of questions to try and figure if I was from a world they'd had a stray from before. They call people who accidentally wander through wormholes 'strays'. Sa Lents is some kind of anthropologist and he says that my description of Earth doesn't match up to the lost worlds previously described and he's looking forward to learning and writing about it. Good for him, I suppose.

Anyway, I guessed right when I said they weren't at that town to rescue me. There's a particular kind of Ionoth called Ddura (massives) which are really rare and from what little I could make out are something like the whales of the Ena. REALLY massive, if that was what was making the incredible noise before I was rescued. They'd detected one on Muina and rushed out to try and study it, but were too late and only got me instead.

I find it hard to believe that the people from Earth are from some other planet. For one thing, you'd think we'd have legends or stories about Ionoth and this Ena place and Muina. And though they talked about this happening thousands of years ago, 'modern' humans have been on Earth for at least tens of thousands. So, not convinced, though since Tare people look just like Earth people there's probably some connection.

Strays count as a kind of refugee, and other than representing a slight curiosity for being from a 'new' world, I'm not particularly unusual. Fortunately, it doesn't seem like Tare has a refugee policy like Australia's, since I wouldn't enjoy mandatory detention. Although they are trying to find all the worlds that the Muinans went to, and so are already trying to find Earth in a way, they didn't seem to think I should get my hopes up about it. Apparently the Ionoth have been really bad lately and they're doing a lot more defensive work than exploration.

Sa Lents is going to be my sponsor. After some more quarantine and testing I get to be integrated into society, and that means a couple of years at least of living with Sa Lents and his family while I learn the language and enough skills to get a job, and he conveniently does a little research project on Earth. He has two daughters – one older and one younger than me – and the older one has just left home.

They started talking about how long it would take me to learn to use the 'Kuna' (a word which also seems to mean 'spaces'), and we had a really confused discussion for a while until I finally figured out what the injection to the temple was for. I don't quite understand the whole 'spaces' thing, but the nearest I can make out the people on this planet are several steps ahead in terms of computers and networks and virtual environments, and before they could give me this internal dictionary, they had to set up an interface in my head.

I'm a cyborg! The Tarens use nanite technology and my head has been exploding the last few days while a computer built itself in my brain. And I'm not hallucinating the dot in the middle of the room or the floating words. That's just the default display of the computer in my head. Before I get sent off with Sa Lents I have to pass basic interfacing-with-virtual-environments training. And currently I have no access rights to anything, so all I can see is a dot.

I just reread all this big long entry and it sounds nothing like the explanation they gave me, which involved showing me pictures obviously meant for children and saying in their language: "Muina. Home. Planet. Home. Lantar. People." And me sitting there looking puzzled, as my injected language tool triggered concept recognition, not words. I'm not sure how much of what I've written down matches what they were trying to tell me. The pictures were more helpful than what they were saying.

It was only when I was taken back to my room and had had a shower that I started crying. Because being rescued and going home are worlds apart. And, weird as this sounds, because I'm not a surprise to them.

Friday, December 21

Say Ah

Another medical exam to start my day – if it is the start. Since it never gets dark outside and the lights don't go out in my room, I'm having a lot of trouble keeping track of time. My meals are all very similar – something fruity, vegetable sticks, either bread or processed fishy stuff – so all I have to go on is when they choose to talk to me, and a watch which tells time for a totally different planet.

Being able to ask questions, no matter how slowly, really makes a difference to the poking and prodding sessions. The doctor is a pretty nice lady. She even apologised for not giving me painkillers, but apparently it can cause problems with the way the interface builds itself.

We had a long, if infantile, chat about the interface, which has left me feeling very dubious. I kept picturing my brain being shredded by little wires, until it dribbles out my nose, but from the helpful illustrations Ista Tremmar showed me, the nanites are so small they build a mesh which coats the insides of veins. Computerised cholesterol? Ista Tremmar said that almost all strays have a naturally strong affinity for the Ena, and for some reason this effects the amount of body 'real estate' the interface grows to cover, which confused me again because I don't understand what the Ena is or its connection with nanites.

Having a large interface may or may not be a good thing, but it sounds like knowing how to use it is what matters. These people spend all their time permanently wired into a really complex virtual world, and they start living there just after they figure out the whole walking thing.

Kuna seems to translate to 'virtual space', maybe. I desperately need a real dictionary, rather than these vague feelings that what they're saying matches something I know about. I still can't quite decide what they mean by the Ena. It could be some kind of other dimension? Or an evil spirit world? The fact that it's involved in travelling really quickly from one planet to another makes me think of hyperspace, but hyperspace is really just a 'magic science' word people made up, isn't it?

Saturday, December 22

Meh

I can't sleep. I'm not even sure I'm supposed to be sleeping right now.

Today was my first session with Sa Lents. I told him I don't think the people of Earth are descended from Muinans, and he said that other Muinan-settled worlds had forgotten their origins too, and that I was definitely Muinan-descended according to my genes. I refrained from pointing out that that could mean that Muinans are Earth-descended.

The rest of the time was spent on geography. I drew a really bad map of Earth with my finger on the tablecloth screen and wrote down the countries I could remember.

I'm supposed to start on interface learning tomorrow, once they're sure there's been no strange issues caused by my language injection, which I reacted to 'poorly'. I am very bored. I wish I'd brought my pippin statue along for company.

Sunday, December 23

Digital mind

No more complaining about being bored. Interface training is giving me some idea just what having a computer in your head means.

The training is aimed at little kids and is as much teaching them to read as it is how to use their interfaces. Just read. They don't teach kids to write. So obvious, but yet so strange. If you can select a letter from the alphabet quicker than writing one out, why bother with writing? I'm being trained by a complex teaching program which looks like a cuddly lady in her thirties. Sana Dura. It took me way too long to realise she wasn't an actual real-time person, but eventually I realised that whenever I interrupted her and asked my scrambled questions, she would answer, but then go back to exactly what she'd been saying, in exactly the same tone.

I did exercises for ages – I want out of this room – and the more the basics settle in, the less straightforward the training becomes. At first it was just me and Sana Dura standing in a colourful room, with her telling me to push buttons which I can see before me. I can't really describe how I push them. I see them floating in front of me and they activate if I want them to. Then I 'graduated' to alphabet and it was a very interactive 'touch the letter' game which put 3D movies to shame. It was as if I was in my room, and also this colourful world of floating letters and flowers and cutesy animals, the two worlds overlaid on each other. I find it very disorienting unless I close my eyes to block out reality.

There are twenty-eight letters in their alphabet.

Monday, December 24

86400

I can turn out the lights! It feels like *such* an achievement, but so far as I can tell it means that this tutorial program thinks I'm about five now. I can also open the internal doors without having to go poke the locks, and I can make the window go dark like extremely tinted glass. All of it's extremely simple – it's just that having run through all these training exercises I've had an upgrade to my status so that I can use some of the minor room functions. My injected language has also settled in more – I'm not going to be able to speak it properly any time soon, but it helps my memory during all the infant lessons I've been having. Accelerated learning, I'd guess you'd call it, and I'm taking big leaps forward – enough to start asking more complex questions.

During yesterday's session with Sa Lents we used my watch to work out how long an Earth year is compared to a Tare one. Fortunately, while they use different squiggles for each digit, their number system is apparently the same as ours. I don't know how I would have managed if they used binary or base three or something. I'm good at maths, but not *that* good.

Even though there's now a calculator in my head, I find it really hard to think in their digits, so I only used it for the large multiplications and divisions, and did the workings in the back of my diary. Sa Lents said he found the way I write very interesting – kind of like cave-paintings to him, I bet.

Anyway, one Earth year is worth about three Tare years. Sa Lents is over a hundred Tare years old. Their 'living day' is about twenty-six Earth hours long, though neatly divided into ten 'hours' of a hundred 'minutes' each. What they consider a second is not quite the same as an Earth second, and there's a hundred of those in each minute. For every five of these days the planet has one solar day (which explains why it stayed dark outside so long). I don't in the least understand how a planet can have a longer day but a shorter year than Earth's, yet similar gravity.

The mind's eye

Den = second

Joden = minute

Kasse = hour

Kaorone = 'living day'

Kao = day (single day/night cycle)

So my name is a bit like a reference to time here. That's better than the Earth meaning by far. Cassandra means 'she who entangles men', which has got to be the suckiest name meaning ever, and that's not even getting into the whole cursed by Apollo and then everyone thinks you're mad and you know everything's going to end up a mess and can't do anything about it part. I've never understood why Mum picked it, since she's usually more sensible about names. I can think of ten million names I'd rather have than one which stands for tragic futility and madness.

That's – it sounds circular saying it, but it drives me nuts, thinking that I'm really nuts. I mean, walking through cracks in the world to different planets and having computers installed in your head? The giggling in a straightjacket possibility seems so much more likely.

And I'm not. I'd know, somewhere deep down, I'd know if this was all imagination. Delusion. I'd never have made up being so sick, for a start, or those blisters. I'm not imagining any of this. I'm not.

...

Must sleep more and practice interface less. Then I wouldn't get so worked up over stupidities.

Tuesday, December 25

From here to you

Merry Christmas Mum. Merry Christmas Dad. Merry Christmas Jules. If there was some way I could make you feel better right now, I would.

Wednesday, December 26

Moving on

I've been released from the Institute! I'm on 'parole' with Sa Lents, after a final medical exam where they decided they don't need to keep me under close observation any longer.

One thing the doctor told me just before she sent me off really brought home what kind of society I've found myself in. I currently have the barest access rights to the systems around me, but the government here has access rights to me. My interface isn't just one way, and I'm not in control of it. It's a school, entertainment, a health monitor and an alarm. It will send a distress signal if I'm sick or hurt, and it can stimulate my brain in a way which regulates hormones. I've automatically been 'regulated' for birth control. Rules about having babies are really strict here, and you have to be given permission to conceive, for each and every baby you want. You have to pass some kind of parental worthiness test and everything.

Having someone else put me on birth control without my permission is just...I feel really strange about it, especially considering the uncomfortable conversation I had with Mum about babies at the beginning of the year, when I went out with Sean J. Sean and I have been friends a few years, and we were trying to see if we could be more, but it was totally a bad idea. We were careful enough, the couple of times we did it before the sheer awkwardness brought us to our senses, but if I'd wanted a baby, I could have walked down that path. I don't get that choice here. I'd have to fill out a form first, and hope someone stamped it APPROVED.

Sa Lents is taking me to his family's home on a place called Unara, which involves a long journey by plane (or tanz, as these spaceshippy flying machines are called – they don't look at all like our planes). It'll take a few hours, but my interface practice comes with me everywhere. I've a whole world of work installed in my head, and it's powered by my own body, so won't run low on batteries – unless I do.

I'm growing increasingly confident using the interface, now that I properly know a few basic words. The concepts aren't very different from email or web browsers, just without a mouse or keyboard. I haven't qualified for some of it yet, but have just stopped to write after sitting through the introductory lessons for how to record everything I see and hear, and keep a personal library. Every person on this planet is a CCTV system. I'm definitely going to have to remember that when I talk to anyone, or am in sight or earshot of anyone. I keep telling myself it's not that different to everyone having a mobile phone and access to You Tube, but it's hard not to be a little creeped out.

Talking to people remains a huge challenge. I'm more or less okay listening, at least to get the general gist, but it's going to be a mid-sized forever before I can talk anything like normally. I don't *know* any of the words. It's not like a proper dictionary. I can't look up cat and find 'nyar'. Instead, I think cat and my head produces an oozy possibility of words and, increasingly, a lot of handy labelled pictures. But it can be hard to tell if it's meant to be a picture of an animal or a predator or hunter or kitten – and abstract concepts are far more difficult. My head fills with pictures and feelings when people talk and an odd kind of certainty of knowing what they said without understanding how I know. The idea comes without necessarily an exact translation. I'm trying to figure out how to annotate my head with words I'm certain of.

Anyway, I'm pretty excited just to get out of that military facility.

Thursday, December 27

Overload

Until today, I'd hardly seen any people. Those couple of blacksuits back on Muina, and a few greensuits and greysuits and the guy who brought my meals. The only people who have spoken to me were Sa Lents and Ista Tremmar. At the KOTIS facility all I really saw were three rooms and a few corridors. And, biggest change of all, my interface was at the most minimal level possible.

During the flight – which was a military flight and not open to the public – Sa Lents taught me the different access options of my interface. This is a bit like choosing to have subtitles when watching a DVD, but so much more. I had to laugh when I turned on the 'Public information: people' option, and you could see people's names floating above their heads. World of Warcraft without the shoulder pads. You can't hide your name, apparently, any more than you can absolutely shut the government out of your head.

There are tons of different display options or filters. 'Open' is full of things everyone can see, and is broken down into different levels – emergency and directional and décor and advertisement and entertainment and so on. Then there's 'closed' or 'tight', which is things only you or a particular group can see. Having made sure I knew how to filter all these display levels on and off, Sa Lents had me turn all but directional and décor off before we reached Unara. This was a good move.

Tare is fantastically crowded. I hadn't realised the extent while I was locked away, but they're seriously packed in. From Sa Lents' description – and the world map he showed me how to display – there are a lot of small islands, but only two decent land-masses, and even those are more Tasmania-sized than Australia-sized. Unara is on an island called Wehana, which is almost all city. Not suburbs, not even sky-scrapers, but this deep below the ground and high above the surface endless blocky whitestone *mass* – the same as the Institute, but monumentally larger, like a beehive of people. External windows like the one I had are really rare and not even very popular because people feel exposed and unsafe. I couldn't tell if Sa Lents meant that windows really did make you less safe, or if it was some kind of agoraphobia.

So anyway, we flew through very bad weather over a lot of dark, uninviting water until we reached Carche Landing, which is a main 'airport' of Unara, and Unara pretty much tops what you'd get if you compacted Earth's biggest cities into a ball. People *everywhere*, going every direction, and even the two display filters I had on were just Too Much. The Unaran idea of décor involves holograms of fishes and clouds and winding patterns shifting all over the place and way too much colour and movement. I shut it off.

Sa Lents didn't seem to mind too much – or probably wasn't very surprised – at the way I clutched at his arm. Thinking back it was really just a humungous shopping centre, but airier and with tons of plants (vegetables mainly) growing everywhere, and reminded me vaguely of the Jetsons cartoon with glass tubes with long train things shooting through them. But the constant movement, the absolute mass of people and the height of the central atrium of Carche Landing had me the most freaked out I've been in ages. And the noise. The hive was buzzing.

We boarded one of the glass-tube trains, which thankfully blocked out most of the noise so I could get my head back and look around just at the people inside of the train. I hadn't realised that not everyone here is Asian (or looks Asian, whatever: with black hair and golden skin and 'Asian eyes' I'm calling them Asian). Maybe one in ten Tarens don't look particularly Asian. I haven't seen anyone really black-skinned or any bleached Nordic types, but there's all shades in between and I'm not the only pinkish, brown-haired girl, so I at least don't stick out completely.

Unless we're less genetically similar than I've been told, the dye bottle is popular, especially colours like lime green. Clothes are almost normal, though formal wear for men seems to involve long coats or robes. I was beginning to think everyone on the planet wore tight-tailored uniforms, but that was just the military, of course. Nenna – Sa Lents' younger daughter – dresses like she's out of a music video, but I think I'll save trying to describe Nenna till later. I'm supposed to have gone to bed.

Saturday, December 29

The teens here are your forties

Sa Lents' daughter Nenna is the Energiser Bunny of talk. Or just the Energiser Bunny generally, since she's always moving about, dancing in place, dashing back and forth. I like her, but I'm glad I'm not sharing a room with her.

The Lents have a three-bedroom apartment in an area called Kessine. They've been very nice to me so far, though Sa Lents has been off working at some kind of university and his wife, Ketta, is what I think equates to stock market broker, and spends almost all her time in her home office gazing into nothing I can see. Sa Lents handed me over to Nenna for a couple of days so that she could help me adjust before we started in on our interviews again. He knows how much harder it is for me to talk than listen, and Nenna's really good at explaining everything we do or see, and asking yes and no questions, and bringing some fun to my infant status. And I guess it's not really worth his time interviewing me until I can string a sentence together.

Nenna finds it all very exciting having a stray to look after, and devoted herself to showing me how to change the wall decorations and access the way-too-much entertainment and telling me all the things she thinks worth watching and listening to and getting me to try on her clothes. What was that song? "We'd Make Great Pets". I do feel a little like a new pet, but really Nenna's just a normal kid and doesn't mean anything by it.

One thing I found out right away is that Nenna's absolutely obsessed with the blacksuits. The Setari. The word means something like 'experts' or 'specialists', and after two movies, all the poster-hologram-things in Nenna's room space, and Nenna going on about them constantly, I've figured out they're some kind of psychic soldier. She was really disappointed that I only saw two of them for a couple of minutes.

The movies are highly useful, though I can't tell if they're supposed to be realistic or over-the-top. One was so 3-D I had to look behind me to catch everything going on, but otherwise they're pretty similar to what you'd get out of Hollywood, which I guess means that culturally it's not that different here, for all that most of what's going on plotwise goes over my head. But watching them really helps with my language mountain: I'm picking up the things people say most commonly, and the way people greet each other. Mixing movies and television in with my interface lessons will make this easier, and more interesting.

Nenna's at school at the moment. Despite all the lessons you can have over the interface, there's still mandatory school attendance for sport and practical science classes and other group sessions. Since the city's not open to the real sun, there's three shifts each day instead of a formal night and day. Nenna goes to Shift Three school, and attends four out of six days, which gives me a useful break. Nice as it is to have someone who wants to talk to me, it's also good to have some quiet to think.

I'm not allowed to go out of the apartment yet, but Sa Lents says that when I'm a little more adjusted, Nenna can take me on a tour.

Monday, December 31

This world is not my world

For every thing I find which is similar to Earth, there's as many which are different.

Tare's not a democracy, for a start, or a monarchy. From what I could tell from my session with Sa Lents, it's some kind of quasi-meritocracy. To be put in charge of anything you have to pass exams on related knowledge and practical competence. It sounds like you have to pass exams to get to do pretty much anything; it's all about demonstrating capacity. The top non-military government jobs are Lahanti (city leaders like mayor, except that they're mayors of cities of tens of millions) and any resident can apply to be a Lahanti. They have to pass all these tests and then a council chooses from the top scorers. I asked Sa Lents if people could cheat, or buy better results, or at least bribe the council if they got top scores and he squirmed around the answer a bit and said that such things were very difficult but that no system was perfect.

I'd already thought about the question of cheating and whether having a computer in your head means that there's no crime, but it's not quite so absolute as I thought. Citizens aren't actively monitored, but breaking into someone's house, for instance, when you don't have permission to be there, will trigger alerts. If you attack someone, they can immediately let emergency services observe what they're seeing. If you're knocked out, your interface will send an alert for help. One of the movies Nenna and I watched showed bad guys using programs which changed who the system thought they were, and gave permissions they weren't supposed to have. Probably as likely as any of the hacker excesses of Hollywood but still based on the possible. Tare comes across as hard-working, orderly, and obedient, but not any kind of ideal society. I'm not going to forget the forced birth control any time soon. And they have monster attacks, of course. All the movies Nenna wants me to watch either involve cute boys or monster attacks or both – so not too different from what I watch at home, hah.

There's no stilettos, either. It was a funny thing to notice. Nenna's wardrobe is full of platform boots, and sandals, and a couple of pairs of court shoes, and that's what they're wearing in the movies too. Haven't seen anyone tottering about on pinpoint high heels. Make-up and hair is pretty similar – other than the popularity of day-glo dyes – and there seems to be a complex tradition involving henna-coloured designs on your face. Geometric patterns on guys, and curly tendrils for girls, usually on one cheek or the corner of the forehead or drifting up from the throat. It seems to mainly be worn with really formal, dressed up outfits.

No printed-out books that I've seen. That sucks. I don't mind reading onscreen, and there's no glare or eyestrain problems if you're reading inside your head, but it's just not the same as a proper paperback. Also, no meat in all the meals I've eaten so far, except for fish. And that not very often. At least, I think it's fish. Maybe they cook up the monsters they hunt.

Though it's common not to change surnames when you get married on Tare, the tradition is for the husband to take the wife's name, so 'Lents' is Tsa Lents' wife's family name. That's kind of cool.

Beyond the stars, rampant consumerism

I have money. The allowance has an official name which is very long and vague, but boils down to "Lost Aliens Stipend". Nenna and her mother are taking me shopping for clothes and to see some kind of sport called Tairo.

I keep swapping between excited interest and an unexpected urge to start yelling. I far prefer shopping on Tare to starving on Muina, and yay relatively benign alien civilisation. But the allowance gave me a loud, clear message that what happens now is I learn the language, find a job, build a life here. Getting me home is just not a priority to these people.

Working on gratitude adjustment.

Making a display

Nenna finds my taste in clothes very boring, but otherwise it was a fun day. It's hard not to enjoy shopping, and I found clothes I liked and managed not to have my head explode from all the layered interface displays everywhere, and didn't gawk too much at the occasional person who looked really outrageous – blue glowing patterns beneath skin, hair extensions that reach out and touch passers-by, clothing that constantly oozes and changes shape. Nenna called these kind of people 'teba', which I think might be the equivalent of Goths. Or avant garde experimental artists. They were certainly an exciting reminder that I wasn't in just any old shopping centre.

Plus Tairo rocks.

Picture a big glass box, with the audience in rows all up against the outer walls. There's a hole in each wall, painted a different colour, and a bunch of poles at different heights – a lot like canary perches. Add four teams playing a kind of extreme handball with three balls at once. Then make the players totally Spiderman Jr, able to bounce up the walls and off the poles and leap and twist and somersault – and fly.

Psychic powers, just like the blacksuits. Psychic powers are connected to this Ena in some way, and apparently almost everyone on Tare can use the Ena to some mild degree, though things like flying is elite athlete stuff.

Or, possibly, the Ena or the interface enhances natural psychic abilities. Nenna's explanation was way too confusing.

Anyway, the Tairo match was great fun to watch. I could feel the players thud off the walls right in front of me, and they do things which would make Cirque d'Soleil green. And we had a really nice meal, and Nenna's mother talked to me after about, well, girl-things and how it all works here. The birth control means I won't have periods, for a start, which is a big bonus. And she gave me a cream which is some kind of super hair remover. Use it once or twice a year and no stubble. Deodorant comes in waxy sticks. She gave me a few tips on polite behaviour, and then made me cry because she reminded me so much of Mum, all dry and calm and comfortable, and she held me while I made an idiot of myself and told me I didn't have to pretend not to be homesick and frightened.

JANUARY

Tuesday, January 1

Triple the New Years!

Happy New Year! I wish I was watching fireworks right now. I wonder if New Year is half as big a thing here, since it happens every four months? Nenna's older sister Liane is going to come over today and we're going to go to the Roof. I can tell Nenna's not really comfortable with the excursion: the outside on this planet is basically cold and stormy or cold and windy, and most people simply never go outside. I tried describing Australia to Nenna, and I think even Sydney Harbour would freak her out, let alone somewhere like the Outback. Tarens are severe indoor types. I'm not exactly bush savvy, but, wow, I hope Nenna never gets zapped to Muina.

Whoosh

As Taren days go, I gather this was a good one. Not raining, only lightly overcast, and winds that you could stand upright in. The sea was seriously far down, and looked like the kind you see in those paintings of sailing ships almost standing on their ends. But even the sea was nothing compared to the overwhelming hugeness of this city. The largest land mass on their planet, and almost all of it one whitestone block, like an unsymmetrical step pyramid that just goes on and on.

There was plenty of outdoor activity, but mostly confined to tanz (airships) arriving and leaving in the distance. But I did spot a few other people standing out on the vast whiteness. Maintenance workers, Liane said.

Nenna's sister is more serious and not quite as nice as Nenna. Not nasty, but she wasn't too good at hiding how impatient my slow, stupid-sounding speech made her.

Thursday, January 3

Fruit of the Sea

Much of the food on Tare is grown underwater. I thought some of the vegetables were like seaweed, but I didn't realise how many were water plants. And then there's plants grown in the big atriums and inside 'parkland', and vats of algae and hydroponic installations. There are a few bits of land which aren't covered by city, but it sounds like they're mostly wind-blasted nature reserves. They farm fish in ocean 'arrays', and red meat is an incredibly expensive delicacy.

Today was spent mainly on interface training while Nenna was at school. Well, it's not really interface training any more, just kiddie school. Lessons designed for six year-olds are still hard for me to follow, and very dull. At times I'm just tempted to watch the entertainment channels instead, but after stumbling into a show which I afterwards discovered was labelled "in-skin", I decided I needed more language skills before randomly sampling the entertainment here. "In-skin" isn't a euphemism for porn, though I bet it's used for that. It means that every sense that the interface is able to record is transmitted to the audience. Sight, hearing, smell, and touch. I never entirely lost track of me, sitting on a couch, but someone else's experience was layered over the top of that and I could only cope with a few minutes of that before I had to stop. Then I went and had a shower.

I keep telling myself that I need to be more responsible about my schoolwork, and then five minutes of basic maths leaves me gritting my teeth with anger. I. Just. Finished. High School. I know addition. I'm hoping to convince someone to tailor this stupid course to me sooner rather than later.

It's clear that the Lents are giving me some settling-in time before starting to push, but soon Sa Lents will want to work on his study of Earth, and of course I can't live with the Lents forever. From what little my ineffectual interface searches have shown me, strays don't have a lot of career options open to them even after they've learned the language. And I can't figure out how long the Taren government will pay for me to try.

Nenna's thinking about careers right now too: she has to do some aptitude tests tomorrow, and is pretending not to be worried about it. She says she's going to be a song star, and doesn't need to excel at this aptitude chain. Song stars are almost as popular as the Setari are, and Nenna's favourite show in the world is one where this girl is a song star *and* a Setari. Lots of cute guys, as you can imagine.

There are practically no images of real Setari. The blacksuits don't do publicity, apparently. They're taken to the KOTIS island when they're really little, and are raised to be paranormal soldiers, with limited visits to see their families. I couldn't work out if they can choose not to go.

Saturday, January 5

Fall apart

Just got my diary back. A lot of not-great stuff happened, and I won't be staying with the Lents any more.

Nenna did well on her test, and the next day she was allowed to take me out on her own to celebrate. Of course she decided to show me off to her friends.

We went to a place which was a cross between a café and one of those video game arcades where people have *Dance Dance Revolution* competitions, except this was a psychic powers show-off arena. There was a table of girls waiting, and a couple of guys, and it wasn't fun being exotic curiosity of the month. It's not that they weren't nice, or sneered at me or anything. They got a big kick of listening to me talk in English and even though my attempts to speak Taren are insanely confusing, they hung on my every word as I told them my 'survival' adventures: they were just as interested in what I'd done on Muina as what Earth is like, which is something the KOTIS people didn't really care about. Being outside, finding your own food, sleeping under the stars: that's all incredibly foreign and scary to Tarens.

They also wanted to know everything about the Setari I'd met. The Setari have some kind of security level which means that you can't film them (using the interface – I expect an ordinary camera would work on them). They show up as outlines on interface recordings unless you have permission to capture their image.

My mobile was a useful way to avoid having to keep talking, though it's running low on batteries again. Nenna's friends recorded all the song ring tones, and made me promise to translate the lyrics, which I guess would be a good language exercise. They seemed to like the two Gwen Stefani songs, and *Mr Brightside*. *Sweet Dreams* by Marilyn Manson weirded them out, but the one they liked best was that closing theme to the *Portal* game – *Still Alive* – and so I guess they have a thing about syrupy-sweet sounding music. That it's a psychotic, murderous computer totally contradicting itself is *not* something that's going to translate.

After a while the two guys had a match on the Psychic Showdown thing and that's where it stopped just being embarrassing and got messed up.

By this time, thanks to Nenna's patient and devoted explanations of all things Setari, I knew a bit more about psychic powers. Everyone has a connection to the Ena, which seems to be some kind of psychic dimension (or world of dreams, or something). The connection manifests as telekinesis or pyrokinesis, etcetera: there's a couple of dozen known psychic talents. The original Muinans were really strong in their connection to the Ena, more so than most of the people on Tare are now. Tairo players are strong, but the most powerful psychics are in the Setari, where gifted children are pushed to extremes to increase their abilities.

However, with the interface and 'circuitry' in certain rooms, even weak psychics can be boosted to use whatever talents they have. The two guys were 'projectors', I guess you'd call it, and they were able to make illusions. Not very clear ones, but it was fun to watch.

Strays are thought to be fairly strongly connected to the Ena, so before we were due to go home Nenna had me try out a couple of things – image projection and trying to float – which involved me standing in the centre of the room thinking really hard about doing those things and nothing happening. I didn't have to worry about accidentally burning or blowing things up since the room had a filter that meant it only enhanced certain kinds of actions, and to be honest I was glad nothing happened because it would have been weird to suddenly be psychic.

Nenna's ability is teleportation, though she's not strong enough to move more than a foot or so even when boosted. But it was amazing watching her flicker from one spot to another: it made her into more than just a talkative kid. Something magic.

If she puts all her effort into it Nenna can take a passenger, and she offered to 'jump' me. And that was a really bad idea.

We jumped to a nearby atrium and fell two floors. I've a broken collarbone and lots of bruises. Nenna's much worse. She hurt her back, and even with advanced nanotech medicine she's going to be in hospital a long while.

She didn't die. I'm so glad. So incredibly – I couldn't have stood it. Because, you see, it was me. They're not sure why, but they think that something about me made Nenna's jump go wrong.

So I'm on the way back to the KOTIS island. Not with Sa Lents this time, but a grim greensuit escort. It was an accident, but I feel so awful. I hurt her.

Sunday, January 6

Back to the Lab

Endless medical scans. Apparently they'd already tested me for potential psychic powers, but the only sign they could find was the possibility of being a projector (perhaps the least useful ability in a world where everyone is their own home movie theatre). When they finally sent me off to get some sleep – back in my old room – I can't.

Part of that's because I'm sore. They use nanites to glue broken bones back together, but it still needs to heal properly, and I have to lie on my back not to pressure my collarbone. The pain meds wore off too quick.

More tests tomorrow. They haven't been able to find any reason at all for Nenna's jump to have gone strange.

Monday, January 7

Turn it up to 11

Today they moved on to practical experiments in a different part of the KOTIS building: a huge, reinforced room with observation windows and massive blocks of greenish metal in a row from small to large. Test Room 1.

First 'they' (voices in my head of people I'd never met) had me stand in the centre of the room and told me to try to project illusions or teleport or move a little box or do anything at all. I couldn't. I felt a complete dick.

Then they sent in a Setari. He was about twenty-five, reminded me strikingly of Johnny Depp, and had the nicest smile I've ever seen. Ever. He told me his name was Maze (or Mase, maybe – all the Taren words I write down are serious guesses as to spelling – the alphabet doesn't quite correlate to the letters I'm used to). He lifted each of the metal blocks in turn using telekinesis, though he was only able to make it halfway through the row. Then he had me stand next to him, and told me to do exactly what I did when Nenna jumped us. I told him I didn't do anything, just stood there while she held on to my hand, and he told me to do that then, and held on to my hand while I tried not to look incredibly embarrassed, or to think how much Nenna would want to be in my place.

Maze began lifting the blocks again. And made it about two thirds through them, and was quite wide-eyed by the time he was done. I would be too, since the last few blocks were bigger than school demountables. They brought a different Setari in, a very beautiful woman around the same age, her hair in a long braid. Her name was Zee, and she did the same thing, except she started out wide-eyed.

After this was endless, boring variations of hand-holding and block-lifting. They found that whatever it is I'm doing keeps working for a little while, even if they let go of my hand, and decided I'm a new ability: a magnifier or an amplifier. Not nearly as fun as having psychic abilities of my own, but I guess it's more good than bad that they were all excited and disconcerted. Back in my room now; time for kindergarten.

Tuesday, January 8

Suckitudinous

They decided to expand my interface. Apparently all the Setari have an interface network all over their bodies, instead of just on one side of their head, because it increases their link to the Ena and thus their strength. They gave me a bunch of 'hypoinjections' – even in the soles of my feet! – and *then* told me what they'd done. And then switched off my interface so that even my language tool went away.

Tare nearly had a Casszilla incident. They could have at least pretended to ask. I went hot and dizzy and said really rude, overloud things in English and only just stopped myself from shouting because I had to work at not crying in front of them. This was horrible enough the first time.

Friday, January 11

O.o

Cannot begin to describe how awful I feel. Contemplating vengeance of the direst sort.

Monday, January 14

For the ones that are still alive

Well, they nearly killed me this time. I've been in the infirmary for the past few days on life support. My expanded interface *really* expanded and I started having convulsions. Apparently. I don't remember too much of it.

I still feel awful; I can barely sit up to write this. It'll be a few days before I'm anywhere close to not-ill.

Friday, January 18

Apologies

Nenna sent me an email. She sent it a couple of days ago but my interface hasn't been on. And when they turned it on, they only gave me my language tool, kindergarten and barebones basic room functions. Ista Tremmar tells me that I'll be given access back after further assessment, and that I can write to Nenna, but I can't explain anything to her, or tell her much about what it's like here. Then she gave me a big file of rules to read, but my head wouldn't be up to it even if it was in English. The interface has stopped expanding but I'm still horribly headachy.

Anyway, Nenna doesn't hate me. She apologised to me. So now we're apologising to each other. I told her what little I guess I can – her father's probably able to tell her more anyway – and promised to translate the lyrics to the songs when I can.

It was so good to get her email.

Saturday, January 19

Blacksuits

Another test session today with Zee. We did basic lifting. Or, rather, I stood around feeling tired and extraneous while she lifted things. Then there was another woman, Mara, who was talkative and had wonderfully sproingy curly hair. She and Zee and Maze are all from 'First Squad': they're the oldest of the Setari, one of the three original combat squads created from children trained intensively to deal with monsters from the Ena.

After they decided the early results were promising, the Taren government vastly expanded the Setari program, and now there's a dozen six-person squads, most of them five to seven Earth-years younger than First Squad. There's also a lot of people in training who haven't yet qualified for active duty on the squads. The Setari program has been running for 60 years (twenty Earth years).

Mara explained all this to me while Zee was working out if being any distance from me effected the temporary increase with her strength. Mara is primarily a Speed talent, but she can also make a glowing light which curls about like a kind of cutting whip. I made her even faster, which she was pleased about, but something about how the whip worked really shocked them. It came out in a different colour and they spent ages studying it and being confused. Then I was put back in my box. I hate being a lab rat.

More Labrattery

After a few hours I was recalled for more experiments with First Squad – all of them this time. There's four girls – Zee, Mara, Alay, Ketzaren – and two guys – Maze and Lohn. All in their mid-twenties, all wearing their black uniforms and looking very fit and smart and...worn. I didn't like to ask if all the years fighting monsters ran together for them, or if they ever get to stop.

The uniform the Setari wear is very interesting. It's flexible and stretchy: solid stuff but not so unwieldy as a wetsuit, and – it's hard to think what it reminds me of. Expensive sport shoes, with their airholes for breathing and all the extra stitching and complexity. It's very tight-fitting and all-covering – the neck part goes right up to the chin and the arms to fingerless gloves, and the soft boots seem to be built in too, and it looks like it must be a pain to take on and off. It's far more layered and complex than the spandex suits of superheroes, but with a cape and a big logo I bet they could pass.

There's something unspeakably tedious about standing about while people act worried and excited, and you don't really understand why. Especially when they started communicating on channels I didn't have access to instead of speaking, which really brought back the whole "you're an experimental subject" feel again.

Maze, Zee and Mara – all of First Squad – are relaxed and friendly, though, which helps. They talked me through some of the implications of the fact that I'm not just enhancing some of their powers, but changing them. It really increases the danger. The accident with Nenna was an example of that – it's possible that I didn't simply increase her strength, but changed the coordinates of her jump as well. They were thinking of it only in terms of an overshoot before, but now they think it was a distortion, and that means that anyone trying to teleport me anywhere would be at huge risk.

I don't seem to distort everything though. Or, at least, it's not noticeable if I am. But Mara's 'Light whip' has a more melting effect when I enhance her, and Alay's Illusion casting goes totally weird. Ketzaren felt dizzy when she tried to make me levitate and Lohn – who gives a good imitation of a *Star*

Wars blaster shooting beams of Light – made a burning wall instead. There was a big pause after that, where First Squad stood about looking disconcerted and listening to someone I couldn't hear, who I guess was having conniptions.

The one thing they did establish is that I consistently distort. So Lohn's beams always became a wall, and Mara's Light whip was always the same. They cheered up after that. They're still going to have to go carefully working out just what effect I have, but consistently weird is a lot better than randomly weird.

And now I'm back in my box waiting for the next test. I think it's the fact that the door won't open to me that bothers me most.

Monday, January 21

Still alive still

I spent the beginning of the day translating song lyrics for Nenna. I am improving. My grammar is terrible, and I had to write a huge amount of explanatory notes to make half the concepts remotely understandable, but it showed me how far I'd come in being able to communicate. Talking to First Squad between testing sessions has been helping. I was feeling very proud of myself, even if I could tell it was a botched job, and had just mailed it off to her when I was brought down for another testing session.

This was more of the same, just working on the limits of me enhancing people. So they had two, then three of the Setari touching me at the same time to see how many people I could enhance at once.

And down I went. I never used to pass out on frequent occasions. I'm not epileptic, and I never had a fit till I came to this planet. Until now they weren't sure if I was being physically stressed by whatever I'm doing to enhance people. And, well, now they know.

They're getting more anxious about killing me, I think. The greysuits, that is, and whoever it is giving orders over the interface. I don't see these at all, just First Squad and greysuits.

First Squad were very upset, and Zee and Maze came to the infirmary after I'd woken up again and we all apologised to each other for nothing which was our own fault. They don't seem bothered by the tests, they just think they should have somehow predicted what was going to happen and prevented it.

Change of pace

Sa Lents came to see me for the first time since Nenna's accident. He didn't act like he blamed me or anything, but it was still uncomfortable. No experiments 'today', just talking with Sa Lents, trying to describe Earth's history.

My sleep schedule is totally messed up. The lack of proper day and night, and the way the people I've been working with all seem to be on different shifts, really messes with me. Their breakfast is my dinner and so forth.

Tuesday, January 22

Zan

Today I was assigned to a girl called Zan. She's from Twelfth Squad and is another telekinetic. She's short and very serious and has blonde-brown hair which is very fine and cut into a soft and wispy bob. Quite pretty golden-brown eyes.

They've decided to postpone further experiments with me because they think I'm too worn down. Being half-starved on Muina and then that bad cold and then the broken collarbone and all these bad reactions I've had are adding up. Even though I've had regular meals and not really done anything since I was rescued, I've not put on much weight and certainly aren't fit. They want me to get healthy and they're going to confine the tests purely to Zan's Telekinesis for a while. She only has the one psychic talent, with no secondary talents at all.

She's also going to train me. In some kind of judo, which is not exactly something I'm keen on. Hitting people is...just not me. They want to study the effect of prolonged exposure to Zan, and at the same time make me a bit more capable of surviving, should they ever decide it's a good idea to use me in combat. I really am a potential weapon to these people.

It's hard to tell what Zan thinks of all this. She's what Mum would call 'scrrrrupulously correct' and even though she's trained all her life to be an incredibly deadly monster fighter, she didn't act as if there was anything odd about teaching some unco beginner how to stand and how to step back and forward over and over again. Must be dull as hell for her.

She did do the wide-eyed thing when they tested how I enhanced her. By herself she's a lot stronger than Maze. With me, she can lift all the test blocks at once.

Wednesday, January 23

Lab Rat One

I spent all of today having test after test in the medical labs. Ista Tremmar is polite and all, but she's still inclined to leave me sitting on an examining table for an hour while they talk about me. If I didn't have the interface kindergarten to keep me occupied I'd go mad.

Maybe that's what Zan does during our exercises – zones out and reads her email. If I ask her questions, she answers in the briefest possible way, and she never asks me anything. I miss Nenna's chatter so much. I miss that she treated me as a person as well as an exciting curiosity.

When I was delivered back to my box today I drew a rat on all my clothes, and wrote 'Lab Rat One' underneath it, making a little logo for my official designation on this world.

Today I particularly miss Alyssa. I've only known Alyssa a few years, but she's the only person I really tell things to. I hadn't realised how important that was to me.

Thursday, January 24

Attitude adjustment

Strange how going around wearing my lab rat logo makes me feel so much better. This morning's session with Zan went well because I felt less like I was helplessly doing what I was told, and was, well, doing what I was told while wearing an ironic comment about it.

We're still working on stances. Step forward, step backward, over and over again, very controlled. I concentrated more on it this time, deciding I at least may as well do the best I can, even if I know that I'm never going to be really good at this kind of stuff, and will only be laughable in comparison to athletic people who have been training since they were five. I'm going to have a go at cracking Zan, too – at least get her to treat me a little less like an assignment. I don't care if she takes a teacher/student attitude, even though she can't be more than a year older than me, but I want some kind of interaction, some kind of response.

I'm really curious about her now, about if she's so serious and unsmiling all the time, and why. First Squad was a lot more open and friendly. And I know I'm not going to get a chance to work out Zan if I'm all sullen and unwilling. I mightn't have a whole lot of power and independence in this place, but I can control the way I act and that will make me feel better.

I've never thought of myself as a 'typical' Australian – that whole laconic and stoic thing – but I'm trying to use that attitude to cope with here. To copy Nick, who is always so calm and unfussed by everything that the world throws at him. Not super-optimistic or unbelievably Pollyanna, but he sets a great balance between dealing with the bad stuff and enjoying all the good bits. Nick would never lose sight of the fact that I'm no longer starving on Muina.

Nick's an ex-step-cousin. His dad was married to my Aunt Sue when we were younger, and we saw a lot of each other – all the family holidays and so forth. His dad started being an ass, so my aunt divorced him, and Nick does a lot of making sure he doesn't go completely off the rails. We still live in the same area, though, and Mum and Aunt Sue keep including Nick in holidays as if we're still related and I see him at inter-school events. He's not quite one of those incredibly popular people like HM, but he has a relaxed focus on what he thinks is fun which makes him really great to be around. Nick would be far better able to cope with being here.

Friday, January 25

Baby steps

I've started looking forward to my sessions with Zan. Not because I like the exercise particularly, but because I'm actually *doing* something. Medical examinations are the worst – sitting around for ages, holding still for the benefit of the scanners, or getting blood samples taken.

Since I'm waiting around *all* the time, either in my box or being examined, I'm damn lucky I have something to do, but kindergarten is keeping me sane and driving me nuts at the same time. I want back the access I had before my accident. I can't watch any of the entertainment channels, or even try to read books longer than twenty words. I asked about getting access back, and they said I had to reach certain qualification levels. In other words, no play until I'm out of school. It's obviously an attempt to push me to improve my language skills, but, heck, I'm sure I'd learn lots of useful words watching that silly singing Setari show Nenna liked so much.

Training, even though it's repetitive and I tire quickly, is like being let out of a cage. While Zan is correct and distant, she's also patient, and I think it makes training some idiot stray better for her if I try. I do feel a complete gangling gawk beside her; she's so small and fine-boned. But quite deadly. I saw her practicing when I came in this morning, and was wholly dismayed at the thought of ever trying to move like that, but it seems she's aiming to train me to dodge, rather than try and hit things. And to be fitter and wheeze less.

Saturday, January 26

Speed trial

I hit a round of tests in my interface kindergarten, and was on the back foot from the start since tests trigger a 'test environment', and it's almost like being in a darkened room inside your own head. I could *just* see the real room. I hadn't realised how thoroughly the interface could impact my senses, and while Ista Tremmar told me later that the interface is restricted from making people completely blind and deaf for safety reasons, that did *not* reassure me in the slightest.

The tests were timed, which made them incredibly hard for me, since I barely have a basic command of the language, and it takes me too long to understand exactly what the question is before trying to formulate the answer. So of course I ran out of time and only finished the maths test. I aced maths, but failed the tests overall. And now I seem to be repeating kindergarten, which sucks, since the questions are incredibly easy. I don't know if I can get better at this language before I die of boredom.

Looking forward to my session with Zan immensely, because it doesn't matter how badly I speak.

Sunday, January 27

Hands off

Today's practice didn't go quite as scheduled.

I was frustrated over failing the tests yesterday, but stepping back and forth is pretty calming, and so is Zan. I was just thinking that maybe I should call her 'Zen' instead when she stopped stepping back and forth and turned to look up.

The practice room is small and bare, with a floor of padded mats and a high ceiling with a window 'upstairs' in one wall so people can watch. Ista Tremmar had been up there earlier, but when Zan looked there were a half-dozen Setari. The most noticeable was a tall blonde guy at the front, his hands raised in fists against the glass as if he'd just hit it. He was glaring down at Zan like he wanted to hit her instead. Then he stormed out of the chamber, most of the other Setari following him.

Two of them stayed, and I was caught up looking at the girl first because I don't think I've seen anyone that gorgeous outside model magazines. She had that antelope look, but athletic rather than stick-thin. Even at that distance I could see her eyes were very black, with big irises and long lashes. Her skin was creamy bronze and her hair was unreal – these two spirals curling down past her ribs. She was almost as unsmiling as Zan, but I think her attitude was mainly curiosity. Not angry, anyway. The guy with her looked enough like her to be her brother (though no long pigtails, heh), and I didn't recognise him until he tilted his head a particular way to talk, and I realised he was one of the two Setari who had found me on Muina.

Just then Zan told me to go stand in the corner, which totally pissed me off. Even though I'd figured out that there was a yelling match coming, I'm not a dog to be told to sit and stay and get put out of the way. But I went, and just in time, as the door to the hall opened and the blond guy stormed in. There were a bunch of other Setari looking in the door at us, but they stayed there.

"This is it?" the guy was yelling (well, in Taren, you get the idea). "This is your special assignment? The reason we're all on downtime is you're playing with some profanity stray?"

Swear words aren't in my language tool. I can tell it's a swear word, but not what it means, so it's like my head says 'profanity' whenever someone swears. I find that funny and annoying at the same time. I need to find someone who is willing to teach me what they mean.

I knew enough of Zan by this time to not be surprised at her complete lack of reaction to some really buff guy standing over her and shouting. She just said: "Stand down," in a curt little voice and went and picked up one of the towels we'd brought in with us.

I'm not so good at not reacting, so when the blond guy turned toward me, I was glad Zan had stuck me in the corner. And I'm pretty sure I did the open-mouthed gaping thing when he suddenly lifted up and was slammed into one of the walls, for all I knew perfectly well Zan was a telekinetic.

"I said, 'Stand down', Lenton," Zan said, and, wow, totally cold voice. She wasn't smiling or frowning, but her eyes had narrowed and I decided then that it would never be a good idea to piss Zan off.

The Lenton guy didn't take the hint though, and looked really offended and told Zan to put him down before he made her regret it. He was calling her "Namara", which is her surname. All the Setari seem to call each other by their surnames. Zan calls me "Devlin" and I generally avoid calling her by either name because I think it sounds stupid to call someone you see every day by her surname. Even First Squad seem to do it most of the time. I think – hope – it's some kind of on-duty thing and that they're more human to each other when they're not being all proper.

Before the shouting match turned into a bigger mess all the Setari except Zan, who was probably expecting it, paused in clear reaction to suddenly getting a message in their heads. Zan put the Lenton guy down and though he glared at her, he strode off without another word.

"Get changed," Zan said to me, glancing back up at the observation room. The two Setari there were still watching, but turned and left when she just stood looking at them.

"Everyone's really competitive?" I asked. "Or just no manners?" Except, given my grammar and how slow I say stuff, it was more like "Compete all much? Manners no?" I really hate sounding so stupid. Yoda with a lobotomy.

Zan didn't reply. She never responds to questions like that, and I sure as hell wasn't going to push her, so I went and changed out of the loose training jumpsuit into my knee-length cargo-style pants and a sleeveless t-shirt featuring my lab rat logo. I really did draw it on every shirt I considered mine – not my school uniform, but the clothes I'd bought with Nenna and her mother. Zan put on her black uniform, which she manages in a surprisingly short amount of time for something so skin-tight.

Next was the big testing room, where every Setari in the complex had obviously been ordered to assemble. Maze had told me there were twelve active squads of six people so the rows six people deep showed me who was in which squad. They left spaces for the people who weren't there – three missing teams and a few random gaps. And then they brought me 'into channel' and I saw that even a few of the missing people were 'there': attending the meeting through their interfaces rather than in person. Little see-through holographic pictures of them filled in some of the empty spots. Lohn from First Squad and Zan were the only ones out of place, over to one side near me.

Since Maze was at the first spot of the first set, it was pretty easy to guess that the squad captains stood at front. The team next to him was around the same age – mid-twenties – and everyone else late teens or perhaps twenty. The gap left by Zan in Twelfth Squad was the first spot, which meant she was their captain. News to me. The blond guy was next spot back and was trying to look super-correct, though his face was tense and set. The girl and guy I'd seen in the observation room were the captains of Third and Fourth Squad respectively.

Even the people in charge had shown up as interface projections: the first time I'd seen any of them. They wore blue, which I guess means 'officer'. No-one was chatting, or doing anything but looking straight ahead. And me the only person not in uniform, sticking out like a sore thumb.

Another interface projection 'appeared'. A woman, compact and stern, her hair clipped really short, with a hint of grey in it. She had the really black, almond eyes of the observation-room girl and guy. The Setari all saluted her – they do a fist to shoulder sort of salute – so it was pretty easy to tell she was in charge.

I can re-watch what happens next, and have a few times, because it occurred to me I could record everything. It's really weird to be able to do that, and I'm glad they've not taken the ability away, since this is a scene it's interesting to play over. So far as I can tell, I can't play the recording for anyone who doesn't have the right security level. It makes me wonder what security level I have.

"This is a level 5 classified briefing," said the woman. "As you are aware, Fourth Squad recovered a displaced person from Muina during last month's mission. Namara and Kettara will demonstrate why this has become important."

Zan went first, turning and looking at the big metal blocks. "Current strength," she said, extra clearly, and lifted the largest block she was capable of managing alone. Then she glanced at me, totally giving orders just by turning her eyes in my direction. I was hard put not to roll my own, but obediently stuck my hand on her shoulder, which she'd suggested as less restrictive than hand-holding.

"Enhanced strength."

I had turned to watch their faces when she lifted all the blocks. Only First Squad didn't react, since they'd seen all this before. Most of them did the eyes-going-really-wide thing. A few shifted from their spots, or were openly astonished or upset, but then went back to stony-faced as quickly as they could manage.

Lohn came forward next, and said: "Intense Light projection," and shot a few of his burning beams into a target. He gave me a little smile and when I put my hand on his shoulder said: "Same skill, enhanced."

The burning wall freaked the Setari out a good deal more than an extra-strength Zan. A lot of them exchanged glances before they went back to being correct.

"Subject Devlin's effect on skill users is still under investigation. As you have observed, it is not simply a matter of increased potency. In addition, multiple simultaneous enhancements causes her lethal systemic shock. Until further notice, the subject has been assigned to Namara. Under no circumstances initiate physical contact with the subject unless instructed. Dismissed."

The woman in the blue uniform vanished, as did most of the other watchers. The Setari squad captains, although they were probably dying to give Zan the third degree, sent their squads straight out the door and then most of them left as well, though a few stopped at the door to talk to each other. Maze came across to me, Zan and Lohn and told me I did well. I pointed out that I don't actually do anything, but he said at least I wasn't doing anything *consistently* and he and Lohn grinned at each other and talked about what would have happened if the enhancement hadn't worked. First Squad is so much more human than the rest of the Setari.

And then the leader of Fourth Squad came over. I was wondering if I should thank Fourth Squad for rescuing me, but if anything this guy was even more unsmiling than Zan is. As an added bonus he seemed to be staring at my chest, which was really amazingly uncomfortable until he said: "Experimental animal?"

Maze thought he was being insulting, and said "Rue-el," in a warning tone, but stopped, probably because he saw my expression.

"You can read English?" I asked – in English – completely disbelieving.

"Don't neglect the psychological aspects," the Fourth Squad captain said to Zan and turned away without another glance at me. Though he added, "It's not inapposite," over his shoulder as he walked away to where the Third Squad captain was waiting.

"How he know what say?" I asked Maze, who was taking his turn chest-staring. "Earth contact after all yes?"

"You've written 'Experimental Animal' on your shirt?" Maze asked, clearly upset.

Zan answered my question: "See Rue-el's primary talents are sight-based. He was reading the symbol, not the words."

Psychic psychic powers, in other words. And Zan was standing stiff and still, with her face so set that I couldn't miss that she was mortified. Because she'd had no idea what my shirt said, and the Fourth Squad captain had dressed her down for that, even if it was just with a single sentence.

There wasn't much I could do to fix that, but I did try to explain. "In Australia – in my culture – important able laugh at self. I–" I tugged at my shirt, then read out the words in English and the closest Taren translation. "Lab Rat One. Is true, is what am me here. Pretend not, that stupid. This–" I shrugged. "Cope mechanism. Sarcasm. Make me feel better wear."

"But it's not–" Maze wasn't getting any less upset.

"I kept in box. Take out for tests. What else call it?"

Maze grimaced, but Lohn laughed. "You have to admit her point. So the people of your world think it's important to laugh at themselves? That's an idea I could get along with. But, Maze, no-one will be laughing if we miss that shuttle, so get a move on."

He dashed off with a wave, and since Maze obviously couldn't think of an argument he sighed. "Let me know if you need anything, Caszandra. Although I suppose it must seem like it, your status is not that." He shot the picture on my shirt a grumpy look, nodded at Zan, and strode off after Lohn.

Zan just said: "I'll escort you back" and took me to my room and left me here.

Being able to record everything you see and hear certainly makes it easier to write down a conversation, though my translation of what they said – and what I was trying to say – is probably not that accurate. I hadn't noticed before, but First Squad all call me 'Caszandra', not 'Cassandra'. Taren is a very zeddy language.

Writing this down took hours, but it's given me plenty of translation practice and time to try and work out which of the three – Maze, Lohn or the Fourth Squad captain – that Zan likes enough to make her mind so much what happened today.

Monday, January 28

Roof

This morning started as business as usual with training. Zan, rather than the greensuits, has been collecting me from my room. We get changed in a side room which has a stock of freshly laundered training outfits and then we do a lot of stepping backward and forward and now side-to-side. Zan had gone back to being imperturbable, and I wasn't in the mood to push her, so I was really surprised when, after we'd changed back, she said: "I've been given leave to escort you around the facility, if there's any parts you wish to see."

"Can go outside?" I asked immediately.

I could see that surprised her. People really just don't go outside much, on this planet. "It's night phase at the moment."

"That bad thing?"

"Well..." She shrugged, and led me to the elevator that led to the corridor that led to the walkway that led to the quickest elevator to the roof. It's not nearly so huge as Unara, but the KOTIS building mound is still pretty damn big. It can't all be Setari facilities, even with all the not-yet Setari who are being trained somewhere.

It was very cold and windy on the bit of roof we ended up on. It feels even more like being on the side of a big mountain than going to Unara's roof did. Unara's more an endless blocky roundness, while the Institute is closer to the water and you can really see the *down*. But you could also see up since the sky was clear for once and so I found a convenient edge and sat down and stared up looking for any constellations I recognised. I would like to at least be able to stare in the direction of Earth.

"This is similar to your world?" Zan asked after a while. Even she can't just sit and not say anything forever.

"Not my part." I supposed Scotland might look like that, if you covered it with buildings. "Australia – big sky, red dirt, blue sea, lots beaches, huge empty inland. Deserts and tropical forests and...harsh, thirsty country. And then flood." I shrugged. "Out here because never not gone outside ever. Walk to school. Go to beach. Garden. What you do when not being Setari?"

I'd asked her before, but she'd ignored the question. This time Zan sighed, ever-so-softly. "If you want to talk, go inside out of this cold. I'm supposed to be watching your health."

But, of course, as soon as we got back inside someone called her away. And it's back to kindergarten in a box.

Tuesday, January 29

Bored Spitless

I suck at learning languages. Other than English, the only one I even begin to know is sign language, and even with that I spend a lot of time spelling words out because I don't know the sign. It annoys me, because I have a good memory, but there's a difference between remembering and knowing something, I guess.

Despite having an entire dictionary in my head cheating for me when I listen to Taren, I'm struggling to 'know' the words. I know yes and no and hello. And new words like Muina and Setari seem to have sunk in far better than 'bed' or 'morning'. Which is all just a whiny lead-up to saying I figured out how to trigger those interface tests and still can't pass because it takes me too long to phrase answers. I need multiple choice answer tests! What kind of planet gives kindergarteners tests this hard?

I can only do the tests once a day, so now I'm sitting around hoping Zan will show up and still be willing to talk. And feeling a bit annoyed with her for not coming back yesterday. And wondering what her other duties are beyond babying me. It looked to me like she doesn't get on with the rest of her squad, or at least not that obnoxious blond guy.

I wonder what they'd do if I drew patterns on the walls? Everything on this planet is so undecorated and white because they use interface 'skins' as their decoration. I've been trying to work out if the buildings are made of the same whitestone as the buildings on Muina. They don't look anywhere near as simple, of course, but they feel the same to touch.

sulks

Bleh. Instead of training, I had medical examinations this afternoon. More scans and blood tests and seeing how my heart is going and dull and uncomfortable as hell.

One thing, though – I don't think any of the Setari have told anyone else what my Lab Rat symbol means. At least, Ista Tremmar didn't pay any more attention to it than last time, and wasn't giving me psych tests or anything.

Wednesday, January 30

Tactics

Zan likes 'classical' music. I should have guessed: it fits in with her being all serious and proper. They call classical music 'orchestral music' (tennanam anam). The instrument Zan plays is called a Tyu and looks and sounds to me a lot like a zither, but is larger than the zither they had in the music room at primary school – about the size of an A3 sheet of paper, but much thicker of course – and has softer strings which she plucks. It's made of wood, which is super rare on Tare. I think it's probably rare to have an actual musical instrument, as well, rather than playing a virtual something in a virtual space.

I was just as interested in her rooms. I had been picturing all the Setari stuck in little boxes like mine, but Zan had a small apartment: one bedroom, but with a separate lounge-kitchen combo and a study nook thing and a larger bathroom than mine – bathtub! I guess I shouldn't have been too surprised. You can apply for adult rights at 50 (almost 17) here, and the Setari are a few steps above an ordinary sort of soldier. Keeping them permanently in barracks or whatever probably wouldn't have worked.

Anyway, I thought Zan's apartment was wonderful. She's decorated it in muted shades of green and blue (the public space, that is) with curling patterns which look a bit like ferns that shift and wind about. And she has a cat! A cat like that screensaver cat that drops down from the top of your screen and wanders about, except this one wanders about Zan's entire apartment, and is blue-green to blend in with the walls. You can sort of pat it, even, because your interface will pretend like you're touching something. I asked if there were real cats on Tare and she said a few brought from a planet called Kolar. Only the really rich can possibly have actual pets.

I'm not under any illusion that Zan suddenly wants to be friends. She's been given me as an assignment, and she still acts exactly like I'm an assignment, just that the assignment has been expanded to my mental health as well as physical fitness and dodging. I don't know whether I like her or not, beyond that she's the only person on this freaking planet that I see on a near-daily basis. I can't remember hanging out with any super-serious girls in the past, let alone someone who is part of the military and kills for a living. She makes me curious though.

After this we went and had another stepping session, and I waited till she was escorting me back to my room before I asked her again: "Setari competitive why?" And when she paused, since this was definitely not the sort of question she was likely to answer, I added: "Your squad, why unhappy, holiday?"

"The Setari don't compete directly," Zan said eventually. "But how we perform effects privileges, which assignments we are given, and even whether we remain on active duty. Fighting in the Ena is greatly preferred to the more basic duty which is usual on Tare, and not simply because being in the Ena makes us feel...twice as alive. Twelfth Squad had only just been activated for Ena assignments, but were transferred to training routines, and are very disappointed."

"Mostly fight Ena, not planet?"

"The whole concept of the Setari is to prevent anything from the Ena reaching this world. And to find a way to fix the fractures which have made it so easy for the walls around this world to be crossed." She looked even more than ordinarily serious. "The numbers increase every year and the fractures are widening. Working on Tare, it's just clean-up unless there's a major outbreak. The war is beyond this world."

That was a good deal more dramatic than I'd been expecting. Where I'm going to be placed in this war is something too large to think about.

Thursday, January 31

A proper history lesson

I passed the stupid interface test! Only just – I still didn't finish a lot of the questions, but I got almost all the ones I did answer right. So I now have a new year of school to plough through. Still no entertainment channels or anything, but a small library of children's 'textbooks', which is good. I much prefer being able to freely read the books than to sit through the pre-set lessons and their snippets of information. A thorough browse has given me a lot more background and a better explanation of just what happened on Muina and what the situation on Tare is now.

So, whatever it was happened on Muina happened thousands of *Taren* years ago. They're pretty imprecise about exactly how long ago it was, because they went through a really rough and chaotic first few decades on Tare, so don't have a very good written record. Kolar is the other main planet which properly remembers being from Muina, but its early records are no better than Tare's. The best I can make out, the evacuation from Muina was between 1500 and 2000 Earth years ago. So ha! to the idea of Earth having been populated by people from Muina – the Egyptian pyramids are over 3000 years old and that barely scratches the surface of Earth's archaeological and fossil record. I guess it is possible that some Muinans came to Earth long before that, but we definitely weren't part of the evacuation dispersal. I never believed that, no matter how similar I am to them genetically. It still makes *vastly* more sense to me for the Muinans to have originally come from Earth, especially because Tare's population also reflects some of Earth's races.

'Lantar' doesn't refer to the entire population of Muina, either, but to a psychic ruling caste which caused the disaster that made Muina uninhabitable. Back then the Ionoth monsters were only an issue for these ruling Lantar (Lantarens?) when they travelled between planets. It's not clear why they were travelling between planets, but it was common enough that they started a huge planet-wide project to make it easier: creating a little network of permanently aligned wormholes. The result of this was like if you decided to stop earthquakes in California by nailing the tectonic plates together: everything started to rip apart around the nails.

The tearing allowed things from the Ena to more easily get to Muina, where they liked to throw themselves on people and eat them. The Lantarens couldn't immediately undo what they'd done because the places where they'd constructed the main supports of their interplanetary superhighway had been flooded with too many Ionoth. So they built these things called Ddura – the massives the Setari are so interested in investigating – which are artificial Ionoth whose job was to clear out Ionoth from the supports and from Muina. But they immediately lost control of the Ddura, and the situation on Muina began spiralling into chaos: whole villages and cities of people inexplicably dropping dead, and more and more Ionoth coming through and eating people.

All the Lantarens on Muina had a big 'teleconference' (hehe!) and decided they had to leave Muina. They couldn't all manage to go to the same place, and it doesn't sound like they wanted to either. There were some who stayed behind on Muina, but no-one's ever found any trace of them, so they were probably killed.

If you stay too long on Muina, something comes and eats you, or you drop dead. I'm glad I didn't know all this while I was busy boiling wool.

Stepping it up

The medics have decided I'm more or less recovered, so Zan says we'll have two sessions of training tomorrow. So funny to be excited about exercising. I wonder if the Setari have to earn TV privileges as well.

I asked Zan what the Ena looked like, and she said that it's incredibly varied, but that the nearest space looked just like Tare, except without the people. It's a shadow of this world. Now that's freaky.

FEBRUARY

Friday, February 1

Frabjous

This morning was routine. Though my lessons with Zan are getting a bit more complex, it's still repeating a set of movements over and over again.

But Zan didn't deliver me back to my room afterwards. Instead we went to lunch in a smallish canteen. It seems to be a Setari-specific place, though I think the kitchen handles more than just this one room.

It's funny how your aspirations change after being locked in a room for – how long has it been? – nearly a month since Nenna was hurt. It makes small things like eating in a very plain canteen so exciting. Being able to pick from a couple of options for my meal instead of having food delivered by a pinksuit under guard made me feel almost human again. The illusion of choice.

Of course anything, even sitting in a room reliving kindergarten, is better than starving and alone. Annoying as this place can be, I'm still glad to have been rescued.

The other Setari in the room weren't anyone I particularly recognised, though I guess they'd all been there for the demonstrate-what-the-stray-can-do session. They pretended not to look at me, and didn't bother us. It's hard to know what they'd think of me – a walking instant power-up that they've been told to stay away from.

After lunch, I was expecting more 'martial arts' practice, but instead we went down to a different changing room and Zan sent me into one of the shower rooms and told me to braid my hair up and strip and get into the shower. And when I did, wondering what was going on, black goop sprayed out of the walls at me and that was enough to make me jump back and want out. And then it started *wriggling*. I sometimes forget that these people use nanotechnology. I ended up with a light swimsuit, sturdier than those I'm used to, and going all the way to the knees and elbows. Thinner than the Setari uniform, but I'm starting to understand how Zan gets changed so quickly.

After I'd recovered from my minor heart attack, we went into the next room and it was this HUGE pool. A big square, maybe forty by forty metres, but incredibly deep, with this underwater obstacle course, all tunnels and circles and things. I couldn't even see the bottom.

"This is something I need practice in, as well," Zan said, watching my disbelieving expression. "The requirement for water manoeuvres only came in two years ago, when some of the nearest spaces became flooded. The medics recommended this to increase your overall fitness, and it will prepare you in case they do decide to use you in the Ena."

"Not that good at holding breath," I said, extremely dubiously. I figured I could make the top couple of tunnels and tubes, and that would be it.

"There's breathers for the deep work. First will be surface swimming. Are you taught swimming at all on your world?"

I gave her a funny look, then dived in and swam across the pool and back. I was a little more out of breath than I expected when I reached her, due to my various medical dramas. But I love swimming. I'm not Ian Thorpe, but water sports are one of the things I've always been reasonably good at.

"If ever go my world," I told her, treading water. "Teach you how to surf."

I'm a better swimmer than Zan is. And they don't use the freestyle stroke, just breaststroke, so she asked me to teach her. And we're doing swimming practice every afternoon until further notice. Today was a great day.

Saturday, February 2

Ructions

Zan is now teaching me how to fall. Or how to throw myself on padded mats without too much bruising or unnecessary giggling. I find it hard to take seriously, and no matter what else I think or feel about Zan, I have to admire her patience. I think that it's causing her a lot of trouble to babysit me, too, unless the Setari are just plain nasty to each other out of habit.

The nastiness came out during this afternoon's swimming session. Zan's picking up freestyle quickly (Australian crawl, really, but everyone I know calls it freestyle), but it'll take her a bit to really get into it, so we were having a race with breaststroke. I'm okay with short races, but if I try and do more than a couple of laps I run out of pep.

But I can beat her in a short dash, and was terribly pleased about it. Problem was, so were the people watching us. Three Setari, two guys and a girl, and one of the guys was standing right on the edge of the pool where we touched. Gave me quite a fright, looking up and finding all this blacksuited leg and chest. I pushed back from the edge, just as Zan reached it, but they were more interested in her than me anyway.

I don't know if Zan had managed to figure out they were there before she looked up, but from what I could see of her face, she didn't act surprised.

"Truly, Namara, I'm starting to feel embarrassed for you," said the guy. He had an amazing voice, really beautiful, and so wasted on such a putz. "Bad enough your squad's been pulled off rotation so you can demonstrate infant-level combat skills, but now you're actually being outdone by a stray."

Zan reminds me of a drowned kitten when she's wet. Her hair sleeks down and makes her eyes look really big. The guy was so tall, and Zan being down in the water must have felt at a real disadvantage. But all she did was move to one side, haul herself easily out, and go pick up one of the towels.

"Can I help you with something, Kajal?" she asked, once she'd dried her face.

"Not swimming, obviously." The guy was irritated that he'd not managed to get a reaction out of Zan, but made out he wasn't bothered, laughing. "Lenton's chances are looking better each day."

The Setari girl standing behind him touched his arm. "It's an unfortunate situation," she said, in a much more reasonable tone. "Twelfth Squad may have lost out on this rotation altogether, and Lenton does need to be taught to keep his temper. Worse still, I doubt the stray will be assigned to Twelfth Squad, if they do use it in the Ena. It's very unfair on you."

I was glad I'd kept moving away, was at least ten metres from the edge. Not only was the girl enjoying a few sly digs at Zan while pretending to be nice, but she'd called me *it!* I'm not totally incapable of understanding the nuances of spoken Taren. Stupid idiots were acting like I was a performing animal, not a person.

It occurred to me then that I no longer had the function which displays all the names of people over their heads. A full month after Sa Lents showed me how to use it, and I'd forgotten all about it since the accident. I don't see what they achieved by making it so I couldn't use it, but it was probably related to me losing almost all the other 'public' functions. I was able to call up the recorded memory of the Setari briefing, though, and work out that the Kajal guy was captain of the Fifth Squad, and the girl was captain of the Seventh. The other guy was also from the Seventh Squad. What they were trying to achieve with all the dick waving I couldn't guess.

At least they left after that, though another person showed up as Zan was turning back toward me. I was too far away to hear what she said, since her voice was soft, but Zan smiled at her, and then shrugged. So she's not totally without friends. I practiced swimming underwater for a couple of minutes, till Zan told me that was enough for the day. It's going to take a while to get used to people being able to talk in my head when I'm upside-down in a swimming pool.

I didn't bug her with questions while she escorted me back, didn't really feel equal to it. Was even glad to be back in my room so I could get in the shower and cry myself sick.

I do almost all my crying in the shower. I'm still not sure how much they monitor me while I'm in my room, and I'm really hoping that I get at least a little privacy. The shower lets me pretend I'm hiding the bad days. This was worse than usual. It's going to be my birthday soon, and Mum had promised to organise a family and friends party at our house, and then Nick, Alyssa and I had permission to go out to actual nightclubs afterwards, so long as we stayed together and friends who hadn't turned eighteen yet didn't come with us. Nick was coming along to 'protect' us, which I of course thought was a fantastic idea for all the wrong reasons. Alyssa and I put so much effort into setting that up, all for nothing.

I will never be Cass here. Even if I was still staying with the Lents, I would always be this 'stray' first and foremost and above everything else. I have this label and there's no way to take it off. Even if I adapt to the stupid language and the nanites, all the things I spent years learning, all the stories and people which shaped me aren't here. No-one's read the novels I've read. No-one likes the music I like. No-one on this planet will be able to score people on the Orlando Bloom-meter, the way Alyssa and I used to do with all the cute guys. The only thing which speaks English is this damn diary, which I guess is why I still keep it.

I'm so homesick I could scream.

Sunday, February 3

A wan shadow

No training today. Zan took one look at me this morning and sent me straight for medical exams. I had to work very hard to convince them that the swimming wasn't the problem, and I look really exhausted and drained just because I couldn't get to sleep. Leaving out the bit about crying half the night and giving myself the hugest headache in the process. At least this let me know that they mustn't be monitoring me too closely in my room.

But I ended up spending almost all the day in the medical section, prodded and poked and sitting in machines while they got distracted trying to figure out how my enhancement abilities work. They've decided that the number of abilities an individual Setari has might increase the strain on my system when I enhance them. Which is why Zan is training me, since she has only the one. The experiment enhancing three from First Squad at once messed up so badly because between them those three had seventeen talents. Maze has eight all on his own, and apparently there's a couple of Setari who have even more.

I took the opportunity to have another argument with Ista Tremmar about why my interface had been cut back so much, and why I couldn't at least have the access I'd had before or straightforward things like being able to see names and so forth, but she just gave me a lecture about qualifying for privileges. It didn't work to point out that standard access was hardly a privilege, and how stupid it is to run tests which are timed for someone who has been learning their silly language since they were babies. Of course, my inability to speak that silly language with any fluidity made my arguments less than comprehensible.

Ista Tremmar is very strict and by-the-book about a lot of things, but she did say she would review the speed of the tests. But she also told me the simplest thing would be for me to improve my language skills. Bleh.

Monday, February 4

Forward/Backward

Even though I slept quite well last night, swimming practice has been postponed for a few days, which meant Zan delivered me back to my box to sit around again. On the up side, a few more of my interface functions were abruptly restored in the middle of stepping practice. No entertainment, but the minor environmental things like the names over people's heads. Still, dull day, especially since interface classes are trying to teach me subtraction now. I wish I could pick and choose what the lessons are.

Kanza

That was an infinitely better afternoon than I was expecting. I'd only been back in my box a little while when there was a text popup in my head which is the equivalent of someone outside my room, knocking. Rare consideration, let me tell you, for a visitor to not just open the door.

It was Lohn and Mara, come to kidnap me for lunch. While this was probably their own version of 'not overlooking the psychological aspects', I had a huge amount of trouble not bubbling over with glee and going completely hyper. Not only did I get to spend some time with the nicest people on this stupid island, but they even planned on taking me outside KOTIS grounds.

The island that the Setari use as a base is called Konna, and is about 20% military facilities and 80% supporting city. The city's called Konna, too, and was here before KOTIS was established. It was really nice to get out to see atriums and shops, and people not wearing uniforms, and there were plants and advertising and snatches of music and scents of cooking food and everything that the Setari base is not. They even do fake skies, and internal parks and while it can't entirely escape Huge Shopping Mall Syndrome, it was such a nice change.

We went to an 'outdoor' plaza, with cafés (no coffee *or* hot chocolate!) arranged around a plant-filled square where kids were running about and someone was busking. Actually busking. Being stuck with the Setari had me convinced that this was such a totally controlled society, though my time with Nenna should have taught me otherwise. I'm guessing there's little chance that they'll let me live out here.

The place we went to eat was called "Mimm" and Lohn sat me in the corner of a big booth and then he and Mara sat either side of me with a careful gap so that we didn't touch. They bracketed me as we travelled through the city too, making sure people didn't bump me. I thought that pretty funny, since it's the Setari touching me which is the problem. Most ordinary people wouldn't have nearly enough talent to hurt me. The food was near enough to fondue as to make no difference (though I've no idea what they make the cheese from, and really would prefer not to find out), which seemed hugely out of place on an alien planet, but very yummy! The rest of First Squad showed up just as it was arriving, and I was sorry to see that Maze's hand was covered in a blue square of bandage tape, and that Zee was walking with a limp.

Maze gave my shirt a quick frown – I'd forgotten about my mascot altogether – and then asked me lots of questions about Earth food and I ended up spending the entire lunch talking. About fondue and then Nordic countries and skiing, a thing they don't do here at all, and then we swapped different sports that there's no equivalent to on either world. Taren sports are mostly indoors, unsurprisingly, except for some kind of air races. There's so many Earth sports that don't fit well here. Golf and skiing and riding just for starters.

They'd booked a Kanza court for after lunch. Kanza is a very strange game like hockey crossed with mini-golf crossed with Pac-man, except the pucks hover and skim and ricochet madly over the surface of three intersecting recessed circles. The court was in the centre of a grassy amphitheatre where people were eating picnic lunches and watching the games. You play in teams of three and you stand on the edge and hit your pucks all out at once and try and not go in any of the holes until you've passed over all the little floating balls of light. If you keep your puck in play you get bonus pucks. It's tremendously fast-paced and silly and Maze is idiotically good at it so I was glad to be on his and Lohn's team. Zee sat out because of her leg, and Mara, Alay and Ketzaren were the opposing team and Ketzaren turned out to be really dry and funny and made this hilarious commentary and Lohn really played up to her. I nearly fell into the rink a couple of times from laughing.

After our final round, while Mara's team was playing, Maze and Lohn went off to get everyone something to drink. I was really tired from all the laughing, and sat with Zee watching the growing audience cheering Mara and Alay playing a duo game when I noticed a couple of people I recognised. The Third Squad captain's twirly hair makes her pretty hard to miss, even when she's not in the black uniform. She was standing up the top of the small amphitheatre with another girl, staring down with a really fixed lack of expression. I wasn't surprised that it was Maze she was watching – half the audience was panting over him or Lohn and most of the rest were drooling over either Mara or Zee. Really, there's hardly any of the Setari who aren't above average in looks. It must be a job requirement.

I made sure to not be looking at the Third Squad captain by the time Lohn and Maze got back with the drinks, but I wondered if I'd earned myself an enemy because Maze handed me a drink and sat beside me and smiled and said I had to concede that this was better than a long walk occasionally hitting little balls, which is how I'd described golf. It's hard not to enjoy it when someone so gorgeous and nice pays me attention. But even though it's only six or seven years' difference, all the people I know on Earth who are in their mid-twenties are teachers, so I do feel out of place around First Squad. I'm fairly sure Maze doesn't mean anything, is just being kind and thoughtful. And there's a sense that underneath it all, he's unhappy. I keep feeling sorry for him.

When I was delivered back to my box, I was on enough of a high to not let the Fourth Squad captain's 'psychological aspects' drown out my thanks. I think they all enjoyed themselves too and were genuinely curious about Earth, so it wasn't like the excursion was a total pity party. And then I napped for what was left of the day and woke up in the middle of the night and really I have the weirdest life right now.

Tuesday, February 5

A very busy day

I had an early appointment with Sa Lents. And I knew about it beforehand! I had a further boost of my interface functions, and found I have an appointment calendar. I can look forward and see what they've scheduled for me for the rest of the year. I literally do have appointments an entire Taren year ahead. Almost all medical examinations. I don't know if the increase in function is down to Zan, or Maze, or even the conversation I had with Ista Tremmar, but it's a relief to almost be a person again.

The appointments with Sa Lents are always uncomfortable. I ask about Nenna, and he assures me she's improving. She only wrote to me a couple of times, and then didn't reply to the last email I sent and I tell myself that she's probably in a lot of pain and not exactly in a chatty mood. It's hard to imagine Nenna not being chatty though, and whatever else happens, I've changed Nenna forever and I think about that all the time when I'm talking to her father.

I tried to hide it by pressing him comparing dates on Earth to the things that are supposed to have happened on Muina, and he conceded that it sounds like Earth is very atypical. I think Earth is beginning to make him really uncomfortable. It's one thing for him to document another 'lost world' which fits the known pattern, and something altogether more difficult to try and fit a 'pre-dispersal settlement' into the mix. Especially when I gave him my theory for Muinans originally being Earthlings.

Tarens clearly resemble both Asian and Caucasian people – or what you'd get if Asian and Caucasian people had babies for a few thousand years. Some people with pink skin and 'round eyes'. Some people with skin in golden shades and epicanthic folds on their eyes. And pink-skinned people with epicanthic folds, golden-skinned people with round eyes, or blue eyes, or darker skin, and every combination you can think of. I tried explaining to Sa Lents that he looks Japanese or Korean, but gave up the attempt because my language skills just aren't up to it, and he was smiling politely and not believing me at all. I'm not sure Tarens even have the concept of race as we do on Earth. Sa Lents acted as if I was explaining that red haired people were a distinct species from blonde haired people.

I don't know. If the Muinans really come from Earth, why isn't Earth full of psychic people? Or why doesn't Earth have stories of cultures ruled by psychics? The Egyptians had their god-kings, true, but they weren't like those on *Stargate*. Hm – must watch Tarens carefully in case their eyes flash mysteriously.

After Sa Lents, it was my regular session with Zan. If possible, she was even more formal and correct than ever, and not at all communicative. I thought about trying some personal questions afterwards, while we were eating lunch in the canteen, but there were a fair few Setari there and though I never saw anyone actually looking at us, I felt very centre of attention, so I played obedient student and asked what few questions I could think of about the training she was giving me. I don't know whether to feel sorry for Zan or not. For all

I know she's done something to deserve people being nasty to her. But I don't see any reason to give them any ammunition.

Next up was the big test chamber, this time with Zan, all of First Squad, and an in-the-flesh bluesuit, a man named Sur Gidds Selkie. Bluesuits definitely seem to be the military people in charge. 'Sur' is his rank. Squad captains are "See". Lots of ranks and titles start with an 'S' sound but with just the faintest 'z' overtone to it. Now that I can display names (title option on) again, I see I've been spelling them wrong. Not an 's' or 'z', so much as 'ts'. 'Tsa', 'Tsur' and 'Tsee'.

Tsur Selkie was a slender, quite short guy who could probably do a great Clint Eastwood imitation if he had any idea who that was. All the wrong colouring and everything, but a totally 'chipped from flint' attitude. And I think he's the one making most of the decisions about me. First Squad were really correct around him, though not nearly as formal as Zan, who scaled new heights of expressionlessness. He didn't speak directly to me at all.

This was the first serious testing of the effects of my enhancement since my health break. They started out with Zan, and I had the distinct impression that there was something about Tsur Selkie personally observing which meant they expected to get more information from watching her again. Once Zan had picked blocks up and moved them around for a while, they swapped to Maze doing the same thing. Then they very warily had Zan and Maze touching me at the same time, and using Telekinesis at the same time. I didn't feel anything, as usual, but Tsur Selkie seemed to find something significant in it all, because he nodded and said:

"The best analogy is an amplifying container. A limited number of talents fit into the container without any particular effect. Too many, and the container is torn. The different 'sizes' of the talents also appears to be relevant. Until further notice, multiple contact is forbidden absolutely. Surion, your squad will move on to testing the effects of enhancement upon each individual talent available to First. A controlled test within the Ena of that category of skills will be arranged. Namara, Twelfth Squad will cover First Squad's previously scheduled assignments for this rotation. Briefings have been transferred to your mission file."

They all saluted, hand to chest. I just watched. Military equipment doesn't salute. After he had left, closely followed by Zan, everyone relaxed and Zee surprised me by hugging me and saying: "Now I don't have to be so anxious about accidentally killing you."

I was glad for once that I was so bad at talking, since my immediate reaction was a sarcastic one about irreplaceable equipment, and First Squad don't deserve that kind of attitude from me. I was really relieved I'd been assigned to work with them, rather than Twelfth Squad. Zan I think I like, or would if she'd let me, but that Lenton guy isn't exactly high on my list of desirable people to be around.

It was a long afternoon. No disasters, but between them they had a lot of talents and they examined them all carefully, finding occasional strange distortions, and drawing two tentative conclusions. If they try to use a talent *on* me when I'm enhancing them it will be distorted in some way, though they can use their talents on me so long as they're not enhanced by me. And the same if they try to use an Illusion talent while I'm enhancing them. They think that my supposed ability to make illusions somehow interferes with any projections they try while they're enhanced. I've yet to be able to produce anything like an illusion and though Alay tried to talk me through different methods people use, I still didn't get anywhere.

Although they were cheerful and upbeat, First stayed relatively formal and correct and I took my cue from the way they were using their surnames and was careful to remember that they were on duty and were probably recording everything to put in reports, or being watched by who knows how many people.

But when Zee, who had to go to medical to have her leg checked, was escorting me back to my box I took a chance to ask a few questions.

"Twelfth Squad, what mean do First assignment? Pick which Ionoth kill?"

"We're assigned particular sections of the Ena to patrol, and clear them of potential threats before they have a chance to find a way into real space. Twelfth Squad will be clearing the sections we would have been working."

Something about the way she said it made me ask: "That not good thing?"

She grimaced. "Twelfth is the newest of the squads, and have little practical experience in the more complex situations you can encounter in the Ena. Our assignment will be an extreme test for them."

Hard to say whether Zan would be pleased about that or not. "Why rest Setari so different First Squad?"

"Different?" Zee asked, but I'd bet she knew what I meant.

"Too serious. Competitive. Less...human."

She thought about it a long time before answering. "The senior Setari started the program later and early on lived with our families, attending KOTIS like it was a school. When we began to show positive results, the program was intensified, the talented living onsite and allowed few visits with their families. The younger Setari started earlier and were pushed harder and further and so are stronger than us. And we will need that strength. But they were given little chance to be children, and like us they're burdened by the magnitude of the task. Without the Setari program, Tare would be a world of street battles and lurking death." She opened the door to my box, and gave me an unhappy shrug. "The younger Setari, don't misunderstand them. They are weapons. But they are not so different from you."

I thought about this for a long time after Zee left. Mainly about how much harder and further they'd be willing to push me. But also about growing up knowing you stood between your family and monsters.

Wednesday, February 6

Outfitting

All my morning appointments with Zan have changed to morning appointments with Mara. For me last week revolved entirely around seeing Zan, and now for all I know I'll never work with her again, and I really can't see her showing up unexpectedly and taking me to eat fondue. The problem fidgeted around my head half the morning, and eventually I composed a little thank you note, doing my best to make it grammatically correct and everything – though I think that made it worse – and emailed it to her. She treated me as an assignment, but she never called me 'it'. And I really enjoyed looking at her apartment, which is something she didn't have to show me and something I bet she's pretty private about.

Mara is far more of a taskmaster with my dodging training. I suppose they've decided I'm healthy enough to step it up a little. She started with stretches and steps and all that stuff, but then she brought out a basket of balls and said I had to dodge them and threw them at me, one after another, harder and faster each time. Not at all martial arts-like, but effective at making me *want* to dodge.

And also very glad to stop, which we did when Lohn showed up to take us to lunch. I get the distinct impression that Lohn and Mara are a couple, for all they don't hang all over each other. Hell, for all I know they could be married. Even in the same canteen, it's very different eating lunch with Lohn and Mara – particularly Lohn. He talks non-stop and makes big gestures with his hands, sprawls back taking up two chairs, and chats with every person who passes by. He's the anti-Zan. All the Setari he talks to unbend to him at least a little. One of the people from Second Squad, a woman named Jeh Omai, joined us. Second Squad is the other 'senior' Setari squad, and Jeh is calm and relaxed and treats Lohn as if he's an overlarge but endearing great dane puppy.

With me she was straightforwardly curious, and asked me quite a few questions about what it was like to live on Muina. She's actually the first person to ask me anything about that since Nenna's friends, so I told her about trying to make a blanket, and that one of the first things I did when I briefly had the wide-ranging interface access was to look up how to make soap (basically oil and ashes, which I *don't* see how it can turn into soap, but whatever). Mara said that very few of the Setari had even been to Muina, that it was considered so dangerous that even the squads who were cleared for an investigative mission there weren't allowed to stay for more than a few hours, and that I was amazingly lucky to have survived. Lohn said First Squad had won itself a good luck charm, and I told him that Devlin actually meant 'unlucky'. I think he thought I was joking.

After lunch, Mara took me off to teach me about clothes. We went down to what I think must be a commissary, and I was given a light, stretchy black harness – a triangle at the back with two straps you slip your arms into and another which went around my ribs and joined like toffee when I held the ends together. Mara had me strip to my underwear in a cubicle and put on the harness and then 'assume the position' – the thinking about doing a star jump pose for spray-on swimsuits. This time I ended up in a Setari uniform.

There's a mirrored wall in the cubicles, and I spent a long time staring at myself. Barely recognisable as the girl who walked home from her exams and missed her path. My skin had tanned on Muina, since I was outside so much, but that's faded a lot and other than a few acne scars and tiny freckles it's looking pretty good. I seem to have developed a jaw line, which wearing a tight throat-hugging collar certainly emphasised, but my figure isn't nearly up to Setari standards. I look like a gawky crow. My hair has gone blonder than I expected, with only the lower layers brown – again that's from being out in the sun so much – and it's grown a couple of inches. I've been wearing it in a loose braid most of the time to keep it out of the way. I haven't suddenly become beautiful or anything – my mouth is still too wide and I've always thought my nose a bit too long – but I was looking better than I expected and not really me at all.

I feel like the longer I'm here, the less chance I'll have of going back, and that putting on this uniform somehow made it nearly impossible. Like I've visited Faerie and stupidly eaten the food.

Mara asked if I'd fallen asleep, so I came out, and something about the way she looked at me made me feel I was right about the Faerie food. No-one's ever asked me to join KOTIS or offered any kind of choice at all. They did rescue me from Muina before I was eaten, though. And they're fighting against monsters and I can help with that, in possibly the most passive way imaginable, but still apparently I might be useful. Just because I've never said yes, or been given the chance to say no, doesn't mean I haven't agreed to anything.

Enhancing the Setari is a better option than washing dishes, which is where I'd probably have ended up as just another stray. They're more interested in finding Earth now, as well, and while I'm not keen on many of the possibilities of being useful to the Setari, I'm trying to focus on the day-to-day and not what the rest of my life is likely to be.

Suits made of nanoliquid are beyond weird to wear. The harness is a specific control mechanism for the nanites which doesn't rely on the wearer's personal interface, and lets the Setari do all sorts of fun stuff with their suits. Make them thicker, give themselves kneepads, make the gloves cover the whole hand or go away altogether. Make pockets. You could probably even stick yourself to another Setari. Mara taught me how to manipulate mine and then told me to play for a while. Tomorrow we're going to go into the Ena to test out how my amplification works there, and to try a couple of talents which don't work in actual space. We're not going to be fighting Ionoth or anything, but it's still all a bit daunting.

Thursday, February 7

Glimpse

The excursion into the Ena was scheduled for the morning, so no dodging practice. Mara collected me, made sure I brought my uniform harness, and took me to the nearest "nano-changing room". I think the Setari must have these in their own apartments, rather than having to leave their clothes in little lockers about the place.

I didn't like walking through the facility in uniform, and almost wished they'd given me my own colour or something, for all that it would make me stand out more. But I'm willing to bet that the black nanosuit is something that these people *earn*, not just parade about in. I was glad I'd made the effort to do my hair really neatly in a French braid, but I still felt vaguely like I was going to be arrested for the equivalent of impersonating a police officer. And for a moment there it felt like Maze and Lohn and Zee didn't even recognise me. Lohn at least murmured "All grown up," before getting serious and professional. Going into the Ena is the most formal I've ever seen First Squad when a bluesuit isn't around. Because, even though we were going to the safest bit they could find, the Ena is dangerous.

The blast doors emphasised that point. KOTIS was built on this island because it's a very 'torn' space and there are lots of places where it's easy to get from actual space to the Ena, and vice versa. Wherever they find one of these torn spots on Tare, they build a metal box around it, with doors that only the nastiest of monsters could hope to claw their way through.

While we were waiting for clearance, Maze set up a group channel or 'space' in the interface for the squad, started a mission log which would record everything we did, and then talked me through what was going to happen.

"We have three objectives today. To test your enhancement on the talents which are only effective in the Ena. To see if there's any variation with the talents we've already tested due to the different environment. And to orient you in the Ena, since you stepped directly from your world to Muina, and you were sedated when you were transported from Muina to Tare. The Ena is a very disorienting place, visually overwhelming in places, and at the same time it intensifies the senses. Tell us immediately if you start experiencing any kind of sickness or distress.

"Annan and Gainer will accompany you at all times while we are in the Ena. Don't move anywhere without them. If we encounter any situation which requires moving quickly, they will move you. Do not run. Above all, do not enter any of the gates without clearance. Do you understand all that?"

"Yes," I said, in such a small voice I sounded about five.

Maze crinkled the corner of his eyes encouragingly at me before going on. "We are unlikely to encounter Ionoth in this section, but it always remains a possibility. Depending on the type, we may choose to deal with it. You'll be kept well out of the way if that's the case. Anything serious, and we'll return you to actual space before approaching it."

By this time the big door had opened, and we moved into the spacious metal box. I couldn't see any sign of visible tears in the world, but then I hadn't when I walked from Earth to Muina either. The interface obligingly drew a triangle of light in the air in front of us, showing where we should walk.

Maze and Mara went first and then me with Zee and Alay on either side of me. I was finding all the surnames confusing, so it's good that I'd been given back name display and could see Zee Annan and Alay Gainer floating over their heads.

I didn't feel any sense of resistance walking through the triangle, but I certainly felt the cold. That was something they hadn't mentioned, that the Ena is perhaps 10 or 15 degrees Celsius. And the weird thing was, we were still in the metal containment box, and the door was closed, but most of the walls were missing – or, not missing. If you've ever seen a drawing someone's made, where they start with the line art and then colour it in, we were in a version of the box where the line art was there, but only half of it was coloured in. Kind of.

Anyway, it meant we could walk out of the box through one of the 'uncoloured' sections of wall. I felt like I was walking into a half-complete animation for *Setari: the CGI Movie*. We were where we'd been before, but with all the people and lots of the 'textures' missing. This was the part of the Ena they call near-space, and it was truly weird.

It did make me feel more alive. I don't know if it was the cold, or a sense that the gravity was lighter there, or just...mystic spooky stuff, but I felt hyper-alert and awake. Maybe the air there has adrenaline in it. Everyone was waiting to see how I reacted, so I smiled and shrugged and Maze nodded and started off.

It took me a while to recognise the gates for what they were, scattered through the construction zone of a world. Some glinted and some were dark. It was only when we rounded the corner into a patch where there was nothing above us but a dark sketch of a sky and...thousands of them. It was like someone had taken an ocean's worth of mirror and shattered it and flung the pieces to spin in every direction, but every piece reflected not what was before it but some other place. Other space.

We didn't walk far, stopping at a jagged rift about the size of a car: all brilliant green intensity. Through it was grass, and rolling hills, and a pale blue sky paling to white. Huge tumbled stones, like blocks for an ancient grey castle. Most of this was intact, coloured in, but the edges of the space were fading out into mist.

"Try not to touch any edges stepping through. Gates can be fragile, and tearing them attracts Iono–"

Maze stepped through as he spoke, lifting his feet carefully, and I noticed that passing through not only cut off the sound, but that 'no connection' had appeared in the group channel display where Maze should be. When I stepped through myself there was a soap-bubble sensation, and the air changed again, bringing an over-emphasised sense of grassiness. There were a lot fewer of the pieces of broken mirror here, which might be why they chose it.

"Spaces what exactly?" I asked, realising how limited the horizon was. This wasn't what I'd pictured at all.

"One day perhaps we'll have a definitive answer on that," Zee said, while Maze and Mara had a scan-the-area-for-enemies moment. "For now, my favourite definition of it is that they're the sloughed-off memories of living worlds, crystallised and decaying fragments of the past tumbling and interconnecting."

I suppose if someone had taken a billion jigsaws and mixed all the pieces together and then had them connect up randomly so you could move from piece to piece you'd get the same effect, but Zee's explanation was much more poetic.

"Ionoth memories inhabitants of worlds?" I asked, and saw I'd managed to surprise them.

"That's one of the possibilities," Lohn said. "Maybe part of Muina's histories survived on your world after all."

"We lots entertaining fantasy," I said. No-one seems to believe me when I say Earth wasn't settled by Muinans.

"Looks clear," Maze said, coming back to us. "Let's get started."

The testing was much the same as all the testing we've been doing, with me contributing a lot of standing about. I wish I could at least figure out how to make these illusions. Still, it was entertaining watching Maze throw the stone blocks at one another, creating fantastic explosions of rock and dust. Most of the skills First Squad hadn't already tried seemed to work, and they were pleased about one which involved the gates, but I was more than glad when they decided it was time to head back.

And then, as we were walking back to the gate we'd entered by, there was a small gate, twice the size of my head. And through it, something so familiar my heart almost stopped. I certainly stopped, and my internal recording shows me how quickly Zee and Alay reacted, shifting around in my peripheral vision, flanking me. At the time, all I could see was It.

"That's what your world looks like?" Maze asked, eventually.

I shrugged, feeling so betrayed I wanted to scream. "Some parts. Australia lots red dirt. Sky – that quality light – I forgotten how big sky is. That right sort tree." Then I scrubbed at my face and added in English: "Crying over a fricking gum tree. How pathetic can I get?"

I made myself stop. Made myself say something that would get them moving. Made myself hold it in, at least until we were back on Tare and I could say I was tired and wanted a shower. None of First Squad were under any illusion about how I was feeling, but they had sense enough to know they couldn't fix it, and were kind enough to leave me with a short stop at medical and then to my room.

I thought it was real. Just for that second, before I saw the fraying edges, I thought that was Earth. I can still feel the way my stomach twisted, the way every part of me leapt through stillness into roaring joy, and then crashed.

All the feelings I've been trying to hold back, all my struggles to resign myself to being this stray, this person out of place and never really belonging, they've risen up to drown me. And tomorrow's my birthday. For a brief second I thought I had a chance, that I could go home and be there for my birthday and I just don't know if I can stand this awful pit that's opened up in me after that moment of belief.

I want to go home.

Monday, February 11

Happy Birthday

I was sitting on my bed when I woke up. MY bed. My bed, my room, my world.

Just, not quite.

Somehow I'd ended up in Earth's near-space. The cold tipped me off immediately, even before I saw the great big sections of wall lacking any substance. I was horribly chilled, cold with a deep ache in my bones, like I'd been sitting outside in Winter. Sydney's Winters aren't exactly sub-zero, but you don't feel happy about life if you sit out in them wearing a pair of underpants and a thigh-length t-shirt.

But, oh gods, cold was the last thing I cared about right then. I had no idea how I'd managed it, but somehow I'd ended up THIS far away from exactly where I wanted to be. I jumped up, and staggered a bit since I was very stiff, like I'd been there a while, then pulled open the door. Touching and moving things in near-space was like being underwater. I could lift objects, but things which should be light needed more push, and things I expected to be heavy were buoyed up unexpectedly.

At first I was just looking. All those trivial domestic things which were familiar and right and how things should be done, instead of the way they're done on Tare. Which were MINE. I started recording it, a thing which is becoming more automatic with me. Storing memories to re-examine later.

A lot was missing. The walls and furniture, the bigger and more permanent objects, were solid enough, but most smaller objects were a haze where I could almost make out the outline of what should be there, but it was more a smudge than any kind of substance. The bookshelves were full of the *impression* of books, blocky and colourful, but there were only one or two shelves – the shelves where Mum keeps her favourites – where I could make out titles or pick anything up.

The back garden was unexpectedly real. Mum likes having a garden, but she doesn't spend a lot of time on it, and goes for a cottage garden look: masses of plants and no neat borders or parts which need to be constantly weeded. The plants, the leaves, flowers, were all there. It even had some of the scent, though everything was flattened by a tinny greyness. No blue sky, but a washed out watercolour slate.

I'd gone outside to look for gates. I'd been able to see the gate we'd used in Tare's near-space, so I figured my best bet was to look through all the nearby gates until I found one which led to planet instead of Ena and then see whether I was able to get through it.

No gates. None visible, anyway. I went out to the street and walked down it, looking for any sign, the bitumen very gritty beneath my bare feet but oddly warmer than most everything else. I knew that Muina and Tare were in an area that is considered 'shattered', which is why they have so much trouble with Ionoth, but it seemed Earth's near-space was signally lacking ways in and out of it.

I don't know why I wasn't more scared. I think the cold had blunted my common sense. I knew on a mental level that, rather than being right where I wanted, I was in serious shit. If ever a world 'memory' would have monsters, it would be Earth's. Monsters wearing the faces of people, monsters which did the most awful things to each other, and that didn't even count current and past non-human predators, let alone the creatures we liked to make up. For all that Australia's one of the safest places you could possibly live, plenty of bad things have happened there. And I was also cold and hungry and could die of that as readily as being eaten.

But I was numb to thoughts of danger, and just returned to the outline of my home and sat down on the back patio steps. I couldn't work out how I'd gotten there, but was sure it wasn't a dream. The most I could think of doing was to try and find something tangible enough to keep me warm, and then to wander around randomly hoping I could find a gate.

The spaces seem to be quiet places, and the only noise I'd heard had been something like wind or static, distant but ever-present. I don't think I heard anything else at all, but I felt a sudden tingle all through me and a sense of something passing. I jerked upright, realising I'd nearly fallen asleep, and stared over my shoulder at the familiar boards of the patio and the sliding door into the kitchen.

Shadows. The patio table and chairs, sketchily half there, and shadows. Just the faintest hint of shapes, of people, which seemed to get fainter or darker as I moved my head. It didn't occur to me for a moment that they might be Ionoth. Filled with hope, I stood and began casting about, walking back and forth until I found the best spot to see them, standing right in the frame of the sliding door, facing outwards. I knew Dad straight away – he's tall and he tends to stoop. Mum was sitting down. The short shadow had to be Jules. Just there, right in front of me.

I knew shouting was pointless – I'd already seen that sound didn't carry across. Reaching out with my fingers and trying to tear a hole did nothing. It was all just air, with no edges I could catch. But with just an odd thickness which reminded me of the gates First Squad had taken me through. I concentrated on that, on the idea of resistance, of there being something between my world and me, something that if I could only touch, I could push against. I didn't reach out again, but leaned, feeling that thickness against my cheek, watching and willing those shadows to take on form, to let me see them properly.

It became amazingly difficult really quick, like pushing against a rubber wall that resisted after only a little stretching, but with each millimetre came more details. The aunts were there, and Nick. It was overcast, but not raining. Everyone had come over for lunch on my birthday, even my Dad and Nick. Nick had bruises all down one side of his face. Mum had Mimmit, our calico cat, on her lap, and she looked so worn and tired and unlike herself and I knew that was all because of me and pushed harder and harder.

Mimmit suddenly arched and spat and scrambled off Mum's lap. And then Aunt Bet dropped her glass and Mum stared after Mimmit, then in the direction Mimmit had been hissing, and then she looked like she'd been stabbed.

Thank all the gods for sign language. I've never been particularly good at it, but what I can't remember I can spell. And I had no problems managing: "Not dead."

Jules reacted first, leaning forward and trying to touch my arm. He said something, while Mum squeezed her eyes shut and opened them again. Dad tried to grab my shoulder, but other than a little tingling I couldn't feel him at all. I tried pushing against the wall, but I didn't seem to be able to go any further, and was feeling really exhausted just staying as far as I'd managed. But at least I could finally tell them what happened.

"Walk through wormhole," I signed. "Other planet."

That made Mum look totally incredulous and everyone started talking and trying to sign back at once. Aunt Sue grabbed her bag and pulled out her mobile phone, pointing it at me. I looked at Nick and signed: "What happen face?"

"Dad," he signed, which was enough of an explanation. When Nick's Dad gets really drunk, he stops recognising people, and thinks he's being attacked. Nick can usually manage him, but it's not his first black eye. Yet he won't leave.

Nick gave me that grin which has always been one of my favourite things in the world, where bad stuff has been happening, but he's decided to sit back and make the most of the good. "WTF?" he added, pointing at me.

Explaining all of what had happened to me seemed so enormous. I tried.

"Walk home. Next, other planet forest. Walk days. Ruins. Empty. Then rescue psychic space ninjas." I shrugged at their expressions as I spelled, but it was the best explanation I had for the Setari. "Many world, monsters. Astral plane? They fight monsters. Found me, took me their planet. Tare. People me, strays. Gates – wormholes – everywhere. Monsters, people, walk through. Earth hardly any gates." I pushed at the air in front of me helplessly. "Looking for gate."

Mum's expression had slowly changed while she watched me sign. She'd decided she wasn't hallucinating, and being her took the story at face value.

"Monsters there with you?" she signed back.

"Not know. Not know how here."

"Why lab rat?"

I was beginning to regret my mascot: I wouldn't have told Mum that. All I could do was shrug. "Too many medical exams. But nanotech computer in head! Download language. Do school in bed."

Mum's expression – everyone's – changed in a way which made me look quickly over my shoulder, and saved me from being scared out of my skin by the Fourth Squad captain. He's even better than Zan at being all business, never surprised or impressed by anything. After glancing past me at my world and my family he just removed some black straps from his arm and held them out to me. My uniform harness.

I only just managed to say "Thank you," because I was being very surprised that the Setari had found me when I couldn't even guess how I'd gotten here.

"Space ninja?" Mum signed, as I slipped on the harness. I nodded and she looked him up and down a moment, then added: "Friend or enemy?"

Hopefully I didn't look *too* doubtful when I looked back. But luckily the Fourth Squad captain was drawing off a pad of solidified nanoliquid which had been attached to his suit, and not looking at my expression.

"There are no tears that I can see in this world's wall," he said. "If you succeed in breaking through here, Ionoth will flood to this point."

I flinched, because I hadn't thought about that at all. "Say I put you danger," I signed, and watched as Mum frowned and Dad looked suspicious. Then the Fourth Squad captain pressed the pad of nanoliquid to the centre of the harness where it crossed my back and the suit flowed over me, bringing immediate warmth. I hadn't realised how cold I'd been.

"Venom!" Jules signed, his face lit up. He loves the Spiderman movies.

I smiled at him, but then said: "Can find gate?"

"There are none in this area, possibly no tears at all into your world. There may be natural gates, but they are immensely rare."

This wasn't exactly 'no', but I doubted I could force him to do anything, even if he could find a natural gate. "What realistic chances Tare find way get me home?"

He was looking behind us now, that attentive survey familiar from my day with First Squad: searching for Ionoth. "Before today's excursion, I would have said none. Especially having seen how far from the centre of the fractures this is. But if you can reproduce whatever you did to track your world, quite obviously reaching this planet's near-space is possible."

The near-space, yes.   But even if I could travel here at will, I couldn't get further, and there was absolutely no way I was going to be the first person to tear a hole in Earth's protection against monsters.

They must have seen it in my face, when I turned back. Dad said something, looking upset, and Mum's hands closed on the arms of her chair.

"Have to go back.   Don't know ever find gate not hurt Earth.   Chance low."   It was getting really hard not to cry. "Miss you so much."

"Can I come?"   Jules signed enthusiastically, and then gaped as the Fourth Squad captain turned – quite casually – and skewered some *thing* leaping at us from the outline of the lounge room door.   It looked like a spider made of rusty nails and old tyre rubber, which really isn't what I expected Ionoth to look like, and as he held it up so he could get a better look at it I saw that he'd made a blade of nanoliquid grow out of the arm of his suit.   I'd seen something like that in the movies I'd watched with Nenna, and it's not that different from *Terminator 2*, so I wasn't particularly surprised.   The Ionoth spider was shock enough.

My Dad's face had changed when I looked back.   He'd wanted to argue, but now he wanted me to get to safety as soon as I could, no matter where safety was.   "Happy Birthday," he signed slowly. "Hugs."

"Love you," I signed back, then looked over at Nick and made an X with my arms to give him a hug too.

He copied me, and added: "Be happy."

"You too," I signed back carefully.   "Tell Alyssa, sorry miss party.   Miss her."

Nick grinned.   "Will do."

I smiled at my aunts, then looked at my Mum.

"Live well," she signed.

It was exactly the sort of thing Mum *would* say.   I nodded, thought for a moment then signed: "Thank you for being my Mum.   Love you always."

That made us both cry and I tried to smile and then stepped back, wiping at my face as my family faded to shadows. I wanted to stay, to say more, to ask questions about a thousand things, but I wasn't silly or selfish enough. If one Ionoth had come to attack us, more would.

I turned to the Fourth Squad captain, who had gotten rid of the spider and who I really doubted wanted to stand around while I played happy families, but was at least managing not to look impatient. "Sorry," I said. "Ready now."

He just handed me a small flask and a wrapped food bar, and said: "Follow close."

It was almost ten minutes' walk to the gate, and I wondered how I'd managed to travel it while asleep, and how he had followed me. We met another of the spider things as we twisted a long path through the outlines of my neighbourhood, but it gave him as little trouble as the first one. Eating and drinking had succeeded in making me feel hungry and exhausted, but I did find a small amount of pleasure in being able to make myself a pocket to put the flask and empty wrapper in.

The gate was in someone's back yard, in what would be a swimming pool if the water had remembered to be there. I could see red earth through it, blue sky, a scatter of huge rocks. It wasn't a clean tear: the edges were surrounded by tiny fragments, thousands of glinting glimpses of red and blue. And at the bottom of the pool were a half-dozen of the spiders and a fraying shadow with claws. Dead. It was hard to follow down to stand among the bodies.

"Gates, particularly the ones you tore wider, are the most dangerous points in the spaces, because the threat on the far side cannot be clearly gauged. If this side is clear, I will go through and you will wait without moving until I signal you to come through. Do not come through without my signal unless you are in immediate danger of attack on this side. Should we need to run, above all things stay close to me, no matter where I run. Do you understand?"

"I tore gate?" I asked, staring down at all the monsters he'd had to kill, just at this one spot.

"You don't remember?" He looked at me, perhaps gauging whether I was lying. His eyes never seemed to show surprise; never annoyed or angry or really interested. "You tore a new rift in Tare's wall, and either struck or widened thirteen gates between here and there."

I stared. "Hole in medical facility?" I could feel my face heat, but rather than go into it further just said: "I wake here."

He'd gone back to scanning the area, then studied the gate for a very fixed and intent moment before stepping through it. Even though I'd been wandering about Earth's near-space by myself, the instant the Fourth Squad captain was on the far side of the gate I felt horribly vulnerable. A half-dozen examples of why I was vulnerable were scattered around my feet, and the edge of the pool was at eye-level so I could have a nice close look at anything scuttling up. That really destroyed any sense of pleasure I could gain from my last few moments in Earth's near-space.

Fortunately he signalled almost immediately, and I stepped out onto a red, flat plain where the sky was the biggest thing ever and there was plenty of distance between me and anything. The space was the memory of heat, and a ribbon in the sky that seemed to twist and shift, but was way too far away to be scary.

In all that space, I could only see two other gates. One was very distant, a glimmering on the horizon, and the other up a slope of rock that was no harder to climb than a flight of stairs.

"The next space is very populated," the Fourth Squad captain said as we approached the top of the rock slope. "They are tola type, not dangerous unless you remain among them, but both gates are thick with them and if enough gather it could be difficult to pass them. They are attracted to sound, so walk quietly and only communicate through the interface. Don't stop at the following gate; we're going to walk straight through."

Tola meant 'thin'. I stared through the gate at what looked to me like vertically striped shadows and couldn't see anything at all that looked like monsters. I remembered in time not to walk through the first gate until he signalled, but he did so almost immediately anyway. It felt like I stumbled into cold cobweb. The space was, I think, a shadow of a forest, so faded that there wasn't really even trees there, just darker stripes. The Fourth Squad captain moved forward, holding one arm before his face and I followed as best I could, though it was a little like when I'd been trying to push my way out of Earth's near-space, just that the resistance didn't get any harder. And it was damn dark. The gate we were heading for wasn't even visible to me, and I immediately lost sight of him. The only reason I didn't freak out completely was because my interface knew where he was and I realised if I turned on names I could follow him far more easily. So I followed a floating 'Kaoren Ruuel' sign through the forest of creepiness, and almost felt like laughing.

[Taren spelling continues to confuse – Maze pronounced 'Ruuel' as 'Rue-el'.]

The next space was totally black, so I was lucky it had already occurred to me to track him using the interface. Zan had said the Fourth Squad captain's talents were Sight-based, which explained how he was able to walk so confidently into pitch dark. I think the space was some sort of cave or tunnel. The ground was fortunately smooth, though, and it was short. The next gate was only ten or fifteen metres away, and I saw silvery grey water and stopped while he passed through.

But again he signalled straight away and I walked out onto a beach at night. That was a strange one – beautiful and eerie, all silver and black, but no moon in the sky to explain where the light was coming from. There was a single line of footprints along the beach, with sand kicked up behind them to show how fast he'd been going. The Fourth Squad captain's, and yet none for me.

"Why not full squad?" I asked, since asking him if I'd been levitating would have been pointless.

"Groups attract Ionoth. Fighting our way through would have been too great a delay."

So he'd come alone through thirteen spaces to find me. I'd seen enough of how First Squad behaved going to a space they'd considered safe to know how dangerous that had to be.

"Thank you," I said. "Save my life."

This he didn't even respond to, which made me feel just wonderful. But of course he hadn't come to save Cass, but to retrieve a potentially valuable weapon. He was taking me back to the place where I was 'the amplifying stray' and something they were willing to risk a squad captain's life to retrieve. I hadn't realised how valuable I was to them.

The next gate opened out onto a city of skyscrapers covered in vines. I could tell by the way the Fourth Squad captain turned his head once he was through that there were Ionoth in there, and I wasn't surprised when he went off to one side and didn't immediately come back. It would be my fault if he was killed.

The question of what would happen if I kept doing this occupied me for the incredibly long time it took my only protection to return, and I was just switching over to what I would do if he didn't come back when he reappeared. He didn't look injured though, or even out of breath when he signalled me to come through, but he said: "Move quickly through here," and strode off at double pace.

That place smelled of death. I don't know how else to describe it. Old blood and rotting plants and the stink of decay and wrongness. Death. I couldn't see what it was which had kept the Fourth Squad captain so long, but I didn't particularly want to, and scurried after him. Whatever world that space belonged to must be a truly horrible place.

There were at least a dozen visible gates there – every space we went into seemed to have more. Every time we came close to a gate, my heart lifted, then fell when we moved past. My need to get out of the smell of it was incredible. And when the Fourth Squad captain finally did stop, at a gate showing only some carved grey stone and a bit of stair, he turned and looked carefully around us and I realised I was going to have stay there alone while he cleared the next space. I had to bite my lip not to say pointless things, and when he stepped into the next world, looked around, then moved away, I nearly ignored what he'd said and went after him.

I think it was the idea of the Fourth Squad captain giving me a lecture on doing what I was told which kept me there. But I felt really sick about it, and stared in every direction, convinced that things were moving toward me. The gate was in the middle of a street, and the leaves overhanging the windows above fluttered and shifted all the time. And I could hear a noise, a scratching, coming closer. I was trying to decide what constituted 'immediate danger of attack' when the Fourth Squad captain reappeared and came back through to my side of the gate.

"We're going to run," he said. "Straight up the stair to the apex and straight through the gate. Go."

Devil and Deep Blue Sea time. I was so freaked out by the smell and sounds of the skyscraper place that I didn't hesitate. The next space was cold and full of a stifled echo, a distant roar. I looked down, and the angle of the stairs was way too sharp to make that a good idea, though what was at the bottom of it certainly helped in getting me moving in the other direction. The grey stone was a stepped pyramid, huge, rising out of an ocean of black...something. It reminded me horribly of the nanoliquid our suits were made of, writhing tendrils of it reaching upward. And all over the sides of the pyramid were shadows of people on spikes, speared through their backs like butterflies, and with tendrils of black reaching toward us from out of their chests.

I am not good at running up flights of stairs. Especially not crumbling stone steps with chunks of recently severed black stuff on them. I can replay the eternal frantic minute it took us to get out of that space, can see the Fourth Squad captain overtake me and cut clear a path, but I don't actually remember too much of it, just this white panic. If the gates didn't have that soap-bubble resistance, I think I would have kept on running, though my chest felt like it was going to explode. As it was, it was enough to break my momentum, and I went down on my hands and knees, gasping.

The Fourth Squad captain walked a little way ahead while I recovered, looking annoyingly unaffected by sprinting up nearly-vertical stairs. Breathing a little deeper. I stared back over my shoulder and shuddered and said: "Cthulhu lives." And could probably chase us through the gate, since Ionoth theoretically could move from space to space. The idea was enough to get me to my feet and looking around.

We were on a branch, wide and soft with moss and lichen, and so far up that if there was any ground in this space it was lost in the gloom below. I became very glad I hadn't kept running. The Fourth Squad captain had walked down to where another branch crossed over the top of the first, and was making handholds in it using another blade made out of nanoliquid. When he climbed up, I followed, though I was starting to feel very rubbery-legged and ill. I'd managed to count through the worlds we had crossed – red desert, tola forest, tunnel, beach, skyscrapers, pyramid, tree – which made six more until we reached Tare's near-space. In retrospect I'm glad the Fourth Squad captain didn't show any sign of caring about my opinions, because I really wanted to stop and hug my knees and rock back and forth for a while, and it was only that he seemed to expect me not to that kept me walking.

Thankfully the next gate was one he immediately gestured me through, and I grew a little more hopeful about getting back without being eaten. That space was a huge one, impossibly tall, with all these white platforms crisscrossing a black chasm and climbing up into stars. There were tons of gates, the most I'd seen in any of the spaces, but I was glad that the Fourth Squad captain seemed to be heading for one on the same level as us, since I wasn't keen on more climbing.

Head jerking upward, he stopped so abruptly that I almost ran into his back. Given it was the first time I'd seen him act at all surprised by anything, I stared too, of course, but all I saw were some distant washes of colour, something like what I'd expect the Aurora Borealis to look like. And there was a faint, vaguely familiar noise which I thought might be whale song. The Fourth Squad captain found it far more interesting than anything else we'd encountered, and was standing stock-still, staring.

Then he said, "Augment me," and held a hand back.

He'd been very careful all along not to touch me, and alone in the middle of the spaces was not a good place to test my effect on whatever talent set he had. At the same time, I doubted he ever gave an order without a reason, so I took his hand without stupidly saying: "Are you sure?" But with great misgivings.

And he fell to his knees. Totally not what you want your sole rescuer to be doing, especially since he was standing near the front edge of one of the platforms at the time, and yanked my arm half out of its socket in the process. And just stayed there, staring upwards.

With his eyes opened wide, he didn't look like he was in pain, more like he was having some sort of religious experience. I thought it was damn stupid timing, but I'd been wanting some knee-hugging time, so I sat on the platform's edge and waited. And waited.

Eventually I lay back and watched the distant light show, and tried to get the suit's fingers on my free hand to turn into knives, which wasn't very successful. I could make them go out to spiky points, but they were soft, rubbery spiky points, just like the rest of the suit. Mara hadn't shown me how to make weapons.

The noises grew a little louder, and I realised that they were the noises I'd heard on Muina, except not nearly so close. The 'massive' that they'd come racing to investigate, and found me instead. And these Ddura were supposed to be some tool or weapon to use in fixing the problem tearing all the spaces apart, so I guess I understood why the Fourth Squad captain was so interested in that one, but if he had stayed like that much longer I would have given in to creeping weariness and passed out, and wouldn't even have been able to shout a warning if something came along to eat us. Fortunately the Ddura faded away, and the Fourth Squad captain closed his eyes and took a long shuddering breath. I wasn't sure he'd even blinked for all of the time he'd looked at it.

"Beginning think your brain melt," I said, and he looked down at me so blankly I knew he'd completely forgotten I was there.

"Not yet," was all he said, and climbed a little stiffly to his feet, keeping hold of my hand so I couldn't stay lying down. "We're going up."

I can't tell you how unenthusiastic that made me. The Ddura had been a long long way away. I'm not sure what the Fourth Squad captain would have done if I'd kicked up a fuss – carried me up, maybe. He hadn't let go of my hand, and started walking without waiting to see what my response was, so I trailed along behind him wondering when the day would end.

But we only went up about three staircases worth of platforms, and stopped before a tall but narrow rift to a white place splashed with washes of colour, with a tall white tower in the middle, big and solid with very familiar arch-shaped doors. The Fourth Squad captain indulged in another staring session, but didn't try to go through the gate, just stood studying everything he could see.

Since the building had some similarities to those on Muina I immediately guessed it was either a space belonging to Muina or one of these extremely dangerous supports that the Muinans had built in the Ena which had caused everything to fracture. The Fourth Squad captain was being intense enough about it to make me think it was something that important, and since the supports were supposed to be incredibly dangerous I'm glad he didn't decide to go any closer.

After he was done looking he held out his free hand, which glowed faintly, and made the gate glow faintly in return. And made him go interestingly pale and squish my hand a bit.

There were five gates between the platform space and Tare's near-space. He did the same thing at every single one of them after we'd passed through, and if there'd been the slightest need for running or killing Ionoth we would have been screwed because whatever making the gates glow was about, it took as much out of him as running up those stairs had me. By the time we'd reached a familiar-looking metal box, I was beginning to wonder if I'd have to carry *him*, which wasn't going to happen since he's six foot two at least. As soon as we stepped through the last gate into the proper world he let go of me, leaned his back against a wall, and closed his eyes, looking so grey I thought he was going to faint.

The shielding door opened almost immediately, after the briefest time for scans. I was swooped on by greensuits and greysuits, while Fourth Squad and a couple of other Setari rushed my rescuer. One of them, obviously a friend since he called him by his first name, said, "Ends, Kaoren, how far did you have to go? I've never seen you like this."

"Never mind that." The Fourth Squad captain was recovering, and had straightened up. "Get Third mobilised. I stumbled across one of the Pillars out there, and even with the stray's enhancement I don't have the strength to truly lock every gate for five spaces."

He could have announced the sky was falling, the way everyone jumped and stared. Me, I was glad I was so tired, because I knew I was headed straight for endless medical tests and I planned to sleep through them. Which I did, except for blearily answering a few questions about no I really don't know how I almost got to Earth. The room I'm in now is even more of a box than before, with scanners constantly pointed at me because they're trying to work out what I did and whether they can stop me from doing it again. They gave me my diary after a day, and it's taken me forever to write this all down, but that's okay because my interface has been shut off almost completely while they run tests and there's nothing else to do.

Lab Rat again. Stray, always. It really hurt to hear that.

But I guess I'll cope. It makes so much difference that Mum and Dad know I'm not dead. That I got to say goodbye. I don't know if I will ever be treated as a person here, but I can follow Nick's lead and look on the bright side of things until I can make them better. I'm not starving. Nothing has eaten me. And somehow, in a way I don't understand, I have the ability to go to Earth. I don't want to kill myself doing it, and I won't ever risk drawing Ionoth there, but now I have a goal beyond being a useful stray. If I can gain control, perhaps I can figure out a way to find a natural gate, and be able to go back to my real life, to being Cass again.

As birthdays go, it could have been worse.

Tuesday, February 12

Psych 101

Maze came to see me after lunch, to talk me through what they'd concluded from all the tests. He didn't tell me anything I hadn't figured out already: that I must have some ability to find Earth through the spaces, and then travel there, bashing open gates on the way. While asleep. It's nothing like any ability they've encountered before, and since they work out your abilities by looking for known 'patterns' in the brain, they've now decided they really don't have any idea what I can do and they don't know how to test me. They think they've probably got it wrong about the Illusion casting, too.

Mainly they're worried I'll keep tearing holes where they don't want them, and vanishing.

Maze asked if there was anything he could do for me, which isn't the sort of thing you ask someone who's been locked in a room for days on end with nothing to do except wait for the next medical exam. There's obviously tons of things they *could* do, but the question is what they *were* doing. Poor Maze must have wondered why I looked so angry, but because it was Maze I managed to not shriek and rant.

"Thing I need is be less homesick," I said. "Is why that happen, guess. Didn't go bed think 'leave tonight'. Not scared, upset. Just homesick. But is different now, plus. Family know where am, make big difference. Plus, would choose not go unless find way not tear hole Earth's shield, bring monsters. Not acceptable. Is found way stop me leaving?"

"In truth, we don't know. You're still here, but that may be because you haven't tried to leave. We don't know if the extra containment on this room is having any effect on you, but it does help some of the more sensitive Setari, who need dampening on their quarters to sleep properly."

"Bigger box soon?" I asked, hopefully.

"Keeping you in high security intensive care indefinitely isn't very practical." Maze gave me what I think of as his 'captain look'. "And stop calling it a box."

"Is box long as door lock. What think I do? Go day trip Unara?" My voice had gone flat and hard, and I sighed and shook my head. "Getting tired silly psychology games. Put Cass in box nothing to do. Cass happy do anything, try hard training. Take Cass outside lunch, happy Cass try harder. Cass leave to Earth. Put Cass in smaller box, take away toys."

"You think that's why we took you to lunch?"

"No." I was embarrassed about being nasty. "First Squad just nice people. But bet Maze report state Stray's mental health."

His mouth squinched a little, so I knew I was right.

"First Squad, Setari, they useful weapons. Lots rules. Choose be Setari because protect home. I here, not my planet, but owe life. Since can't go home yet, willing help. Right thing do. Accept rules. But. Kept in box, annoying. Have interface cut back, stupid. If testing, need reproduce circumstance. Different circumstance nullify test. Someone petty? Or punishment? All achieve is grumpy Cass. Then Maze sent talk me."

"Do we seem that manipulative?" He looked really sad.

I shrugged. "Don't know sure. Could just be big stupid machine forget Cass person. Or is idea make very obedient? Don't know. Tolerate it, just annoyed." And I didn't want to push them to worse treatment, the possibilities of which I'd had more than enough time to dwell on. I'd had this horrible nightmare where I'd dreamt there was a scar on my stomach, and found out they'd harvested my ovaries and were trying to breed more amplifiers. And since that really was a logical approach, I'd been freaked out half the day about it, caught between desperately attempting to leave again and telling myself not to over-react. Which was probably why I said any of this stuff to Maze. "Sorry. Not Maze's fault. What happen big tower?"

I think I'd really depressed him, but he brightened up at the change of subject.

"That was truly spectacular luck. The Ionoth are symptoms, while the Pillars are the disease. Ever since we've been able to travel among the spaces we've been searching for them, and that's intensified a great deal over the past five years with specialist Setari squads. Only twice before have we managed to get anywhere near one, and both times the shifting of the gates meant we barely viewed them before they were cut off. To capture information on a Ddura and a Pillar both is the most progress we've ever made. We're about to lose the path to this one, despite everything we can do to lock the gates, but have been able to deploy a number of drones in the space, and they went ahead yesterday afternoon and sent Third in to make a preliminary approach, which went without a hitch. Best of all, they think the gate we're losing is a rotational, and the rest relatively stable, so we should be able to return regularly and unpick its mysteries."

"What happen if just explode it?"

"Good question. We've no idea. But it could be catastrophic, so we're not going to rush anything." He smiled, a less sad smile this time. "Now if you could be convinced to become homesick for the Pillars, wouldn't that be an interesting development?"

"No thanks."

He left then, with a little wave and no words of reassurance. I didn't miss that he hadn't denied any of my little paranoid theories, but I was also sorry I'd made him feel bad.

-

And it's an hour or so later and my access rights have returned. Back to the way they were when I was living with the Lents. And because I appreciate the gesture I'll keep pushing through kindergarten, and will make sure I work before I play. Maze really is a nice guy.

When the bell rings, drool

It's a very odd thing to be able to record all your conversations so easily. I wonder if I'll run out of 'hard drive' to store them on. But I love that I can replay my conversation with my family, which was about the only thing that made up for having barely any interface rights for so long. Even going back to having a full interface – with all the news and television and entertainments I didn't even know existed – I replay pieces of my 'birthday party' over and over again. I can see all the nuances I didn't catch the first time, can look at their faces, look at the garden Mum loves. The Aunts are watching Mum, looking relieved. Dad bites his lip. Jules is just loving the whole thing, thinking it all so cool. Mum is...Mum.

I'm exasperated, though, about other parts of that day I keep replaying. Maybe it's because he saved my life, or because I spent a good two hours holding his hand. I keep telling myself not to and then watching my log of the Fourth Squad captain gazing off at the stars. A stupid thing to do: he didn't make a positive impression personality-wise, not to mention calling me a stray right in front of me. Kaoren Ruuel. Not the usual type I daydream about, but I seem to be far more excited about him in retrospect than I was when I was clutching his hand.

Other than not having enough willpower, it's been an eventful day. Mara came after breakfast, dressed in casual clothes instead of her uniform. We collected my belongings and she took me to my new box. Which wasn't a box at all.

"This is the latest expansion of the Setari living quarters, intended for Thirteenth and Fourteenth Squad," she said, as we walked down a short, empty corridor. She stopped at the end, triggering the door. "The rest of us are on the floors below. Until the new squads are qualified, you'll be the only person here."

It was a whole apartment, the same layout as Zan's, except no decorations displayed in the public space and incredibly neutral coverings on the whitestone furniture. Mara smiled at the expression on my face and said: "The doors will open to you. I'll take you on a tour of some of the areas you're permitted to go, and then into the city, if there's anything you'd like to buy. Outside KOTIS is completely off limits to you without an escort and clearance."

"What change their minds?"

"Maze suggested your intelligence be re-evaluated. Before you decided to stop being obliging and cooperative."

They thought I was stupid. I chewed on that one for the rest of the day, but otherwise let myself enjoy the change. There was more to the KOTIS facility than I'd expected, including some actual leisure areas populated by large amounts of people my age and younger, making me realise just how many Setari they're trying to train. But the exciting thing for me was going shopping. I'm not exactly a mall devotee, but when you've had everything supplied to you for weeks, simply buying a dressing gown or choosing your very own bedspread becomes a big event. Fortunately my displaced person allowance had been accruing.

Mara was really tolerant, and answered my endless, scrambled questions as if she had nothing else she'd like to do. We had lunch together and, just as I had back when she was showing me around KOTIS, I kept noticing people recognising her. A member of First Squad. Even if people outside KOTIS can't record her image, in the facility's support city there were a lot of people who knew who she was, or were from KOTIS taking a break. It put the Kanza game in a different light. I knew but hadn't really thought through how very much all the Setari are faceless celebrities on this world, the people everyone wants to know. And I get to spend all this time with them, and can't let myself buy into it.

I'd told Maze that I thought First Squad were nice to me because they were nice people. But I am just as much an assignment to them as I was to Zan; they simply approach the task differently. Every time I start thinking about how nice they are and how much I like them, I hear: "Don't forget the psychological aspects," and remember that I'm part of their job. Helping them feels like the right thing to do, but it's not necessarily the right thing for me.

I really miss Alyssa, miss having someone I trusted absolutely, and I wish I knew whether Nick has told her everything that happened, and if she believed him. Mum's not silly enough to announce to the world that her daughter is off on another planet, no matter whether they succeeded in videoing me. I'd give it a week before Jules posts that phone video on YouTube, though.

I thanked Mara carefully when she delivered me back to my brand spanking-new apartment, putting a lot of effort into pronunciation. I might be an assignment to First Squad, but I appreciate that they don't rub that in.

Mara told me where and when to meet tomorrow, since we had a lot of training to catch up on, and then left me alone. With a door I can open. It's a test of sorts, I guess. From practically no freedom to quite a lot, to see how I'll react. I went out straight away and up to the roof, where it was evening, and blowing an absolute gale – not raining, but super windy. Fortunately, I'd taken my brand new jacket with me, and found a corner to tuck myself in to think, and read through the instructions Mara had shown me on how to change the public spaces in my rooms. Simply loving that I was able to walk up there on my own, and I could go back when I wanted to.

I don't trust them not to take this away from me again. So far they've chopped and changed their approach to me several times, and could easily decide it's better to keep me in a box.   In its way this is just another bit of positive reinforcement training.   But I'm happy enough to keep being cooperative in return for an unlocked door.

I'm missing home a lot today.   But I really really hope I don't wake up tomorrow and find that I've gone tearing off through the spaces again.   I need a better understanding of just what the spaces are, what natural gates are, before I even begin to think of experimenting.   There's an entire world of information which I've just been given access to, and I need to go do more kindergarten so I can hope to understand some of it.

They thought I was *stupid*.

Wednesday, February 13

Settling in

So, my apartment has three and a bit rooms.   The bedroom is a little larger than my original box in the medical facility, with a lot more cupboard space.   The bed's a double bed, too, instead of the narrower 'hospital-type' bed.   I had a lot of trouble deciding on what kind of bedspread to buy, and ended up with a dark green one with a pattern of leaves and tiny white and pink flowers.

The kitchen part of the main room has a small refrigerator and cooker and a sink, plus bench and cupboard.   Given the Setari can get all their meals from their canteen, there's no need to do a lot of food preparation in the apartments, but at least it's possible.

There's a 'coffee table' and a matched pair of two-seater lounges facing each other over it.   All very plain, and nothing you wouldn't find in any Australian home, though made with a light, possibly hollow frame that seems vaguely related to whitestone.   Wood is far too rare here to be used for basic furniture.

I think I'd like to get some throw rugs to put across the lounges.   There's no television or sound system or anything like that because all that's inside your head, which makes the lounge look rather bare. The study nook is not really a study nook, I think. After all, I haven't seen a printed book or file yet, let alone anyone writing by hand, so why would you need a table designed for writing? Maybe it's meant to be a breakfast table? An upright chair and a table, anyway. It's a good place for me to write in my diary, even if it's not what it's meant for.

I really wish I'd brought my pippin statue with me. I only had it for a couple of weeks on Muina, but it was almost like having a pet.

I love the fact that I have a bath, and I did a lot of soaking in it last night, trying to read one of the novels I found in the vast array in my head. I should have bought some bubble bath, presuming it exists here. Bath oils and bath salts and maybe a rubber ducky. The shower is both a shower and a nanoshower. When you tell your nanosuit to go away, it drains down to your legs then kind of spins together and shoots out a special 'drain'. It makes me wonder if all the Setari are all using the same 'pool' of nanoliquid, which is a grotty and funny and disgusting idea. One size fits all taken to new levels.

I'm dressed in my uniform now, waiting for it to be time for me to go to training, and hopefully not get lost! Mara told me that if I have any kind of official assignment – training or meetings or even a medical exam – I'm to wear my nanosuit. I still wish it was a different colour, so people would know I'm not pretending to be a Setari.

Combat Room 3

Full day of training with First Squad today, both before and after lunch. We met at 'Combat Room 3', one with lots of shielding, and they borrowed a guy called Nils from Second Squad to make illusions of common sorts of Ionoth attacking us while they worked out the best way to use my enhancement while not putting me in too much danger. It was like an elaborate game of tag, and I felt so useless and awkward, especially when Nils had some really nasty illusion-Ionoth swarm the spot I was standing, and had to be rescued. Nils' illusions can't really properly show the effects of the Ionoth being hit, since they have no substance, but I didn't like a dozen of them pouncing toward me.

Ketzaren is my 'primary minder', since she has strong Levitation. If they need to move me quickly, she gives me an order and I have to put my arm around her shoulder. She grabs me around the waist and binds our suits together and then she levitates herself and I get brought along, which overcomes the fact that they can't put Levitation directly on me when they're enhanced. Her other talents are Ena manipulation, which seems to be what they use when they're trying to lock the gates, and Wind manipulation. Wind is a slow-build talent, so only occasionally used in combat.

First Squad was really pleased with how the training went, and they met up with some more of Second Squad for dinner afterwards and talked through strategies and possibilities. Maze was good at making this not an uncomfortable conversation for me, and I was okay with it anyway, since I'd decided that my role was like a caddie for a bunch of professional golfers. I don't do any of the hitting of balls, but I make the day a little easier for them.

The leader of Second Squad is called Grif Regan, and he's a very serious type who likes to listen more than talk. Nils, by contrast, is overwhelming. If you took the lead singer of The Doors (forgot his name) and crossed him with Marilyn Monroe, you'd get something like Nils. A really pretty guy who oozes sex. He treats Zee like she's a particularly delectable mouse, but Zee just ignores him. He also asked me if everyone on Earth could speak with their hands and I explained about my aunt being deaf and we sidetracked into a long discussion about Earth and things which are different between the worlds.

But the question was a useful reminder that everyone here can record everything they hear and see, and even feel, though that's an extra setting and not one I'm keen on using. And when Setari are on missions, what they record they put in mission reports, so everything Ruuel saw me do or say in the Ena has apparently been reviewed by whole bunches of people. It made me very glad I hadn't kept trying to talk to Ruuel, and hadn't done too much shrieking or squealing while panicking. And means I'm sure as hell not going to say *anything* during official assignments that I couldn't bear being watched by a hundred people.

No wonder Zan wouldn't gossip.

I went up to the roof again after dinner, just because I could, and because I could see stars up there now that the sun's fully set. Tomorrow will be more training, but Maze said that if they're happy with how it goes they'll consider going into the Ena with me again, this time to kill things.

Must remember to work the conversation around to different types of gates.

Thursday, February 14

Bubble worlds

Morning was dodging practice with Mara, which went well except for when I dodged in precisely the wrong way and got a ball in the face. I'm not very good at predicting where she's going to throw the things and that seems to be half of what dodging's all about.

I asked her if I was allowed to go swimming just for fun instead of it being for training, and she laughed and said yes and told me where to look to see whether anyone had booked the pool. But then later she said that for now it'd be better if she just added the pool into our training schedule, so I guess she checked with someone who decided there was too much chance of me drowning or something.

Over lunch, she explained a little more about spaces and gates. Spaces shift about. Some move only a little, bobbing up and down. Others apparently rotate, like planets. A few even zoom about: little comets on an astral level. And when they move, the connections which were the gates between them shift also, vanishing altogether, or linking up with other spaces, or just phasing briefly out of alignment. Setari with Ena manipulation skills are able to 'lock' the gates, preventing them from shifting, but unless it's between two relatively stable spaces, it's immensely difficult to hold them for more than a day or two, and there's even an argument about whether it's a bad thing altogether, given that it's similar to what the Pillars do.

Four of the gates back toward the Pillar we found are stable, shifting only a little, and it's become part of the regular 'rotation' of the Setari teams to go and firm the 'locks' up.

The gate into the space with all the platforms is gone. There's a different talent which allows you to 'read' the gates, and tell how long they will last, but they can't tell for certain if and when that gate will rotate back. They *think* (are hoping really hard) that the platform space is a rotational space, and that eventually the gate will realign again and they'll be able to lock it for another few days. Until then they check every day and puzzle over the readings they took from the space with the Pillar.

I didn't want to press too obviously about natural gates, how they're different, and how hard it might be to find one.

After lunch we joined up with the rest of First Squad, and this time all of Second Squad joined us. After testing the effect of me on their talent range, they worked with First Squad on a really big game of tag-team combat. They've been set a minimum time they have to wait between each person touching me, and then they have to keep track of how long the enhancement will last, which is a little over five minutes, always. Nils made illusory monsters again, and the two squads worked through fighting and enhancing while keeping to their rules. Then we took a break while Maze and the Second Squad captain, Grif, talked through different ways of managing me, and which talents it was best to enhance.

I was sitting on a bench next to Lohn and Nils and asked: "Is worth it? Stronger, maybe, but so complicate."

"Definitely, absolutely," Lohn said. "When I think of some of the situations we've been in, when the problem was sheer lack of fire power! The effect on some of the more esoteric talents, like Combat Sight, is incredibly hard to quantify, but I wouldn't give it up."

"Just the speed alone is worth it," Nils added. "It almost makes the thought of doing Columns Rotation bearable."

"Think how that last massive battle would have gone," Lohn said, and they glanced at each other and looked away.

"Massive?" I repeated. The word they used was 'kadara', but it seemed to have the same meaning as 'ddura'. "Ddura?"

"Different sort," Nils said. He lifted his hand and conjured an illusion of a four-legged black thing as tall as the three-story room, with swarms of miniature Setari buzzing around its long, spindly ankles. Everyone else in First and Second

Squad jumped and gave him a look, but he just waved at them. "They turn up very occasionally, crashing their way between the spaces rather than travelling through them, and end up in near-space. It took eight squads to take this one down."

"If we don't spot them, they can reach real space. That was a bad year." Lohn scrubbed a hand across his face, then smiled at me. "It's not so complicated, either – we're just taking turns patting you on the shoulder on a timer. So what do you say, Maze?" he called. "We going to do this for real tomorrow?"

"Pending clearance by medical," Maze said, coming over. "And clearance by you, Caszandra. You've seen something of what we can run into out there, and that was neither the weakest nor the worst thing we might encounter. Are you ready to do this?"

I'd seen enough by now to know that none of the Setari were completely confident of returning when they went into the spaces. Maze was asking a really serious question. And the spaces I'd gone through with Ruuel had scared me, had made abundantly clear that there was danger and horror involved. I didn't want any part of that.

"Long as don't have ran up stair," I said after a moment. "That hardest bit."

Maze smiled, but gravely, and nodded at me. "It will be one of the more straightforward rotations," he said. "I'll schedule it, dependant on the results of the medical."

After the medics cleared me, Alay and Ketzaren took me to dinner. Alay's the most quiet and reserved of First Squad, but really lovely when she laughs. She's what people call 'gamine', and wears her hair short, though little random curls sproing out. I think Ketzaren, who is very dry and sardonic, was deliberately setting out to cheer Alay up, and it was only after they'd delivered me back to my apartment that I thought about why, about the reasons First and Second Squad often look tired and sad.

I don't want to go into the spaces hunting Ionoth. I'm scared about the trip tomorrow. And of all the trips after that which I'll be in for if I let myself be conscripted by an alien military organisation to fight a problem which has been growing steadily worse. I fully intend to go home.

But then there's First Squad. They've been doing this for years. Fighting nightmares. And getting hurt. I haven't missed that there were originally three senior Setari squads, but now there only seems to be two. I can't bring myself to ask what happened to the other one.

And I've been writhing silently at the thought of saying: "Thanks for saving my life, but not my problem. I'll go home now and try not to think too hard about whether you're dead yet".

But I want to go home.

Wearing the Setari uniform makes me feel so fake.

Friday, February 15

Rememories

I started out the day by spotting Zan in the canteen. She was eating dinner – Twelfth Squad is on a different shift than me at the moment – but after I picked out some breakfast I asked if I could join her and she of course was polite and said yes.

"You look tired," I said, since I refuse to be all stilted and formal with her. "Is rotation bad?"

"No injuries so far," Zan said, being her usual correct self. But then she actually asked me a question, which is progress. "You're scheduled to start a rotation today?"

I nodded, wondering if for the rest of my life people would know more about what I'm doing than I do myself. "When Setari off-duty?" I asked. "Never know if what say go into mission reports."

"It would be truer to say we're off-shift, not off-duty. All time in the Ena is fully logged, and most training sessions, but I would have no reason to report on this conversation, for instance. Besides, you're on second level monitoring."

The way she paused made it clear that she wished she hadn't said that, so naturally I asked what second level monitoring was, and appreciated that she didn't avoid answering.

"It means your life signs monitor, along with everything you do, you're recording internally – separately from any private recording you make. The record isn't reviewed unless there's an incident which needs verification or investigation, such as when you vanished into the Ena."

I suppose I wasn't that surprised deep-down, but that didn't stop me from feeling absolutely exposed. I must have gone brick red.

"Everyone can look at?"

"No." Zan made her voice as firm and clear as possible. "There are very strict rules about such reviews, and they can be performed only for a clear reason, by those with the very highest security clearance. No-one in the Setari has anywhere close to that level. But a selected extract of your record was appended to Tsee Ruuel's report on your recovery, showing your attempt to open a gate into your world."

"Monitoring used criminals?"

Zan was looking distracted, but nodded. "Or children considered at risk."

Or conscripted strays, I thought. In a way I'm almost glad, because every time I start to think about being heroically self-sacrificing, the words "second level monitoring" are going to help me immensely.

I looked up as Maze put a tray on the table next to me and sat down, his mouth set. I was willing to bet he was the reason Zan had been distracted, that they'd been having a silent conversation about what I'd asked and how she'd answered.

"Do Tare have saying here," I asked, before he could say anything, "'Who watches watchers'?"

He blinked, then gave me one of those tired, super-nice smiles: "I think I've heard some variation of that. But the restrictions on monitoring are very tight."

"Is ever likely be less monitored?"

"I don't know. Perhaps if we gain a proper understanding of your talent set. And you stop nearly dying."

I felt like arguing, demanding that I be taken off, but I could see by the way he was steeling himself that there was no hope so I held my tongue. "When everyone talk using surnames, that when official recording, right?"

"Usually. Or habit. Formality is a discipline." He glanced across at Zan, who was being super quiet and proper while she finished her dinner. "Unnecessary, I suppose, but the competitive atmosphere fosters it."

"During rotation, consistent naming is common sense," Zan said. She paused, then stood up, lifting her tray. "Good luck today, Cassandra." With a nod to Maze she left.

A first time for everything. *And* she'd pronounced it correctly. Pleased, I made myself forget about starring in my own reality show, and concentrate on eating my breakfast. And toyed with the idea of asking Maze if he knew or cared that half the younger Setari had the hots for him. Or why they bullied Zan. But it would be unfair, since Zan was really bothered by Maze, to go talking about her with him.

After we'd eaten, Maze gave me a lesson on extra equipment we would take while on a mission. A little food and water, a very tiny medical pack, and the breather, in case we encountered a flooded zone. Zee joined us, and reminded me practically to go to the bathroom, and then we went down and met the others at another of the sealed-up gates. I could tell by the way Zee was watching me that she and Maze had discussed second level monitoring before she arrived, but by that time I'd moved through annoyed to resigned, and switched back to being worried about gallivanting through the Ena killing monsters.

"Is all spaces okay atmosphere?" I asked, making a pocket for my breather.

"Usually," Ketzaren said. "Sometimes the air is not very pleasant, but we've yet to encounter one which was toxic. The theory is that only certain atmosphere types create a truly living world. Or that we are not truly breathing."

"Why this easy rotation?"

"Because it's short, there's nothing smart, and it never changes," Lohn said, grimacing in the middle of some slow stretches. "And it leads to Unara, as at least a quarter of all rotations do, so there's usually not much going on in near-space either."

Maze took over talking, in captain-mode. "In addition to Tare's near-space, we will be travelling through four spaces. The first is always bare. The second will be insects – small, and in swarms. We are not likely to allow any to get close to us, but if one strikes you, the antidote to their poison is in your medpack. After the second space we will return to Tare's near-space and search for any Ionoth which have reached it from neighbouring spaces. The first space on the return trip is only occasionally inhabited, and the Ionoth which spawn there are large and quite slow. The last space contains three winged Ionoth. Spel will move you if necessary. Ready?"

I nodded, though my breakfast was considering not coming along. That sick feeling stayed with me the entire time, for all the mission itself went exactly the way Maze said. We crossed through near-space to a baked and dying field of plants, then to a meadow crawling with over-sized bugs which made the mistake of gathering into groups and coming at us. Lohn touched my elbow and fried them instantly, his Light wall blocking any chance of them getting close.

And then we were somewhere in the bowels of Unara, in a wind-blasted tube taller than a house which Mara said was one of the air channels which power Unara and keep it breathing. We walked along it, not finding a single Ionoth, then stepped into the bottom of a canyon with a thin stream running down the middle, and a hulking bull with wide horns crashing along one bank. All of First Squad simply went up, Ketzaren hooking me into her side and lifting effortlessly. We floated above as it ramped about, crashing and snorting, until Mara dropped down and finished it with a single, swift stroke of her Light whip. I could smell it, burnt flesh rising to cut through rank, musty animal scent, and decided to eat smaller breakfasts as we lifted up further to a gate into a forest clearing. Lohn, who was unenhanced by this time, shot three Light bolts at three precise points around the clearing, and three feathery things crashed to the ground. Then back to near-space, and through to the KOTIS facility.

Though they were as crisply professional as always, it was clear that the run had been incredibly easy for First Squad, that they knew exactly what to do before entering each space, and had been most interested in testing out their altered abilities. Maze and Zee escorted me down to medical so that all three of us could be scanned for side-effects, and discussed the effect on Combat Sight, which picks up hostile intent. They were very pleased that this doesn't seem to be distorted. It was a good introduction, and I'm not quite so worried about the next rotation. Nothing came even close to me, and though I didn't find the killing easy to watch, I can perfectly understand not wanting any of those things running loose on Tare.

But it's endless, this fight. Because for all they kill off the Ionoth, the spaces still remember them, and they come back and have to be killed again. Memories. The Unara Rotation was so easy because First had done it hundreds of times, and knew exactly what the Ionoth would be and how they would behave. Over and over, an infinite number, and First Squad's already been fighting them too long.

Saturday, February 16

The Watched

This morning I found myself avoiding looking down while dressing, and staying turned away from the mirror. Then I made myself look, because what did I have left to hide? I'd spent the night wondering if second level monitoring logs were ever deleted, or if there'd be a permanent record of me farting in the bath and laughing at the bubbles. Inspecting my armpits. Every single thing I do in the bathroom.

I don't think I'll ever dare masturbate again.

It didn't occur to me to look up the laws concerning second level monitoring until breakfast. I'm too used to being kept in a box with no view of the outside. Second level monitoring is almost like parole here, far more common than I expected. There's layers and layers of rules and controls about when the logs can be uplifted, but it's an accepted part of the Taren justice system. There's even a third level monitoring, where you're basically live-streaming your life. Some people here actually do that for the kicks.

The encyclopaedia entry I found handily told me the history of the laws which had led to second level monitoring, and I guess it's a logical progression from things like the CCTV and GPS bracelets, and I can understand why they'd put a lab rat like me on it, but NOT HAPPY, JAN.

Until I can figure out how to safely get home, I'll just have to put up with it, but I did need to degrump myself before leaving to meet Mara. The Setari are assigned rotations every second day, so I'll be going into the Ena again tomorrow, and I'm scheduled in for three more rotations with First Squad after that.   Between   I   have   training   and   medical appointments. In a few days I also have a session scheduled with Eighth Squad and later Third Squad, to review my effect on their talent list. Then a day with nothing scheduled, but I'm not sure if it counts as a day off or they just haven't put anything there yet.

This morning I had swimming with Mara, and Zee and Ketzaren came along as well. They're all so incredibly fit. I can just about beat them if I swim freestyle while they breaststroke, but even though they've only been swimming a couple of years they outpace me easily if we're doing the same stroke. Mara's such a taskmaster – after we played around for a while she made me do laps while she monitored my heartbeat. And then she scheduled in some running for me as well, for afternoons, though she says I don't have to wait for any of them to join me for that. Running is *not* my idea of fun, though I think maybe I could do my schoolwork at the same time as running, which is useful, or watch television or whatever.

I'm doing quite well with this year's schoolwork, though I'm not pushing through it nearly as hard as I did the previous year's. And I'm starting to find my way around all the vast array of the parts of the interface which I now have access to. I watch news programs, and am constantly surprised by stories of violence. I kept imagining this place as relatively crime-free, especially thanks to second level monitoring, but bad things still happen here. And there's sports reporting, and gossip and politics and business, all of which is this mass of confusion to me because they don't explain who the people are and I have to look them up to work out what's going on. I usually don't bother, just let all the sounds wash over me while I look at the images.

With the entertainment options and discussion boards and games there's so much out there that I've been too overwhelmed to do more than browse. I read the beginnings of books, watch the beginnings of shows, follow links, but keep moving on.   Schoolwork comes as a relief after that because it's so structured.   I started watching that Setari/Songstar show that Nenna liked so much, but it's really silly and young.   I found a different one called *The Hidden War* which is also about the Setari, but much more serious and with no singing so far.   There are years and years of it, though, and while I found out how to watch it from the beginning, I've only skipped through a couple of episodes.   It starts out with this girl called Nori being in the not-yet-qualified-as-a-Setari part of KOTIS, and I'll probably go back to it when I'm in a better mood.

The planet is seriously obsessed with the Setari.   It's not surprising.   Earth would be the same, but give them less privacy.   [I can't believe I just wrote that.]   As it is, I've found these huge discussion boards which are all about people talking about sightings of Setari.   They can't take photographs of them, and their name display shows random names, but every sighting of them is tracked, and people draw pictures using art programs.   It's very rare for Setari to be seen anywhere except Konna, and rarer still for them to go out in uniform.   Hordes of people want to live on Konna, just because of the Setari.   I already felt, the couple of times I've been into the city, the sense of lots of people watching, and the extra-smile factor of shop assistants, but it's apparently against some kind of rule to run up and ask the Setari for autographs, which is fortunate or they probably wouldn't be able to go out at all.

There were descriptions of our Kanza game on those forums.   There were great big dossiers on First Squad.   They don't know what they're called or anything, but they've given them all code names and link the sightings together, and now there's a dossier started on me.   They think I'm a Kalrani or newly graduated Setari, or possibly just a relative of someone in First Squad.   I spent lunch reading through a bunch of posts of people giving really frank opinions of what I looked like (6/10) and how I acted.   6!   I think I'm a 7, really, but I guess I was standing next to Zee a lot of the time.

It amazes me that any of the Setari ever poke their noses out of KOTIS.

Sunday, February 17

Lights Rotation

Today's rotation was called Lights Rotation.

The first space was up on a mountain, all grass and tumbled rocks and flowers on a slope so high there was cloud below. We're settling into a routine for being a squad-with-useful-stray. Before going through each gate, Mara and Maze, who both have Combat Sight and Speed talent, touch my arm to enhance themselves, then take lead. They go through as close together as they can, and just like when I was with Ruuel, the rest of us only come through when they signal.

This time, as soon as Maze was through, he dived abruptly left – so fast it was almost like he vanished – and something flashed after him. Mara followed in a rush, and just as quickly ran right, her Light whip striking out from one hand. None of the rest of First Squad enjoyed staying put, but they did, very tense and prepared. I was wondering how long they had to wait before going without a signal, but Mara came back almost straight away and Lohn and Zee went through followed by me and my Ketzaran/Alay escort. Lohn brushed a hand against my arm and was off.

The things they were fighting were like gargoyles. Or bats with wolfish faces, all grey-skinned. The sky above the mountainside was thick with them, and they dived like hawks, incredibly fast. Ketzaren's Wind manipulation abilities were really useful there. It's not the same kind of instant-hit that Lohn's Light wall is, but if she sets up enough movement in the air, it grows to cyclonic levels. It made it incredibly hard for the gargoyles to fly, and funnelled them together really handily.

That space was huge, too. It took almost an hour for First Squad to chase down all the gargoyles, and I noticed a few escaped through other gates, and that one of the things First Squad were trying to do was prevent that, although they wouldn't chase them through the gates. It was also by far the worst time I'd had with First Squad, because there's no way slaughtering a couple of hundred animals could be anything but awful. The Ionoth might just be memories, but they still don't want to be killed. Being Setari is a really horrible job.

It was only when the very last of them was gone that First Squad said anything more than "There," or "To the left". Maze called for a break, and we all sat down on some rocks and had a drink and some of the molasses-tasting food bars. Using their powers takes an awful lot out of the Setari, especially over such a long period of time, and they were sweating and looking drained. In a way it annoys me that it doesn't take me any effort to enhance them. I'd feel less like a useless spectator if it at least made me tired.

"That was more than twice as many as the last time we did this space," Zee said, after drinking thirstily.

Maze nodded. "I'll recommend reclassification of the rotation."

"Don't understand how ecology work here," I said. "Do Ionoth need eat? Or just attack people out habit?"

"It varies," Lohn said. "In some spaces the Ionoth don't have any apparent food source, and we've never verified if they *have* to eat, but they often turn on each other or start to roam, preying on whatever they can find until separation from their home space causes them to fade. There are others, roamers and static, which are not aggressive and don't have any interest in us at all. If we do Boulders Rotation, you'll see the Tenders. They 'notice' but never attack us, so we leave them be, as we do anything not classified as a threat."

"It's a big job keeping up with all the known types," Alay said. "But a lot easier dealing with types already encountered than new varieties."

Maze called the end of the break then – they don't like to hang around in the spaces unnecessarily – and we went into the next space, which was a single short corridor with a couple of gates in it. All the doors were outlines, showing only blackness. and First Squad were really tense as they passed through it. They said that they'd occasionally encountered very unusual Ionoth in there, but there was nothing this time.

Next was the reason it was called Lights Rotation. It was a night time space with lots of huge overarching trees by a lake, and there were floating balls of light everywhere, about the size of two fists together. It was the coldest space I've been in yet, and everyone's breath came out smoky. The lake was black and mirror-still and reflected the glowing balls. Maze had explained before we went through that there were usually only one or two creatures in this space, but that they were fast, and clever enough not to just jump out and be killed. That was a rather nerve-wracking space, because after enhancing themselves, Lohn, Mara, Zee and Maze all disappeared off into the dark and Alay and Ketzaren and I waited by the gate. I turned on the names in my interface again, but could only see where Maze and Zee had gone. And then, while I was craning to see the others, Alay leaned forward and the chilly silence was ripped apart by a high vibrating sound, followed by a shrieking yowl accompanying a black shape falling out of one of the trees. Alay has a sonic talent which seems to only be useful when she can take a few moments to build it and, importantly, none of her squad are anywhere near what she's trying to take down.

The last space was like a ghost town in a Western: old, falling apart, little more than the shells of buildings on a dusty plain. In the middle of the town were square wooden frames, and tied to the squares with barbed wire were the shapes of people. Black shadows with no features at all, like a person had had all their skin had burned away and then been covered in dusty ink. They looked like they were in pain, being tortured like the shadows on the pyramids. First Squad approached incredibly cautiously, scanning every building as we approached the frames, making sure nothing was lurking, and stopped at the edge of the central square with the frames.

"These are seen in a number of spaces," Alay said. "Most notably on the Columns Rotation. They are one of the most dangerous of the Ionoth, and frequently reach near-space and sometimes real-space."

One of the shadows reacted to the sound of her voice, eyes opening to slits. And then a mouth appeared on the darkness of the face, out of nothing like the Cheshire Cat's does in Alice of Wonderland, but stretching up into the nastiest grin you could imagine. It was all light inside, the shadows burning white within. And what I'd thought was pain was a kind of exultation.

Then Maze set the entire thing burning, all the frames and the shadows on them. He was still enhanced, and called down a pillar of flame in an absolute Wrath of God moment, shocking me. First Squad, except for Mara who continued scanning the area for anything coming, all stood and watched in silence. It was pretty clear they hated these things.

"Most monsters my world are people," I said, feeling inadequate. "These memories of people?"

"Not anything I'd class as a person," Alay said, very firm and sharp for someone usually so quiet. "Time to head back?"

Maze nodded, and we went back through the same set of spaces, with Ketzaren pausing at every gate and enhancing herself before locking them as much as possible. Even though we'd just been through them all, First Squad stayed alert and ready for attack right up until we stepped back into real-space.

This time, an alert flashed in our mission display when we were being scanned. "You've got a stickie, Zee," Maze said, and she groaned and walked away from us to a corner of the box.

"Stickie is?" I asked.

"A very weak variety of Ionoth, but with an ability to conceal itself even from Sight talents. They're parasites, feeding off human hosts. When they're stronger, they can copy themselves to new hosts through physical contact, and–"

"Are a plaguish nuisance," Zee put in, arms crossed.

"If they're left too long, they begin to corrupt their hosts," Lohn added, grinning.

"They're removed using sonics," Maze continued, as if they hadn't interrupted, then gave Zee a sympathetic smile. "Also known as an Instant Headache Treatment. Hopefully the rest of us won't finish the day so uncomfortably."

We split up then. After missions, showers and rest are very high on First Squad's list of things to do, and I guess Maze gets to file a mission report. The rotations seem designed to last only a couple of hours, and there's never training or anything like that afterwards because it takes so much out of them. I showered, ever-amused by my nanoliquid uniform, and then grabbed some 'portable food' from the canteen and went up to the roof.

It's still night, but it was very clear and not too windy and it was nice to sit and watch the stars. I wasn't really surprised when Lohn and Mara showed up. They take babysitting as seriously as they do killing Ionoth.

"What's the attraction?" Lohn asked, sprawling down next to me. "Black, black, black and some stars?"

"The wind," I said, after thinking about it. "And there insects here – they sound crickets – insects from home. And temperature changes. And different smells."

"Not many would consider these things positive," Lohn said. "Besides, we had all that in Lights Rotation, didn't we? Except perhaps this chirping."

"Too busy being nervous enjoy."

"You hide it well," Mara said. "Maze wanted us to check how you're holding up to all this."

I like Mara for being very open about Stray mental health checks. She's a really straightforward person.

"Is awful," I said. "Killing things. Spaces very interesting, Ionoth horrible. Obvious." I shrugged. "But not overwhelm. First Squad not scared. Save panic for when First Squad is."

This made Lohn laugh. "Worse philosophies, I suppose."

"One night Muina, most scared ever," I said. "Been walk eleven days, sick eat bad fruit. Sleep on hill under mat made leaves. Something big walk up to me. Foot came down mat, right next head. Sniff me. Lay there listen to it. Then it go away. Lots panic. Watch very deadly Setari toast bugs easier."

They both shut up at that one, then Lohn slung an arm around my shoulders and squeezed tight. "You've a way of putting things in perspective. But you'll let us know if there's anything troubling you?"

"Sure." Since I'd succeeded in putting second level monitoring into perspective for myself as well, I thought about other things I could ask them, then said: "What Eighth Squad like?"

"Ah, you're due to do enhancement testing with them tomorrow, right? Well, Kanato's solid, very level-headed.

Eighth is one of the 'big punch' squads, so we can expect some exciting damage to the test areas, I'd bet."

"Have decided long-term what do with me?"

"Too early. There's a lot of debate, and some competing interests. They won't have you actively working with the younger squads for quite a while, since having a talent set so increased and then reverting it might have a negative impact on them. In theory we're too old and wise to have our heads turned as badly." He laughed. "I gather Seventh Squad is not very happy with Eighth for being selected to test with you."

I drew my knees up to my chin. "Cloning legal Tare?" I asked carefully, and felt the depth of their silence.

"Cloning will not reproduce a talent set," Mara said eventually. "Kolar tried it not long ago, and although there's some pattern similarity, it seems that there's more to talents than simple genetics. Since they haven't found a way to make clones with an adequate lifespan, there's a ban on human cloning here."

But there'd obviously been 'a lot of debate' about quite a few things.

"Be really good way make me want be anywhere but here," I said softly. "That good thing to add today's report." And then, because I hated making First Squad feel bad, I added: "Six billion people my planet. Bet Cass not only one enhance skill. Hope they look harder for natural gate, get chance show First Squad my home."

Mara put a hand on my shoulder. "We'll do that. Besides, the real solution's the Pillars, not increasing our ability to kill Ionoth. You can be sure we'll be throwing all our resources into taking advantage of the stroke of luck your visit home brought."

It isn't necessarily an endless war. It's good to remember that.

Monday, February 18

Eighth Squad

It's a weird feeling to have a group of strangers all eager for me to show up. Or really eager to try out what their powers are like enhanced, anyway.

Eighth Squad is one of the Setari teams 'stacked' with high impact talents instead of being more all-round. They're not usually used for spaces that require close fighting: there's apparently some spaces where you don't want to go in and make things explode because parts of the spaces explode right back. Memories of oil refineries, perhaps. And there's some Ionoth that you have to kill by hitting them because it's a bad idea using psionics on them.

Eighth's captain is Ro Kanato. He tracked me down about half an hour before I was due to meet them, to introduce himself, show me the way to a new test room, and double-check my preferences for people grabbing hold of me. He kept making references to the rules which had been set up regarding my 'handling'. I'd love to be able to read these rules, and the reports and things filed about me, but though I've access to the public parts of the interface, there's an awfully large amount of the KOTIS network which I can't look at. I'd like to be able to look up more information about the rotations I'm assigned to before going into them. Although maybe that would be a bad idea and give me nightmares. Hard to tell.

Kanato is about my height, with long black hair which he catches up in a ponytail, and he comes across as unfussed with a mild-mannered efficiency that turns mountains into molehills. I kept wondering where I'd heard his voice until I recognised it as the person who'd first spoken to Ruuel from Fourth when we returned from my 'excursion', just sounding considerably less surprised. He's not quite as correct as Zan, but all sensible and by-the-book, which kept me feeling less embarrassed than I might otherwise have been.

Test Room 2 is built for testing the high impact talents, divided into two by a massive amount of shielding, with the larger side full of angled walls of metal – targets – and the rest of Eighth Squad waiting on the 'safe' side of the shielding.

Two girls and another three guys, all polite and professional, with an edge of underlying excitement. Kanato introduced them in the order they were standing: "Henaz, Kade, Trouban, Bryze, Hasen. We'll do a complete run of each skill set per person, starting with Hasen. Remember your instructions regarding contact. Anyone who fails to keep to the restrictions will spend the rest of the day on a training run."

Hasen was a tiny, bird-like girl with soft black hair cut really close to her skull, gorgeous dark brown eyes and darker skin than most Tarens. She stood before a hatchway which was the only opening to the other part of the test chamber and did the whole 'current strength' base level test first. Her primary talent is Electricity, and she shot a fat bolt of it at a target a third of the way down the long length of the test chamber. It wasn't like Lohn's Light bolts, which are short bullets, but a literal lightning bolt, stretching all the way to the target. It left her breathing deeply, and there was a sharp ozone scent in the air and if it wasn't for my uniform I think the hair on my arms would have been standing on end. The target made a thooming noise, and I watched through the thick, distorting viewport as some residual lightning played around the metal wall. There was an afterimage of it across my eyes.

"Now enhanced," Kanato said, after it had died down, and Hasen brushed the back of my wrist with her fingers. First Squad had decided it's better for the Setari to handle the contact involved in the enhancement because there's less communication lag, and they have far better reaction times than me. I was relieved that Eighth Squad had realised that they didn't need more than a slight touch to be enhanced.

I think she was aiming for the same target. It was a little hard to tell since instead of a bolt shooting from her hand this huge round ball of white appeared about a quarter of the way into the room, arcing and spitting and drifting slowly away from us. The noise and smell of it was incredible, and I turned away and covered my ears, but could still feel the vibration of each strike. It didn't last too long, fortunately, and died away to this stunned silence.

Kanato wasn't quite managing to hide that he was having exactly the same "Whoa" reaction which Jules would have to something particularly cool and unexpected, which all of them were having, I guess. But after blinking a couple of times, he said: "We'll target to the far end of the room in future, I think. Either of you experiencing any side-effects?"

I shrugged, and Hasen slowly shook her head. She looked so small and slight to have done so much.

"Re-test that at the far end of the room, then, so we can see if the result is the same."

It was. I did my usual weird things to Eighth Squad's talents, but again the distortion remained consistent whenever it showed up. Fortunately most only had three or four talents each, but I was still feeling hungry and tired by the time Kanato called it a day and sent me off to the medical exam they make me go to after test sessions. The medics couldn't decide whether I was feeling the impact of the enhancements or was just normally hungry and tired. Eighth Squad all looked exhausted after blasting all-out like that, so comparatively it's still a negligible impact on me. I did snooze for a lot of the afternoon though, and slept through when I was supposed to go jogging (too bad, so sad).

Even though Eighth is closer to my age, I'd rather stay with First Squad, given the choice. I know that Eighth Squad was being all business and distracted by excitement and whatever, but Kanato was the only one who said a word to me the entire time. They weren't being deliberately rude or anything: I think maybe they're not sure how I fit into this very structured world they've been raised to accept. Like they haven't been given permission to be social.

I didn't mind them, though. It was funny watching them being so excited and trying not to show it.

Tuesday, February 19

Maze Rotation

'Tsennel Rotation' actually, but tsennel means labyrinth/maze. I've found a proper dictionary, to supplement my vague injected one, and have taken to looking up words and trying to fix the real definition and making annotations to connect to English.

Breakfast was with Maze, Zee, Mara and Lohn, to talk about the day's assignment. Lohn, of course, thought it very funny when I said that in English 'maze' could be labyrinth or 'corn' if you just go by the way it's pronounced, though it was a bit hard to describe what corn was beyond it being a yellow vegetable. Or grain? The Taren alphabet is really strange with its 's', so I'm not entirely sure whether Maze or Mase is correct. They have an 's', but use it mostly at the beginning of words, and then they use this 'ts' letter a lot of the time, and there's an awful lot of 'z' when I would expect 's', like how they pronounce my name 'Caszandra'.

Anyway, Maze Rotation is what they consider a fairly tough assignment, partly because of its size and the need for close combat, and also because they've encountered new types of Ionoth there from time to time. Lohn was saying that the spaces we've worked in this week have been reasonably straightforward, and that now they were going to try me out in the 'weird and confusing' territories. The way he talked about it made me wonder if the spaces weren't so much the memories as the nightmares of planets.

"What toughest rotation?" I asked, as we walked to our assigned gate-lock.

"Unstables," Zee said. "Spaces which have moved up against Tare's near-space, but which we haven't encountered before. For everything else, even Columns, we know what we're going up against, and they choose which teams to assign based on that. If we sent Eighth into Maze Rotation, for instance, they'd kill themselves in the first few minutes. While Ninth couldn't handle Lights Rotation because you need strong ranged abilities for that mountainside. We can manage either, but at the same time neither is as easy as it would for a team with exactly the right talent set. It's been a big step forward, having specialist teams."

"How long, younger teams active?"

"About seven years, for Three to Six. Eleven and Twelve, coming up on one year. Thirteen and Fourteen will be made active in the next year. The aim is to have sufficient squads to keep the near-space clear, and increase exploration and searches for the Pillars."

It took me a minute to remember that a 'year' here was only four months. "How many Pillars are there?"

Zee lifted her hands, then let them drop. "We only confirmed three years ago that they truly exist. And, presuming that rotational space does realign, we're only just coming up to our first chance to properly examine one. The knowledge of how the things were constructed, and what exactly they're doing, has long been lost."

"Exciting days ahead," Lohn put in cheerfully, and then we reached our gate-lock and it was time for the mission to be officially logged and to call each other by surname and be all serious.

There were only two spaces involved in the Maze Rotation. The first seemed to be the inside of a house, all cramped walls and sketches of furniture and a shadow by a corner which might have once been an old lady. And then there was the maze.

It was exactly that: a huge maze of white stone covered in a climbing plant with small almond-shaped leaves. The walls looked to me to be really similar to the stone which the Taren and Muinan buildings are made of, so I guess it was a memory of one of those worlds, or another where the Muinans had gone. The walls were really high – twenty feet at least – and right above it the sky looked scratched and rubbed out. But there were clover flowers in the grassy paths below and it had an austere English garden feeling which made me like it despite it being dangerous.

"The walls have a resistance to talents," Maze said through the interface, once we were all through the gate. "Reflecting or dampening them unpredictably. We will be close-fighting almost exclusively in here, and keeping very near to each other. Avoid touching the walls; we've found that seems to draw increased attention from any Ionoth in the space. Follow Spel's lead, staying on her left, and communicate only through the interface."

I nodded, and he started off, getting even more focused. First Squad is always serious while in the spaces, but I could tell by how tightly concentrated they all were that they'd meant it about it being tough. Everyone except Mara made long blades out of their suits, the first time I'd seen anyone except Ruuel use that. I still hadn't figured out how to make any bits of the suit be more than tough rubber.

Staying on Ketzaren's left put me in the centre of the six of them, and I noticed that Lohn, on my left, had his blade on his left arm instead of his right. I was only just within arms-length of any of them, so that they could reach to keep up their enhancements without risking accidentally bumping me.

"Coming up, mark seven, twenty in," came Maze's voice over the interface. "Three rush."

Three rush apparently meant Maze, Mara and Zee would suddenly leap forward, while Lohn, Alay and Ketzaren closed about me and followed at a slower pace. We reached the corner just as something I couldn't properly see leapt off one of the walls at Maze. Maze, Mara and Zee all have the Speed talent, and unenhanced they move amazingly. With enhancement, they come close to blurring instantaneously from one place to another. Plus both Maze and Mara have Combat Sight, which so far as I can tell is an ability to detect attacks almost before they happen. The thing didn't really have a chance, in other words.

I only saw it properly when it was dead, and stopped being so difficult to look at. A lizard, like a gecko except with some uncomfortably humanoid lines to its scaly white body. And too much claw. Chameleons with attitude.

Even before it was still, Maze added: "Two coming fast from mark two," and they shifted about me to cover an opening on the opposite side.

It went on like that for way too long. The maze space is huge, and we weren't just walking through it to a certain point, we were systematically searching out all of the chameleons and killing them.

The bright spot of the space was in the centre, the heart of the maze. It was an open, circular garden, with lots of grass between us and the walls, and beds of purple and red flowers which looked like cosmos. We'd been going about two hours by that time, and had cleared most of the chameleons. Maze ordered a break, though still to stick to using only our interfaces, and we sat down in the very centre, resting but on guard, Zee and Maze watching in opposite directions. Everyone was looking worn, and ate silently, so I decided not to bug them with questions and chewed on my entirely unappetising molasses bar. And then there was this cat.

Half-grown kitten, really, long-legged but not properly grown up. It was one of the slinky, big-eared type I'd seen on Muina, smoky grey with unexpectedly dark moss-green eyes. It was just there, sitting in front of me, drifting into visibility in an eye-blink. And, yeah, I was stupid, but my automatic reaction to cats, even ones which pop up out of nothing, is to hold out a hand, fingers unthreateningly down, and see if it runs away.

It acted just like a cat should, delicately sniffing, touching a cold nose to one knuckle, then rubbing its face against my hand. I had scratched it behind one ear and under its chin and felt the slightest buzz of a purr before it even occurred to me that maybe I shouldn't, and carefully took my hand back.

"Can I pick it up?" I asked over the interface.

First Squad's reaction would probably have been comical if, well, if the Ena hadn't been a life or death thing for them for so many years. Ketzaren was closest to me, sitting at a right-angle, and turned her head only to leap up as if scalded. And then they were all on their feet, the nanoliquid blades appearing, along with Mara's Light-whip, and the cat very sensibly leaped away and vanished, leaving me sitting there staring up at them.

I remembered, at least, to keep talking over the interface. "Kittens are evil?"

None of them answered immediately, but Mara touched her hand to my shoulder and stared about, searching. "Nothing," she said.

"Checking the log," Maze said. When we're on mission, as well as second level monitoring I'm on mission log, which he can access as team captain, so he meant he was looking at my recording of the cat. And then he looked at me a moment before scanning the area again. "Gone now, at any rate. Or completely undetectable." He looked back at me, and though his voice wasn't angry his mouth was a flat line as he said: "If anything approaches us, no matter what it looks like, warn us immediately. We can't judge by appearances here."

I felt a prize twit, of course, and could only nod and try really hard not to screw up any more on the mission. Which took another hour of tense maze-trekking and by the time we finally got back to KOTIS everyone looked like they had stress headaches.

"Another increase in population," Mara said, after the scan had cleared us of stickies. "I'm starting to reconsider the proposals to double-team."

"Dealing with swoops on top of that?" Lohn pulled a face. "I'll pass."

"The trade-off is too great," Maze agreed, sounding terribly tired. He gave me a worn smile. "You made a big difference to that space's difficulty. If it wasn't for the population increase, we would have easily set a record completion pace."

"And you claim to disapprove of the pace records," Lohn said, heading to the showers.

"Lunch with me?" Zee said as we followed him, and I knew I was in for a talk well before we were sitting in a quiet corner of the canteen.

"Are kittens evil?" I asked, as soon as I'd swallowed enough of some yellowy mashed stuff (which tasted a lot better than it looked) to no longer feel painfully hungry.

"I've not read any reports featuring them," she said. "But there are Ionoth which can disguise their shape, and Ionoth with appearances entirely innocuous and intentions which are not. The problem with that one was that we did not detect it. There's very few things that can get anywhere near as close as that to someone with Combat Sight without notice, threat or not." She reached over and rapped the back of my knuckles with her spoon. "And petting the thing was entirely idiotic." But she smiled at me, and shook her head to take the sting out of the words. "He was angry at himself, not you. Just be sure to be more sensible in future."

I nodded, still cringing internally. There was no way I was going to upset everyone like that again if I could help it. I watched her eat, not missing the shadows under her eyes, and finally managed to ask: "What happen third senior Setari squad?"

"A kadara." She said the word so softly I could barely hear her. "One which broke into real-space three years ago. We lost nine, most from the senior squads. They renumbered us all afterwards. The original First Squad captain, Helese, was Maze's wife. He's been very hard on himself ever since."

"Very sad guy," I said, and could only promise myself to not be entirely idiotic in future.

Wednesday, February 20

Third Squad

Third was a difficult squad to test with. Not because of any attitude, but because they had such a range of talents, which required three test environments to get through. I'd been a little nervous about working with their squad captain, Taarel – the spectacular one with the unlikely hair – just because I'd taken the impression she was really intense about Maze. But she was totally professional, so either it was my imagination or she's not a petty sort.

But before Taarel there was Eeli. After breakfast I'd gone up to the roof because I'd figured it was around time for dawn, and on Tare dawn lasts a really long time and is well worth watching. I was sitting through a lesson on Taren geography, keeping an eye on the horizon, when a girl a year or maybe even two years younger than me arrived. Eeli Bata, according to the interface, looking like a string bean in her Setari uniform.

"Sorry to interrupt you," she started out, her voice high and enthusiastic. "I thought I'd introduce myself since we're working with you today. I'm Eeli. I'm the path finder in Third Squad. I've really been looking forward to this. We all want to see how far you can take us."

This was definitely a different sort of Setari. "Hello."

"I can show you the way to the test room, when you're ready," she continued. "Why are you up here on the roof? Are you not used to being inside buildings? Is this much like your world?"

Eeli is what Nenna would be if Nenna had uber psychic powers. She'd sometimes stop asking questions in the hopes I would remember them all to answer them, but then new questions would bubble up and she'd be off again. I wanted to see if she would act like that once the training session started, and was pleased that, though she shut right up and did exactly what she should, she kept looking really excited the entire time.

We started in Test Room One to go through the combat talents. In terms of sheer fire power Third Squad is nothing compared to Eighth, but they're not shabby either. We moved on to testing sights next. There's six sorts of sights: Combat, Path, Gate, Symbol, Place and 'Sight Sight', which is two different words, but both mean sight. Third Squad has all but 'Sight Sight', which is really rare and is apparently something to do with divining the 'nature of things'. According to Eeli, the bluesuit who came down in person to look at me, Selkie, has Sight Sight and so does Ruuel. Eeli is a great source of information. I don't even have to ask her questions.

I could tell Taarel's squad really adores their captain, the way First Squad respects Maze, but with an extra level of worship. She's definitely one of those people like HM, a tiny sun, though she leaves HM in the shade. She has the strongest Ena manipulation talent, and when we went into the Ena to test my enhancement on her talents, she was able to partially close one of the gates. She has a calm reserve, but I can really picture her giving a Battle of Agincourt type of speech, inspiring everyone around her to follow and admire and commit great acts of nobility.

Reading back that last paragraph, it sounds like I have the hots for Taarel. Funny. I guess she impressed me. This whole entry is really confused and out of order and I think that's because of Eeli's gossip and because Taarel really reminds me of Ruuel. I haven't had any reason to write about him, but I've developed a tendency to look closely at any squad I happen to see, hoping it might be Fourth. I think about him a lot more than I've written about.

And it occurred to me, while I was watching Taarel and being impressed and seeing Ruuel in the shape of her eyes, that I might be on second level monitoring for the rest of my life. No wonder none of the Setari want to have informal conversations with me.

Thursday, February 21

Let's try that again – Third Squad

Yesterday's entry reads as amazingly garbled. The shorter and less confused version is that Eeli collected me and we went to Test Room One. We tested combat skills and Combat Sight and then went to a smaller room where we tested Symbol and Place Sight. Then we went into the Ena and tested Path Sight, Gate Sight, and Ena manipulation. The fact that, enhanced, Taarel was able to partially close a small gate was a fairly major thing apparently. There's a few gates in very inconvenient spots and, though it sounds like it would take a lot of sessions to do it, I had a strong impression that I'll be assigned to Third Squad at some point in the future to go and close one or two that they really don't want open.

Path Sight is a tracking ability: not seeing footprints, but knowing the direction of something. Gate Sight allows you to tell how long a gate will remain open. Place Sight is a very vague and all-encompassing sight that lets you see invisible things including things like auras, "the remnants of touch", whatever that means, or the way things used to look. Sometimes Place Sight will even show stickies. It's considered a difficult Sight to cope with: painful, with bonus nightmares. Symbol Sight is a "specific interpretative" ability that reminds me of my injected language: see a word, and have an impression of meaning, while 'Sight Sight' is a vaguer but more profound comprehension. They're all called 'Sight', but it's really more 'awareness'. Combat Sight, for instance, means you're aware of creatures around you, even if they're behind walls, and gives you a strong advantage when trying to anticipate movement and attack. Both Third and Fourth Squad are Sight based exploration squads with duties focused around establishing new paths through the spaces to 'hot spots' where Ionoth are infesting Tare's near-space and real-space. But also trying to find and investigate the Ddura and the Pillars, and even to do investigative work for real-space crimes (psychic detectives!).

I suppose I must have some form of Path Sight, to have found my way to Earth's near-space, although Eeli made it very clear that what I did was way outside their idea of the talent. Back when I first returned, and was in medical again, their attempts to test me for Path Sight were a complete failure, and I think they're a little wary of pushing me too hard to do it in case I have another 'excursion'.

There's been no suggestion whatsoever that I try and train or focus my ability to jaunt off to Earth, no matter what Maze said about finding Pillars.

Castle Rotation

Today was my last scheduled rotation with First Squad, though I think that may be because they haven't decided yet how to allocate me next week. Tomorrow I have nothing scheduled and to my delight Ketzaren said she was going into the city and asked if I want to tag along. Then I have a training day and a few more squads to be tested with (Fifth, Seventh, Tenth), but no more Ena rotations listed, just blank days every second day where they're probably going to put missions once they've decided what they will be.

I feel strange about being a resource which is shared between dozens of people. There's some teams I'm not looking forward to working with, but now that I'm not being kept in a box it sometimes feels like a positive way to live. I'm making their job a little easier, even if all I actively do is follow them about. I managed not to make an idiot out of myself this rotation, too, and First Squad were looking quite cheerful at the end of the day.

Lohn says that Castle is his favourite rotation. It was definitely different from the ones we've already done, and for the most part made me feel more than ever that I've strayed into some kind of computer game. It had NPCs! Maze explained beforehand that there would be two types of Ionoth in the Castle space, and that one we would be attacking while the other we would avoid. This would require me to move quickly whenever Ketzaren told me to, and there would probably be occasional levitating to different spots so I needed to be ready for that.

They didn't warn me about the stairs though.

Castle Rotation is literally that – a castle. On a cliff-like rock. And we started at the bottom and worked our way to the top, chasing a mass of invading shadow people and cutting them down wherever possible. There were defending shadow people fighting against the invading shadow people and I see why Lohn likes it because it's like you're helping them. They even react sometimes as if they're surprised to see the Setari and one looked like it was thanking Zee.

But, gods, we went up a lot of steps.

I think Ketzaren did a lot of extra unnecessary levitating, for which I will be eternally grateful. I really don't know if I can get as fit as everyone else, and talked to Mara about it afterwards, especially about the way I keep falling asleep after the testing sessions instead of doing the jogging I was supposed to. She pointed out that I'd been hospitalised twice the previous month, and that walking up all these stairs probably counted for more than the jogging anyway. The interface lets them monitor my heartbeat all the time, and they're really more interested in keeping me alive than trying to make me into a watered-down version of a Setari.

Not that this let me out of dodging practice the day after tomorrow. Mara says she's planning to make sure I at least have a chance to survive if a bunch of children try and beat me up. I gather she thinks I'm pretty hopeless so far.

Saturday, February 22

Can I keep it?

I'd made a list of things to look for during my trip to the city, like throw rugs for the lounges, and some snacks to keep in my apartment. Although I'd realised I could purchase most things through my interface and have them delivered, it was more the idea of going out and looking around which had me excited. Besides, I wanted a haircut, and Ketzaren hadn't seemed at all bothered about the time involved in taking me to a hairdressers, even though it meant she would have to sit around waiting for me. She has long, shiny black hair which is super-straight and neat and makes my current collection of split ends look even worse by comparison.

It was also nice to have a reason to wear something other than my uniform, and to see Ketzaren in a pretty dress. I often wonder if First Squad does much socialising outside of KOTIS. Do people not in the military seem annoying or refreshing? How do they get the chance to meet them? Are there rules about whether you can date someone in your own squad? I guess it must be okay to get married, since Maze was.

I was toying with the idea of seeing how many of these mysteries I could unravel while spending a day just with Ketzaren, but when we met up she was with Jeh from Second Squad, so I shelved the idea for the moment. Jeh is so comfortable and relaxed that I didn't mind her coming too, though having to be escorted about does mean that shopping is always going to feel like wasting someone else's time to me. We were just at the big doors which mark one of the exits out of KOTIS, and are one of the few places which are actively guarded by greensuits, when an alarm (bip-bip-bip) sounded. Actual noise, not just in the interface, which is really rare here. The emergency space of the interface abruptly filled with 'Lockdown' and 'Incursion 1' messages. And the doors to 'outside' began to close.

I'd really love to know what would have happened if I'd been up on the roof when the lockdown started, but I'm hoping no-one else thinks of that because then they'd probably tell me not to go out there all the time. As it was, Ketzaren and Jeh both froze and looked really surprised for a second, then went very alert.

"In here," Ketzaren said, pointing to a waiting room area just to one side of the entrance. She and Jeh had flanked me, looking all dangerous and prepared despite the nice dresses. Jeh touched me on the shoulder as we moved, and said: "Nothing in my range," when we stopped in the centre of the room. They stayed on either side of me, scanning for movement.

"Is Ionoth in KOTIS?"

"Not confirmed yet," Jeh said, but then the message change to 'Incursion 2'. "Confirmed now."

Then there was an exceedingly tedious period where Ketzaren and Jeh stood guarding me and obviously talking to people over the interface. I didn't like to ask any more questions when they were tensed for attack, and after a while I gave up and started playing around with interface settings. I still hadn't decided on the decoration for my rooms, and had found a vast array of images I could purchase to use, and yet couldn't settle on any of them.

Ketzaren made a sound, so I stopped playing with the interface and looked at her only to find her looking back at me with a strange expression.

"They found the incursion," she said. "That Ionoth cat from the Maze Rotation must have followed—"

She broke off. I guess I must have done some sort of major colour change. I certainly felt sick right through: lightning nausea. "It hurt someone?"

"No." She gave me a quizzical frown. "Don't jump to conclusions. Here, have a chair." She steered me into the nearest and shook her head at me.

"Probably simplest to show her rather than explain," Jeh said. "I'll route it."

Perhaps the oddest thing ever about living on Tare is that when you watch what people have recorded with their own eyes and ears, you not only have it filtered by factors like bad hearing or red-green colour blindness, but you also see it through the frame of their face. Just as how you can see the edges of your nose but usually tune it out. Whoever had made the recording Jeh sent me blinked a lot, had a long fringe, and wore a stud in their nose.

The recording started out with the Ionoth cat, sitting on top of a high cabinet in a huge and busy industrial kitchen, staring down at something below it. It was all coiled and intent, tail twitching, and the person who was recording called out to the other people in the kitchen, drawing attention to it. The cat didn't seem to care, staring down at this guy standing just beneath it. Some girl made a joke and the guy looked up and looked confused, and stepped away. The cat's tail twitched even faster and then it leapt at him, making a lot of people shout and shriek, and it would have landed right on his chest, except it went right through him. And he gasped and shuddered and sat down in a heap and there was the cat on the floor on the other side of him, with something in its mouth that looked like a big silverfish with octopus tendencies. The cat shook the thing briskly, then held it down with a paw and bit it in a particularly final way, crunch. Then it picked the body up, jumped up to the nearby counter and on top of another cabinet, and vanished.

"Is stickie?" I asked, still feeling sick about the whole thing. The Ionoth cat had followed me home because I'd petted it. If it had attacked the cook instead of the bug-octopus, then it would have been my fault.

"A new type." Ketzaren sat down with a sigh, apparently deciding we weren't in immediate danger of attack. "One that's beyond the current scans, which is a huge problem. It's too much to hope that that's the only one. It's far more likely that there's a more developed originator, and that we're looking at a minor or even major plague of the things. And that could get extremely nasty. Stickies don't kill you quickly, but they're fatal left unchecked, even if the host doesn't have a psychotic break. And if we can't detect them, we can't even tell how far they've spread."

"What happen now?"

"We stay in lockdown. They'll start with the kitchens and try every kind of scan available to see if they can detect any Ionoth. If that fails, they'll randomly treat some unlucky volunteers with unpleasantly painful sonics and see if anything falls out. And if it does—" She wrinkled her nose. "More attempts to find some way to detect them. And if they don't, a very high chance they'll treat everyone in KOTIS with sonics, and issue a general health alert so civilians have the option of being treated, which most of them won't because it's unpleasant. And then people will start to sicken and die and the majority will get treated but a few won't and there'll be an endless cycle of infection and outbreak hotspots."

I stared at her. I think she meant it.

"Lohn was right," Jeh said, placidly

Ketzaren lifted her eyebrows and said: "Only rarely. What this time?"

"He said Caszandra is lucky. Which she is, to have survived Muina. To have been rescued. To have put Ruuel in the right place to find that Pillar. And now for meeting a cat which eats stickies." She smiled at me, but then added: "Not that you should ever go petting any other Ionoth which come walking up to you. That truly was—"

"Dumb." I sighed. I can tell I'm never going to live that down.

We stayed in the waiting room for three hours. Ketzaren and Jeh told me about the last major stickie outbreak, which happened nearly fifty Tare-years ago, and then a few stories about stupid things they'd done early in their training. Jeh had been really good at falling off things whenever she went into the Ena and Ketzaren had once walked through the gate next to the one everyone else went through.

When they finally figured out a way to scan for the new type of stickie, we had to report to be scanned and I was really glad to learn there was no octopus-silverfish living in my chest. But they've found something like five hundred infected people so far, and have extended the scans to the rest of the island and they'll be part of 'elevator security' on all of Tare in the future.

But they haven't found the cat yet. And I'm glad.

Saturday, February 23

Bring out the whips

Mara took my training seriously today. Dodging right after breakfast (ow), and then we went jogging slowly around a running track which had an obstacle course in the middle which a bunch of kids were scrambling their way through in a terrifically professional kind of way. Setari of the future.

The whole squad met up for lunch, and talked about the progress of the stickie cleansing. KOTIS have found what they think was the original infection point – a food supply place out in the city – and the number of cases has risen to thousands. KOTIS only had a secondary infection hub. I'd already seen some of this on the news, but the real numbers involved aren't publicly announced, and all of First Squad were looking relieved and worried both. From their point of view this is just another sign of the increasing strength of the Ionoth, in numbers or in ability, and no-one understands what's changed which has made the problem increase so much these past few years.

I feel more a part of the team rather than a guest now, settling in to that caddie-type role I was thinking of earlier.

But my assignment to First Squad isn't going to last, which sucks. I've got testing with Seventh Squad tomorrow. Their Captain was the one pretending to be nice to Zan at the pool, the one who called me 'it', so I'm not looking forward to having anything to do with them. I'm really not sure what I'll do working with squads who have people I'm not comfortable with or who make me feel bad. Especially if we go out on rotation in the Ena. What I said to Lohn and Mara is close to how I feel: going out there is scary, but I'm not panicked by it because I trust First Squad. I wonder if I'll ever be given any choice about who I work with?

After lunch, all First Squad did swimming training with me. Maze says we might do some of the flooded rotations, and so we swam in our full uniforms with the breathers, and had little races through the underwater obstacles. Underwater battles have whole new levels of complications: talents like Fire and Wind are useless. Telekinesis is still viable, but you handle it differently, since picking up a rock and throwing it has an entirely different effect underwater. Lohn and Mara's Light powers still work pretty much the same, and there is apparently a water manipulation talent, though no-one on First Squad has it. But most water environments are close-combat, except harder.

I was so tired afterwards. I keep having afternoon naps, and then waking up in the evening. Hopefully when I'm fitter I'll be able to handle all this better.

Sunday, February 24

Seventh Squad

I shouldn't have been surprised that the Seventh Squad captain, Atara Forel, was totally professional. Back when she was being nasty-sweet to Zan I'd already seen that she was the type whose attacks aren't open, and she definitely wasn't the sort to show herself in a bad light during an official testing session which was being recorded. So when I reached the testing room, all she did was nod at me and say: "Good, we can get started now. Same routine as Kanato's squad. We'll start with you, Mema."

Seventh is another of the big-hitter squads, and just like Eighth, were caught up in the sheer excitement of being enhanced to super-destructive levels. It's spectacular to watch the big-hitter tests, but at the same time kind of dull, so I spent my time studying them instead.

Forel is like a cat: lithe and slinky, with a pointed chin and big eyes. I can just picture her purring and digging in the claws. Her primary talent is Lightning, and she saved her testing for last. It was important to her, I think, that her overall result was higher than Hasen's from Eighth. When she's pleased her eyes go all slitted.

The other guy who was with her at the pool is Pol Tsennen, primarily an Ena manipulation talent, with a secondary in Fire. He seems mainly interested in watching Forel. Then there's the smug twins, Mema and Residen. I don't think they're really twins – they don't look precisely alike, and they have different surnames – but their hair is cut the same way and they seem to use the same mannerisms and they're very pleased with themselves and keep exchanging looks. They had a swag of talents, with a primary of Ice for Mema and a variation of Light manipulation for Residen.

Dahlen is their Sight talent, with both Gate and Path Sight, along with Telekinesis. She's tall and strong-looking and I don't know if it's just because of her height, but I kept thinking of her as a tree. Cats might sharpen their claws on trees, but they've got plenty of bark, and don't really care.

The last squad member, Saitel Raph, was the only one who caught me watching them. Him I couldn't make out at all, other than an impression that he's smart. He's also the only one who spoke to me outside Forel's strictly correct instructions, and then just to say "Thank you," before heading off.

Is it really the second level monitoring that makes the younger squads so disinclined to interact with me? Or do they think of me as human machinery, there to perform a task? With the notable exception of Eeli, the younger Setari never seem to consider the possibility of just chatting with me.

Or – just occurred to me – they're all competitive with each other, and there's an advantage in having me assigned to them. Maybe they're all determined not to be seen 'pursuing' me, so to speak. But...no. No-one's ever acted like any of my assignments will be my decision.

Speaking of which, when I woke up from my inevitable after-testing nap, I had another bunch of rotations assigned. All with First Squad, so I have something to be happy about.

Monday, February 25

Bridges Rotation

I spotted Zan again, having dinner when I went for breakfast, and wasn't slow to ask to join her. She had circles under her eyes, but almost sort of smiled at me as I sat down. I asked if she could recommend any novels to read, and tried to explain fantasy to her. I don't want to read stories about Setari — I was getting more than enough of them in real life and from television — but hadn't succeeded in finding any good stories which were based on mythology rather than reality, so to speak. We had a really interesting conversation about the origin of myths and the kind of stories people tell when they know what's "out there" compared to when they don't. I almost forgot to meet up with First Squad for the day's mission, and had to dash off, but she emailed me a list of books to try.

Bridges Rotation is only one space, although we had to walk through an awful lot of Tare's near-space to get to its gate. Near-space is usually fairly clear, because the Setari spend such a lot of effort killing off everything in the surrounding spaces, but we've a couple of times encountered things on the way to the gates and today there was this swarm of razor-tipped rabbits (O.o) which First Squad chased down and killed on the way.

The Bridges space itself was very strange. The bridges are all made of bone; the starkly curving ribs of giants. But the space is twisted, distorted, and perspective plays tricks with up and down and where things end and begin. A space designed by Escher, which I should have appreciated, but it made me dizzy, so I eventually had to concentrate just on the section of bridge in front of me.

There were three types of Ionoth there. Quite large ones, about the size of a car, that had attached themselves to the underneath of the bridges and were very similar in colour. I suppose the idea is that they wait until something walks above them and then they close these massive filigree claw-things over the top. An odd kind of Venus fly-trap. Combat Sight made these immensely easy. Maze or Zee would spot them well ahead, and then Maze just pried them loose with Telekinesis and held them up so Lohn could shoot them with unenhanced Light beams.

The rest of the time we chased about after long-legged, metallic storks with curving, sword-like beaks. They would run if they met us alone, collect in groups, and then try and rush us. The walls of light and columns of fire came in handy for them.

And there were two dog-things, rather like afghan hounds, but with possum-type claws to grip the bridges as they raced along. They trailed a pearly rainbow light, and looked strange and dangerous. Since they were a new type, First Squad paused to observe and document them, waiting to see how they would react when they sighted us.

They stopped, and sat down, heads angled toward each other as if they were talking. First Squad waited, and made no move to prevent them when the dogs loped off through one of the gates.

I was glad First Squad doesn't indiscriminately slaughter everything they encounter, but curious as well, and asked Zee about it over dinner. I've learned not to ask too many questions while in the spaces. First Squad will usually answer me, but I think they'd rather keep their attention on scanning for attacks.

"Fortunately, the Castle Rotation was one of the first spaces we encountered," Zee told me. "It's an obvious lesson: some of the Ionoth can act as our allies, if only by lowering the number of our opponents. Combat Sight allows us to judge intention to a degree, and those two today sparked no reaction. Wary, but no more. If they attack unprovoked, they'll be put on the kill on sight list, but not until then. In some of the spaces, if we tried to kill everything there, it would take us a week, and it only makes sense to focus on Ionoth which pose a tangible danger. Still, don't-"

"-pat cats," I finished resignedly. "Has been seen again?"

"Not yet. Hardly an ideal situation, having an Ionoth loose in KOTIS, no matter how useful. It *is* pushing us to develop newer and better scans. If you see it at all, contact one of us immediately."

I nodded, though I can't say I'd particularly want to help get it captured. Tomorrow is Fifth Squad testing, worse luck. Not looking forward to it.

Tuesday, February 26

Fifth Squad

Fifth Squad are fuckwits.

Their captain is that Kajal guy with the voice, who was making an ass of himself to Zan. I was lucky, I think, that I'd had that warning about what he was like: smugly pleased with himself and the type who is really interested in proving himself better than everyone else, even for small things. I don't know if his squad started out as unlikeable as he is, but he seems to have infected them pretty thoroughly. It's a five guy, one girl team, but I can't say that the girl, Elwes, is any nicer than the rest of them.

They're a generalist squad, so we met in Test Room One to start with. They were all standing in the middle in a circle, and didn't glance at me as I came up. Kajal's a big guy, maybe 6'4", and the rest of his team are pretty close to as tall. Even though I'd learned from Seventh Squad that I shouldn't have to worry about official on-the-record test sessions, I still felt a bit nervous. And then annoyed, because even though there wasn't a chance they didn't know I was there, Kajal left me standing at his elbow while he finished telling his squad something not particularly interesting-sounding about their next day's rotation.

"Right then," he said, at last. "Let's get started. Nise, you're first up."

They moved away, only one of the guys staying near me (he had great hair: spiky with dark blue tips). He waited till Kajal nodded at him, then grabbed my shoulder for a moment and began testing a Telekinesis talent. It went on like that for all of them. None of them spoke to me or nodded to me or anything like that. Every one of them gripped my shoulder in the exact same way – not roughly or hard or anything, but enough for me to feel it through the uniform's padding. All the other squads, since the first day with First Squad, have barely touched me, usually brushing the back of a hand against my arm. It couldn't be coincidence that every single one of Fifth Squad approached enhancement so differently, though it's really hard to imagine them sitting around deciding this would be a worthwhile exercise.

Then we went into the Ena to test Ena-specific talents. Since Kajal continued to address all his remarks generally, so they could be interpreted to include me, I followed along behind, wondering if what he was trying to do was get me to kick up a fuss or act upset or what. We always do Ena tests in the grassy space First Squad took me to, which is both easy to get to and seemingly permanently clear of Ionoth. There was nothing different about what Fifth Squad did for their testing there, except they walked in front of me on the way, striding along at a pace I didn't expect, so that I trailed them by a few feet.

That was a mistake, I think. Sure, there was pretty much no chance anything was going to attack me, but it looked like they were being lax and had forgotten they were supposed to be protecting me. I hope they get demerits. And when we were back in real-space, they just walked off without another word.

I took myself off to medical, and tried to figure out why Fifth had bothered. To intimidate or upset me, yeah, but why? What does it gain to make me feel uncomfortable? It did work. I spent most of the time feeling embarrassed and angry. They acted like my enhancement was something bad, a thing causing them inconvenience. Like they were barely tolerating that they had to work with me.

Perhaps they expect me to complain? For a lot of the time I felt like it, but I don't even see the point. I don't feel safe working with them in the Ena, but I'm unlikely to be assigned to another generalist squad if they do change who I work with. I figure I'll either be kept with First Squad or swapped between the big hitters and the Sight specialists as the need arises. I don't know. I want to bitch and complain about it, but there's no-one I can do that with. Everyone on First Squad would have to deal with it officially if I whined about it, and so would Zan if I laid it on her.

I guess, if I brood on it too much, they'll have won. So I'll try to forget all about it, and not worry unless they show up on my schedule again.

It's occurred to me that, in gaming terms, I'm an escort quest. So funny. And Fifth Squad are hardcore pvp-ers who think quests are a waste of time. Tools.

Wednesday, February 27

Cancelled

Today was supposed to be Boxes Rotation, but when I woke up this morning I had no appointments for the rest of the week. I've gone all paranoid that this means they've decided to assign me away from First Squad.

I guess this is an opportunity to catch up on all the school work I've been ignoring, which I will get to right after I'm done with some important worrying and sulking.

MARCH

Sunday, March 2

Aether

'Aether' is an Earth word, I'm sure of it. Or, at least, 'ether' is, and I know that's an anaesthetic, but there's another definition. I've read it in fantasy novels, used for the 'atmosphere' in one of the afterlifes or something. There's a phrase, 'off in the aether' isn't there? Aether is a word on Tare, as well. I found that out...it's four days ago now, I think. The day which was supposed to be Boxes Rotation.

I spent the morning on the roof doing homework and enjoying the sunshine. It was a rare cloudless day, really nice. After lunch I lolled about on my bed, watching news and sampling dramas and trying to read the descriptions of online games I'm considering subscribing to because no-one would treat me as a stray in a game – just a noob. But they all look a bit daunting because it's played inside your head and though they're not 'in-skin', they'll still be vastly more than I'm used to. The things you might do in a 'full' virtual reality are more than I'm willing to take on just yet.

I was labouring through the description of one when an appointment was entered into my calendar, and I had just looked to see that I was supposed to be doing a 'Retrieval' starting five minutes ago when Zan "opened a channel" to me, which is Tare-speak for calling me, except that when someone opens a channel you don't get any choice about answering your equivalent of a phone – their voice is just abruptly there in your head. Only people with a certain amount of authority can do that, generally for emergencies. This was a big one.

"Cassandra, come as quickly as you can to Green Lock," she said. "Ready for entry into the Ena."

I was glad I wasn't still on the roof. "Something happen?" I asked as I quickly stripped off the clothes I'd been slopping around in.

"The Pillar investigation teams have gone down," Zan said, which was enough to make me run along the corridors, after I'd made a lightning-quick bathroom stop and had my uniform sprayed on. I was too scared to ask what exactly 'gone down' meant, just hoped 'retrieval' meant something more positive than bringing back bodies. First Squad are pretty much making this planet bearable for me, and the idea of anything happening to them made me sick.

I wasn't the last to arrive. Both Twelfth Squad and Tenth Squad were gathering, more than a few of them looking mussed and sleepy since they were on an earlier shift than mine and would have been in bed when the call came. The only person I'd worked with before was Zan, and the implications of that kept my mouth shut altogether as they waited for the last stragglers to arrive. To use two squads who had just come off-shift, and to put me with them when they're not squads I'd tested with, was more than enough to underline how bad it was. I didn't even need to see the worried glances they kept exchanging.

This was the first time I'd seen any of the Setari really fretting. The Tenth Squad captain is a guy named Els Haral, who looks incredibly laid-back and speaks with a soft voice. He was having a really good calming effect on everyone else, but the situation wasn't one you could tamp down on thoroughly. And there was one guy there from Sixth Squad called Juna Quane, who had brought the news back and was barely able to stand the delay while everyone assembled. Haral created a shared space for both squads, Quane and me, and began briefing everyone as the last few were heading toward us – one of the advantages of the interface.

"Following our regained access to the Pillar space at the beginning of Shift Two," he said, "all but one of the monitoring drones were recovered intact. These revealed an unvarying energy signature from the Pillar, but no other activity. The space itself is exposed to deep-space and heavily frequented by roamer Ionoth: primarily swoop-type, and some larger. Third and Fourth Squads were deployed to perform an external examination and, if satisfied, to commence investigating the interior. Given the calibre of Ionoth, First, Sixth, Seventh and Eighth were assigned as support.

"Sixth Squad was stationed in the adjoining entry space to observe, and the primary teams entered without incident and commenced the external examination. Here is the schematic of the Pillar prepared following external scanning and observation. We'll move into the near-space now."

We broke neatly into our two squads and Tenth Squad went through the gate-lock first. Zan had kept her call to me open and said: "Stay on my left as we travel, and tell me on this channel if you can't keep pace, or feel any threat."

There wasn't much I could say to this except "Yes," and I looked over the schematic during the brief pause while we waited to go through.

The Pillar was a lot bigger than I'd realised. With nothing around it except white or washes of rainbow colours, I'd judged its height by the door. If the schematic was correct, then the door was nearly three times as tall as 'normal' doors. The Pillar seemed to have a hollow inner tube running all the way from top to bottom which was marked 'power core'. The gap between the inner and outer wall didn't seem to have any stairs or levels or more than possibly some structures on the ground floor. Built, if anything, like a giant thermos.

Once we were all in near-space, Haral and Zan both gave the order for a quick march in formation. The squads each settled into three pairs and we started off, with me settling beside Zan and Lenton, while Quane played offsider with Tenth Squad.

"During the external examination," Haral continued, "three groups of swoop-types and one tarani attacked. These were well within projections, and easily dealt with. A little over one zelkasse ago, the decision was made to open the Pillar."

A kasse is about two and a half Earth-hours long, and a zelkasse is a quarter that, so it had started less than an hour before Zan collected me.

"There was no apparent locking mechanism, and the doors were opened easily using a drone. When no negative reaction was detected, Third and Fourth engaged in another set of scans preparatory to entering. They had not yet completed when this happened."

We'd reached the first gate out of near-space, and though all these spaces would have been recently cleared, Haral and his partner did exactly the same pause, scan and clear through that had become familiar, but he gave us all a fragment of recorded memory to digest first. It had a 'mission display' overlay and had "Quane" written in the lower left and a little 'life monitor' for the rest of the squad along the right side, which of course made me think of gaming in a far from positive way. No infinite lives or save games here.

The first image was of the Pillar space through the gate from the Platforms space. Quane had looked left, where there was only white flatness with a rainbow-tinted backdrop, and a handful of Setari. Then he'd looked right, back past more Setari to the tower in the distance. It *was* a lot further than I'd thought, maybe a hundred metres away. The doors were open, and Third and Fourth Squads were standing well back from them, playing with a drone.

I saw Ruuel just before he moved. He turned his head sharply and I think he shouted, but it was too late.

White light. A massive beam of it, roaring out of the open doorway, spreading to completely block sight of the Pillar and the Setari. For about ten seconds nothing could be seen and Sixth Squad bit back startled comments. Then the whiteness began to lift, or drain down, quickly clearing at the top. The hazy outline of the Pillar came visible first, and then black shapes, lying in a settling mist.

"Kormin sent Ammas in, and confirmed aether effects," Haral went on, while we were still watching the end of this. "He was able to reach Tsennan with talent and return, bringing him out, but even that brief exposure left him debilitated. Tsennan's vitals were steady, but he showed no immediate sign of recovery. At that point Kormin sent Quane with the emergency call."

We reached the next gate, and after we were all through Haral switched to handing out orders.

"On reaching the Pillar space, Kantan will enhance and create a vortex, drawing up as much of the aether as possible.

Then the Telekinesis talents will enhance and bring out as many of the fallen squads as can be reached. Our major challenge will be successfully reaching the most distant squads while suffering the effects of aether. And Ionoth."

That was a big 'and'. I wasn't sure what swoops were, but it was obvious that they'd deployed a lot of squads to ward them off. At about this point I was starting to really have to work at not slowing down, and was glad the space before the Platforms space was this short remnant of a flagstone road, all tumbled and broken and not the sort of thing you can jog straight across. And then we were in the Platforms space, and Sixth Squad weren't waiting for us.

"Twelfth, stay with me," Zan said curtly, as Tenth and Quane doubled their speed and dashed up the criss-crossing white squares. She increased her pace, and lifted me easily with Telekinesis. Then Tenth reached the top and someone cursed, my interface only telling me "(Profanity) (profanity)."

"Mane, that's in your normal range," Haral said, unflurried, but with just a hint of tightness in his voice. "Ignore the swoops and pull them back here."

One of the girls from Tenth Squad stepped through the gate. Another turned to a trio of blacksuited figures lying unmoving on the platform just above the one next to the gate. Zan, jogging up, glanced through the gate as she returned me to my feet, and said: "Ice seems safest."

Haral nodded, eyes narrowed as he watched over Mane's shoulder. I could see what seemed like a pair of pearly pterodactyls, but less awkward-looking. Swoops.

"Lenton, enhance and stop them before they follow," Zan said, adding a hand gesture to tell her squad to spread across the nearest three platforms. Me she had stand just to the right of the gate entrance.

Lenton, who seemed to have left his temper behind today, brushed a hand against my shoulder and stepped through immediately, slipping past Mane as she returned. She had three limp Setari hovering behind her, and everyone moved back so she could bring them through, Haral catching her by the shoulder as she looked likely to fall over herself.

The nanosuits are good protection, really resistant to piercing and cutting, and automatically self-repairing, but they're not invulnerable. And they left the faces bare. Of the three Setari Mane brought back, two had gaping rents down their fronts, slick and wet, and the third looked like something with a wide, small-toothed mouth had tried to bite off his head, and not quite succeeded. I recognised Dahlen from Seventh, but not the other two.

"Kantan, enhance and start," Haral said.

Kantan was a tall, fairly dark guy. He touched me on my back, stepped around the cluster of people trying to do something about the injured, and walked resolutely out into the knee-high mist. Lenton had made two massive balls of ice with swoops in the centre, which fell to the ground and stayed still. He paused a moment, looking around, then stepped back through, staggering as he came but managing to stay upright. He was sweating, but said steadily enough: "Another cluster of swoops to the left, approaching fast, and what looks like a stilt in the far distance behind the Pillar."

"Darm, enhance and take care of the swoops," Haral said. "And tell Kantan to come back in before he collapses. Namara, will you go after?"

Zan nodded as a curvy Setari went through the gate and turned left. Kantan was a Wind talent – I could see the stirring agitation he was causing in the mist thickly covering the ground. Like Ketzaren he needed time to set up anything really strong, but managed to start up a twisting spiral, sucking the mist toward it, before he returned obediently and stood shuddering and shaking his head. "That will draw for a while," he said, as Zan touched my arm. "But more was flowing from the Pillar."

"Rest," Haral said, watching Zan step through. "You may be able to strengthen it later, and it's at least pulling some of it away from this gate. Drysen, prepare to enhance. Status on injuries?"

"Dahlen and Roth will keep," said Nels, the Setari who had been doing most of the medicking. She'd somehow made most of the wounded's uniforms move aside, and was busy spraying what I guess was liquid bandages everywhere. "Ammas is critical and getting worse."

"Quane, Sherun, get him back to base," Haral said. "Drysen, go through. Tens, Charn, get ready to take some of these."

The difficulty was not the weight of the Setari, but distance and numbers. I'd already learned from testing that picking up multiple small objects is harder than one big one. Zan, the strongest of the telekinetics, had gathered eight fallen at once, and started feeding them quickly through the gate into the waiting arms of the two Haral had ordered forward. Others stepped up to ferry them further away from the crowded entrance, and then Zan came through, stumbling. "Darm's down," she said, voice slurred. "Drysen's fetching her. One swoop of that cluster still coming, no more in sight."

"Kiste, take care of it and come straight back in," Haral said. "Mane, how's recovery?"

Mane, the first of the telekinetics who had gone through, was sitting two platforms up, looking green, but she stood up when he spoke and came back down to the gate. "Doesn't wear off quickly," she said, grimly.

"We'll pause when Kiste's back in," Haral said, surveying the still forms around him. They'd managed to get less than half out so far. Drysen, when he returned, had Darm and three others. One of them was Zee, which made my heart give a little joyous skip, but the toll on the two rescue squads was obvious. They'd brought in every Setari who was close, but almost all of First, Third and Fourth Squad were still out there.

And all that time I'd been staring at the glowing mist and remembering moonfall on Muina. Liquid light. But moonfall hadn't hurt me, as it was so obviously hurting the Setari.

"What aether?" I asked Zan through our shared channel, since she was sitting down with her eyes closed and was probably the least busy that I'd get her.

"A form of energy," Zan replied, opening her eyes, but keeping her answer in the channel. "We encounter it occasionally in the spaces, though I've not seen any reports of such concentrated amounts outside the major interplanetary gates which cut through deep-space. It's very common around them, and we need to use vehicles to survive passing those gates."

"It do what you?"

"Initially pain, like being burned or frozen at the bones. Interference with control of movement and talents, then loss of consciousness, increasing paralysis. Death within a kasse, if you remain in it." She closed her eyes again, but added: "We'll reach them yet."

"Is other sorts aether?"

She gave me a puzzled look, but then Kiste came back into view and fell through the gate, landing on his hands and knees. "That stilt's heading this way," he said, panting. "Circling, but definitely coming for here, and not slowly."

Haral was looking grimmer by the second, but his voice was still relaxed and calm as he said: "Kantan, enhance again and do what you can. Mane, be ready to follow. Signal if the stilt's in my projected enhanced range." He went on as Kantan touched my shoulder. "Given the effect of the aether, we can't take a stilt lightly, no matter how enhanced. We'll try an initial group of myself, Lenton and Tens. If everything we can do doesn't bring it down–" He paused, and I suspect he'd realised he'd run out of conscious heavy-hitters. "If we can't bring it down, Kiste, make whatever attempt you can while Namara and Drysen pull everyone they can reach to the gate."

Mane followed Kantan through before Haral finished speaking and Haral waited a few seconds then touched my arm, watching without change of expression as Kantan collapsed at Mane's feet. He'd managed to strengthen the wind vortex, but the glowing mist didn't seem to be getting much thinner. Lenton waited the bare minimum of my prescribed delay before enhancing himself as well, while Tens stepped up to help Mane, who was struggling not to fall while bringing Kantan and another – it was Alay – through the gate.

"Stilt will be closing in a count of twenty," Mane said, folding into a panting tangle almost on top of Alay. "Gainer was the only one left in my range."

Tens touched my shoulder, and exchanged a glance with Haral. I think they were trying to accept not succeeding in getting everyone out.

I never saw the stilt myself. Only later, in extracts of the mission report which Zee showed me. Black, nearly as tall as the tower, with a long, sloping body and spindly legs like vine tendrils. The underside of it was all covered in more tendrils, long ones and short ones, and I think that's where its mouth was, because its head was just this sort of triangle with eyes. Haral, Lenton and Tens concentrated their attacks on its underside, anyway, with Ice and then two balls of lightning. The first was a little low, but the second was placed nicely, shattering frozen tentacles in a spectacular orgy of blasts. One of its legs was blown apart, and it fell.

Lenton passed out, and Haral and Tens carried him back between them, staying upright themselves but moving very slowly. "Go," Zan said to Drysen, who touched me and headed out, face bleak. I saw the same expression on Zan's face as she waited her turn. Everyone who'd gone in a second time had collapsed. With the continuing Ionoth attacks, it was no wonder all of Sixth Squad had ended up unconscious. The few Setari remaining had no chance of getting the other squads out. When Drysen didn't even manage to bring back one more person before going down, Zan lifted her hand toward my shoulder. And I caught and held her still, just long enough to take advantage of her surprise and step through the gate myself.

I'd almost convinced myself that it would hurt. Genetically, I'm the same as these people, and every one of them had flinched a little walking into the mist and then acted like it was slowly crushing them. But it was just the same as Muina's: chilly but bringing a pleasant warmth, a feeling of wellbeing. The wind from the vortex made it swirl around me ominously, but I felt fine.

Drysen wasn't a little guy. There was no way I could carry him through the gate, but I could drag him closer and lift him partway so that Zan and the one called Nels could haul him the rest of the way through. I paused before following, taking a good look about, but could see no sign of more Ionoth for the moment. I was wondering if not trying to go through before was a big screw-up on my part, but it's not as if I would have been able to fight off the Ionoth. Besides, I would have had to waste time arguing with everyone, and the picture I was presenting was definitely worth a thousand words.

"Try close door, best thing?" I asked, after stepping back through.

"That doesn't effect you?" Haral sounded totally nonplussed.

"Is – moonlight feel is alcohol. Light-headed, bit dizzy." I shrugged. "Not hurt, such. Is close door help?"

Zan and Haral exchanged a long glance, then Zan said: "I don't see any other positive options," and Haral pulled a face and nodded.

"Run," Zan said to me.

That I didn't need encouragement to do. If any more Ionoth came along, I'd be the one with my face scraped off. And I hadn't properly worked out just how much time was left before people would start dying from exposure to the aether.

I don't recommend taking on Serious Business while tanked. It's not so much that I was incapable of running (well, jogging) a hundred metres, even though I became ever more pixillated with each step. I saw Mara as I ran past and became madly convinced I was going to let her down, and I really didn't want to. It was a damn good thing that I wasn't out to do anything more complicated than close some doors. And I remember this whole obsession growing up about the size of the doors and that I wouldn't be able to move them when I got there, but then I was there. I actually collided with the right door, which was one way to learn that they moved really easily. I pushed it shut, suddenly feeling good again, and started for the other half, and that's when my head shut down altogether.

As I was waking up, I was thinking that since I was waking up I must have shut the other half of the door. Then I was noticing a fuzzy fence which seemed to be holding the fact that I felt very very bad at a bearable distance. And a weirdness about my face, which made me lift a hand, and I found that one of my eyes was covered up. There was something else which was even weirder, but I couldn't immediately figure out what it was, so I turned my head and saw that Maze was on a chair beside me, but asleep, slumped against the wall.

I heard someone shift on my other side, and that was harder to look at because of my covered eye. Without understanding why, I didn't want to move my hand, and kept it over the bandage, but eventually I managed to shift round enough to see Zan, who I think must have moved so I could see her. She plainly needed to sleep a lot too, but mostly she looked incredibly relieved and happy-upset.

I wanted to say something about she should smile more often, but that's when I realised what was really weird. No interface. Not at all. Trying to talk and not having suggestions for words coming in my mind really threw me. I couldn't even remember really common words which I'd actually *learned*, my brain was so mushy. So I just tried to smile back at her, and said: "Stupid language," in English in a really croaky voice, and most sensibly passed out.

Next time I opened my eyes, Zee was there instead, and I was a little more capable of stringing two thoughts together. And seemed to be in less pain, but also on fewer painkillers, so I felt it more. I was pleased that I could remember a few words of Taren this time, and managed: "No interface?" but my throat really didn't like me talking, and my chest felt all congested and my mouth tasted foul, so I coughed until Zee fetched a greysuit who helped me spit out black stuff and drink some water – from which I figured that the Setari again have orders not to touch me.

I hate being in the medical section, especially anything which involves drips and catheters and tubes. Tare's technology seems to be pretty similar to Earth's in respect of tubes, and the greysuit sent Zee away and did a bunch of tests, and fed me about a half a cup of a horrible salty-sweet drink, but thankfully removed the tubes. Some time during this I caught sight of my arms, and was holding them up and staring at them when Zee came back with Maze and a different greysuit.

"I look like the world's worst junkie," I said, still in English, turning my arms to better appreciate their purple and blue glory. I'd never seen anything like it. Even my *palms* were bruised.

I couldn't understand what they said back, of course. Maze looked like he'd had a proper rest, so I'm guessing it was a lot later than the first time I woke. They were being pleased I was awake, but serious at the same time, and Zee said something to me slowly which had the word for interface in it a couple of times. I just shrugged, though I was finding that moving hurt and staying still hurt, which didn't really seem fair. Then I felt all tingly for a moment, and like I was catching up with myself.

"Can you understand now?" the greysuit asked, and I nodded, but put my hand back over my bandaged eye because it had started hurting rather more than anything else. "Some lingering malformation there," the greysuit said helpfully, but did something which made it stop hurting. "It'll be a few days before the remedial work is complete and the remnant toxins are flushed from her system," he added. "But there doesn't seem to be any loss of function."

"Mission log's intact," Maze murmured to Zee, and nodded to the greysuit, who gave me a last glance and went away.

"Everyone alive?" asked, and saw the 'no' in their faces before Zee answered.

"Ammas from Sixth Squad died during the return to base," she said, and we all looked down at the same time, as if it was rehearsed. "You remember what happened?"

"Up to door." I glanced at my arms again. "It fall on me?"

"No." Zee wrinkled her nose. "Your interface started growing again, destructively beyond prescribed limits. It became non-functional and had to be shut down and pared back." She indicated the purple patterns beneath my skin. "That's partly the damage and partly slough from the repair work. Your left eye suffered the most, but they don't expect permanent problems."

Nanotech. I sighed. Convenient as it is, I'd really appreciate it if my interface didn't keep trying to kill me.

"We've only had the outside view of what happened after you reached the door," Maze said, passing me across a log file. From his faintly abstracted expression, I guessed he was reviewing mine, a thing which always makes me feel totally weird.

The log file was Haral's, watching through the gate as I jogged with a curving wobble toward the end to the Pillar. It wasn't *too* obvious at that distance that I ran into the door rather than deliberately stopping, but I stood there for at least a count of five before my brain caught up and I pushed the thing shut. I turned to cross to the other door in a business-like way, but paused in the gap, looking inside.

And then another wave of light came pouring out, filling the entire space with white, and I heard the Setari who'd been watching me gasp, and Nels said: "Tzatch," which Lohn tells me is a shortened version of Tzarazatch, a spiritual concept on Tare kind of like Ragnarok: the destructive end of everything. I can't get Lohn to tell me any real swear words, but he explains the milder ones.

For about thirty seconds there was nothing but whiteness, and it didn't even look like it was going to settle as it had the first time, but then it thinned abruptly and was sucked away to nothing, back into the Pillar, leaving the space as clear and empty as it had been the first time I saw it, except for all the unconscious Setari. I was noticeably absent from the doorway.

The fragment of the log finished, and I looked back up at Maze and then blinked, confused. His face was set and furious, a muscle working in his cheek. Zee was staring at him, as surprised as I was, and when she touched his arm he flinched away, then said: "Watch her log," and turned his back, getting himself under control.

Of course, that immediately made me watch it myself, jumping straight to the last bit I remembered: closing the right half of the door. It's highly disorienting to watch things you don't remember doing. I only remember stepping forward, don't remember at all looking into the interior of the Pillar. Most of it was taken up by the central core, with empty space curving off to the right and left. There was a rounded rectangular hatch just about at head height on the internal column, with two big white levers set into the stone below it. By big I mean almost as long as my leg, sticking out of grooves that ran to the right around the Pillar's core.

The hatch was designed to slide, and was open a crack on the right hand side, making a brilliant white vertical line from which aether drifted down. And as I looked up at that, something interrupted the vertical line, a few black spots blocking the brightness. Fingertips, claws, curving around the hatch from the inside. Then it pulled it open, the movement accompanied by a shifting rumble from the levers, and everything went white.

A black hand shape appeared in view: my hand, trying to block out the light and not really succeeding. And then I must have gone forward, under the main intensity of the blast into the drifting mist of aether falling down from it. The top lever had gone left as the hatch opened, and I seem to have tried pushing it back to the right but wasn't succeeding. Then I looked upward, into the spotlight glare of white coming out of the hatch, and there was this barely visible human shape, just the head, and shoulders, the arm hooked over the edge of the hatch, reaching. The scene dropped down abruptly – I must have ducked – and then moved right, pushing the lower lever instead of the top, with an accompanying rumble which was loud enough to suggest huge boulders grinding together, stopping with a nicely final thud followed by a hiss and a howling wind noise. The only thing I was looking at, at this point, was the floor, really close to my face. I levered myself partially upright, turned toward the door, and dropped again; must have fallen flat on my ass. Then my hand came up and covered my left eye and lifted away to show rather a lot of red and I bent forward, the scene becoming barely visible. I guess all that aether wasn't doing enough to block whatever having your eye self-destruct feels like. The last moments of the mission log don't show much, because I'd closed my eyes, but you can hear me panting and then I say, "Rage, rage against the dying of the light?" and let out this confused-sounding laugh and then the log stops abruptly.

"Glad don't remember that," I said, after a moment. Maze had stopped looking upset, but Zee had taken his place: not so angry, but eyes wide and mouth pale. "Is thing in Pillar same Lights Rotation?"

"Cruzatch," Maze said, and you could hear the hate in his voice, and see him make the effort to put it aside. The word means "burning", with overtones of destruction.

"There are several spaces they appear, and they also roam. They're not the only human-form Ionoth we encounter, not the only ones which intelligently react to us. But we have – for a long time there has been discussion about the level of their awareness of the Setari, and whether they retain and learn from previous encounters with us."

"The last massive to break into real-space was accompanied by a Cruzatch," Zee explained. "Almost as if it was riding it. Guiding it." She sighed. "The idea of there being organisation among the Ionoth is not accepted by many."

And certainly hadn't been mentioned in any of the stories and movies I'd so far seen. "Organised not, that one bloody annoying. What happen it?"

Maze made an equivocal motion with one hand. "No sign. We think you closed the intake of the Pillar's power stream. We're not entirely certain why all the aether was pulled back, but the entire Pillar seems to have shut down as a result." He smiled at the expression on my face. "No need to look like that: it's what we would have tried eventually, if not so soon, and the only thing we've really lost is the chance to study the Pillar in more depth. Everyone's off-rotation, only clearing near-space, because it seems that the surrounding spaces are shifting, and we can't trust the gates. But you did well, Caszandra. And were very brave."

Although that was hugely gratifying, I doubted it was true. "Blind drunk panic more like," I said. "Don't remember either way."

"What was it you said before the log cut out?" Zee asked, leaning forward to touch my leg and then stopping. Definitely orders not to touch me.

"Is line famous poem about dying." I repeated it in English, because it makes it slightly easier to work out a translation, then did my best to render it in Taren. "Funny thing say but fit guess. Was *really* drunk."

I must have fallen asleep then, and had uncomfortable dreams about what I'd seen in my log, and about Maze being angry, and of running and hiding from something chasing me. None of it pleasant, in other words. I keep having dreams like that. Otherwise, being in the med section is the same tedious crap that it always is. The greysuits say I have to stay here because all the bruising means I'm at risk of blood clots. I spent the first couple of days sleeping and coughing up black stuff – blood and phlegm and discarded bits of interface, apparently – and having to move about a lot because it's good for my circulation.

Everyone from First Squad came to visit me, as well as Zan, still looking tired, but no longer all stressed out. I asked her if she would bring me my diary, and she did, and sat and talked with me a while and was all proper and Zan-like, but just that tiny bit more human than before. I think if I'd died she would have felt responsible, because she'd ultimately given me the order to go. And maybe that she does like me, a little bit anyway.

I've been doing school lessons. I don't really feel like watching shows or the news because the news is full of the impact of shutting the Pillar down, even though it's been kept secret. The Setari squads have been distributed over Tare because that's the only way they can effectively patrol the near-space when they can't use other spaces as shortcuts to get about, which means that there's more sightings of them, and more outbreaks of Ionoth into the real world. I did that.

I still feel pretty horrible too: tired and sore. Every time I get close to being fit, I nearly die and go back to the start again. And I look like a pirate junkie panda, with a patch and a huge ring around my uncovered eye. It was purple, but now it's going green with hints of yellow.

This is the longest entry I've made in this diary yet, and I've passed the halfway point. Will have to do some research on whether there's any way I can get another one custom-made.

Still alive.

Monday, March 3

Ghost

When I woke this evening (for the second time today – I'm still doing a lot of napping) my chest felt heavy. I was half-awake noticing the weight and worrying that I was getting sicker instead of better and would be stuck in here forever. Then it filtered through to me that my chest was also purring.

I didn't do anything stupid like jump or shout, but I must have moved, because the purring stopped abruptly. The weight was still there, though, and I lifted a hand carefully and felt the shape of the cat I couldn't see. The purring started again, and after a while it stopped looking like I was petting my own chest and there was the Ionoth cat.

It was just like I remembered: dark green eyes and short, smoky fur. A half-grown cat, not creepy or scary in any way. For a little while I just let myself enjoy it, petting and playing with it, and establishing that it looked like it was a girl cat, but eventually I had to give in and be responsible.

There's lots of different ways you can talk to another person over the interface, most of it nothing too different to Earth's internet. You can't just open channels to random people, unless you have certain rights, like squad captains during mission time. Usually you can only send a channel request with a text message and it's up to the people you want to talk with to accept or not, and for the Setari I think most normal people can't even do that: you have to be in their 'address book'. Or you can email, leave a voice message, or chat just by text. I'd never tried opening a channel before: I'm too aware of how overworked the Setari always seem so if I need something or have a question I send an email.

Since, so far as I know, I'm still assigned to First Squad I sent Maze a channel request: "Is time ask?" Gods I hate my screwed-up grammar. I doubt the baby English I write in my diary even comes close to how dumb I sound to the Tarens.

Anyway, Maze answered right away. "Something bothering you, Caszandra?"

"Is visitor," I replied, and sent him an image of the Ionoth cat sitting on my lap. Then, before he could respond, I quickly went on: "If capture what happen her?"

He paused a long time before answering, then said carefully: "They'll find a way to scan for it. Then I'll personally return it to the Ena, since I suspect you'll accept nothing less."

Maze really is the nicest guy on the planet. "Is big thank you," I said, and he laughed.

"I'm out in the city at the moment, but I'll send someone to you. You're not feeling any negative effects?"

"Purring cat good thing."

"Won't be long."

Stray

He left the channel active, in case I started screaming about evil kittens, and I took the opportunity to play with my temporary pet a little more. I've decided to call her Ghost, which definitely fits. I didn't absolutely believe that no-one would try and kill her, but I trusted Maze to do his best to make sure that didn't happen. I wasn't entirely sure she would cooperate at all, but I figured that if I stayed calm and no-one made any sudden moves, she'd probably at least not run off the second anyone showed up.

I wasn't expecting Ruuel, and reacted all out of proportion, stiffening so that Ghost stopped purring, and probably going pink beneath my bruises. What Mr I-Have-Every-Kind-Of-Sight-But-No-Visible-Sense-of-Humour made of my expression I couldn't tell, but he took the container the two greensuits were carrying and shut them outside.

"Place it in here," he said, moving the container so it was flush with the bed. It was an ominous-looking box, metal and plastic with a rare physical control panel on one corner. And warning signs about containment fields.

I didn't move immediately, carefully stroking Ghost, who hadn't scrambled off, but mightn't like me after this. "Come back and visit me again," I told her in English. "I'm only going to turn you in this once." Scooping her up with a hand beneath her chest, I carefully lowered her into the box, saying, "Her name Ghost."

Ruuel just turned the containment field on, which made Ghost look upset. She vanished, but I don't think she was able to get out. At least, he didn't act like he thought she had, turning and opening the door again and handing the box to the greensuits.

I busied myself telling Maze that Ghost was safely in a box, expecting Ruuel to go away again, except he didn't.

"I had a question for you," he said, when I looked at him. "You referred to the aether as 'moonlight'. Was that simply your ineptitude with our language?"

I could have lived without 'ineptitude'. Ruuel doesn't dance around shortcomings.

"Is because aether look feel like moonlight Muina when building make liquid," I said, as clearly as I could manage,

188

and had the satisfaction of making his eyes open to more than halfway.

"Building make liquid?" he repeated.

"When moon rise Muina building light..." I had to search around for a word which fit. "Draw? Focus? Become? Thicken? Look feel same aether."

"The buildings on Muina turn moonlight into aether?" I nodded and was given a full-on 'captain look' in return. "It didn't occur to you to tell anyone this?"

"Is your planet," I said, struggling to keep annoyance out of my voice. "How know what you not know?"

"Wait," was all he said back, developing that gaze-into-nothing look people get when they're talking over the interface. I took the time to remind myself that these were life-and-death issues, and that there was no point glowering at him just because he'd made me feel in the wrong. I did wish that I hadn't given him a starring role in so many daydreams, or at least wasn't sitting in bed dressed in a flimsy patient gown, looking so damn ugly.

Then I was added to a channel with about ten people already in it, a bunch of names I didn't know, as well as Ruuel, Maze, the Third Squad captain Taarel, and the bluesuit, Selkie.

"Devlin, please explain your experiences with aether on Muina in more detail," Selkie said, all brisk and businesslike.

"Is...moment." I hadn't expected to be dumped into some high level meeting, and reached for my diary as the simplest way to handle it without sounding defensive. Flipping through a few pages, I said: "First time saw moon, Muina, seven night there. Was still walking river then, no buildings. Just seem like moon to me, bit bigger bluer Earth moon, three quarter full." I paused. "You know has hole in yes?"

"Yes. Go on."

I flipped a few more pages. "Reach village thirteenth day. Moon come out every eight day, so came out after been there couple day, was full. Was sitting on roof tower when rose. Buildings began glow. Faint first, then too strong normal. In centre all roof there circle – rosette? Pattern. All building there have. It glow much strong than rest building. Light – aether – start flow out from circle. I right next circle, touch flow light. Was cold, but made feel warm. Effect like alcohol. After while saw that bigger light centre village. Followed aether there. Think it was flow up hill. In centre village there amphitheatre. Very big circle there. And cats. Cats not there that night, just huge lot liquid moonlight. Centre circle make column light. Very drunk by then. Went stood in column. Passed out. Woke there next day. Felt good."

I sighed, flipping more pages. My moonlight adventures made me sound like a total idiot. "Few days later, sick. Cold all time. Liquid in chest. Fever." I paused, thinking back over the few confused fragments I could call to mind. "Was maybe die. Not conscious most time, several days. Then again moonfall. Too sick move, don't remember much that. Could see aether fall past window. Made feel warm. Easier breathe. Much better next day. Able move."

The next entry made me frown, and I said doubtfully. "Not sure this. Eyesight strange after. Some things blurry, some not. Thought had damaged. Next day, thought being watch. Feel something behind, see movement corner eye. Thought go insane, imagine monsters. Next day, lots noise, like hills wailing. Ddura, guess. Couldn't see where come from. Sounds go away, so did feeling watch everywhere. Eyes still blurry. Two day later, Setari show up." I glanced at Ruuel, who had gone back to being impassive, but was watching me very closely. "Don't remember eyes blurry since ten thousand injections. Is all."

"You could hear the Ddura from real-space?" Selkie asked, with a queer note to his voice.

"Loud. Loudest thing ever heard. Like unhappy mountain."

"I cannot–" someone began, sounding hugely pissed off, but stopped, then said in a sharp but less obviously hostile tone: "Have you observed any other relevant phenomena?"

The 'speaking' indicator told me the person's name was Lakrin, but I don't have the access to look up more details about people.

I was wary of just saying 'no'. "Not obvious," I said eventually. "Ddura. On Earth have polar aurora, look like Ddura, but lot bigger. But not make noises. Nothing about Ionoth. Is just, uh, something do radiation from sun? How know whether relevant? Is relevant every place go have cats? Nothing obvious relevant."

"And two worlds' worth of observations an expansive topic," said another voice, a woman called Notra. "The youngster is still in the medical facility, is she not? I will revisit the question of other detail with her separately."

"Very well," Selkie said, and then I was cut from the channel. Military people are like that.

I started to close my diary, but Ruuel slid it out of my hands. Military people are like that, too.

"Symbol Sight can let read?" I asked, sounding nearly as unenthused about that idea as I actually was.

"Not usefully."

He turned several pages back, then pressed two fingertips to one of the pages and closed his eyes. Whatever he was doing – presumably using one of the 'Sights' – didn't seem to be easy, and little lines of effort or pain appeared around his mouth. But he didn't do anything more dramatic than that, and after a while opened his eyes and handed my diary back.

"Since Tare found a way to travel through the spaces, we have not encountered our equal in technology," he said, voice measured. "It leads to an assumption that there is little we can learn from those who have not the same achievements. Base stupidity not to debrief you fully about your experiences on Muina. But no sense on your part to assume in return that we know everything about a planet that we are only permitted to visit under exceptional circumstances for a few short hours."

It was hard to argue the point, so I said: "Fair enough," and he nodded and left me to feel annoyed at him for producing even-handedness. I'll bet he's considered a strict but impartial sort of squad captain.

Not that 'strict but impartial' is something I ever thought I'd find attractive. And not having a sense of humour should make him totally not worth it. Though I suppose that comment about my lab rat not being inapposite might have been a very dry humour, and I could appreciate that.

He has really nice hands.

When he was gone I went to check myself out in the mirror of the tiny en suite, and confirmed that I was the worst I've ever looked. After a while Maze came to visit and told me that Ghost was still in the containment field but not yet scannable. The information I'd given them about Muina is pretty major, apparently, though he doubted they were going to be able to decide exactly what to do about it any time soon.

A weird day, altogether. I'm sick of the medical section.

Tuesday, March 4

Muina Debriefing

I spent a lot of today with Isten Sel Notra, who is some kind of senior scientist. I think she'd be a variety of physicist, if physicists believed in psychic talents, spaces as well as space, and moonlight which could be converted into mist. The main thing I could tell about her is that she's really smart, a Taren Einstein-type, and she's kind of a cross between everyone's favourite grandmother and the strictest headmistress in the universe. She has minions, too, who came along to fuss about her until she sent them away, and she told the medical staff to bring me some better clothes and took me to a kind of 'meeting lounge' so that we could both sit comfortably.

Old age is a little hard to judge on Tare. They're quite happy to use their nanotechnology for cosmetic purposes, and it's really rare to see anyone with any kind of blemish or birthmark or more than fine wrinkles, though they don't seem to have figured out how to stop their hair going white. They can get rid of, or at least reduce, most cancers, but they still get old and frail. Best I can tell, 'retirement age' would be between eighty and ninety, and a good lifespan would be a hundred and twenty. Their oldest person (I just looked this up) lived to be a hundred and forty seven (well, four hundred and forty-two). Isten Notra is old. Frail-old, though still able to get about, and still sharper than I'll ever dream of being.

Isten Notra is also interested in absolutely everything. She asked a lot about the moonfalls, of course, wanting to know what happened to the aether once it reached the amphitheatre (I think it drained away underneath – not sure) and whether it felt exactly like alcohol or just similar (kind of) and whether the aether in the Pillar space felt different from the aether on Muina (no) and whether I thought I was sick because of the first exposure to aether (no) and if I really thought the second moonfall had helped me recover from being sick (yes). Whether I ever saw the buildings glowing at other times (no). Whether the roof decorations had felt unusual or different to me other than during moonfall (um). Whether there was any unusual noise during moonfall (I think mainly I remember an absence of noise – all the animals had gone very quiet).

Then we moved on to what I'd eaten on Muina and what I'd eaten on Earth. Things I'd seen in the village. Animals I'd seen. Animals that appeared to belong to both planets. What level of psychic talent there was on Earth, if at all. Whether there was anything resembling Muina structures on Earth, or legends about Muinan culture. The only thing I could come close to thinking of in terms of psychic legends was Atlantis, and I'm sure Mum told me once that the original stories didn't have anything about magic or strange powers in it, that they were added later.

Isten Notra is also the only person on this entire planet who has ever corrected my grammar and pronunciation, or made me repeat sentences until I get them right. She started our talk by giving me handy tips about ways to better manage verb-forms and sentence structure. And then went off on a huge tangent about language, and Earth's languages and development of communication and what I would have been doing on Earth if I hadn't ended up on Muina, and she pried out of me that I thought studying the origin of myths would be an interesting thing to do but didn't think it would be very likely to get me a job. And all the while turning the whole discussion into examples of how to handle trying to talk in a language I don't really know, not letting me be sloppy, and insisting I work the sentences out properly before trying to say them, no matter how long that took. Isten Notra's minions kept popping in with snacks and lunch and to ask her if there was anything she needed and to give me scandalised looks because they heard me talking about vampires and zombies to someone Lohn later confirmed was one of the most respected scientists on the planet.

It was a great day. Isten Notra's a really special sort of person, with not a lot of time to spare, and she gave a whole heap of it to me.

And I was outside of my medroom box, which was also a bonus.

Wednesday, March 5

Someone call the wahmbulance

Ista Tremmar took off my eye-patch today. They've been changing the big adhesive covering daily, but my eye was taped shut underneath. Today they lowered the lights, pulled off the tape, and shone little torches at me. Then, after another tedious medical exam, they released me. I have check-ups and tests scheduled, and nothing else whatsoever, not even training.

I should have been happy. Not so much at the nothing scheduled, but being let out of my latest box. Glorious illusion of freedom. But, you see, my eye is wrong.

I have hazel eyes. Brown and green with some flecks of blue. I still have hazel eyes, but flecks of purple and violet have been added to the left one, and combined with the blue it drowns out the brown and green. It looks pretty cool, but I hate it. Because it's not my eye any more and every time I look in the mirror it's telling me I don't exist any more. I'm not a girl from Sydney who loves reading and games and was about to start uni and hadn't quite decided what she was going to do in the long run. I'm not Cass here. Devlin most of the time, and Caszandra occasionally. I'm a stray, and it's not just what people call me, it's what I am inside: something out of place. My main goals are to learn a tiresome language, and to avoid getting anyone killed until I can figure out a way to get home. Not dying is also a goal. I don't like to count up the number of times I've nearly died since I was rescued. At least this last time I achieved something before falling apart.

So now that I've finally been released and can wander about, I've spent the day moping on my couch. I should be grateful for having an eye at all, but instead I'm busy trying not to let myself get too upset, because I might take another sleep-walking excursion to Earth and I'd hate to have to be rescued again, but at the same time I can't help but acknowledge that I haven't done anything at all to try and work out how I reached Earth's near-space, and how I can get home safely.

Hiding how unhappy I am right now is important to stop them from monitoring me more and more, especially since my immunity to the aether makes me an even more interesting lab rat. I have no wish to confide in the greysuit who has had a session with me every day since I woke, 'chatting' with me in a way which screams 'psych evaluation'. Or perhaps they're a trauma counsellor, but in that case I can't like them for not coming out and saying so.

I wish I could stop having nightmares. I guess I really was in a blind panic back in the Pillar since my dreams are filled with scary things snatching at me, and I wake sweating and panting, with a hand clutched over my eye. I don't think I'd make the grade as a Setari, even if I had psychic powers, and it's a good thing that they have no plans to put me back on active duty any time soon.

First Squad is off on some island called Gorra. I really appreciate that Zee emails me every so often and lets me know what's going on with them, and with the shifting about caused by the Pillar shutting off. They're slowly checking which of the known routes still exist, and trying to work out ways through the spaces which allow them to easily get to the same locations in near-space that they could previously access. Everyone's scheduling has been thrown madly off, and they're all working double-time trying to make up the ground they've lost.

Bleh – this is not a fun day. It needs to hurry up and be over.

Thursday, March 6

Professionally sozzled

This morning I had aether tests. Now that I'm no longer in danger, merely covered in yellow bruises, tender and stiff and occasionally shaky, they've decided to try and find out why I react so differently to aether from everyone else. Which means I spent this morning getting drunk.

Since they're wary of setting off my interface, and are trying to work out why it started growing again, they only gave me enough aether for a minor buzz. So I was bored but cheerful. I swear I must have had more brain scans than anyone on any planet. At least I had the warning signs in the containment room to entertain me. "Danger – toxic substances!" plastered everywhere, in and out of the interface.

They released me around lunch time, but I was in no mood for school work. Mildly defiant, or perhaps still a little drunk, I went swimming. Nothing too strenuous, just to get the kinks out, and I think I'll keep going unless someone remembers I'm supposed to have an escort.

While I was floating about pretending that was exercise, I abruptly gained a brand new level of access, accompanied by an email from Isten Notra directing me to a huge collection of files. "Your assignment while you're in testing and recovery is to review the information we've collected on Muina and to notify me of any possible relevant parallel with your world."

Homework! I haven't the foggiest idea if I'll find anything useful, but it's definitely something new and tangible for me to do.

The Muina collection, however, was not nearly so interesting to me at first glance as everything else this access level let me look at. They've reclassified me as a Setari, and now I can see things like everyone's calendar, the space, rotation and Ionoth libraries, squad profiles and a general noticeboard. After months of being a mushroom, this is a serious adjustment.

I have to admit the first thing I wanted to do was indulge my increasing curiosity about Ruuel. It was only the recollection of playing "Browser History of Shame" over at friends' houses which held me back. Instead I checked out First Squad's profile, opening Zee's details first. Talent set and ratings, mission history. No doubt plenty of stuff I couldn't see. Next I methodically opened and read the details of each squad captain in order, and if I lingered a little longer over Ruuel then that might be excused by the fact that he has eleven talents. All the Sights and Speed rated high, then low ratings in Ena Manipulation, Telekinesis, Levitation and Light.

That pointless piece of self-indulgence over with, I turned to the Ionoth library (the Bestiary!) to look up cats. And found out that Ghost has escaped. Yay Ghost! I hope she comes to visit me again, but I expect that she won't be trusting me any more.

After browsing randomly for a while, quite overwhelmed by how much information there was, I glanced over the Muina collection. And pounced on a report from a few months ago. An expedition to Muina to investigate a Ddura detected in the planet's near-space.

I was in 'Additional Notes'. "Displaced person, young female, recovered from secondary site. Uninjured, condition poor. Stickie scan negative. Not from known language group. Submitted for processing."

My so momentous rescue. The attached log was fascinating though, giving me some idea of how the Sight talents operate. After arriving at the town, Fourth Squad started out near my wool-boiling operation, which made it obvious straight away that someone was there. Those with Place Sight could see glowing footprints everywhere: mine and those of different animals, and even my handprints all over the bowls. The squad split into pairs, apparently confident there was no major danger nearby.

Watching my Muinan town through Ruuel's eyes made me feel both stalker-ish and hypocritical, and really brought home to me why the Setari are so damn proper most of the time. I expect it's a rare thing for anyone to review entire mission logs, but you sure as hell wouldn't want to spend your time checking out a squad member's butt while out on mission, or gossiping about other teams.

It was also beyond confusing seeing as Ruuel does. Auras everywhere, and strange patterns where patterns shouldn't be: art nouveau heat hazes. And that was only visual input. Most of the Sights are far more than visual, so I hate to think how much information someone with six Sights is processing, and can better understand why Ruuel nearly collapsed staring at the Ddura while enhanced. I don't think all the Sights are on all the time, though, since there were times when my Muinan town looked entirely normal. Perhaps it's like changing channels, and he flicks through them.

I felt no nostalgia seeing my tower again, was simply glad not to be there as my trackers easily cleared away my makeshift door and passed the clutter of junk I'd kicked down the stair, then the second floor I'd been in the process of clearing. Then they were on the third floor, Fort Cass, with my bowls of washews and red pears carefully lined up, and my pathetic collection of tools in their corner. My bag. My blanket. Me.

Huddled in my stained and worn school uniform, with my hair greasy and lank, I looked bony and ill. 'Condition poor'. Ruuel looked at me with normal sight first, then one which made me light up in dull greens and blues and reds.

"She's been here some time," said Ruuel's partner, Sonn, over the interface.

"Weeks, not days," he agreed.

"The time limit's close. What do we do with her while we look for a gate?" An edge of irritation had crept into Sonn's voice. They weren't there for me.

But Ruuel didn't seem overly concerned, turning from studying the ceiling to look at me as I stirred groggily. "Put her down at the lake's edge for the escort to collect."

I watched myself perform this magnificent recoil worthy of a scalded cat. So scared. Ruuel just changed whatever Sight he was using and started looking around the room again, seeing a strange overlaid image of rubble, and a few different fragmentary ghosts of me.

"Do you understand me?" Sonn asked in Taren, then said almost the same thing, but pronounced the words differently.

"Who are you?" past me said, staring back and forth between them.

Sonn tried again. I swapped later to watch her log, and she was carefully sounding out the same question using a "Stray Encounter Guide" which had a little stock of useful phrases from the languages of strays which had been picked up in the past. They're all wildly varying dialects of Muinan, which is something I couldn't tell at the time.

"Nothing you're saying sounds like anything I know," past me said.

"Not getting anywhere," Sonn murmured.

"Just use gestures," Ruuel said. "We don't have the time to waste with this." He left to go up on the roof, telling the rest of his squad to keep scanning for gates.

The time limit for visits to Muina is strictly enforced. Looking over the whole of the mission report, they'd started out miles away, at the ruins of a major city where a network of scanning drones had been installed both in real-space and near-space.

Robotics here are more advanced than Earth's but the AI is still nowhere near *real* AI, so there are limitations to tasks drones can perform. The news about the Ddura had involved a complicated chain of drone messages. They have drones seeded about the spaces near the big interplanetary rift on Muina which stay powered down most of the time, waking themselves up on a regular schedule to scan. Another drone wakes itself up and collects the scans, and yet another drone travels back and forth between Muina and Tare with the collected scans. A Ddura had passed by the scanning drones, and that was enough to get Fourth Squad hurriedly sent out, two days later, in the hopes that it was still about.

Once they reached the city, they'd gone straight into near-space to get the latest information from the drones there and to try and track the Ddura. They were able to calculate the direction it had moved and had chased off after it in their ship, finding my town as a consequence, where they'd stopped to see if they could find a gate and look for it there. And found me instead.

Leaving me sitting on the lakeshore, Fourth Squad had located a gate a short distance south of the town and gone through. After two days they weren't surprised that the Ddura was gone, but they'd been able to identify which gate it had gone through, though how something as big as that aurora 'goes through' those little gates I don't know. They'd tried tracking it until the constraints of their time limit had forced them to return.

I think I'm going to have to go through the Muina files from beginning to end rather than jumping about. Why, for instance, aren't they searching that big city for records? Sssso much technical jargon: it's like someone gave me everything NASA has ever written.

Friday, March 7

tl;dr

I decided, before I started on my file review, to read more generally about Muina and Tare, now that I had access to more than the 'primary school' textbook version of the past. Establishing a timeline will help. I'll write it down in Earth years because Tare years are just too stupidly short.

@ 1500 years ago – The Lantaren caste on Muina screw up royally by creating Pillars which start tearing apart the fabric which divides real-space from the Ena. And then they're almost completely wiped out trying to fix their screw up. I missed this little detail before – the people who set up the Pillars died almost at the outset, leaving a serious information and leadership vacuum.

@ 1500 years ago – Entire towns and cities begin dropping dead, and Ionoth plague the rest. The remaining Lantaren caste frantically evacuates everyone they can to other planets by walking thousands of people through the Ena (some through the kind of spaces I've been to on rotation, and others through something called deep-space).

@ 1500 years ago – One group arrives on Tare, which is a wet rock constantly pounded by storms. They run for the nearest cave and struggle to survive underground. The Lantarens as a distinct caste disappear at this point, but the bloodline remains mixed into the general populace. Plenty of minor psychics about being useful, but they're treated as a necessary evil because for centuries it was considered a bad and tainted thing to be linked to the Lantarens, who are blamed and hated for what happened to Muina.

@ 1400 – Muinans finally start to get the upper hand on Tare, and their life becomes less of a desperate struggle for survival. The population starts to go up instead of down. Proper written records start being kept, or stop being lost. Even at this point the Tarens have a kind of nanotech – all those white buildings on Muina are basically grown, not built, from a kind of 'living mud' developed by the Lantarens. The Tarens managed to bring some with them and maintain a seed stock of this mud and have built structures with it ever since, even though they had no real understanding of how it worked until the last couple of centuries. House-building here is ultimately bizarre: they start with a big vat of white goop which they feed with raw material to make more white goop which they then 'instruct' using little models to create big versions of the same. So long as they kept some of the white goop 'unformed' they could always make more white goop. Since the white goop hasn't absorbed the whole planet yet, I guess it has a mechanism to stop it spreading everywhere.

@ 900 years ago – Tare has a strong and stable civilisation at this point, and is starting to branch out from the original island, Gorra, and establish on other islands. World exploration phase, somewhat hampered by extremely violent oceans.

@ 300 years ago – The attitude toward psychic ability finally shifts enough that it's considered a good rather than a bad thing, and the Tarens actively try breeding for it. Later, once they figure out how to boost it with machinery, they find that psychic talent of some sort is almost universal in the population, although they don't have anyone who can even come close to the level of the old Lantarens.

@ 200 years ago – Computer age begins.

@ 120 years ago – Advanced nanotech age begins. At this point they've passed Earth's current level of technology and are beginning the first roll-out of the bio-powered interface.

@ 100 years ago – Tarens build 'spaceships' which will allow them to travel through the interplanetary gate again. This gate (or rift) goes to deep-space and is thick with aether and doesn't seem to be like either the gates I've travelled with First, or the gate which took me from Earth to Muina. The Tarens start hunting for habitable planets/Muina, which is by no means easy. They send off and lose a lot of drones.

@ 90 years ago – A planet called Channa is located, which has an ex-Muinan population. It's a rocky, arid world and not very attractive as a colonisation prospect, so the Tarens set up some mines on an unsettled continent, and indulge in long ethical debates about what to do about the ex-Muinans who are living a harsh, nomadic hunter-gatherer life. Instead of stepping in and trying to take over, the Tarens disguised themselves, learned the dialect, and have been feeding them small technological advances, turning them into a more agrarian culture. Since Channa's Ionoth infestation was relatively minor, they've left it at that until recent years when, like all the other known planets, Channa started to suffer from much increased Ionoth numbers. Now there's a huge argument about whether Tare should lend more outright assistance or even try to remove several million Channans from the planet.

@ 80 years ago – Located Nuri, a moon-sized planet with a small but stable population (tech level probably equal to the Romans). The Nurans seem to consider Taren technology a contaminant, and though there's been some diplomatic exchanges, the Nurans really don't want to have anything to do with the Tarens, and won't share information. They also seem inclined to hold the Tarens at fault for the recent increase in Ionoth infestation. The Nurans have the strongest 'natural' psychic powers of the known planets, and have been able to handle Ionoth up till now, but are thought to be struggling with the increase.

@ 60 years ago – Located Dyess, which has the remains of Muinan-type habitation, but it seems Dyess was overwhelmed by Ionoth long ago. It's a watery world with a string of tropical islands crawling with things that consider humans tasty with ketchup. There's been quite a few expeditions there focused on collecting useful plant life, but the slivers of land mass are not considered worth colonisation.

@ 50 years ago – Located Kolar, which is a dry but reasonably habitable world where ex-Muinans have been busy having wars with Ionoth and occasionally themselves. It's the most advanced technologically of those Tare has encountered and though they would have been more primitive than Earth at time of contact, they're now a little more advanced thanks to Tare's help. The Tarens and the Kolarens don't have a very warm relationship. The Kolarens really want the Tarens to share more of their technological secrets, while Tare likes Kolaren resources but not the prospect of them standing on an equal footing. Kolar has an internet, but the Tarens won't give anyone except the Kolaren Setari the interface. Of course, large portions of Kolar don't *want* the interface, and loathe all the potential violations of privacy it would bring.

@ 30 years ago – Muina rediscovered. Much rejoicing till entire expeditionary force wiped out in an explosion. Repeated expeditionary attempts invariably wiped out, although in different ways.

@ 30 years ago – KOTIS formed: theoretically a joint venture between Tare and Kolar, but in truth mainly Tare. This was in response to a noticeable increase in Ionoth presence across the known worlds, and also wanting to 'fix' Muina. Both Tarens and Kolarens consider Muina 'home' and there's this grand ambition to move back there.

@ 18 years ago – Tare is suffering from more and more Ionoth coming through to real-space and has to devote a lot of time and manpower to fighting them. They begin a big push to increase the strength of psychic talents, formulating the Setari program in the hopes of moving the battle out of the cities. Which has been very effective, but in no way fixes the larger problem.

So that's the interplanetary situation. I can see why Ruuel doesn't think there's much chance of them finding Earth, since it took them so long to find their own home world. Thanks to the strays which have shown up on Tare and Kolar, they know there's at least three other inhabited planets of Muina-descendents, and they haven't even been able to find them.

Thirty years ago when they found Muina, the Tarens didn't know very much about why they'd had to leave Muina in the first place other than "everyone's dying, run away!". Why the Lantarens felt interplanetary travel was so important is a mystery, and so is how the Pillars were created. Not a single one of the 'core' group of people involved in setting any of this up on Muina made it to any of the known worlds.

There are endless stories about the Lantarens, most of which make them out to be arrogant mystic masters, but beyond being really great psychics, the true scope and nature of their powers isn't known.

So there's my context for starting Isten Notra's project, though I'm not sure how quickly I'll get that done when my mornings involve getting drunk and then sleeping it off. And still feeling tired in the evening.

Saturday, March 8

Early Muina Expeditions

Thirty years ago a drone returned through the rift gate having charted a path to a new habitable planet. The exploratory ship *Lonara* was despatched with a crew of twenty to survey the find. As planets go, Muina's a juicy one. Large polar caps and a few arid splotches, but the rest a very habitable green and blue gem. Lots of lakes. Massive cities of empty, white blockish buildings. The *Lonara* did a quick aerial survey of the first big city they found, and could see no sign of human life, though plenty of animals. They set down on what looked like a parade ground, left a few drones, and reported back that the home world had been located at last.

Both the *Lonara* and another ship, the *Tsaszen*, were sent to begin a more detailed exploration. Fifty crew altogether, a mixture of military and scientific specialists. The Tarens had known that Muina was dangerous – or had been when it was evacuated – so they'd expected to find it infested with Ionoth. But even before the Setari program began they'd developed plenty of effective anti-Ionoth weapons, and without their own cities and citizens in the way, that first expedition wasn't really expecting major problems.

They didn't report back.

A third ship, the *Maszar*, discovered only smoking rubble where the expedition was meant to be. The *Maszar* searched for survivors and found none, then returned to Tare. It was really sad reading the reports from that time. They had no idea what had happened. Had the ships been attacked by massives? Some kind of weapon? Sabotaged? There was a strong undertone in the reports that Kolar was suspected. The *Maszar* hadn't even been able to find the drones.

There was a lot of debate about going back in force or sending a small and very quiet mission. Small and quiet eventually won out. A ship called the *Danna*, carrying ten people. They tried to be sneaky, staying in the air a long time, landing well away from the city, scanning, scanning, scanning, and deploying a dozen drones. Half of them stayed with the ship and the other half went on a sled ('sled' is roughly what 'deeli', their name for their hovering transporters, translates to) to the site of the other crash to investigate. They arrived without incident and began sifting through the rubble, performing scans and searching for what seems to be the equivalent of a black box flight recorder. They were making good progress, not troubled at all by Ionoth or any other sign of attack, when they lost contact with their ship.

When yet another ship was despatched to investigate why the *Danna* hadn't returned, they found the five from the investigatory group camped beside the *Danna*'s shattered hulk. They had no idea why it had exploded. There'd been no attacks in the two days since, and they'd continued to do their scans and investigatory work and were very glad to be rescued, thank you very much.

It took another exploding ship, the *Netz*, before KOTIS instituted a rule about ships only being able to remain on the planet for twelve hours. For their next attempt they established a camp of people on-planet and left them there, with regular two-day check-ins. That worked really well for about a week, and they made good progress on exploring the city, looking for records and important structures and anything to unravel the mysteries of the past and present. It seemed smaller machines didn't explode as quickly. Drones tended to not last more than a few days, but their sleds proved quite robust.

Then a massive attacked them. About half the thirty people there died – were eaten. They tried again, a different site with more people. Four days later they vanished entirely, not even the bodies remaining, and no signs of battle.

That all in the first year after Muina was re-discovered. And, twenty-nine years later, not much has changed. The Taren government reduced the permitted time on the planet to only three kasse. When they began to understand near-space a little better, they found that drones they set to power down instead of being constantly active usually didn't stop working. The drones trundle about, a bit like the Mars Explorer, recording everything they see for an hour or so, and then transmit their recordings to a collection drone and shut down for the day.

Satellites in orbit don't explode, at least, and they've one up making a complete aerial world map. GoogleMuina! I could even look up my village. I still haven't scratched the surface of the reports, just skipped through the main details. There's too many for me to ever hope to read everything. And I haven't found a single thing that seems worth telling Isten Notra. I guess I'll keep glancing at the files, but I've lost my initial enthusiasm.

On other fronts, more getting drunk in the morning to no visible benefit. They rather over-exposed me, and I passed out mid-session. There is a complete lack of fun in getting drunk while a bunch of serious people watch you and take notes.

I did better swimming today: I'm starting to feel that exercise isn't a thing of horror. I sent an email to Zan telling her that if she's ever bored, or not exhausted, and wants more swimming practice to come join me and she replied with "I'll do that." But since she's on a different shift, I guess the chances are pretty low.

Sunday, March 9

Not Clint Eastwood

This morning Tsur Selkie came to watch me be drunk. After observing through a viewing window, unenhanced and then enhanced, he had some poor junior greysuit stand next to me while they gassed us both. The greysuit was this short, very pretty guy who sweated and gritted his teeth even before the aether was piped in, and then shot me these outraged looks when I just lay there being bored while it was obviously hurting him plenty. He passed out fairly quickly.

Then Tsur Selkie had them pipe just a puff of aether over his own hand and my hand, watching with those flinty black eyes. He continues to remind me of Clint Eastwood, even though he doesn't look at all like him.

"Is same reaction, but reversed," I said helpfully, while Tsur Selkie was watching our hands. "Both lose fine motor control, reaction time slow, plus judgment, plus pass out. Is just way feel different. And healing or dying, guess. Are there any famous actor this world that people say you look like?"

That made him look up. I suppose it'll go in the mission log file. I can only be glad, since they'd decided to try out Sight Sight, that they hadn't used Ruuel for it. Who knows what I might have said to him?

"The difference is not in your reaction," Selkie said, after a moment. "But in the behaviour of the aether. It is attacking me."

That made me stare. "Is alive? Or more nanotech?"

"Possibly. The Nurans claim that we made Muina itself our enemy. The next question is why it recognises you as a friend."

"Everyone like Australians," I said, with a short laugh, but then sobered a little. "People from Earth, not good for own planet. Don't see why another would like."

He just turned away, signalling for them to open the doors.

"Wait." I reached out and grabbed his wrist, trying not to look too embarrassed about it. "Try test again."

Clint Eastwood's not the sort of guy you go about grabbing. And Tsur Selkie definitely isn't. But after a moment's thought he told them to try again, and stood there without changing expression as the jet of aether gusted out to cover his hand. Then he said: "Increase the amount."

I wasn't in the channel where most of the discussion was happening, so lay there working on the retention of minor shreds of dignity while watching Tsur Selkie get squiffy. He handled it well, but you could see the change, the gradual unfocusing of his eyes, the line of concentration appearing between the brows. Prime target for a random breath test.

By then I was finding most everything amusing, so I piped up with: "Drunk on duty. Ten demerit points." And laughed at the way he frowned at me, but sneakily went on: "Going pass out soon. Can stop?"

First he had to test what happens when he was no longer in contact with me: an instant return of all the negative effects. I didn't even trust myself to stand up, and let myself go to sleep again. Waste of half the day and now I'm too wired to sleep.

Monday, March 10

Sacrifice

The parents of Setari candidates give up their children to the government. There's lots of movies here about that. About families who are like soccer moms, who want the prestige of their kid being taken into the Setari program, no matter what. About others who try and hide that their kids have strong psychic abilities, who do everything they can to discourage them from excelling. I watched a sad story a few days ago, about the sister of a girl who was taken into the Setari program, who had to fight to have anyone acknowledge her as anything more than that girl's sister. She killed herself in the end.

I spent today thinking about Sixth Squad, about the guy called Ammas who died, and how his parents must have felt when they were told. Were they angry? Had they pushed him into the Setari program, or resisted his conscription? Had he been given leave to go see them recently? Did he have any sisters, or someone he was in love with? Were there things he wanted to do other than kill monsters?

The Setari aren't by any means without rights, and there's several oversight committees, but to develop their talents they're pushed in a way which hovers between strict and cruel. While they're not allowed to be sent into battle until they pass their adult competency exam, and they really are given chances to leave the Setari, there's no way they can gain truly strong talents without giving up most of their childhood. It's useful remembering that whenever I get into a grump and feel like complaining.

With the severe increase of incursions into real-space, and the repeated sightings of Setari on the main islands, there's a lot – seriously a *lot* – of speculation about what's been going on these last couple of weeks. That they've found a Pillar and shut it off is one of the many things rumoured, but nothing about so many teams coming so close to dying, and nothing about me. The Setari might have oversight committees, but KOTIS is by no means open to public curiosity. I wonder if there's an Unexpectedly Useful Strays oversight committee?

No getting drunk today, just a regular medical exam, so I swam in the morning and didn't manage too badly. I think the aether sessions might have helped my recovery along. I tried to be super-virtuous and go jogging after lunch, but there was a sports carnival on. Well, a competition with at least three hundred kids aged all the way from little six year-olds to people my own age. If I'd bothered to check the scheduling I would have seen that the 'park' was booked.

They had uniforms, too, though not black nanoliquid ones. Brown and cream, obviously designed for sports. I hastily sat down after walking in, glad that I was back from the action, but too embarrassed to walk straight back out again when all the people nearby had seen me. I always feel like such an impostor in my black uniform, because I've seen enough of the TV series about the girl trying to qualify as a Setari to know how much of a mark of achievement it is. Though I suppose it's possible most of them knew what I was anyway, and maybe that's half the reason they were looking at me. I'm not sure if the matter of useful strays has been allowed even outside the main body of the Setari.

They were so deadly serious about the competition. They did cheer, and barrack for their friends, but even the little ones scrambled over the obstacle course as if their lives depended on it. I guess it does. I wasn't in whatever channel they were using, and didn't try to find it, using the time for more flipping through Muina reports instead. I didn't turn the name display on, because some of these kids are probably going to end up like Ammas.

Tuesday, March 11

Little to contribute

I'm not getting anywhere with Isten Notra's assignment. After reading endlessly I can't think of a single thing to tell her which doesn't sound lame, so there goes my hidden ambition to point out that the dog didn't bark in the night, or the parsley hadn't sunk in the butter, or any other Sherlockian observation. I was sticking to it, though, paging through increasingly tedious reports, but more than a little relieved when Mara came and kidnapped me for dinner in the city with

First Squad, who have finally been posted back to KOTIS headquarters.

It was a great outing. We went to a place which sold food pastes similar to hummus and refried beans, with different edible 'spoons' ranging from hard brown bread to the now-familiar vegetable sticks. I immediately thought of it as the "Hot and Cold Dip Shop". Lohn was being very funny, and kept saying: "Ten demerit points" whenever anyone accidentally knocked a glass. He says he's my eternal slave forever, just for the expression on Tsur Selkie's face.

"Is Setari allowed drink alcohol?" I asked, since I'd only ever seen First Squad drink water and juices.

"Not in any quantity," Alay said, tilting her glass. "Even if we weren't actively serving, the risk is too great. I've *tried* alcohol, but the rule against control-diminishing substances is only good sense."

"Tsur Selkie main guy in charge Setari training?"

"A dominant force in our development, say." Maze seemed even more tired and worn-down than usual, but he produced a wry smile at this. "I have to admit to re-watching that testing session more than a few times. So Selkie looks like a famous actor from your planet?"

I tried very unsuccessfully to explain Clint Eastwood, and then moved on to Johnny Depp, and now all of First Squad except Maze have sworn to find a path to Earth so they can watch *Pirates of the Caribbean*.

Afterwards, Zee took me to have my hair cut. There are apparently hairdressers available in KOTIS for the brownsuits, who are properly called Kalrani ('juniors'), but they're what you'd expect for school barbers, and so Zee took me to the place she uses. I had my hair neatened, without doing anything fancy to it, but I feel much less of a scruff now that the split ends have been cut out and the ends aren't so jagged. Not that it makes much of a difference, since I've taken to braiding it.

As we walked back I talked to Zee about my eye changing colour. I've moved past my first reaction to it, and was able to tell her that it makes me feel uncomfortable, without transforming into a rampaging drama llama. And I told her about my nightmares, which I felt safe to talk about now that I'd stopped having them every damn night.

Then I asked Zee about Nils in Second Squad chasing her, and she said: "In his dreams." And changed the subject.

Wednesday, March 12

Fun

More getting drunk on aether. Though I wonder if I should be writing 'high' instead of drunk, since I'm breathing not drinking. I guess I don't like the idea of 'high', which is very contradictory of me since alcohol is just another drug. 'Party oil', as Perry called it: no big deal, just something to make things go. Alyssa had made me promise never to drink without her, which I haven't technically, but even though I'm legally old enough now, I don't think Alyssa – let alone Mum – would be impressed with my current career. There's something less than special about having breakfast, then lying on a couch being all tingly until I pass out.

On the flip side, I have lots of medical supervision, and I'm even trying to be conscientious about exercise. This afternoon I went both swimming *and* jogging, though I'd have skipped the jogging except Zan came and joined me for the swimming (yay!) and I asked her if there was somewhere I could jog which wasn't quite so visible and well-populated as the obstacle-course park. She showed me a different training area, an endless maze of corridors and stairwells and the occasional ladder. This is probably a better thing for overall fitness than just jogging lightly in a circle, but gods I barely managed one circuit going at a pace which really wasn't more than a walk. Way too many stairs. My legs were jelly afterwards.

Zan kept pace with me, not looking like it was costing her the mildest effort, and told me afterwards that I shouldn't try and run the circuit at all, just walk it once a day, taking as much time as I needed. I can't say I'm eager, but at least I would be without an audience, barring other people doing the course overtaking me.

We ate together after, and talked over one of the books she'd recommended: a historical novel set in Tare's past, before they had the interface. Pre-Setari too, with an epic

tray

quest to uncover lost Muinan records in caves deep below Unara. She made me miss Alyssa so bad. I just can't bring myself to ask Zan to rate the smex level.

Instead I asked about the sports event I'd walked in on, and Zan explained that winning those things, while it gets you some nice privileges, doesn't count toward whether you qualify to become a full-fledged Setari. And that's what the Kalrani are very focused on at the moment: they're choosing Thirteenth and Fourteenth Squads from those who have reached the right age and passed the aptitude tests. There's about twenty-five of them who are of age, one of whom will have to be slotted into Sixth Squad. Fifteenth and Sixteenth Squad won't be formed for at least two Taren years.

"Does anyone not qualify ever? What happen them if that happen?"

Zan answered in the extra-neutral tone she uses whenever the internal politics of the Setari are involved. "While there are some still Kalrani who are more senior than the members of Eleventh and Twelfth Squad, if it was felt that it was not possible for them to qualify, they wouldn't have reached this stage of the program. But forming a balanced and effective Squad is more complex than matters of age and qualifications. They'll be brought into active service when there is the right team for them."

I wondered if this touched on the reasons some Setari were so nasty to Zan, but kept my mouth shut about that and instead thanked her for showing me all the torturous stairs. She said she'd come swim with me if our schedules matched up again. Definite progress on the Zan front.

And now, while I was writing this, I've been scheduled to test with Fourth Squad tomorrow. I think I'm looking forward to it, but I have to wonder if Ruuel's too-many Sights mean that he'll look at me and see right through to all the shivery anticipation the thought of him creates. Alyssa used to say that time spent with impossible-to-achieve guys is time well spent because it gives you a chance to find reasons not to like them. But I don't feel equal to dealing with Ruuel right now.

Ah well – the worst that can happen is that I can make a total idiot of myself, and have that immortalised in mission reports forever. Such a lot to look forward to.

Thursday, March 13

Fourth Squad

There was an email from Ruuel when I woke: "We'll be combining this test with productive work, so be prepared for an extended session."

Given how sore my legs were after all those stairs yesterday, my first reaction was to use what Dad would call "ripe and illustrative words". But I decided it was a good thing. Setari exploring the Ena aren't going to be the slightest bit interested in my internal monologue.

The contrast between my last squad testing session and this one was massive, but it started out almost identically, with Fourth Squad standing in a circle in the middle of the same test room. The difference being that as soon as I walked into the room, Ruuel brought me into a squad channel and began the briefing, moving so that his back was no longer turned toward me. Tiny things, but underpinning a vastly different attitude.

"We'll test in the same order that we will rotate enhancement, starting from myself to Sonn, then Auron, Ferus, Halla, Eyse. Ferus, you'll be primarily responsible for ensuring Devlin's safety, with Auron as your flank. You've observed the techniques Spel used to bypass the resistance to enhanced Telekinesis and Levitation. We'll save testing Combat Sight and Speed for the combat simulation rather than individually, and concentrate on the attack elements. Devlin, report any new or unusual reactions immediately."

Ruuel would have been a disconcerting team captain to start out with: he basically sets the bar high and expects you to get over it. I suppose he would have taken it slower if I hadn't worked with First Squad already, but he sure likes to get through things quickly, testing unenhanced Levitation, Telekinesis and Light talents and then enhancing and going through them again in less than a minute. Unenhanced he can lift maybe a hundred kilos, and enhanced about four times that. With his Light talent he created a curving spike from his arm, much the same as the nanoliquid swords. Enhanced it distorted the same way as Mara's whip, shifting colour and becoming more intense, but not too spectacularly different.

It's more interesting for me doing these tests now that I can look up squad information before each person tests. Fourth Squad is evenly broken into guys and girls. The girls are Fiar Sonn (primaries of Ena Manipulation, Combat Sight and Electricity), Charan Halla (Place Sight, Gate Sight) and Mori Eyse (Path Sight, Combat Sight, Teleportation). My two minders are both guys. Par Auron is very tall, about six foot four, with primaries of Path Sight, Gate Sight and Levitation. Glade Ferus is my height, with primaries of Telekinesis, Combat Sight, Symbol Sight and Speed. They both have minors of Ice and Fire and I get a bit of a buddy sense from them.

Personality-wise, there was no-one outstandingly off-putting. Ferus has an evil gleam in his eyes occasionally: not nasty, but I bet he gets up to mischief when he's not on mission log. Auron seems quiet and calm. Sonn is serious with an impatient overtone. I found Eyse interesting: she smiled at me once, a nice wry smile. I guarantee she has a sense of humour. Halla I haven't figured out. She had a bit of an edge, but not directed at me I think. Overall, although they were nowhere near as open and warm as First Squad, Fourth's one of the easiest squads I've worked with. I think because they all treated me like a visiting consultant or something. Like I understood what was going on.

Nils from Second Squad showed up while we were still testing the 'elemental talents'. I still haven't decided how serious the thing is between Nils and Zee. Or what I think about Nils, who does a good impression of a walking sex-god. While the last of the elemental testing was going on he kept leaning down and telling me completely innocuous things in this incredibly husky voice, totally doing it to see if he could make me blush. I don't think I'll ever be gladder that Ruuel seems to think that one minute is the maximum time needed to master any new skill, and that he soon sent Nils over to one side to summon illusions for Fourth Squad to chase.

Having Ferus cart me about with Telekinesis is not at all the same as Ketzaren doing it, and I probably would have been more embarrassed about that if I wasn't so relieved not to be at Nils' mercy any more. Ruuel took more time and was far more exacting about getting everyone used to working with me and the rotations of enhancement in combat, but he still decided we were ready to go into the Ena in under an hour. By then I wasn't nervous about it. It was obvious they were as totally professional as First Squad, and that Ruuel hadn't allotted himself enough time to study me for signs of awkward lust.

We kitted up at Red Lock. Getting ready to go into the Ena involves grabbing a little food and drink, a tiny med-kit, and one of the breathers in case of water-logged spaces. And going to the loo. I have no idea whether it's considered a bad idea to go in the spaces, but given the mission log I'm sure everyone wants to avoid the need, so it's part of the ritual of 'gearing up'.

"We will be mapping the gates off the new High Forest space," Ruuel said, once everyone was ready. "Additionally, we will see whether Devlin's enhancements will bring us any closer to relocating Columns, or a reliable path to Hasata. This is still a test situation. Do not push limits."

High Forest space is beautiful. Really. Tall, slender trunks, branches soaring far overhead, silvery leaves drifting down to form a shushing carpet. And, although I suppose someone might have killed them earlier, it doesn't seem like it's inhabited by any Ionoth. There's a ton of gates leading off it, and I think the idea was supposed to be that we document where each of them led, but Auron, who is the strongest Path Sight talent in Fourth Squad, said he had a suspicion of a short line to Unara, and so we went off through a very low gate onto a rocky path winding up a hill (my aching legs!). Just like with First Squad, Ruuel and Sonn go through the gate first as a pair, and the rest of us can't go through until they've signalled us. With the hill space, Ruuel signalled us through straight away. There were things there a lot like wargs, six of them in all, and they looked strong, but they weren't nearly fast enough. Fourth Squad seems to prefer using close-combat methods.

After Auron found the next gate he was looking for, Fourth paused to survey the hill space and the other gates leading out of it, and Sonn used Ena Manipulation to ensure the gate we'd passed through and the one we were going to pass through were absolutely solid. The next space was a cliff-top beside an angry ocean, and full of weather, grey and pounding wet. That was a quick signal through and then a slog through damp bushes. There were Ionoth there, misty grey horses which ran off as we approached, but though Fourth Squad were very alert, there was nothing that they seemed inclined to slaughter.

The gate Auron took us to was a new type for me. It was as vague and unreal as the horses and you couldn't really see through it, except in occasional flickers showing the outline of buildings.

"Phasic," Auron said. "I've never managed to track through one before." And he gave me this solemn sort of nod which was more successful at making me go red than all Nils' teasing.

Then it was Sonn's turn, enhancing and frowning at the gate. Phasic gates aren't steadily aligned, and thus are only open in short bursts. Sonn frowned at it for a short age, nearly collapsing in the process, but looked pleased with herself when she was rewarded with a clear view into Unara's near-space. Ruuel had Ferus pair with him to go through since Sonn was so clearly drained, and then signalled us through again, out of the downpour.

Leaving Sonn and Auron guarding me, the other four went hunting, tracking down a number of Ionoth in the area. I stood about and dripped and tried to picture the people who owned the apartment we were standing in.

When they were back, Ruuel checked the status of the gate once again, then said: "We'll retrace now. A good result." I swear, he talks like he's being charged a dollar a word. But that judicious dollop of approval succeeded in making his whole squad, even me, stand a little straighter.

At least, with Fourth Squad being dauntingly competent, I didn't have a lot of time to fret about crushes. Other than sending me off to medical afterwards, Ruuel failed to do anything to either make me dislike him or fall at his feet, and I ended up focused on business. I really did like when he said it was a good result, though.

Friday, March 14

Planning an outing

Today while I was swimming I was brought into a meeting channel by Isten Notra. "Just listen," said her invitation text, so that's what I did, floating slowly about the pool.

There were about twenty people in the channel, most of them people I'd never even seen their names before. But also Maze, Ruuel, Taarel and Selkie.

Someone had been speaking when I joined, but stopped abruptly and said: "Notra-" in a protesting tone.

"Since our young ally's contribution will be central to this venture, it's best to keep her abreast of the issues, don't you agree, Minera?" Isten Notra said, sounding like she was having fun. "Do you wish to speak further, or shall we move on to the question of numbers?"

"Sentimentality mixes badly with survival, Notra," said the one called Minera, but then shut up.

"It can only be a large force," someone else said. "When small forces have been attacked, they've been destroyed completely. Larger contingents are rarely without survivors."

The meeting went on for ages, and I'm too tired to write even a tenth of it. They were planning an expedition to Muina to investigate the aether-making, and were trying to work out a way to do it without everyone, particularly me, dying. Especially since one of the things they wanted to investigate was why the aether/Muina/whatever doesn't 'hate' me. Eventually they decided on four squads – risking both of the exploration squads, which was another argument in itself – with only a small contingent of greensuits. From a few of Selkie's comments, he thought it likely the Setari would end up protecting the greensuits rather than the other way around.

After I'd told them about the aether they had sent a lightning-quick expedition of greysuits and greensuits to set out a few scanning drones at my village, very carefully timed to try and avoid them all being destroyed, and won themselves lots of nice footage and readings of a moonfall, which were transmitted through today. Now that the Setari have nearly stabilised the situation with Tare's neighbouring spaces, KOTIS is planning the first extended expedition to Muina in years, with a day-trip excursion in three days, and then another two days before the next moonfall. They're also searching their satellite scans for any other settlements which have the same circle patterns on the roofs, and have found one already.

When they were done, Isten Notra asked me on a private channel why I hadn't provided her with any comments on the reports and when I explained that I hadn't found anything to say told me to always keep the question in mind, and to not be backward in passing on observations during the upcoming expedition.

Afterwards I talked to Maze, but didn't ask directly about what they'd been discussing before I'd been brought into the meeting. Isten Notra had shown me that they definitely were arguing about my irreplaceability, which I guess also means there's not yet little copies of me growing in a vat somewhere. She was underlining a point, calling me an ally. I'm lucky she seems to have decided to defend me.

Or maybe Isten Notra just understands that I really would try to leave, no matter how dangerous my jaunts are, if I believed that's what they were doing. Making Muina safe is a far bigger thing than me being able to increase the strength of a handful of Setari, and I'm willing to help however I can, but just me. Letting them make copies of me, or try to breed little amplifying tools, that would be a moral failure on my part.

That sounds ridiculous and weird. But I know it's something I couldn't put up with.

Saturday, March 15

Rain thoughts

The weather outside was finally calm enough that I could go up to the roof today after another morning of being zonked out with aether testing. Tare really is prone to horrible weather so it's no wonder the Muinans arriving here had such a struggle: constant cyclone-level storms made surface-dwelling almost impossible. It was still windy and spattering occasional raindrops when I went up, but nothing so bad I couldn't enjoy it.

I'd managed not to think particularly of Ruuel for the whole of yesterday, but I dreamed about him last night, and the rain reminded me of the dream, which had been of a moment during that session with Fourth. So easy to look up my log, to go back to a brief glance I'd taken of him while Sonn was working on the phasic gate. He was in profile to me, gazing out into the greyness – looking at one of the Ionoth horses – with the rain pouring down his face and his hands loose at his sides. Ungodly beautiful.

As crushes go, this one's starting to verge on girly-obsession.

It's really interesting comparing how I write about Ruuel now to the first few times I saw him. I didn't mention his looks at all, except in passing, but it's not like I didn't notice what he looked like. Well, maybe back on Muina I didn't, since the light wasn't good and I was just so overwhelmed by the sheer fact that there were people. When I saw him and Taarel together, I thought them both very good-looking, but only really focused on her. He surely can't be steadily getting prettier. Is it just that I like him more each time I see him, or wasn't I paying proper attention before?

His eyes are his most dominant feature, dark and clearly drawn. His face is delicate around the temples, and he has a clean, not very heavy jaw line. Arched brows, better shaped than mine, which is unfair. He keeps his hair clipped short, shaped to his skull. A swimmer's build, lean and not heavily muscled, with wide shoulders. I think I like his hands best. Last night was the second time I've dreamed about him, and both times have been about his hands in some way, about how careful he is not to touch things, and how precisely and sparingly he moves.

I think maybe I understand a little more why I'm stuck on someone who is really not my type, and who has barely spoken to me. Not just that he's good-looking and dangerous, though I expect that helps. Not that he was professional during the testing session, or even that he crossed thirteen spaces to save my life. I think it's because of the way he behaved when he caught up with me. He didn't treat me as stupid, just told me what would happen if I tore a hole into Earth's real-space, and let me make my choices about it. Nor did he tell me to hurry up, giving me the time to say goodbye. I don't know if he was being considerate, or thought that the best way to handle my 'psychological aspects', but I appreciated it.

Once I'd had my fill of gazing at Ruuel-in-the-rain, I reviewed his report from that session. I quite like reading reports for the missions I've been on, though I avoid viewing the log extracts overmuch. It still seems too invasive to peer through someone else's eyes, for all that it's a fact of life for everyone here. After a lot of debate, I did play the hypocrite and access Ruuel's attached log, skipping to that same scene and looking through his eyes at the Ionoth horses, trailing streams of invisible light which curled and plumed like an impossible mane behind them. All those Sights. Then I went back to the very beginning of the testing session, and saw that he'd started the mission log from just before I walked in the room. I watched for a few minutes, up until Nils arrived, and gave up at a point where Ruuel was looking at me. Nils was talking, bending toward me, and I was obviously squirming, giving him an irritated, amused glance, face red.

I looked very human. Not too bad, I guess, but...mortal. And writing that pisses me off. These people aren't gods. Heroes, maybe. Asses, quite a few of them. Soldiers. Killers. Specialists.

And I'm a very useful stray. I have to remember that Ruuel was just as ready to call me 'stray' as those idiots from Fifth and Seventh. I don't even use his first name in a diary written in a language that only I understand because, well, he hasn't given it to me to use. Even with First Squad – gods, Maze was in a meeting where they were discussing *breeding* me or something. So was Ruuel. Even if I can manage to learn this language enough to stop sounding ridiculous and they can better understand the kind of person I am, they have no choice but to always treat me as 'the useful stray' above everything else, because that's their job. On this planet I will always be more tool than person.

I've put off any attempt to cut and run until after they've had a chance to poke me at Muina and see what happens. It just wouldn't be fair of me to go before that. But it's Dad's birthday soon. Easter's coming up. Mother's Day. I've been gone about four months. I think that meeting yesterday upset me more than I realised. I didn't do anything at all today except sit on the roof. And this diary entry sounds like I'm bipolar.

I don't know. I probably should have exercised, so I was too tired to think. It's a pity First Squad is being kept so busy trying to get things back to normal. I miss the training schedule I had with Mara. I need the structure.

Sunday, March 16

Night Visitor

I woke up in the middle of the 'night' because my chest was purring again. I was so glad. Even though it's occurred to me that Ghost might be interested in me for exactly the same reason that the Tarens are, that for all I know I'm enhancing her the same way I do the Setari, I don't care. She doesn't mind if I talk to her in English. And I can hold her and play with her without feeling that she's been assigned to me, or that she's going to write a report about it after. She acts *exactly* like every other cat I've known, digging claws in inconveniently, chasing bits of paper and all. After a while she bored of me and went away, but I'm pretty sure she'll be back.

Ghost made the rest of the day bearable. Hour upon hour of tests and scans, and the worst medical exams yet. Half-dressed and trying not to cry while a fresh set of greysuits took bone marrow and spinal fluid samples. They mightn't have cloned me yet, but it won't be for lack of material. The greysuits are still trying to figure out what made my interface start growing again, and searching for differences between me and Tarens. Pretty soon they'll have a complete genetic map of me, but they still don't understand why Muina likes me.

I spent the time between whimpering reading up on the cloning debate on Tare. They are really against it, because the clones invariably have shorter life-spans and are prone to sickness. And there's a measurable downgrade of intelligence, too. After a day researching Taren morals and laws, I still can't decide what they might do if the situation grows worse. Tarens don't have any strong belief in a Creator-God, and are split between the idea of planet reverence, or pure scientific evolutionary theory. So they don't have things like the Ten Commandments, of laws which have been handed down from God. Laws are either based on an idea that you must be grateful your planet makes it possible for you to exist, or on a fairly clinical construct of ethics in a functioning society. Funnily enough, most of the laws are very much the same as Earth's, though there's a real emphasis on personal responsibility. 'Social contracts'. Doing what's right for both yourself and for others.

I'm feeling all social contracted out at the moment. My arm and back won't stop aching.

Monday, March 17

Too much aether

Aether sessions in the morning and then late in the afternoon, which meant I didn't really have a day today and now don't feel remotely tired. Which is great given that I'm supposed to go to Muina tomorrow. I'm going to go and swim a thousand laps in the hopes that I can get a few hours sleep afterwards.

Stupid greysuits.

Wednesday, March 19

Loud

We weren't scheduled to leave for Muina until nearly (my) midday. I'd not been sure if I could get any rest before we went, but had abruptly fallen asleep a little before I would usually have had breakfast. I'd set my alarm for a half hour before I was supposed to meet up, but it was maybe an hour before that when Zee sent me an 'override' channel request. The interface tells people if you're asleep, and so when you send them an override, you're deliberately waking them up. I don't remember this conversation at all, but reviewed it later from my ever-present internal log to confirm just how embarrassing it was.

I answered with "Nnngh?"

There was this long pause, then Zee said: "Caszandra? Are you ill?"

"Tired," I said. "Your medics are all sadists." Since I was speaking in English, that was meaningless to her, but I helpfully added in Taren: "Too much profanity aether." Using the Taren word for 'profanity' – I still don't know suitable Taren swear words.

The even longer pause after this gave me an opportunity to fall most of the ways back to sleep, and when she did speak, asking if I thought I needed to go to medical I didn't respond until she repeated herself. And then with more unhelpful English: "No more fucking tests." But then I woke up a bit more and managed to stick to Taren to say: "Sorry, tired. Is leaving earlier or something?"

"No, we were just going to take you over the ship beforehand, but that can keep. I'll send someone with breakfast for you a zelkasse before we're due out. Go back to sleep."

I seem to have said: "Margle margle," back at her, and have no idea what I was trying to say. When my alarm went off I didn't feel much better, but stumbled into the shower and put it on full-force icy, and was trying to do something with my hair when Lohn and Mara showed up with soup and chewy black bread and a hot, sweet milky drink.

"Nice circles," Lohn said, flicking my cheek. "There's plenty of time to get to the hangar, so don't feel rushed."

"How long flight Muina?"

"Nearly a kasse, if you take into account all the pre-flight fussing and actually getting to the gate and deep-space, and then we have perhaps another kasse getting from the gate point to your village. Maze was planning to use the time for a briefing, but I suspect he'd rather you slept than listened at this point. He'll email you an outline." Lohn grinned, stretching himself out on one of my couches. "I wish I could hear whatever he's saying to Research."

"Three different teams were working with you, two specifically on the aether effect," Mara said. "It had become something of a competition between them. And since Muina expeditions are considered so dangerous, they appear to have felt they should do as much as they could in case they didn't have a chance to test you further."

At that point I only had a vague impression that I'd somehow been swearing at Zee, and asked: "Has First Squad been Muina before?" while I looked back at whatever I'd been saying to her.

"Just once. Even though the Setari have a far better chance of survival than any of the previous expeditions, at the same time we've been considered too valuable to risk. Knowing about the presence of aether is a major step toward understanding at least a few of our losses." Mara shook her head. "It's still a gamble though, and since half the reason we're going is to observe how the planet reacts to you, it really would help if you were more than barely conscious. There'll be some revision of how you're assigned in future to inject some continuity and common sense."

"Don't know why tired," I said. "Sleep all yesterday, should be too awake now." But everything seemed a lot of effort, including trying to speak in the wrong language, so I concentrated on eating and then trying to get my hair less tangled. Lohn chattered along blithely, but I can see in retrospect that he was watching me closely.

We headed down in plenty of time, arriving maybe twenty minutes before the marked boarding time, but I wasn't the least surprised to see a lot of people already there, if not yet on board. Parts of Third, Fourth and Seventh Squad, for once not all standing apart in their own little groups. The ship was either the same or very similar to the one I'd first seen on Muina, with a big boarding ramp lowered, and a bunch of greensuits fussing about.

Eeli from Third bounced over as soon as she saw me, ecstatically happy and enthused about the excursion. I really wasn't equal to dealing with her, the stream of comment and questions washing over me as just noise, and it was only when she paused and Mara said "I'd like to hear that too," that I had any chance of catching up. She'd been fascinated by what I'd said in the Pillar and wanted to hear the rest of the poem.

"After mission?" I offered. "Will try work out translation."

Eeli mainly wanted to hear it in English, apparently, because she wanted to 'feel' it with Symbol Sight, but was satisfied with a promise to recite it on the trip back. Given I was having trouble remembering my own name, multi-stanza poetry in any language just wasn't going to happen. But Lohn and Mara rescued me from further enthusiasm and took me onto the ship, which was called the *Litara*, only to deliver me up as a sacrifice to Ista Tremmar.

I don't mind Ista Tremmar. She's pretty strict, but nice enough, and not one of the people who had been doing experiments on me. Not lately anyway. She gave me a quick, thorough exam, asking lots of questions about how much I'd been sleeping and when, and what I'd been eating and doing and whether I dreamed after passing out during the aether experiments or felt strange or bothered on days when there wasn't aether experiments.

When Maze arrived I was saying, maybe a bit shortly, that no I didn't think I was addicted to aether.

"Not for want of opportunity it seems," he said. "What's your verdict, Ista?"

"Beyond straightforward exhaustion, and perhaps some mild anaemia, I've found nothing of note. The best I can suggest from Harl and Luar's early results, is that the aether is acting as a stimulant." She turned back to me. "When you lose consciousness under the influence of the aether, your brain activity monitor doesn't show any of the patterns of sleep. Better considered a type of paralysis, perhaps, and though I don't see any record of an energy expenditure analysis being performed, I'd be willing to bet it's more than an 'at rest' state. In the previous tests, you've had the rest of the day for the aether to wear off, and have slept normally. Yesterday would have represented a massive overdose of stimulant, on top of several days of steady exposure. Your system, although not apparently negatively effected by aether, needed to rid itself of the aether's effect before you could sleep, and then of course you crashed quite severely." She switched back to Maze. "I don't see any reason not to go ahead. I'll re-examine her after she's rested, but consider her cleared for duty."

"And even on schedule," Maze said and when Ista Tremmar left looked at me a long moment, then said: "This won't be allowed to happen again, but I will ask that you speak to one of us if you're being pushed unreasonably." He didn't give me a chance to respond, just started walking, gesturing for me to follow. "The only thing I had meant to check, before this happened, was to confirm that you had seen an entrance below the central amphitheatre, but hadn't ventured into it."

"Too dark," I said, shrugging.

"Did you have any sense of threat from it, or the amphitheatre in particular?"

"Amphitheatre where all cats live," I said, pausing in the entrance of a room with the tiered pod-seat things I remembered from my first trip. First and Third Squad were sitting about sideways on the seats with the covers up. "Super feral unfriendly cats. Don't have to worry about petting them."

"I know," Maze said, and gave me one of his awesome smiles. "You won't make the same mistake twice. Get some rest now."

There were only the two chairs still empty, in the corner on our left. I picked the upper tier one, smiling at Zee across the way, and then squirming as the chair began moulding itself around me. I was too tired to care much about anything else, not even that Taarel was watching from the opposite corner. Maze closed the cover of my seat as soon as I lay down, and I pretty much passed out instantly.

Zee woke me up with another override channel request. "Human yet?"

"Maybe half." I started to sit up and almost whacked my head on the seat cover, then finished the movement as Zee opened it.

"Back to medical. I know you're looking forward to that."

"Zee's turn be comedian." I did feel better, though. Groggy, but no longer like I was being sucked down into a black pit. Ista Tremmar looked me over, told me I had to eat a high-energy, high-protein diet until further notice, and pointed the way to the nearest bathroom. Washing my face helped, and Zee nodded approval when I came out.

"Next stop, a little food. We'll be landing in about twelve joden. Read Maze's mission outline first, and let me know if you have any questions."

There's a hundred joden in a kasse, so that was a little over twenty minutes. I just nodded. I was feeling placid, really wanting another day or two of sleep, but willing to go along with whatever was asked of me so long as it didn't require too much thought. I read Maze's email, and Zee's from early that morning about taking a tour of the ship. It really is a big ship, with all those little 'pods' used when travelling through the gate, enough to cover a sizeable greensuit and greysuit complement. There's the infirmary and a kitchen and canteen and laboratories and assembly areas.

The mission was pretty basic. All four squads would go ashore in my town, split into two groups and do an initial reconnoitre and check the drones. I would be with First and Third Squad, answering any questions it occurred to them to ask me, and their Sight talents would be paying a lot of attention to whether there was an unusual reaction from the places around me.

They were very interested in the amphitheatre, but also wary of it since the aether had drained there, so it would be part two of the outing. We'd all meet up there and poke our nose cautiously underneath and see whether anything bit it off. In other words, the mission outline was "wander around looking for anything interesting, try not to get killed".

Four squads makes for a lot of people in the mission channel, along with two non-Setari people staying on the *Litara*, whose names were Kensan and Tehara. And me. Greensuits ferried us ashore using the hovering sled things before returning to the ship, and I wondered vaguely why they didn't leave any for us to escape with as I followed Ketzaren off onto the rocky bank.

It was the same spot I'd been picked up from – it seemed like an eternity ago – and since Sonn was standing right next to me I caught her eye and said: "Full circle," but though I think she understood what I meant she was being all serious and didn't respond.

Ferus, though, was a different kettle of fish. "What was it you were cooking here?" he asked, nodding at the faint remains of my fires and the three massive flat bowls. "I've often wondered if you could possibly eat that much."

"Boiling wool," I said, shrugging. "Clean it, make blanket." Come to think of it, I don't think I actually *cooked* anything the entire time I was on Muina. I never managed to catch any fish, or find any eggs. Survivor Cass was barely making a passing grade.

It was colder than it had been when I'd been living there. Autumn-ish, with a sharp wind blowing over the lake which made me gladder than ever that I'd been rescued. If the town has a proper European-type Winter, I would not only have needed a whole lot more wool, I'd be facing some real food challenges.

I've written all of this entry so far without mentioning Ruuel, mainly because I hadn't seen much of him. But he was just a little way down the shore from me then, and said: "No sense of threat," and sometimes I wonder if he goes around deliberately striking dramatic poses, because whenever I let myself look at him he seems to be being particularly photogenic. Though I guess gazing intently into the distance is part of his job description.

"We'll take the half to the left," Maze said. "Be vocal."

I was glad the squads were divided the way they had been. Not so much for controlling my urge to gaze at Ruuel, since I'm more or less managing that, but because that shot Forel from Seventh Squad had taken at Zan was a good way to get me to distrust her totally. Other than looking even more cat-that-got-the-cream than usual, she was being very correct, but I was happy to be with First Squad and Third Squad.

Particularly because Eeli was very fun to watch, so overjoyed at her first time on Muina that she practically vibrated. Occasionally a little comment would burble out, but mostly she was just eyes everywhere. Once, Taarel touched her shoulder and gave her a little smile and she settled down a bit. We walked about the town, not seeing anything other than small abandoned town. Sefen, Third's strongest Place Sight talent, could see only a faint after-image of aether, just a haziness.

I spent the time reminiscing, working on a translation of "Do Not Go Gentle" for later, and wondering if Ruuel was annoyed with himself for not having seen anything significant about this town when they chased the Ddura here.

Maze's 'be vocal' apparently meant to communicate a lot as we explored, but I only heard Forel, Auron and Halla say anything from the other group. Eventually Maze told everyone to return to the shore to collect the new drones they'd left there, and head toward the amphitheatre.

The drone left by greensuits before the last moonfall had exploded. They'd been expecting this, since it wasn't transmitting, but spent a small age doing examinations and taking readings and putting another drone in its place. I watched the cats, which had all retreated to the far side of the amphitheatre and were watching us back, tremendously annoyed.

While Third Squad messed with the remains of the drone, Fourth and Seventh Squad took me down to examine the extra-big central circle. Even enhanced, none of them could make out anything more from it than an after-image of the aether. Having me stand in the middle made no difference.

"Should we clear these animals out?" Tsennan asked.

At the time I just thought he was a gung-ho idiot, and only glanced at him as Sonn straightforwardly said: "No threat." It's only thanks to my ever-present log that a later review gave me a peripheral view of Forel shifting to watch me beforehand. They were seeing if they could get a rise out of me because of Ghost. My log also showed Ruuel turn his head in Forel's direction, but he didn't react otherwise. Still, if I was her I wouldn't play petty games in front of Sight talents. Particularly since she seems pretty keen on making herself look good in front of that particular Sight talent.

The four squad captains on this trip were a soap opera in the making. Forel seems to want to impress Ruuel. Ruuel, well, I don't know for sure, but he seems to spend an awful lot of time with Taarel. I'm trying to pretend that doesn't really mean anything. Taarel, at least that one time while we were out in the city, seems intense about Maze. And Maze isn't playing romance any more.

Not having seen this at the time, I just shrugged off the whole thing and went back to thinking about poetry translations and the embarrassment involved in walking around my town with an escort of twenty-four psychic space ninjas who all seemed to think far more was going to happen than I did. I can't say I ever held great expectations for the outing, given that I'd lived there for a month, and the Setari had already gone over the place, if only casually. I wasn't the least surprised when we all went down underneath the amphitheatre and found no monsters, just a short white corridor which curved down to an empty circular room with a round, thigh-high platform in the middle. I was pondering the less-than-fun prospect of returning to do this again, except with me probably having to get drunk on aether again, when Sefen from Third looked across at Ruuel and said: "I don't even begin to understand what I'm seeing here."

"It feels like a gate," Taarel said. "But–"

"No, not a gate." Ruuel moved to my left and touched my arm, frowning. "Far more complex. The Ena is tangible here."

Maze, who had been toting one of the replacement drones about with Telekinesis, lowered it to the ground by the outer wall. "We did expect to find an outlet for the aether, after all." He checked that the drone was stable and turned it on, verifying with the *Litara* that the ship was receiving the drone's transmission. "If it's some sort of device in addition to that, what's your evaluation of function?"

There was a bit of shifting about, as the rest of the Place and Symbol Sight talents took the opportunity to enhance themselves and view the platform from different angles. Maze was running scans with the drone. To me it looked like nothing more than a platform: there were even steps up one side.

"Communication," Ruuel said eventually, and there were a few hesitant nods of agreement.

"Getting an aether reading from it," Maze commented, then said over the interface: "Orders?"

The bluesuit in charge, Tehara, said: "Take contact readings, but no more until we return. Analysis of the scans taken in the interim may give us a better idea of how to approach it."

Between them the two Sight squads had four Place Sight talents. "Go unenhanced, Sefen," Taarel said. "We're still not entirely certain if there is any distortion in play for enhanced Sights."

He nodded while the other three – Ruuel, Halla and Marana – made their gloves flow back into the sleeves of their suits. Place Sight talents often go about fully gloved, since touching an object can give them a deeper reading, like when Ruuel was handling my diary back in medical. I've seen enough of *The Hidden War* now to know that Place Sight talents have a great deal of difficulty with the information they can sense, and avoid accidentally touching people and objects. The actor on the show is always being fraught and sensitive and locked down.

Marana, a short but muscular girl from Third Squad, was first to try, but drew her hand back immediately. "Aether effect," she said, frowning.

Halla and Ruuel both tried, but you could see it was hurting them just pressing their fingers lightly against the stone surface and they quickly stopped.

"Try nullifying the negative effects with Devlin while reading," Taarel suggested, but then she – everyone with Combat Sight – went on alert, saying: "Threat," out loud.

Most of them stepped back away from the platform, creating the nanoliquid blades from their suits. I stepped back as well, aware of Ketzaren and Alay shifting to flank me, and then covered my ears at the sound which followed. Whale song has nothing on it.

"Approaching rapidly," Maze said, fortunately in a pause in the noise. "Overwhelming threat. Get Devlin out of here."

Ketzaren started to move, but Ruuel was faster. He didn't have time to be careful, just grabbed my wrist and yanked me forward, pressing my hand down on the platform. The noise changed, just as loud, but a different pitch, and everyone reacted as if they'd missed being bitten by a shark. Ruuel said something, eyes gone all narrow and extra-black, and I didn't even try and raise my voice to respond, saying: "Can't hear you over Ddura," even as I realised that I was the only one acting like I'd been trapped in a belltower at the wrong moment.

"It's a communication device," came in text through the interface. "Communicate."

The logs attached to the mission report have twenty different views of the look I gave him in response. An "Are you high?" caption would fit it well. I was actually thinking "In whale song?" But what was I going to do? Say no? Especially since everyone was acting as if the shark was circling for another run.

Being suddenly expected to do something instead of standing around was disconcerting to the max. I bought some time closing my eyes and trying to sort out what I was hearing. The Ddura noise was so drawn out and huge it was hard to encompass it. But I was sure it wasn't words, not anything I had a chance of recognising. It was repeating the same long 'hhhhuuuuuuuuuuuuaaaaaaaaaaaa' over and over. It felt like a question. The Ddura had stopped attacking when I touched the platform and was asking me something. So I tried to guess what an artificially created aurora cloud built to kill monsters would ask someone who showed up and tried to talk to it.

As always it sounded sad, mournful. I had no idea if it really was, or if it that was its noise for growling boisterously, but the idea led to one obvious possibility: everyone on the planet had left. If I thought of it as a big (huge-mungous) dog which had been bred to protect the Muinans, and then abandoned, then it would be all where is everyone, what should I do, I'm so lonely, please love me. Sheer guesswork, but treating it like a dog was the only thing I could think of in the middle of all that noise.

Since the noise was apparently in my head, I didn't bother trying to speak, just started thinking over and over: "Shut up! Shut up! Be quiet! Shut up! Quiet! Quiet!"

To my eternal surprise it tapered off, making a brief eager hhhhhaaaaaaa sound. "Good Ddura," I thought, feeling mildly idiotic. "Good Ddura. Be quiet. Good Ddura."

I opened my eyes, trying to think while my head recovered from its noise-pounding, and looking across at the Setari on the far side of the platform, who were watching me intently. Immediately the Ddura made a hhhhiiiiiiiiiiii noise, not nearly so loud, but all anxious and fretful and then, "mmmnnnnnnnnnnnnnnnnnnnnnnnnnnn".

"Threat rising," Maze said, tersely.

"Stop!" I thought. "Down. Friends! Friends!"

It made the hhhiiiiiiii noise again. It wanted to protect me, I think. And that was the problem: it didn't recognise the Tarens, it thought they were the enemy the same way the aether did. And it's pretty hard to convince a dog that the scary strangers all poised to attack are friends.

Keeping my right hand on the platform, I reached to the left. Ruuel had let go of me – I later found some nice bruises where he'd grabbed me – so I took his wrist and pressed his hand to the platform, keeping hold the same way I had Selkie during my aether testing. "Friend," I thought, then carefully let go of Ruuel, watching him wince as the aether in the platform immediately began reacting to him.

"Friend," I thought, but was getting the hhhiiii noise again. "Friend," I repeated, putting a lot of command into it. "This is a Muinan. He belongs here. This is his home. He belongs."

I felt something, not from the Ddura, but the platform itself seemed to go icy and slick beneath my hand and then settle down. Ruuel straightened, eyes opening very wide, and he said: "It's not reject–" but then the Ddura started going "Hhhhhhhhhhaaaaaaaaa!!!!!!!! Hhhhhhhhhhaaaaaaaaa!!!!!!!! Hhhhhhhhhhaaaaaaaaa!!!!!!!!!" so loudly I swear every blood vessel in my head considered popping. Ruuel didn't act like he could hear it, but he had both hands pressed to the platform and was talking, eyes still all wide and surprised.

"Shut up, shut up, shut up, shut up!" I thought over and over at the Ddura and it quieted down a little, but kept going hhhhhaaaaaaa! in this mountainous burble. A lot happier about Ruuel than it had been me.

"Everyone put hand," I said out loud, not even able to hear myself speak. One thing about Setari discipline is they're quick to obey a command. According to the logs, Maze said: "Do it," and everyone did, despite the pain it caused.

"These are Muinans," I thought, to the Ddura or the platform or both. "They belong here. This is their home. They belong."

The Ddura exploded into hysteria – it really did behave a lot like an abandoned dog – and I had to resort to this kind of mental shriek in return: "SHUT UP!!!!" which startled it into pausing. "Bad Ddura. Be quiet. Be quiet. Good Ddura. Yes.

Quiet. Okay. Good Ddura, you can protect the Muinans, can't you? That's a good Ddura. Protect the Muinans." I paused, then looked over at the drone on the far side of the room. "These drones belong to the Muinans. Protect the drones. Good Ddura." I tried mentally picturing the *Litara* as well, but my head was pounding like anything, so have no idea if it was any use going on about: "This is a Muinan ship. Protect the ships. Good Ddura."

It started doing the hhhhhaaaaaaa thing again, far more interested in the Setari it could sense touching the platform than anything I was saying to it, so I sighed and gave up, rubbing my temples instead.

Ketzaren took my arm. "Do you need to sit down?"

"Need Ddura shut up. So loud."

It seemed that I was still the only one who could hear it, which I considered very unfair. A lot of the Setari were looking shell-shocked, fingering the platform cautiously. Eeli was crying in a happy, overwhelmed kind of way.

"First, return Devlin to the *Litara*," said Hara. "Third, Fourth, Seventh, finish your contact readings and then return."

I didn't need any encouragement, coming close to dragging Ketzaren out of the room. Back in the amphitheatre, the only thing I noticed was that the cats had all gone. First moved into formation around me, though Ketzaren stayed letting me lean on her. I wasn't in a falling-down state, but my head was pounding so incredibly that it was hard to concentrate on where I was walking. I ignored everything they said to me, since the Ddura was still enormously loud all the way through the town, calming down only a little. The greensuits were waiting for us and of course I was taken straight back to medical, but for once I didn't care because I really wanted some painkillers. I'd dropped out of the mission channel as soon as I was on the sled, and really wanted quiet and dark.

"I'm accessing your log, Caszandra," Maze said, while Ista Tremmar unkindly made me sit through a scan before even thinking about giving me drugs. I watched his face, and was meanly pleased to see him start and grimace.

"Loud," I said. I could still hear the damn thing, all the way out on the lake, but fortunately fairly dimmed by then. He nodded but didn't respond, watching the log presumably with the sound lowered while Ista Tremmar finished her scan and finally consented to fill me up to the eyeballs with painkillers. She said I could go so long as I drank a lot of liquid and lay down, which was exactly what I wanted to do. Maze, face all abstract, led me back to the canteen, and I found the rest of First Squad waiting, a meal already set out, though they were only picking at theirs. I think they were listening to my log as well, from the way they kept almost-wincing. My thoughts weren't recorded, so it was all Ddura-noise.

"Can you describe what happened from your point of view?" Maze asked, while I drank down a lot of cold, tingly drink.

"Ddura thought you were Ionoth, think," I said, wishing the painkillers would work quicker. "Didn't understand what it was saying, but guess from tone of noises. It like big pet, missing Muinans, kill anything it not recognise. I try tell Ddura that Ruuel was a Muinan, and the platform did something, and then the Ddura realise Ruuel not an Ionoth and get all happy. And even louder. Is Ddura thing been making ships explode?"

"That's been brought up as a possibility in the past." Maze shook his head. "It was certainly approaching with intent to kill. When you touched the platform, it withheld the attack, but was still clearly hostile to us. And then very strongly the opposite. The Place Sights could feel something of its emotions through the platform, once it stopped reacting against them."

"It knew I not Muinan," I said, thoughtfully. "Much happier about Setari, once stopped thinking you Ionoth. But it was platform which changed way reacted to you."

"Ruuel is using an analogy of security clearance. The device allowed you, who for some reason have clearance, to identify us to the 'system'."

"Our turn to have aether tests now," Lohn said. He had his arm around Mara, which was the first time I'd seen them publicly behave like a couple. I think everyone was pretty overwhelmed.

"My turn laugh when Lohn say silly things." I smiled, then sighed and rubbed my temple. "I try tell it that should protect drones and ships and things, but don't think it listen. Too busy being happy. What happen next?"

Maze lifted one shoulder. "We exceeded the mission brief by an order of magnitude. The result is very good, but completely beyond what we were expecting or had planned for. I don't know if it will delay or bring forward the proposed second trip."

"What happens next is you catch up on your rest," Zee said, squeezing my shoulder. "This is a large development, but in the short term there's a two kasse journey back to base. And then at minimum a day of argument, tests and analysis."

"Still huge changes," Lohn said. "We mightn't have solved the overall problem, but our progress on Muina has been entirely stifled by this...security clearance issue."

"The Ddura doesn't explain all of the deaths," Alay pointed out.

"But most of them," Ketzaren said. "Almost certainly most of them, if it's what has been causing ships to explode. Even massives are minor compared to that, particularly when KOTIS can use weaponry without risk to structures. My guess is that there'll be an attempt to establish a serious foothold around this town of yours. And from there we'll search for information about the Muinans of the past, and the way the Pillars were constructed."

"One thing Lantaren not know but," I said. "How *their* security clearance wiped? They understood all that, they made Ddura. They supposed to be more powerful psychic than Setari. And it kill them. What happen, built settlement here, then security clearance wipe again?"

"Very good point." Maze had been playing with his food, and I was willing to bet he'd been thinking over the same possibility. "I certainly won't be recommending any rush."

"Could Setari fight Ddura?"

"Not a chance." Zee glanced at Maze, then repeated. "Not a chance."

"It's the first time we've been close enough to one to get some estimate of what level we'd face," Maze said. "It's a massive made from pure energy which, it seems, can attack in real-space from near-space. I am very glad not to have had to try. And on that note, go lie down. I don't want to see you again until you've stopped looking like you've been stepped on."

Zee came with me, waiting while I hit the bathroom and then seeing me settled back in my chair-pod.

"You're upset about something," she said, one hand on the pod's lid. "More than just the headache."

"Didn't want become more important," I said. If I'm the only one who can give people security clearance, no-one here will ever be willing to let me leave.

Zee gave me an unexpectedly amused look. "I thought it was something like that. Just consider the alternative, if you hadn't been able to stop it." She gestured for me to lie down, adding: "You can make the cover opaque, if the light bothers you. Get some sleep."

It was a fair point. We would have all died. Zee definitely knows how to quash signs of self-pity.

I figured out how to make the cover opaque, but dozed more than slept until after we'd taken off because the Ddura just wouldn't shut up, though it calmed down a lot. Even worse would have been if everyone had died *except* for me. I don't know if I would have been able to cope with that. As it is, I'm not sure that I can cope with what I did totally by accident. Every time I try and think through the consequences of that 'security clearance' my mind runs away.

I must have needed more sleep than I realised, since when Zee woke me up again we were back on Tare. And then it was more scans in medical, and a long attempt to describe exactly what I'd done and thought after I touched the platform. My sleep patterns are totally messed up, but until I have something scheduled, I guess it doesn't matter what shift I'm awake during. Other than the medical scans, I've stayed in my room, just writing and trying not to think of everyone dropping dead in front of me because it hadn't occurred to me to try touching the platform.

Change

Mara came by to tell me the results of the scans on the Setari who were on the Muina mission. Aether has the same effect on them now that it does on me. Just those four squads, though. It still attacks anyone who doesn't have 'security clearance'.

"How are big arguments going?"

"Lively. I doubt they'll change the scheduling of the next mission, but there's a good chance they'll alter the numbers. It's all very well to talk of taking things slowly, but whoever says that also fully expects that they'll be included." She pulled a face. "And that's only in KOTIS. It will be impossible to keep this from going public for long, and then we'll be factoring in a thousand special interest groups and the media. Muina is such an emotive issue."

"Can't imagine Tarens actually living Muina. Never go outside."

"A huge adjustment," she agreed, kicking me lightly for the teasing. "Though I agree that some of those insisting on joining the next mission are going to find all that horizon a challenge. The Setari have the benefit of environment training, but other parts of KOTIS aren't nearly so prepared."

"Looked like the leaves were turning. Will be very pretty."

She didn't know what I meant, and we spoke for a while about Autumn and Winter – Tare doesn't seem to have seasons beyond stormy and really stormy – and then about the potential pressure on the Setari of trying to work on two different planets. All of the squads which went to Muina yesterday are on rotation tomorrow, and the next day is the start of the extended mission. Mara warned me that while Third and/or Fourth will certainly be sent, they're likely to use other squads to support them.

"Taarel and Ruuel are both people you can be confident with. If something happens that worries you or makes you uncomfortable, overcome this tendency to keep it to yourself. Object if there's things you don't want to do."

At that particular moment I was watching Ghost walk across the room behind Mara, and hoping she didn't turn around. I wonder what she made of my expression.

"Will object if think will make difference," I said, reasonably enough. I didn't want to have a needle in my spine, after all, but was sure that if I'd objected it would have meant being stuck in medical even longer until someone came and explained to me that it was important. "Would you live on Muina, if able?"

She didn't answer immediately, then shrugged. "I find it very hard to picture being able to. But it's certainly nice to know it might one day be an option."

Thursday, March 20

Interlude

Today I finally tracked down a place where I could buy a new diary: paper products do exist on this world, they're just rare. It was amazingly expensive, and won't be delivered before I leave for Muina tomorrow, but I think I've enough book left to last. I'm taking this one with me, since we're 'packing' for an extended stay. I'm bringing my old school backpack, which amuses me a lot.

They've assigned the squads: Second, Third, Fourth and Eighth. So no new squads, and none of the ones I really don't feel comfortable with. I wish First was going though. Who am I going to chat with?

What happens this trip is incredibly important to me. I really need for it to be possible for someone else to give people security clearance.

Friday, March 21

Poetry, Death

I succeeded in being well-rested and on time for today's mission. It's scheduled to last three days and we're currently about to go through the big gate into deep-space. Eeli took care of any initial uncertainty I had by glomming on to me the second I showed up and taking me on a tour of the *Litara*, though by this time the only areas I hadn't seen were the flight deck, the research labs, and the 'airport lounge' meeting areas.

There was still some time before take-off by the time she brought me back to the pods, but most of Second and Third

Squad were already sitting waiting. You have to stay in your
pod for take-off and landing, and when you go through the
gate to deep-space.

"Are you able to tell me the rest of the poem now?" Eeli
asked, as soon as I'd sat sideways on my seat. I could have
wished she'd not waited till we had an audience, but at least it
was only two squads.

"Guess. Is poem written by man name Dylan Thomas.
Wrote for his father who was dying." I felt marvellously
uncomfortable, adding: "My voice really not suited to this,"
but making an effort to put some feeling into it. I only know
the poem because it was one of the few that we'd had to read
in Eng-lit which I didn't outright hate. I certainly don't go
round reciting at the drop of a hat.

I got through it by looking only at Eeli, but my face felt
very red at the end. "That what wanted?" I asked, feeling
even worse when I looked around and saw that I had all the
captains watching me from the far door, along with those
who'd been in the room when I started.

Eeli was enthralled, and said: "You sounded totally
different! Like a different person!"

Annoyed, I told her: "Can actually speak own language,
after all."

"But what does it mean?" Nils from Second asked,
watching from the pod directly opposite. "A part of that was
what you said in the Pillar, right?"

"Yes. Translation very bad, sorry." I read off the
translation I'd been working on, wishing the captains would go
away. If that gets put in the mission report I'll be extremely
peeved.

"I got quite a lot of it!" Eeli said, excited. She cast a
beaming look over at Taarel, like a kid who passed a hard
test, then back at me. "Thank you for telling me the rest. It's
so sad and at the same time beautiful, isn't it?"

I just smiled weakly at that, and was glad that the
command came to prepare for launch. And I wrote this up
while they did lots of prep-checks and then took off and now
we're heading toward the interplanetary gate which, for the
first time in four trips, I might actually be awake for.

Today's Assignment

The gate was dull. You can't properly see it from real-space, and once you're in deep-space there's just whiteness.

It took maybe twenty-five minutes to reach the exit to Muina, and once we were through Grif – Grif Regan, the Second Squad captain – briefed us for the first part of the mission. Unsurprisingly this involves going back to my town, and the Setari taking me down to visit the communication platform. They're going to see whether anyone but me can give people security clearance (I am hoping so hard) and then, whatever the case, they're going to clear everyone on board, offload a heap of equipment and set up a camp just outside town, keeping anything explodable separate. Then the *Litara* is going to leave us here. After that the Setari are going to explore more, including in the near-space, while the greensuits guard the greysuits as they analyse everything they can get their hands on. There's also a few non-KOTIS scientists of an archaeological extraction, brought in to begin the enormous task of recovering Muina's history.

Of first importance is the Ddura, of course, and whether it can be made to not blow up equipment, or if equipment can be given security clearance.

I think I'll need earplugs for the inside of my brain.

Saturday, March 22

Reprieve

The Ena manipulation talents can give people security clearance! I'm so happy. I didn't even hide my relief when we were on mission, and Taarel gave me the same sort of smile she gives Eeli, which was both nice and a little annoying, since she treats Eeli like an over-eager kid.

The Ddura didn't show up immediately, and we had finished clearing the ship's crew and were working on all the people who were going to be left here for the mission, before my ear-drums were blasted. It was all hhhaaa and hhhhiiiii at the same time, because there were lots of people it recognised as Muinans and lots that it thought were Ionoth, and it came charging up in this huge hurry to kill all the evil non-Muinans threatening its precious people.

The Ddura is really kind of stupid.

I had to keep telling it to stop ('sit!') over and over until everyone was given clearance. Then I had another shot at telling it not to make the things belonging to the Muinans explode, since all the drones from the last expedition had been exploded. Just picturing the drones and the ship didn't seem to mean anything to it, even when I could get it to pay any attention to me, so we tried putting a new drone right on the platform and tried giving it 'security clearance' and that may perhaps have worked, they're not really sure. The Ddura stopped treating it as a threat, anyway, so we did that for all the drones and any other largish bits of equipment we could get into the room. Then it was time for me to go visit medical on the ship just before it left, since the best equipment was there, and then back to shore, all drugged up to rest on a cot in the temporary medical tent while they started the business of setting up camp. I waited to watch the ship leave before lying down.

And now it's the middle of the night. Fortunately Grif had sent me a summary of the camp arrangements, or I would have had to go stumbling about looking for the portaloo tents. One of the greensuits on guard took pity on me and showed me how to get to the food which had been stored.

I'm going to try and go back to sleep now that I've written this. At least the Ddura shut up eventually. I don't much like spending all my time in uniform, either.

Dawn

When I gave up on sleep this morning there was a mist rising off the lake in the pre-dawn dark. The camp has been set up south of town and it's really impressive how much they've established in such a short time: mess hall, infirmary, sleeping tents, a central command, research and working areas. Lots of canvas, but they'd brought a vat of their nanite building materials along and some 'real' buildings were starting to take shape. When the Tarens make camp, they don't do things by halves.

There were lights on in the command tent. The person in charge of the expedition is someone called Tsaile Staben, who I may or may not have been introduced to during the extreme-headache phase of yesterday, and one of the research tents was bustling with people who were obviously used to a different shift.

There's nearly a hundred people here. I had no idea the mission was that large. Now that everyone has been cleared by the platform, the Setari are support on this mission, not the main focus. The greensuits are taking care of camp security, with the Setari acting as a kind of advanced warning system thanks to Combat Sight. My role's been reduced to trying to communicate with the Ddura, which is no problem right now since it seems that the Ddura has recovered from its excitement and gone away. Now that everyone has the same reaction to aether, I don't even have to worry about tomorrow's moonfall.

I was feeling oppressed and restless – I'd had way too much sleep – and decided to go down to the lake. There was a greensuit posted on the lakeside edge of the camp, but I got past her just by nodding as I walked by, like no-one would think of objecting to me going anywhere by myself. It's not as if the lake was very far away: the guard would have been within sight. It was incredibly quiet, just a few birds starting to think about it maybe being dawn, and so long as I kept facing the lake it felt like I was alone.

Before too long a tiny clatter of rock warned me that wasn't true and I turned my head to see the leg of a person standing on the rock behind me, and a hand in fingerless Setari gloves. And that was enough to know it was Ruuel. It amazes me that I can recognise him from his hands. Since Ruuel moves like a cat, I guess he must have made the noise deliberately, to prevent me from shrieking and leaping in the lake out of shock. Heh – I can't help thinking what an epic fuss that would have made in the camp, though.

"Is there something further along the lake?" Ruuel asked, which was less of a lecture than I'd expected, but also warning that I'd been looking south a bit too speculatively. But then, who am I to overlook an opportunity when it walks up and presents itself to me?

"Show you if want," I said, looking up at him. "One of things I miss about here."

His eyes went that abstract way people get talking over the interface, and then he nodded. I was pretty surprised, and then doubtful since it didn't seem likely I was going to be able to walk along the lake with Ruuel without obsessing over the fact that I was walking along the lake with Ruuel. But it didn't really work out that way. I was super aware of him, of course, but it was a beautiful morning, cold and crisp, and barely light enough to see, so I had to concentrate on not breaking my ankle.

It was a twenty minute walk, and was just getting on for proper dawn by the time we arrived at a small, deep stream draining into the lake, about a third of the way to the river that I'd walked along originally. When we were in sight of it I murmured: "Have to be more quiet now," which was a fairly redundant thing to say to Ruuel.

I stopped at the cluster of rocks I'd used last time I was there, notable for the cairn of rocks I'd constructed on the tallest one, and made a sit down gesture at Ruuel. My goal was there, fortunately: I spotted them straight away and pointed and then just watched.

That's going to be a memory I'll keep forever, even without my log. Dawn, the water glinting ever brighter, the sky mixing pastels. Birds starting to call and sing as the mist dissipated. And the otters which live in that stream dancing in the water as they dug little crayfish out of the rocky bed. I only snuck a single look at Ruuel, and while I have no idea if he enjoyed any of that outing, he at least was watching the otters attentively. Maybe he was thinking of the best and most efficient ways to kill them.

And then the *Litara* showed up, which most effectively destroyed the mood. As spaceships go, I expect it's relatively quiet, but it sure can freak out the wildlife.

"Are called otters, on Earth," I said, standing up. "What is range interface transmission, when not on Tare?"

"About five times further than this, when there's a relay." He was watching the *Litara* rotating for a landing position out above the lake. "Without a relay, not quite this far."

We started walking back, not hurriedly, though the *Litara* was well ahead of what I'd thought was its scheduled return. I thought of quite a few things I felt like saying, but kept them to myself, and Ruuel disappeared with a nod when we got back to camp.

Spaceships are an even better wake-up call than shrieking Earthlings, so there were a ton of people up and about. I'm sitting in the mess hall writing this and eating an extended breakfast while I wait to find out what's going on.

Construction Project

The *Litara* had returned early because the research techs wanted to try out a simulated security pass. So back to the platform. The Ddura turns up reliably once someone starts fooling with the platform, but must have been at a fair distance this time because it took a while. The techs got impatient with me for that, like I have any control over what the thing does.

What does the Ddura think I am? I can hear it and I guess it can 'hear' me when I'm touching the platform, but it knows I'm not Muinan and when the Taren Muinans are around it's just not that interested in what I'm 'saying'. When it finally showed up this time, it reacted to the drone with the simulated security pass in a confused sort of way – anxious and uncertain but not hostile. It can tell there's something not right about it, but the fake pass makes it familiar enough that it doesn't attack. That made everyone happy, including me in a "I'd smile if my head stopped hurting" way. They're still cautious, but they think this means that the Ddura probably won't go exploding all the equipment, and they'll be able to get new visitors to the platform without having to worry about the Ddura killing them on the way. They brought with them two small 'shuttle' type aircraft and they've staked them out as bait. One has the fake pass and one doesn't. They're on the east side of town on the crests of two different hills, so everyone can enjoy the show if they explode.

I wish it meant I could go back to Tare (I nearly wrote 'home', and felt awful), but I'm stuck here at least until the end of the original mission, even though they're probably not going to involve me in the moonfall. I wouldn't mind so much, except they swapped out Second Squad for Fifth Squad.

I guess Kajal must be stable and not completely stupid if they made him a squad captain. Just because he's a prick and treats Zan and me as if we shouldn't exist doesn't mean he's not good at his job. He's still doing the completely not acknowledging my presence thing, which suits me well enough, and it's not really obvious since there's so many people here.

Third and Fourth have been off most of the day exploring the near-space and surrounding spaces; a task made easy by the Ddura's hunting. Fifth and Eighth are assigned to guard duty, split up in pairs around the entire camp, in case something shows up to attack. Fifth is on now and Eighth has night duty. Having Setari squads guarding in shifts seems a real waste of their abilities. You can sure as hell tell that's what Kajal thinks, anyway.

Tomorrow night is moonfall, and they're in a huge rush to set up before then. There's nowhere good to hide away from all the activity. Before Third headed out Taarel mentioned that I shouldn't leave the area of camp, so it doesn't look like I'll get away with another excursion. I spent the bulk of the day in the infirmary recovering from my Ddura headache and the afternoon sitting on a rock down at the shore wishing that if I'm not allowed to leave, everyone would be quieter. I'm not even allowed into the 'old town'.

Cloudy today, but then windy. It'll probably be clear for the moonfall tomorrow.

Sunday, March 23

Boom

One of the shuttles exploded last night.

The right one, fortunately, and I could hear the Ddura being all happy about it afterwards. Funny that people could be pleased that a perfectly good piece of equipment was destroyed. I was in the infirmary, having carefully hung around the medic's tent in the evening looking tired and headachy until Ista Leema, the settlement's main medical person, started running tests on me and kept me in for observation. I have an assigned 'bunk' in with the Setari, which I didn't mind when my neighbours were Second and Third Squad, but found less amusing when it involved Fifth Squad one row over. Even the prospect of perhaps seeing Ruuel asleep wasn't enough to outweigh my dislike of Kajal.

I was reading when the shuttle went boom, and in a bit of a mood, so pretended to be asleep when I heard the noise in case they wanted me to go talk to the Ddura. Headaches are making me less than cooperative. I was thinking that it was useful to be able to read books with my eyes closed when I remembered that the interface would also show them I was awake, if they looked.

Oh well. Now that they've confirmed that the fake security clearance will work for their machines, I'm pretty sure that I'll be sent back to Tare tomorrow. Less important again, thank everything. I can start thinking about cautious 'going home' experiments without feeling guilty.

Male Posturing

Late afternoon, and everyone's keyed up about the moonfall. It's been a good day for me, since it didn't involve a headache, just a couple of private attempts to see if I have a path-finding ability by trying to locate Ista Leema. Otherwise, I found a great spot where I could sit on the lakeshore and read: snugged down between two rocks, out of the wind and almost out of sight.

Eighth Squad, who had been asleep all morning, came down to the water's edge with Fourth Squad and practiced the martial art which is the basis of their close-combat. That was a lot of eye-candy for me, heh. In terms of fire power, Ruuel's one of the weakest of the Setari, but knowing his talent set I wasn't the least surprised that he seemed able to avoid the blows of anyone matching with him. Eighth's captain, Kanato, had him breathing hard though, which I greatly appreciated.

They'd kept a businesslike atmosphere during the training session. Ruuel was his usual tersely-efficient self, of course, and both captains only made suggestions for improving weaknesses, gave the occasional nod of approval, and then dismissed their squads. They were standing together talking when Kajal, trailed by Nise, strolled down to the grassy bit of bank they'd been using as a practice ground.

"Sticking with the easiest targets still, Ruuel?" he asked, that really rich voice making every word double-mocking. "Why not try a real challenge?"

Ruuel barely spared him a glance. "You're on duty, Kajal."

"Is the complete absence of threat here a real concern? These continuing excuses begin to smack of cowardice."

"Take it however you like." Total indifference.

Ruuel walked off, and though Kajal looked really pissed he didn't do anything about it. Drama falls flat. Doesn't surprise me in the least that Kajal's like that, though I'm not sure why Ruuel refuses to spar with him. I expect Kajal wouldn't care unless Ruuel had beaten him in the past. Who knows? One thing I've never been is competitive – I'm too lazy – and I don't really understand the people who are.

Monday, March 24

Machismo redux

Moonfall started out as a real non-event for me since I wasn't involved in it at all. The greysuits had set all sorts of instrumentation monitoring and scanning different parts of the village, particularly the rooftops, the amphitheatre and the platform.

Third Squad had been sent into the near-space to observe from there, which was considered the most dangerous facet of the experiments, so they'd sent Eighth Squad to support them. No-one was allowed in the town during the beginning of moonfall, and then they were going to send in a few test subjects and Fourth Squad. Theoretically Fourth Squad were going to avoid getting drunk, though I had my hopes up.

The moon rose late and I was tired of sitting around in the chill. But it was pretty to watch from a distance, and I was very glad that the night hadn't gone the way I'd expected it to when we set out on this mission: me getting extremely drunk while everyone watched. After a while I bored of the light show and sat at a table outside the mess tent reading until people started to trickle back; greysuits and greensuits, Third and Eighth Squad, and then a disappointingly sober Fourth.

All in all I don't think they learned anything momentous. Certainly not how the whole thing works. People started to drift off, Eighth heading out to take up their guard posts while Ruuel and Taarel did their usual stand together talking quietly and looking like they're very much on each other's wavelength. I was busy trying not to watch them, and also realising that I hadn't arranged an excuse to spend the night in the infirmary.

"You've managed to be awake all day," Taarel said to me, coming over as Ruuel started off. "Quite out of character."

"Trying to make habit of it," I said. Taarel somehow always makes me feel a bit young and embarrassed.

"Working with the night-day cycle here is very interesting. It makes it considerably more difficult to keep shifts."

I was looking at Taarel, and didn't see the start of it, just the way her eyes went wide. I turned because there was a scuffling noise behind me, and there was Kajal taking a kick at Ruuel, who simply leaned out of his way, and did the same again when Kajal aimed a blow to his face, before moving abruptly backward out of reach.

"Report to the infirmary, Kajal," he said. "You've inhaled too much aether."

"Fight, you cursed gelzz," Kajal spat. "Are you so afraid I'll prove the better?"

"I haven't the faintest interest in measuring myself against you." Ruuel looked and sounded supremely bored. "The only thing you're proving is your own insecurity."

Kajal went all out then. And he was fast, really good (in as much as I am feebly able to judge, which is not at all). Ruuel just kept moving out the way. Quite a few of the Setari and random green- and greysuits had noticed but kept back. Taarel looked irritated, which is unusual for her, but she didn't interfere. Finally, there was a blur too fast for me to follow and then Kajal was sailing through the air and twisted to a landing just in front of the tables. The grass is trampled muddy there, and he didn't come down too hard.

"Give up this game, Kajal," Ruuel said, his voice incredibly cutting. "I won't hold back if you try to play it again."

It was a pity Kajal was facing in my direction when he stood up. I saw the change in his face when he realised who I was. Taarel saw it too, and said: "Don't be an idiot," but it was too late; she wasn't quick enough to block him. His hand to my shoulder knocked me into the table and then he really was a blur.

Ruuel rolled with the blow to his face, not fast enough to avoid it altogether. Nor the kick to his stomach, the smash to his knee. And yet the second bout ended the same way, with Kajal sailing through the air and this time slamming hard into the ground in front of the tables. Ruuel walked over to him, and it was very easy to remember that the Setari were trained killers as he stood looking down at Kajal, face haughty as hell. But all he said was: "Infirmary," and walked off that way himself, limping.

I don't know what the fall-out from that's going to be. It's not like the greensuits came and marched Kajal away. Does aether effect count as enough of an excuse? I decided not to mention the really nice bruise on my arm where Kajal pushed me into the table, and this morning everyone was acting as if nothing had happened.

I'm just glad to be heading back to Tare. Eighth Squad have been left behind as guards, taking it in pairs since there's been no sign of any Ionoth attacking the settlement. They think the Ddura is 'based' there and thus keeps it far clearer than the rest of the planet. I'm listening to the faint change in the hum of the ship as we prepare for take-off and trying not to be too obvious in watching Third and Fourth Squad in their pods.

Ruuel has the *best* black eye.

Out of the box

We had a side-mission before we returned through the rift gate. I didn't find that out until we were on the way there and Taarel started the mission briefing. We were going to look over the second of the towns with 'circle roofs' which the satellite had found. I was assigned to Fourth Squad, who were going despite Ruuel's slight limp. Sefen from Third toted a drone which floated along behind him like a kite.

This town was on a river, not a lake, and the *Litara* didn't land, but sent us out in a small flyer-shuttle-thing and then, I guess, flew around in a circle. The town looked so similar. Almost the same plants, a similar layout, central amphitheatre, blockish houses. But at the same time, very different.

"Threat."

We were well away from the edge of the town, following the remains of a road in the process of being undermined by the river. I'd been looking doubtfully at the very large number of paw prints laid over each other, so wasn't particularly surprised. Sefen of Third indicated the first of them, standing well uphill. Muina's version of a wolf, perhaps, though it was more like a border collie than the pictures of wolves I've seen. Black and white, not long-haired, ears upright – a bit larger than border collies and not nearly so amiable-looking. Not snarling, but watching in an attentive way, and the Setari wouldn't be talking threat unless it was thinking about attacking us.

"More ahead," Ruuel said, glancing at Taarel.

"We're not here to clear," she said. "Respond to attacks."

That was an uncomfortable journey. The dogs didn't attack, but we kept seeing them on the tops of buildings and at the end of streets, watching, following. I was left with a strong impression of organisation and intelligence, and Auron and Ferus stuck very close to me. To my relief it looked like the dogs didn't like the amphitheatre. Since the main reason we were there was to check out the platform, the emptiness was a big advantage.

The platform room, other than suffering from a lot of ground grot, was just the same. The Setari took some touch readings, and set up the drone, and then the Ddura arrived. Completely hysterical.

"Different Ddura," I said, under all the Hhhhhaaaaa!-ing.

"In the ecstatic phase," Ruuel said, using text over the interface. They all kept talking in text after that, which I thought was nice of them. And better still that Fourth Squad took me back up top while Third finished the final tests. It was still horribly loud, but nothing like as painful as being in the same room as the platform.

There were a ring of the dogs at the upper tier of the amphitheatre, just watching. Stephen King had come to town. I tried to figure out which dog was the pack leader, but there were quite a few candidates.

One thing about communicating with text is it's only my grammar which sounds bad. I don't have to worry about my dreadful pronunciation and can write a lot before I transmit it.

When Third Squad came up to join us, I sent: "These maybe descendant domesticated working dogs. Similar type to species my planet. Very intelligent animal. Very strong herding instinct."

"How many of the animals on Muina resemble those of your world?" Ruuel asked.

"Hard to tell with birds, bugs. The sheep, the cats, these dogs. Domesticated animal. Otters, not domesticated animal, though did see once documentary people use them to fish. And the people, of course." I was tempted to ask what he thought of my idea that the Muinans had originally been Terrans, but decided I could live without that being on the mission log.

The dogs 'saw us off', totally like a tribe making sure strangers left their territory. That was their town, just as the first town belonged to the cats. Had belonged.

I was thinking about that a lot and watching scenery as we flew to the rift gate when Tsaile Staben sent me a channel request, a thing which surprised me since she was back at the first town and because bluesuits as a rule don't talk to me.

"Devlin," she said, when I opened the channel. "It is traditional for the person who discovers a location to name it. The town where you were located was provisionally named at your retrieval, but the new settlement now needs a label. What will it be?"

"Pandora." I didn't even have to think about it, just translated it into Muinan text.

"Recorded," she said, and closed the channel. Bluesuits make Ruuel look chatty. A few minutes later the new name popped up on the settlement's map, giving me a fine sense of power.

Eeli had left me alone for the start of the flight back – I'm pretty sure Taarel gave her a lecture about bombarding me with questions, especially when I'm in headache recovery mode – but not long after I spoke to Tsaile Staben she came up to the corner of the observation lounge area where I'd parked myself and asked how I was feeling.

"Is good," I said, smiling at her eager expression. She really is too sweet and funny. "Would go lie down if headache drug wasn't working."

She lit up. "I wanted to ask about the name of the settlement. Is Pandora the name of someone special to you?"

I laughed at that. "Don't know anyone name Pandora."

Ferus from Fourth strayed over. I never seem to have these conversations without an audience. "Do I get to guess too? Maybe it's the name of the place you live on your world?"

"Is creation myth from part of Earth called Greece," I said, suspecting Ferus of wanting to make a few entertaining suggestions. "Pandora was first woman, made by the gods. They gave her a box, told her she must look after it, but never open it. No-one ever seems to invent sensible gods. Pandora couldn't resist, lifted lid a tiny crack to peek into box. But lid burst open and all the bad things in the world came flying out – hate, misery, greed. Pandora frantically try and shut box, but too late. Pandora in tears, seeing way she wreck the world–" I broke off, because Eeli obviously had no trouble working out why I'd called the settlement Pandora and was looking incredibly hurt and upset. I shouldn't underestimate her. "Story not over," I said, patting her arm. "Pandora in tears, when she hear noise from box. Something still inside. A voice, pleading to be released, make her brave enough to open box again. The last thing in box is Hope, which is the thing which makes possible to endure all the bad things."

I smiled at her. "Is story of doing something irreversible. I unlock Muina. Bad things will come of that. But good things too. Point of name is that cannot be undone. Been feeling very small, thinking about that."

"What bad things?" Ferus asked, rubbing Eeli's shoulder.

I pulled a face. "Did you look at building they making there? Great big box. Tarens don't know how live with outside any more."

That made Eeli laugh, and surreptitiously wipe her eyes. "It's a right name, isn't it? One that fits."

"Thought so when Tsaile Staben asked me. Was thinking of those dogs, and the cats at first town, and other animals on this planet. For them, would be better if box stayed shut? Even though Seventh Squad make bad joke about killing them, the cats at Pandora won't be let stay at amphitheatre. They already starting move away because not like so many people where kittens are. That been their place for centuries. Feel sorry for them. But this world belong you. Not my place to say, no shouldn't be here."

I'm pretty sure the Tarens couldn't screw up Muina nearly half as badly as we've done to some parts of Earth. Though I have my doubts about them understanding the concept of balconies and a nice view any time soon.

Tuesday, March 25

The art of doing nothing much

A nice quiet day. Not even a medical exam after the one I had after the flight yesterday. I went swimming, and walked the torture stairs, but otherwise just lolled about being glad to be wearing something other than my uniform, and trying to magically transport myself into the bathroom. It's hard to work out just what it is I did to get to Earth.

I seem to have a rotation with First Squad tomorrow. I've missed them.

Wednesday, March 26

Unstable

Unstable rotations involve a lot of fussing over how long the gates are going to last. The spaces were flooded, which meant using the breathers and telling our nanosuits to be more like wetsuits. The first flooded space was a memory of trees, where sharp leaves whirled around like faceless fish and Lohn's enhanced Light talent came in handy because Fire is not a useful talent underwater, and you sure as hell wouldn't want to use Lightning even if First had that talent. After the aggressive leaves there was a big cavern filled with scaffolding around a monstrous Greek-style temple.

This was a space First Squad had only seen once before, one of a series which switched into this position. The Ionoth which was there was one they'd never encountered, a long, flat and frilly thing, like something you'd see on the Great Barrier Reef, but larger. It curled and wound its way through the scaffolding, trailing afterimages of itself.

Maze and Zee came back to the drowned forest space instead of signalling us through. "Kettara, come through with me. Remainder, hold here."

They both enhanced and went through. The brilliance of Lohn's Light wall lit up the gate, but then he returned through it, shaking his head. Maze stayed just in front of the gate, then lifted both of his hands. The scaffolding broke apart and dived toward the Ionoth until all I could see was a pin cushion of metal and a spreading darkish cloud of blood. Telekinesis is dangerous when there's things to pick up.

Everyone looked tired when we got back, and very wet and cold. That rotation had been a lot of swimming, and the leaves especially had been hard to deal with – Lohn hadn't been able to keep up with the swirling clouds and when they got close the Setari had to kill them with their suit weapons.

While we were being scanned for stickies Maze said: "News of Pandora has leaked."

"That took longer than I expected." Zee gazed abstractly into nothing for a moment, then said: "They're making the official announcement in response."

"Will news cause any problems?" I asked as we all headed for the showers. I find it funny to have a shower and have a conversation with six people at the same time, but the channels make it very easy to do.

"Not for us. The demands of people insisting they be taken to visit will cause other sections of KOTIS a few headaches, but they were really only holding off the announcement because they weren't completely certain the camp wouldn't meet similar disasters to the previous attempts." Zee paused. "Check Far Channel."

I didn't know what that was, but managed to find it just as Mara said: "Will they confirm?"

"Partially," Maze said. "It was inevitable details of Caszandra's existence would be known eventually, especially given the role she played on Muina. The factor which we knew would cause controversy is the relationship between Earth and Muina."

Which was exactly what was being discussed on Far Channel, a news and rumours service with attached forums. That Muina had been unlocked was the biggest news, but Far

Channel added that they'd learned that a stray working with the Setari had been pivotal. The news service itself didn't say much more than that, but the forums went far further. That the stray was from a parent world older than Muina, and possessed immense powers. That she was called Pandora, and could control the Ddura, had already located and destroyed one of the Pillars, and was teaching the Setari the secrets forgotten after the abandonment of Muina. Nine parts wild speculation, in other words.

"People will have strange idea of me," I said, after a short silence during which I'm sure everyone was reading the same interesting stories.

"Venerable Sage Caszandra," Lohn said, but added more seriously: "Some of this is a trifle vicious."

"No Heart Mind follower will embrace the idea that Muina is not our original home," Alay said. "I have to admit I find it strange myself. But you truly believe that, don't you Caszandra?"

"Earth has fossil record going back millions years," I said, coming out of my shower-room, still working on my hair. I've been considering cutting it short lately, because even though the showers are very fancy things that blow gales of hot air at you for drying, it's getting annoying having to work out the tangles. How Taarel manages those twirly pig-tail things I don't know. "Suppose possible Muina has one too, that people came from Muina to Earth millions years ago. Not very likely simultaneous identical evolution two different planets."

"Would that bother you?" Mara asked. "If your people were truly Muinans?"

"No. Lot of people Earth would think that great fun. And lot of people Earth wouldn't." I shrugged at Maze, who was watching me closely while we waited. Heart Mind was the main Taren philosophy/religion based on venerating Muina as a mother, and there seemed to be quite a few followers who were calling 'me' interesting names. "Unless upset Heart Mind follower likely get in KOTIS and push me down stair, don't care what say. Don't know anyone but people here. They not likely make me talk to media yes?"

"You're covered by the same privacy arrangements as the Setari." Maze gave me one of his approving captain nods, glad I wasn't going to be upset. "And I think I can safely say that KOTIS isn't going to let the media anywhere near you."

"I once volunteered to be a sacrificial offering to the media," Lohn said, coming out to give my shoulder a squeeze. "The interest in us is so voracious that a couple of us gave strictly anonymous interviews to a few selected representatives. KOTIS also releases details of spaces we clear to ease the hunger."

"Do you watch the fictions about Setari?"

Maze pulled a face, but Lohn shrugged. "Sometimes. *The Hidden War* keeps close to the actual issues we face. I don't think I've seen or read anything which hasn't included some wild improbabilities for purposes of drama. KOTIS isn't nearly so rife with intrigue, and we don't bend the rules half so often."

"Let alone take trips into the Ena for romantic interludes," Mara said, fluffing her hair as she and Alay came out. "Hurry up you two; my stomach is eating through its lining."

We went off to lunch. First Squad, particularly Lohn, were really tired, but I realised they were sticking with me while they looked through more of the discussion about me, and until they had some official direction on what the response to that would be. Which was to announce that a displaced person had indeed been part of the Setari mission which had unlocked Muina, and that this person originated from Muina's 'sister planet' Earth, which unfortunately did not possess developed talents or the knowledge of the Lantarens.

And I'm absolutely not allowed to go out into the city for the foreseeable future. Bleh. Mara says we can do more dodging practice to make up for it.

Thursday, March 27

Behind the news

Mara worked me into the ground today. First dodging, and then jogging around the obstacle park. Later she showed me more things you could do with your suit: how to make the weaponry and even covering your head. Then we swam.

I've another rotation with First Squad tomorrow, then another day of Mara, then another rotation. After that there's nothing booked except my inevitable medical exams, but Mara said that I may be sent to Muina again.

I'm thoroughly bored of reading stories of the unlocking of Muina and the increasingly unlikely descriptions of me. The bits I don't already know are the bits which make me feel bad. I don't think these Heart Minders are really likely to try and hurt me, but it does make me uncomfortable to have upset people just by existing. I'm glad that I'm assigned to First Squad for a while, and that Mara's left me too tired to fret too much.

Which is probably why she's doing it.

Friday, March 28

Roaming

Today's rotation was the closest I've come to being in danger working with First Squad. Another unstable rotation, which took us to a space full of these big metal containers stacked in rows, like you'd see at a port. It wasn't the space First Squad had been expecting, and it was the first time they'd encountered the type of Ionoth we met there.

They were humanoid, but covered with a white-grey hair, and they seemed to have made themselves a home in the containers; a busy township. We were still outside the gate, looking through, when two of them leapt out, slashing at Maze with rusty metal pipes. As a dozen more of the hairy people came rushing at us, Ketzaren grabbed me around the waist and hauled me backward through our current space, which was an awkwardly low set of tunnels through pearly-cream rock.

It was bloody, horrible. The attackers were fast, armed and very determined, but First Squad were well-practiced at close combat, and enhanced. They'd been surprised by the rush, but didn't come close to being overwhelmed.

"Withdraw to the entrance," Maze said, as soon as the last had fallen. He cast a quick glance into the container space, then followed as rear guard as everyone immediately obeyed.

"Broken?" Zee asked, watching him roll his shoulder and wince. They'd not been able to avoid being hit entirely.

"Seems not. Anyone else?"

"Nothing major."   Lohn was clenching and unclenching one hand, and took out his med-kit to spray some bandage over a cut across his knuckles.

"Any chance to read the gate?"

"It looked solid. Days, at least," Alay said.

"We'll go for a clearing entry approach," Maze said. "One blast from Kettara until we have a chance to evaluate."

The hairy people looked smaller in death, and the spreading pool of their blood made the gate entry both unpleasant and slippery. But none of them were lurking on the other side, and so Maze gestured us through and we moved to a defensible corner while they tried to estimate numbers.

"Dozens," Mara said, at last. "A few outliers circling, but most congregated that way." She nodded toward what seemed to be the centre of the space, where the containers were piled highest.

"I'd prefer a height advantage here," Zee murmured and Maze nodded his agreement.

The tops of the containers were rusty and pitted, and a couple of times crumbled alarmingly underfoot. But being up high allowed us to see the trap a few moments before it was sprung. A higher row of containers trembled, then became a tilting wall of metal which threatened to squash us and take out the containers we were standing on.

Maze had said "Up," before I even saw that, and we rose immediately and swiftly as the trap took out the entire area between the gate and the centre like a row of dominos. And before the noise had even settled they began shooting at us with crossbows, one catching Alay in the leg before Maze and Lohn between them created a mini-cataclysm in the area below. There were only a few left alive after that, and Maze and Zee chased them down while the rest of us gathered on top of a slightly tilted container to check Alay's leg.

"Two made it through a gate," Maze said, returning. He surveyed the bolt Mara had removed from Alay's leg. "Any sign of poison?"

"Nothing apparent," Mara said. "I've sealed the bleed."

"We'll short-survey, then. Gainer, let us know if you start experiencing any symptoms."

Alay, Ketzaren and me stayed where we were while the others made a circuit of the space and inspected the bodies of the Ionoth, crisped though most of them were. They didn't dawdle over it, and we were soon heading back out. Maze paused at the gate, then crossed to a kind of wicker cage tucked in one corner, cutting it open.

There were a half dozen little Ionoth in there. They reminded me faintly of ET, and all of them were in pretty miserable condition, like someone had been poking them with pointy sticks. They moved slowly, blinking fearfully at Maze, who stepped away, then signalled for us to leave.

"The original inhabitants of that space, I think," he said, following us through the gate. "These must be roamers." He surveyed the corpses again, extra-thoroughly, and then we headed back at double-time, with Zee carrying Alay using Telekinesis.

A truly horrible day. The Ionoth in that space, both types, were different from those I'd encountered before, more...real for want of a better word. Well aware of the gates between spaces, ready to defend themselves against attack, and a far cry from animals or shadows. And they drew blood.

I'm beginning to understand why Maze always looks so tired, beyond the strain of using psionic talents. It's from worrying that someone in his squad will get killed. I need to stop asking myself how bad First's injuries would have been if they hadn't been enhanced.

Saturday, March 29

Competition

First Squad's off rotation for a few days to give them a chance to recover. I asked Mara if squads ever went out with less than six members, and she said it's rare, but possible so long as all the required talents are covered.

"Did it seem to you those hairy people prepare that ambush and trap particular for Setari?" I asked.

"It certainly felt that way, didn't it?" Mara said, straightforward as usual. "But the type isn't in our records at all, so it's more likely we stumbled into some kind of inter-Ionoth dispute. Perhaps a different band of their own kind."

"That happen a lot?"

"No. Many Ionoth do move to nearby spaces seeking food, but usually return to their own after hunting. Roamers that are systematic explorers, or make any attempt to dominate other areas, are rare and most will fade if they are too long away from their home space. Those were well-organised. Formidable."

Mara has moved on from just throwing balls at me, and in today's lesson was trying to get me to block attacks. She'd told me that I had no instinct for combat but that that was no reason I couldn't be taught to defend myself. I still have my doubts, but I accept the value of trying to learn. She's not soft with me, but she doesn't ever say nasty things or make fun of me for being so bad, and in a painful way I'm enjoying being back with her.

"Who is best fighter in Setari?" I asked, thinking over the battle between Kajal and Ruuel.

"A question best not asked, as you apparently learned."

"Did Kajal get punish for that?"

"He would have lost privileges. The aether effect is not enough to excuse his behaviour, but does mean he's not likely to lose captaincy over the incident."

"Maze doesn't like Setari competing against each other, because of scene like that? Ruuel could have defuse situation by agree to fight him. But Kajal would never been satisfied, right?"

"Not unless he won," Mara agreed. "Maze doesn't like anything which focuses our energy on each other rather than the Ionoth. While we were still Kalrani it was useful, but it's becoming an unhealthy distraction for a few of the younger Setari."

Ruuel's been on my mind a lot today (not that he isn't usually) because now that First Squad's on sick leave, I've been assigned to Fourth Squad for tomorrow's rotation. I wonder how the black eye's progressing?

He was really annoyed about it. More being forced to fight than the injuries. And he didn't think Kajal had the slightest chance of beating him. That moment of anger, of disdainful arrogance, caught me by surprise. I've been putting a lot of thought into what Kaoren Ruuel is really like: whether he's a humourless robot with a rod up his ass, or the Taren stereotype of a Place Sight talent, all sensitive and haunted and needing always to keep control. That fight showed me that I don't know him at all.

I need to spend more time practicing ways to get home.

Sunday, March 30

Touchstone

I made sure to be early down to Red Lock for the rotation with Fourth Squad, and then had to wonder if I was trying to impress Ruuel, and what I thought that would achieve. I need to be sensible where he's concerned. Anyway, turning up early was more about not being on the receiving end of one of those brief glances he gives people when they waste his time. Just a momentary look, not even a change of expression, and I know I'd shrivel.

The point was moot this morning because I was there in plenty of time and Ruuel was almost late. That gave me a chance to chat with Ferus and Eyse about the kinds of missions they usually do and how they're still playing catch up from when the Pillar's deactivation shifted so many spaces about. Both of them are really easy to talk to, with actual and apparent senses of humour. They're looking forward to going back to Muina, to do exploration work in the larger cities.

Ruuel brought us all into mission channel and gave us the two sentences he considered a briefing just before he came into view. "In addition to on-going goals, we'll be looking for the new type of roamer which First Squad encountered. Tracking their source space has been marked priority."

Triggering the gate-lock to open, he passed us to collect the usual rotation gear, and was back just as the lock was fully open. His black eye, sadly, had receded to a faint yellowish shadow, and he didn't seem to be favouring his knee. But mission efficiency hit a snag before we'd even stepped into the Ena. Ruuel paused as the gate-lock was closing behind us, and then Selkie joined the mission channel.

"Devlin," Selkie said, making me feel exactly like someone called out of class by the school principal. "Does the word 'Gea' mean anything to you?"

"Gear?" I repeated, since that's how he'd pronounced it. "Part of machine?"

"Specifically, 'child of Gea'."

"Oh. Gaia, maybe? Gaia is the same as Earth, or Terra. Different names for my planet in different languages. Gaia is Greek mythology mother-planet-goddess, a bit like how Muinans think of Muina. Child of Gaia would either be myth people called Titans, or anyone from my planet, depending on which way look at it. Did you find record Earth in histories?"

"No. An emissary from Nuri has walked out of deep-space and asked that the child of Gea be brought to speak with him."

Even Ruuel reacted to that one, frowning, and there was a little pause while Selkie was probably talking to someone else. Then he said: "Continue your rotation, but return within a kasse." He dropped out of the channel, leaving Fourth Squad looking at each other and at me, very startled.

"Focus," Ruuel said, eyes narrow, and sent us through the gate. I don't think he was at all pleased to have such a big distraction waved under his squad's nose at the beginning of a mission. It was lucky that the most I have to do is stop and start in time with my escorts because I'd certainly been given plenty to distract me from the rotation.

Nuri is the moon world with the Luddite ex-Muinans. It was located around eighty years ago and when the Tarens turned up the Nuran response was pretty much: "We don't want to have anything to do with you. Go away." Since then they'd unbent only enough to say the same thing in rather more detail. They felt the Taren use of technology, particularly the interface, made them a corrupting influence and they could not risk exposure. No, they would not join an alliance to find or investigate Muina. No, they did not want to share their knowledge of Muina's disaster. The last time Tare had sent a delegation to discuss the apparent increase in the severity of Ionoth incursions, the Nurans had barely stopped short of accusing the Tarens of being responsible.

So having a Nuran turn up on Tare asking to talk to me was big news.

I had a couple of hours to stew on that while Fourth Squad headed back through the same spaces First Squad had cleared last rotation. Ruuel was taking an extreme-caution approach to each space, since traps had been encountered last time, but we reached the container space without any sense of threat. And once in there, we found only the little greyish people watching us from a fortification they'd built.

There were over a dozen gates out of that space, and Fourth Squad examined every one. Although the one which the hairy people had run through had shifted out of alignment, they were able to detect signs of them at three other gates, and Fourth chose the most-travelled gate and headed through to the next space. It was a small island, no bigger than a couple of house-blocks, with exposed sandbars around it. Lots of sand-coloured mice lived in burrows beneath the tufty grass. And there were sharks in the water, given the stinking pile of butchered carcasses we found.

Again Fourth mapped the gates, and picked the one which was the most frequented. The next space was big, some kind of multi-story car park full of vague memories of cars, which made it very confusing. From what I could make out of the blurs, they were low and large, with what looked like chimneys in swirls of chrome. Ruuel and Sonn paused a long moment before gesturing us through, and when we were in Ruuel said over the mission channel: "Next level up, perhaps a dozen. There was a lookout."

There was a trap, too, but Ruuel could tell it was there before it was set off. He had Sonn send an enhanced ball of lightning up the ramp to the next level and we all stayed well back listening to the noise. Then Ferus pulled the trap apart with Telekinesis, and we went up. Eight stories of car park, and scads of gates, but once we'd tracked down and cleared the last of the hairy people and mapped the gates Ruuel said: "Not their home space either. We'll pick this up another day."

I've no idea how long they would have gone on if not for the time limit caused by me and my Nuran visitor. They didn't seem particularly annoyed about stopping, at any rate. We returned, not neglecting caution just because we'd been through the spaces already, and stepped back into real-space about ten minutes short of the full kasse.

I wasn't altogether surprised to find Maze waiting for me. He nodded at Ruuel as we came through the gate-lock and said: "You and I are on escort duty," then added to me: "Put this on." He handed me a white dress and a carry bag with shoes and things inside, which I accepted automatically, then realised what they were.

"Serious?" I said, far too aware that even Fourth Squad weren't capable of not staring.

"The liaison branch is very eager to ensure that the Nurans continue dialogue with us, and they've decided it might be impolitic for you to be wearing our uniform. The clothes are Mara's."

"Lohn somewhere right now laughing a lot, right?"

"Very much so." He smiled, amused. "Don't worry, we'll be with you."

"Wearing dresses?" I asked, but decided it wasn't worth arguing about. Sighing, I went and had a shower, keeping my hair dry, and then put on Mara's sundress and sandals, which were only slightly too big for me. She'd included a hairbrush, and some nearly-clear lip gloss which I smoothed on, then let my hair out of its tight braid, pulled it up into a high ponytail and looked at myself in the mirror.

I really loved the style of dress, and will have to remember it next time I go shopping, but I didn't understand why a dress at all. Why not any of my own clothes? Yeah, the dress looked better than my casual, practical outfits, but I felt like I was being set up on a blind date and I seriously didn't like the implications of that. Alyssa once told me that I'm too obliging, that I objected to things way too late, but that dress handily jumped me straight to stubborn doubt.

Then I remembered my lab rat.

Trying not to smile at the idea of showing up to an important diplomatic meeting wearing an "experimental animal" label for anyone with Symbol Sight to read, I stuffed my uniform harness in the bag and went out.

"Does know yet what Nuran want talk about?"

"Your planet, apparently." Maze brought me into a channel with him, Ruuel and someone called Tarmian, ushering me toward the nearest elevator. "He hasn't been waiting long. It took some time to convince him that he'd have to come here if he wanted to talk to you, and the flight landed just before your return."

"If you can succeed in getting him to speak at all it will be progress," said Tarmian, who was a woman with a deep, husky voice. "The most I've managed is to be told I don't need to know his name."

Selkie and someone called Ganaran joined the channel, and I had a sinking realisation that I was supposedly going to have a conversation with a planetary emissary while a bunch of people made helpful suggestions to me in my head. It made me wonder if Alyssa was right about the whole too obliging thing, because it hadn't seemed to occur to any of them that my interests in such a conversation might not coincide with theirs. Or maybe it had, but they were hoping no independent thought would cross my mind. I listened without comment to Tarmian and Ganaran, who are from KOTIS' liaison branch, telling me to let the Nuran lead the conversation, but to try and encourage him to expand on topics he was willing to discuss. Maze and Ruuel kept quiet, though they did both enhance themselves just before we went in, something I should be used to, but which was really disconcerting with my arms and shoulders bare.

Preconceptions are fun. I was expecting someone like a Buddhist monk, complete with bald head and orange robes. The closest I got were the robes, and they were more maroon and white, and not really robes. He had the same sort of colouring as Ruuel and Taarel and Selkie, but wore his hair long, with the sides caught back in a high tail except for strips before his ears. He looked like a manga samurai, complete with two swords tucked into a belt sash.

The other person in the room was a curvy and sweet-faced woman with a lot of curly black hair which kept trying to escape her hairclips. She was wearing a reddish-plum uniform, a new type to me. Liaison branch.

"This is Caszandra Devlin," the woman – Tarmian – said and the Nuran turned and looked at me. His expression was appraising, not particularly warm or pleased or anything, and he bowed, barely more than a nod of the head.

"Hello," I said, in English and then in Taren. I wasn't going to attempt bowing.

"I am indebted for your time," said the Nuran. He spoke with an accent, and just enough hesitation to suggest that Taren was at least a different dialect to his own language.

"Sit down, please," said Tarmian, gesturing to a coffee table and couches arrangement. The room also had a more formal table and chairs, and a couple of corner clusters of seats and smaller tables, and even an actual long window giving an excellent view of a massive storm outside. That was disorienting; weather is so separate from daily life here.

The couches were the firm, solid sort. Maze and Ruuel stood behind my couch, Tarmian had a smaller chair to my right and the Nuran sat in the centre of the couch opposite.

"How did a child of Gaia reach this world?" he asked. And then there was a tickly feeling in my head and I could hear his voice add: ~Are you able to reply this way?~

~Yes?~ I tried thinking, all too conscious of Maze and Ruuel standing behind me, neither of whom were likely to have missed me suddenly sitting up much straighter. I've no idea what Ruuel's Sights would have shown him, and I stumbled on into answering the verbal question to buy myself time. "Walked through a gate from my planet to Muina. Was there until people from Tare found me, brought me back here."

~My name is Inisar.~ His eyes, long and dark, were watching me very steadily. "Can you tell me what knowledge Gaia retains of Muina?" ~I have been sent to offer you Nuri's aid.~

~Aid?~ "None. I had never heard name Muina before Tarens told me it. There are no stories, no recognisable stories, about people my planet going to other planets. Were Muinans first from my planet?"

"I do not know." ~Aid in the form of haven.~ "That Gaia and Muina shared a bond is remembered. It is an ancient one, stretching far beyond any record." ~I see that the distortions the people of this world inflict on themselves have been passed to you.~

~The interface?~

"The path to Gaia had long been lost, however, even before we departed Muina. Had there been any unusual events in Gaia's Ena preceding your arrival on Muina?" ~I am sorry that I am unable to undo their distortion, but I can offer an escape from this place. First to Nuri. And then to your own world.~

Both Tarmian and Ganaran said something over the interface at this point, but I didn't pay any attention to their suggestions, just giving Tarmian a blankly distracted look.

"The...my planet, psychic talents are considered fiction. We have forgotten everything, if ever knew. Don't know Ena, don't access it." I felt unreasonably angry. Holding two conversations at once while someone else talked at me was beyond stressful, especially when my home was dangled under my nose as some sort of bait. I could feel Maze shift behind me, and didn't know whether to feel comforted or threatened by his presence. ~Nuri able locate natural gate my world?~

"How greatly are the children of Gaia troubled by Ionoth?" ~With a link of both birth and heart to Gaia, a path can be found. Natural gates are not constantly open, but if you were able to travel to Muina, it will be possible to find that gate and return you.~

"Ionoth not able reach real-space on my world. Their existence, existence of spaces, none of that is known. Are spaces memories of worlds, or nightmares of worlds?" ~Nuri wants something in exchange?~

"Both." ~You have opened Muina to Tare. That cannot be undone, although we would ask you to balance the act.~ "Memories, nightmares, dreams. They are the expression of the living, imprinted on the Ena." ~Beyond that, we prefer not to see a touchstone in such misguided hands. Returning you to Gaia will remove the risks you pose.~

~Touchstone is me?~ I paused, because it was getting really hard to keep track of the conversation, and the person called Ganaran was saying something excitedly about some theory being validated. "Do you know if all people my planet have this enhancement talent?" ~Why does Nuri think Tare people so bad?~

~They repeat the arrogance of the past, seeking to reach beyond what is born to them. Without balance, without wisdom, they are twisting themselves outside nature.~ "You are something which appears perhaps once in ten generations. Not unique to Gaia." ~Will you allow me to remove you from this place? You need only take my hand.~

~Are you Nuri equivalent of Setari? Protect Nuri from Ionoth?~ I was struggling to decide how I wanted to react, the idea of perhaps being able to go home shrieking at me, along with a great deal of resentment that they couldn't just offer to do it openly. But I at least realised that he probably wasn't going to be able to do what he planned. "Do you know why it is some talents I enhance strength, and other talents I make different?"

He hadn't expected it. He was Ruuel-level in terms of difficulty to read, but when he heard that he drew back his hands from where they had rested unmoving on his knees.

"I first found out was enhancement talent when someone tried teleport me," I went on helpfully, glad to be sticking to just out-loud talking for a minute. For one thing the in-my-head talking itched. "We ended up in totally wrong place. Fell down. Most talents, stronger, but some go very strange."

"The distortion inflicted on you by these," he said, lifting his eyes past my shoulder. "Calling themselves Setari with no understanding of what that title means."

~Even if could go with you,~ I told him silently while he gave either Ruuel or Maze a long survey, ~I do not think could accept offer. I miss my home, but it would be selfish of me to place homesickness above helping stop people be eaten by nightmares. Although I know Tare not place my interests above theirs, they mostly treat me as civilised people should. Also, I think Nuri not helping fix problem by acting as if Tare people too stupid to learn. If child is about to walk off cliff, what point saying they lack wisdom and watch them fall? And interface is a tool. No less unnatural than those two blades you wear.~

~Well said.~

To my surprise he was looking at me with something approaching approval. Then he stood up.

"I will communicate your answers to the elders. Thank you for speaking with me."

And he vanished. Teleported. I guess he had no reason to stick around once he knew he had little chance of getting me out of there. I would love to know whether my refusal would have counted if teleporting me away had been an option.

"Nurans even weirder than Tarens," I said, wishing I could scratch somewhere just behind my frontal lobe. I accessed my own log, but wasn't really surprised to see that, unlike the Ddura, the Nuran hadn't been 'audible'.

"That was a shorter conversation than I expected," Tarmian said, blankly.

"You couldn't hear rest," I said, with an internal sigh. "I make transcript, give me minute write."

"He was speaking using a similar method to the Ddura," Ruuel said, as expected.

"That would explain why your heart rate kept spiking." Maze leaned forward to examine my expression.

"What was his true purpose?" Selkie asked, the first time he'd spoken.

"Came rescue me from misguided and corrupt Tarens," I said, risking a glance up at Ruuel, but he was more expressionless than ever. "Let me concentrate now or will forget bits." I dropped out of the channel and shut my eyes, relieved when they obediently moved away. I was actually really upset and stressed and didn't want to talk to them or even see them while I thought about turning down going home.

Ever since my jaunt to Earth's near-space, I've had this plan to work out what I'd done, and find a way to do it properly. As I'd told the Nuran, I know that the Tarens won't put my interests above theirs. Going home isn't just about homesickness, it's about choosing the best option for me.

I blame *Doctor Who*. Mr Spock. The Scooby Gang: both the ones in the Mystery Machine and the ones with the stakes. I've spent my life with stories of people who don't walk away, who go back for their friends, who make that last stand. I've been brainwashed by Samwise Gamgee.

Even though I'm no longer critical to unlocking Muina, I still made a difference to First Squad's encounter with those roamers, and the way things are going, it won't be the last time my enhancement could save lives. There's just no way I can cut and run simply because I'm an assignment, and a test subject, and I can't absolutely trust the entire hierarchy of KOTIS. Even second level monitoring isn't a big enough reason to abandon First Squad. They matter to me, so much. I can't go back to being me if I have to spend the rest of my life ashamed of myself.

So when I wrote down everything the Nuran said, I didn't leave anything out, and by the time I was done and had re-read it a few times I'd calmed down and accepted that I was choosing to do this, that I wasn't trapped, hadn't lost my only chance. Good or bad idea, I mean to see this out.

Something cold touched the back of my hand at the end of all this decision-making, which nearly had me leaping out my skin, but it was only a glass. Ruuel ignored my expression, and made me take it, saying: "You haven't eaten since before the rotation."

Ever the captain. Drinking did make me realise I was really starving, though, and I was glad to see a tray of food at one of the corner clusters of table and seats. Giving in to the inevitable, I forwarded Ruuel and Maze the transcript in return and went and picked over the food while they, and probably every bluesuit in KOTIS, read it through.

Ruuel went out of the room, leaving me alone, but he and Maze came back while I was still eating, and joined me sitting around the little table of food.

"Feeling better?" Maze picked up one of the chewy sticks of bread.

"Just tired. Are people from Kolar likely turn up and want talk to me as well? Can I pretend not speak language if they do?"

"They haven't focused on you, and will not if that can be avoided."

"Distracted by our failure to communicate any of these developments to them," Ruuel added. "Kolar heard that Muina was unlocked from the news services."

"Same Nuri, maybe? Think interface bad, but big coincidence if didn't hear about me through it."

Maze shrugged, and the faintest wince crossed his face: his shoulder was still hurting him. "Very likely they've cultivated local informants. We vastly underestimated the Nurans, had no idea they had the ability to travel through the Rift without vehicles. No wonder they were so disinterested when Tare announced that we'd located Muina."

"Will Tare unlock Muina for Kolar and Nuri?"

"Kolar, very likely. I've no idea how it will be handled. I don't like the idea of divvying Muina up into territories, but the trade agreements we've established are far too important to try and deny access to the Kolarens. I wouldn't care to guess what's going to happen with Nuri. They did just try to...rescue you."

"Can you estimate how much of what he told you was true?" Ruuel asked.

"No. Or, he seemed all 'my honour not permit lies' but then act pleased when I told him I thought Nurans stupid hypocrites. He didn't act like he lied, but guess he didn't necessarily agree with what ordered to do. Think he meant it about Setari."

Ruuel gave me a dry look – quite the most reaction I've ever had from him – then said: "Did you believe he would be able to return you to your home?"

"Believe he thought he could." Remembered anger made me frown. "Semantics, really. He said he here to offer me Nuri's aid. Was here to remove inconveniently located thing called touchstone from hands of people Nuri not want to have. Would still count as rescue, of sorts, but was for their benefit, not mine. Don't see that they'd think me any less corrupt and misguided than Tarens. Is Setari some sort historic title?"

"Not so far as I was aware," Maze said. "The word wasn't created for us, and has a long-standing meaning of 'specialist' with an overtone of 'special guard'."

"And touchstone?" Dalenset – dalen for touch and set for stone. I think touchstone is a word on Earth, too, but don't think it refers to people.

"Not even in the dictionaries. Though I can see how the name might come about for a talent like yours."

I sighed. One in ten generations was not something I'd been happy to hear. "Will I more restrictions because this?"

"I don't know. We made a mistake, letting the Nuran meet with you. He knows your face now." Maze wasn't happy about it.

"Think he try rescue me again? Risk teleporting?"

"It comes down to a question of what is more important to them." Ruuel had reverted to being super-shuttered, but opened his eyes properly as if I was a symbol he was trying to decipher. "Did they want to use you for some purpose we don't understand? Or simply ensure that we could not?"

Since I was falling asleep, Maze took me back to my rooms after that. He didn't give me any speeches about staying or going, just told me that if anything even slightly unusual happened I was to send an alert immediately. An alert is a personal panic button, sending a broadcast message to whoever is on security detail. I don't count Ghost as anything unusual any more, and was very glad she showed up after my nap, sitting on my desk shamelessly begging for attention while I've filled up the last of my diary writing this down.

So today I met a psychic space samurai called Inisar, who did me no favours by making it clear to the Tarens that I'm even more interesting than they suspected, and who may or may not be sent back to kill me. As a result I decided to not be 'just Cass' any more, and I know there'll be times I'm going to regret that so hard, just as I know that the people who are important to me here will have spent some of today discussing strategies for making sure I don't have reason or opportunity to leave, and finding a balance between me wanting some privacy and their wanting to keep watch on me at all times.

And after ninja and samurai, I'm wondering if next up will be psychic space pirates.

Continued in Part Two: "Lab Rat One"

Glossary

Agowla	The (fictional) high school Cass attended in Sydney.
Aspro	Aspirin
Carche Landing	The main airport in Unara.
Casszilla	Rawr!
Cruzatch	A dangerous humanoid Ionoth, shadow burning white.
Ddura	An enormous energy being created by the Lantarens.
Deep-space	The large portion of the Ena which exists between the 'memory spaces'. It is white in appearance, and filled with gates which open directly to real-space worlds.
Deep-space Ionoth	Ionoth which are formed and dwell not in the relatively small Spaces, but instead in Deep-space.
Diodel	One of the ships KOTIS uses to travel between Tare and Muina.
Do Not Go Gentle	"Do Not Go Gentle Into That Good Night", a poem by Dylan Thomas.
Drone	An advanced robot, usually used for scanning and monitoring.
Ena	A dimension connected to the thoughts, memories, dreams and imagination of living beings.
Ena manipulation	A psychic talent which can change the substance of the Ena, particularly in stabilising gates between spaces. It can also be used in a limited way to change 'reality'.
Escort quest	A mission in an online game involving protection of a non-player character while they travel.
Fan service	Revealing or provocative shots of characters in anime/manga.
Fanfic	Fiction based on the stories of others and/or fiction involving a person of whom the writer is a fan.
First level monitoring	Interface monitoring which triggers an alert if certain conditions are reached (eg. loss of consciousness, heart attack). All residents of Tare are on first level monitoring.
Gate	A tear or rift between spaces/worlds.
Gate Sight	A psychic talent which can judge the status of gates between spaces.
Gate-lock	An enclosure built around a gate from near-space to real-space to prevent Ionoth from passing through.
Gelzz	A now nearly-extinct cave-dwelling Taren insect noted for its tendency to admit a lingering rotten odour as a defence mechanism.
Goralath	The name originally given to the ruins where Pandora is later established.
Gorra	The first island settled on Tare.
Hasata	A city on Tare.
HSC	Higher School Certificate. Received when graduating from high school in Australia.
Ian Thorpe	A famous Australian swimmer.
In-skin	An immersive interface experience where most of the senses – sight, hearing, touch, smell, taste – are stimulated.
Interface	An in-body nanite installation used by Tarens as personal computers/the Taren internet.
Ionoth	Creatures which form in the Ena, usually remnants of the dreams and nightmares of inhabited planets.
Ista	An honorific for medical doctors.
Isten	Professor.
Joden	The Taren equivalent of a minute, though the unit is longer than an Earth minute. One hundred joden equal a kasse.
Kadara	Naturally-forming massive Ionoth.
Kalrani	Trainees not yet qualified as Setari.
Kasse	The Taren equivalent of an hour, spanning approximately two and a half Earth hours.
Kasse	Two and a half Earth hours.
Kolar	A hot, arid world settled by Muinan refugees, and advanced technologically by the Tarens.
Konna	Both the city and the island where the main KOTIS base is located on Tare.

KOTIS	An acronym for the "Agency for Ionoth Research and Protection".
Kuna	Supplementary memory provided by the interface.
Lahanti	Leaders of the cities of Tare – an equivalent to a 'mayor' of a city-state.
Lantarens	The ruling class of Muina before the disaster. Powerful psychics.
Litara	One of the ships KOTIS uses to travel between Tare and Kolar.
Massives	Ionoth of unusually large dimensions.
Muina	A world abandoned after a disaster brought about by the Lantaren psychics.
Nanites	A machine or robot on a microscopic scale.
Near-space	The envelope of Ena immediately surrounding a world, full of reflections of the world as it currently is – and it's most recent nightmares.
Noob	A new gamer who does not fully understand how to play.
Not happy, Jan	A popular phrase taken from an Australian television commercial for Yellow Pages.
NPCs	Non-player characters – a gaming term for characters in a game which you are not expected to fight.
OMGWTF	Oh my god, what the fuck?!
Pandora	First Taren settlement on Muina.
Path Sight	A talent for location.
Pippin	A small animal of excessive cuteness.
Public Space	Virtual décor visible to all interface users/anything accessible to all interface users.
PVP	Combat in online games where players fight other players rather than computer-controlled opponents.
Rotation	Setari missions in the Ena designed to cover Ionoth respawn near Taren cities.
Rotational space	A space in the Ena which moves so that its gates regularly align and move out of alignment.
Sa/Tsa	An honorific for academics.
Schoolies	Australian highschool graduates celebrating the end of school during "Schoolies Week". Primarily located around the Gold Coast in Queensland.
Second level monitoring	A safety/security interface setting causing all sights and sounds experienced by the monitored person to be retained in a secure log which can be accessed under exceptional circumstances.
Setari	Psychic combat 'Specialists' trained since childhood to combat Ionoth.
Sf&f	Science fiction and fantasy.
Shared Space	The interface equivalent of a conference call.
Spaces	A concept used in multiple contexts on Tare, covering 'world', 'dimension', 'area', 'region of the interface', and many others, but most particularly 'a bubble containing a fragment of a world remembered and reproduced by the Ena'.
Stilt	A spindly-legged deep-space Ionoth.
Stray	A person who walked through a wormhole through the Ena to another planet.
Swoops	A variety of deep-space Ionoth resembling a pterodactyl.
Tairo	A kick-ass ball sport.
Talent	A psychic ability.
Tanty	Tantrum.
Tanz	Taren air transport.
Tarani	A many-legged deep-space Ionoth reminiscent of a caterpillar.
Tare	A harsh, storm-wracked world settled by Muinan refugees. The highly technologically advanced inhabitants live crammed into massive whitestone cities.
Taren year	One third of an Earth year.
Third level monitoring	Active observation of everything a subject sees and hears.
tl;dr	Too long; didn't read.
Tola	A classification of Ionoth which have little physical substance.
Toolies	Adults preying on teenagers during Schoolies Week/pretending to be a Schoolie.
Touchstone	The subject of the story.

True-space	The world, not the Ena.
Tsa	A general honorific similar to Mr/Ms.
Tsaile	Commander.
Tsee	Setari Squad Captain.
Tsur	Director.
Tyu	A zither-like musical instrument.
Unara	The largest city on Tare, located on the island of Wehana.
Unco	Uncoordinated.
Unstable rotation	A rotation where the spaces are more likely to change and bring unexpected situations.
Wehana	The largest island on Tare, almost entirely covered by the city of Unara.
Whitestone	A building substance formed with nanites.
Zelkasse	A quarter of a kasse.

Character List

Squads

First Squad	Second Squad	Third Squad	Fourth Squad
Maze Surion (m)	Grif Regan (m)	Meer Taarel (f)	Kaoren Ruuel (m)
Zee Annan (f)	Jeh Omai (f)	Della Meht (f)	Fiar Sonn (f)
Lohn Kettara (m)	Nils Sayate (m)	Eeli Bata (f)	Par Auron (m)
Mara Senez (f)	Keer Charal (m)	Tol Sefen (m)	Glade Ferus (m)
Alay Gainer (f)	Enma Dolan (f)	Geo Chise (m)	Charan Halla (f)
Ketzaren Spel (f)	Bree Tcho (f)	Rite Orla (f)	Mori Eyse (f)
Fifth Squad	**Sixth Squad**	**Seventh Squad**	**Eighth Squad**
Hast Kajal (m)	Elen Kormin (f)	Atara Forel (f)	Ro Kanato (m)
Dorey Nise (m)	Sten Ammas (m)	Pol Tsennen (m)	Pala Hasen (f)
Faver Elwes (f)	Juna Quane (m)	Tez Mema (m)	Seeli Henaz (f)
Kire Palanty (m)	Del Roth (m)	Bodey Residen (m)	Zhou Kade (m)
Tralest Seet (m)	Meleed Aluk (f)	Aheri Dahlen (f)	Kye Trouban (m)
Seyen Rax (m)	Kester Am-roten (m)	Saitel Raph (m)	Zama Bryze (f)
Ninth Squad	**Tenth Squad**	**Eleventh Squad**	**Twelfth Squad**
Desa Kaeline (f)	Els Haral (m)	Seq Endaran (f)	Zan Namara (f)
Zael Toure (f)	Loris Darm (f)	Kire Couran (f)	Roake Lenton (f)
Rebar Dolas (m)	Sell Tens (f)	Yaleran Genera (m)	Dess Charn (f)
Oran Thomasal (m)	Joren Mane (f)	Palest Wen (m)	Sora Nels (m)
Kahl Anya (f)	Fahr Sherun (m)	Zare Seeth (m)	Tenna Drysen (m)
Terel Revv (m)	Netra Kantan (m)	Den Dava (m)	Tahl Kiste (m)

Other

Alyssa Caldwell (f)	Cassandra's best friend.
Cassandra Devlin (f)	An Aussie teenager not enjoying her big adventure.
Clere Ganaran (m)	KOTIS liaison.
Deen Tarmian (f)	KOTIS liaison.
Elizabeth (Bet) Wilson (f)	Cassandra's aunt.
Helen Middledell (f)	aka Her Mightiness or HM. A well-off and popular girl who goes to Agowla School.
Helese Surion (f)	Original First Squad captain, killed by a massive.
Ista Kestal Leema (f)	KOTIS medic assigned to first Muinan settlement.
Ista Noin Tremmar (f)	KOTIS medic assigned to Setari.
Isten Sel Notra (f)	Pre-eminent scientist researching the Ena.
Jenna Wilson (f)	A friend of Cassandra's in Sydney.
Julian (Jules) Devlin (m)	Cassandra's younger brother.
Ketta Lents (f)	Wife of Orren Lents - stockbroker.
Laura Devlin (f)	Cassandra's mother.
Liane Lents (f)	Daughter of Orren and Ketta Lents.
Michael Devlin (m)	Cassandra's father.
Nenna Lents (f)	Daughter of Orren and Ketta Lents.
Nick Dale (m)	Sue Dale's stepson.
Sue Dale (f)	Cassandra's Aunt.
Tsa Orren Lents (m)	An anthropologist working part-time with KOTIS.
Tsaile Nura Staben (f)	Commander of Muina settlement.
Tsana Dura (f)	A teaching program.
Tsur Gidds Selkie (m)	Senior coordinator and trainer of Setari. Sight Sight talent.

Printed in Great Britain
by Amazon